TRAVIS

KALEIGH CLARK

Published by Whitby Bay Publishing 2022

Cover design by Wicked by Designs, Robin Harper

Kev Murtagh,
I love the marrow of you.
xx

PROLOGUE
CLAIRE

"FIRST OF ALL...PULL your head out of your ass," Piper scolded over video chat. "You're twenty-three years old, which means you're perfectly capable of doing things on your own."

I rolled my red, puffy eyes in annoyance. Since seventh grade, Piper and I had been best friends, so there was no reason she wouldn't back me up in what I considered the second most devastating moment of my entire life.

"And don't roll your eyes at me. Listen, if I didn't love you, I wouldn't say anything at all. I'd simply let you sulk and cry until you ran out of time to do anything." She was right, but I refused to back down just yet.

"You're not supposed to kick me when I'm curled up in the fetal position, broken and at my lowest."

"Really? *This* is your lowest?" The crook in her otherwise perfect eyebrow told me she thought I was ridiculous. "I thought that was last year when Waldo dumped you."

"His name was Oswald, and that *was* my lowest...until now."

Without warning, she slid off her bed and disappeared from view. At first, I was taken aback, but I quickly reminded myself that this was Piper Dodson. She knew all my deep, dark secrets, so if she'd walk away from our friendship, she would've done so over the many poor decisions I'd made in the last eleven years.

"Well, in that case..." She came back with a pint of ice cream. "I need sustenance for this. Start from the beginning because I think I missed something. I mean, you *were* sobbing rather uncontrollably, so perhaps I misunderstood most—if not all—of what you told me."

"He kicked me out." The waterworks started once again, garbling my

1

words. So I cleared my throat and made another attempt, calmer this time. "He said I rely on him too much, and I need to learn to spread my wings and fly. Can you believe him? This has to be all *her* fault. He has no other reason to throw me out like yesterday's trash with barely *any* warning."

Piper licked her spoon clean before pointing it at the camera. "You can't think of *any* other reason? None at all?"

I wiped my eyes with the corner of my favorite blanket and shook my head. In that moment, the severity of my situation dominated every thought. I would literally be on my own, so if someone broke in, I'd have to fend them off all by myself.

I had never lived alone.

I wasn't even sure if I could.

"For Christ's sake, Claire, you're acting like you were dumped on the side of the road. Are you listening to yourself? Can you not see where you might have *some* responsibility in this? If you want my opinion, the way you're acting completely justifies his decision."

Now I was insulted *and* hurt. She was supposed to be on my side—not *his*. And *hello*! I was being ripped away from everything I'd ever known and abandoned—not by the side of a road, but it still stung. "After the accident, he swore he'd take care of me. How is this taking care of me?"

"Isn't he, like, eighty-something? How much longer do you expect him to wipe your ass?"

I reached into my nightstand and pulled out a jumbo roll of Sweeties. "Now you're just being mean."

"No, I'm not. I'm being realistic, and I think you need blatant honesty right now. Any other time, I'd pat your back and tell you how right you are about whatever you're rattling on about, but not this time. You're twenty-three, and you haven't even had a job."

"Not true. I worked at that boutique in the mall once," I interjected.

She stared incredulously at me. "Okay, fine, I stand corrected. You haven't been able to *hold* a job longer than a week and a half. Is that better?"

"Marginally," I mumbled under my breath, slumping in defeat. When the words came off her lips, I had to take them as truth, because she would never steer me wrong.

"He's your grandfather, and he adores you. I'm willing to bet he didn't do this to be an asshole. If anything, asking you to move out was probably harder on him, but he figures his time is limited, and the older he gets, the more urgent things become. If he doesn't teach you how to take care of your-self now, what'll happen to you after he's gone?" The sincerity in her tone settled in my chest, calming the remnants of my hiccupping sobs.

She was right. *Again*. But I still wasn't ready to concede.

"I don't need a job; I have lots of money. Well...I *had* money. He's taken that away, too."

Piper belted out a sardonic laugh. "You're hilarious. Didn't you say earlier that he'll be giving you a monthly allowance?"

"Yes, but only for six months. Then he cuts me off cold."

"So why are you acting like he's leaving you penniless?"

Normally, I wouldn't discuss these deeply personal things with anyone. But Piper wasn't just anyone. She was the only person on Earth who knew everything about me—finances included. "Well, considering what my parents left me, the allowance he's offering is chump change."

Piper laughed, which caused me to bite my lips. I didn't find any of this funny in the grand scheme of things. However, I couldn't deny how irrational I sounded. I was lucky she loved me and allowed me to have moments of complete absurdity.

"What'll happen to the rest? Legally, he can't keep that from you, right?" She *finally* sounded like she was taking my situation a little more seriously. About time. Hopefully, she was about to switch sides and tell me how to dig myself out of this mess.

I popped the last two Sweeties from the wrapper into my mouth and shrugged. "Technically speaking, I should have full access to my trust fund on my twenty-fifth birthday. But I'm not sure what authority my parents gave him when they set everything up."

I'd lost both parents in a tragic skiing accident during winter break of sophomore year. They'd gone to Colorado with friends while I stayed back with Piper and her family. That entire year was nothing more than a massive blur in my memory. Everything was up in the air, mostly because my parents' will had been written when I was much younger.

According to that document, I was supposed to live with my Aunt Shelly and Uncle Beau...except they were no longer married, and my uncle had since moved to Germany. That was when my grandfather graciously stepped in to take care of me.

"So all the money is yours in two years?" she asked before shoving another spoonful of ice cream into her mouth.

I could see where she was going with this, but I didn't care to hand the argument over to her and admit defeat. Especially when I felt close to having her on my side. "Providing he doesn't spend it all, yes."

"You're so dramatic. He's never touched a red cent of your money, so I highly doubt he'd start now."

I clicked my tongue and shook my head. "Maybe *he* wouldn't, but what about *her*? Huh? Right after that conniving bitch came into the picture, my grandfather kicked me out and cut me off financially. Coincidence? I think not. And no one can deny the power of the puss."

"*Ew!*" Piper gagged dramatically. "He's old. I doubt he can even get it up at his age."

"Three words, Pipes... Little. Blue. Pill."

"You're disgusting."

Biting back my smirk, I shrugged. "Doesn't detract from the truth."

Everything had been perfectly fine until he'd started dating the woman from the gardening center in town. Maureen Gilfreid. The elderly lady appeared innocent enough, except I wasn't stupid. She couldn't fool me with her white hair, pink cheeks, and wrinkled hands. There was no other explanation why Gramps would make me move out at the same time *she* was set to move in.

"Believe what you want, Claire, but hell would freeze over before he took a penny from you for *any* reason. He's fought off all the family vultures since he became your guardian, which means this entire ordeal is completely temporary. You'll be back to spending your days shopping online and inventing new ways to waste money in no time."

"Yeah, but what am I going to do until then?"

"Oh, gee, Claire, let me think...how about get a job like the rest of us?"

I disregarded her mocking tone and whined, "Easy for you to say."

She tilted her head and pulled her lips to one side. This was her sympathy stare. While it appeared disingenuous to most, nothing was more sincere. "Don't worry, Claire...I'll help you. You won't have to do this on your own."

I had to admit that, with her in my corner, I felt less alone.

But alone, all the same.

CHAPTER 1
CLAIRE

"PLEASE HELP me welcome our next contestant to *You Can't Buy Love*, Claire Hansen." Bob Archer was the best game show host in history, and I couldn't believe he stood right in front of me.

"Nice to meet you, Bob." I let out a nervous giggle and waved at the audience.

"You're here to find love, so let's bring the single guys to the stage!"

Upbeat music filled the studio as a line of men walked out from behind a giant, red velvet curtain. I jumped up and down to the beat, unable to pull my attention away from the washboard abs and defined pecs that paraded by. Each specimen was more gorgeous than the last. There was a good chance I was drooling, but for some reason, I didn't care.

My heart pounded against my ribs so loudly the sound echoed around the studio.

They all stood before me with killer smiles and eyes that urged me forward, inviting me in.

"Say hello to our contestants. This hour is going to fly by; I can tell by the look on Claire's face!"

I lifted my hand to smooth out my hair—something I subconsciously did when I was nervous—and immediately gasped. This couldn't be right; I was on national television with a frickin' topknot on my head.

What the hell?

That *really* made my heart slam against my ribs, the harsh thud filling my ears.

Riddled with anxiety, I clicked my heels against the floor, surprised they made no noise whatsoever. I glanced down and discovered my fluffy pink slippers that I wouldn't be caught dead wearing outside the house.

First my hair, now my shoes.

This was getting worse by the second.

"Claire, go up and meet our hunks of the hour. You can ask them anything, touch them, or run your fingers through their hair." The women in the audience hooped and hollered, and suddenly, I forgot all about my disheveled appearance as my body propelled forward.

Booming echoes filled the studio again, though I became aware they weren't heartbeats this time. I glanced around and discovered a construction crew building a set behind the audience. They battered the wood with their hammers, but no one seemed to care. So I ignored the noise and returned my attention to the man with a giant *T* on his name tag.

Good God, his turquoise eyes should be illegal.

My knees grew weak, and a little bit of drool pooled in the corner of my mouth. I held out my hand to him and moaned when he kissed my knuckles.

"What a prince!" I crooned and turned to the audience. They cheered for me. They supported me. *They loved me!*

T pulled me closer and whispered, "I need to taste you."

I hummed and leaned into him until—

Thud! Thud!

"What the—" I screeched and covered my head with a fluffy pillow. I was in the middle of the best dream I'd ever had, and I wasn't ready to wake up yet. I willed myself to go back to sleep. But unfortunately, I couldn't, because the construction crew wouldn't stop building the...

Thud!

Wait. The construction crew was part of the dream.

Thud! Thud!

However, the banging was real.

I bolted upright, my feet hitting the bare floor before I could process the time. The clock on my nightstand must've been wrong because the glowing blue numbers said it was barely seven in the morning, which couldn't be right. After all, people didn't bang on each other's doors before the sun came up.

Thud!

"Oh my God, I'm coming!" I screamed in frustration as I stalked down the hall. I grumbled beneath my breath with every step from my room to the front door—which wasn't far, thanks to my tiny, one-bedroom duplex.

However, once I opened the door and saw what was on my stoop, my grumbling ceased. As did my breathing and all brain function. The ability to think in the presence of such a gorgeous specimen was nearly impossible.

Honestly, I doubt I'd ever seen anyone as beautiful as the sex god in front of me.

His dirty-blond hair looked a little overgrown, but the unruly, wispy strands that covered most of his brow suited him well. They made his Caribbean eyes stand out, too. The color was hypnotic, pulling me into a trance as I continued my mental examination of this perfect stranger. I followed the slight slope of his nose down to the most beautiful scowl I'd ever seen on another human being.

Wait—that couldn't be right. *A scowl?*

I checked again, ignoring the words coming out of his mouth. And sure enough, this guy could even make a very annoyed glower sexy.

"I'm sorry…" I stammered while shaking my head, hoping to rid my brain of the fog. "Can you repeat that? I'm still half-asleep."

Those blue-green eyes rolled in a perfect half-circle. If he didn't stop with his sexiness, I'd never be able to understand the purpose of his morning wake-up call. "Your truck is blocking my driveway, and I have to leave for work."

"You must have the wrong house. I don't have a truck. I have an SUV that's parked in my garage. But good luck figuring out who else to wake up at the ass-crack of dawn." I slowly began to close the door, ready to climb back into bed and revive my dream of half-naked men wanting to do naughty things to me. But he stopped my exit, preventing me from closing the door by slapping his large, manly hand against the solid wood.

"So that doesn't belong to you?" He hitched his thumb over his shoulder to a small U-Haul, which was indeed blocking the driveway.

"Oh. I'm so sorry! I didn't realize that was in your way."

He dropped his arm to his side and blinked several times while staring at me. The longer he stared, the more exaggerated his blinking became until he finally closed his eyes and ran his fingers through his unruly hair. I might've been lost in a sleepy fog, but I was pretty sure I saw him tug at the roots a bit —which made me imagine doing the same while he had his head between my thighs.

Thankfully, he spoke again, which broke the spell he'd put me under.

"Can you move it? I have to leave," he said, sounding *extremely* annoyed.

His harsh, masculine voice might as well have been a slap across the face, completely knocking me out of the sleep-deprived haze I'd been lost in since rolling out of bed. "Oh my God, yes. Absolutely. I'm so sorry."

Well, maybe not *completely* waking me up, considering I slammed the door in his face without saying anything else…such as *bye*. Oh well, at least he was getting what he wanted—the ability to back out of the driveway.

I barely had the keys in my hand before I realized a few things…one, I was still in my pajamas, which consisted of booty shorts and a tank top that did absolutely nothing to hide my pointy nips. And two, blocking *his* driveway meant he was my neighbor.

My *direct* neighbor.

Which was both good *and* bad. Good because I'd have plenty of opportunities to take in his sexiness without having to talk to him. Bad because I'd ruined my only chance for a good first impression. Not only did he see me look a hot mess, but he didn't seem very happy to have me live next door.

THE LAPTOP SCREEN in front of me refused to provide the answers I sought. I'd managed to download a sample résumé, but I stalled after filling in my high school information. My mind went blank as I contemplated whether or not I should include the boutique I'd worked at for a week. Doing so would look bad. But if I didn't, I was stuck with a big fat nada in the experience section. So I skipped over the part for my previous work history and went to references. That's when I realized how accurate Piper was—there was no hope for me.

I couldn't even manage to write out a simple résumé.

A depressing thought crossed my mind—if my mom were here, she'd know what to do. She'd be able to get me out of this mess. Then again, if she were here, I highly doubted I'd even be in this situation to begin with. Not only would she *not* have kicked me out, but I probably would've had a few more life skills to draw from.

Damn… I really missed my mom.

My stomach grumbled as I caught a glimpse of the darkening sky through the window. Somehow, I'd completely forgotten about dinner. I'd been too busy trying to make myself sound hirable to even care about nutrition. At this rate, I wouldn't be able to afford food, so I figured I might as well start the starvation diet now.

Suddenly, a knock resounded from the front door, freeing me from my depressive thoughts. I'd never been more grateful for a distraction. I'd sent Piper a rant-filled message about an hour ago on how adulting was impossible and whoever invented it should burn and rot in hell. So I assumed she'd decided to stop by on her way home from work to help me bullshit my way through this arduous employment process.

"Ohmygod, it's about time you—" My cheery tone cut off mid-flow when I realized my visitor wasn't my best friend, but instead, my hotty neighbor. I was *not* prepared for round two.

"Hey." The smirk growing slowly on his face melded into his deep baritone.

"Oh. You're not Piper."

I quickly closed my gaping mouth and shut the door halfway, using the heavy wood as a barrier between us. He'd already seen me half-naked; he didn't need to see my hobo look as well. After all, I'd been busy moving and unpacking—more like shoving boxes into closets. And once I ran out of space to hide stuff, I went to work finding a job. I didn't exactly have much time to pretty myself up. Plus, I didn't expect anyone other than Piper to come knocking.

He seemed to have a knack for showing up when I looked my worst.

"Last time I checked, no, I'm not." He held out his arms and glanced down at himself, as if making a show of verifying his identity. When he lifted his chin to regard me once more, the flash of his brilliantly bright teeth caught my attention. His ability to make panties drop was *completely* unfair.

"Can I help you?" I asked, trying to act and sound busy when, in reality, I was simply embarrassed by how I'd answered the door. "I've already returned the moving truck, and my car is still in the garage, so if someone's blocking your driveway, don't look at—"

"Oh, no…that's not why I'm here," he interrupted with amusement lining his lips. That smile successfully made me forget I was dressed like a slob. "I only dropped by to apologize for this morning. I was running behind and wasn't very pleasant, so I wanted to see if we could start over. I'd love a chance to prove to you I'm not always a dick."

"Depends…" I pointed to the bottle in his left hand. "Is that your peace offering?"

"Yes," he answered with a soft chuckle that made me weak in the knees. Then he held out a delicious-looking homemade pie as if the vino wasn't enough. "My name's Travis. It's nice to meet you."

Between those sea-blue eyes of his, the bottle of wine, *and* dessert, I couldn't come up with a single reason to reject his offering. So I shrugged off the uncertainty and opened the door wider. "I'm Claire. Come on in."

He followed me to the small kitchen in the back of the house and took a seat at the table in the corner while I grabbed the wine opener and two glasses. Luckily, I didn't go anywhere without my trusty electric opener, so at least I didn't have to hunt one down—seriously, nothing in this kitchen was at all where I would've put things.

Once I finally found some stemware, I popped the cork and poured us each a glass. Despite my stomach fluttering with nervousness, I didn't spill any. Granted, Piper and I had spent that last couple of years perfecting the art of flawlessly pouring wine. In fact, there was a good chance I could fill glass after glass on a boat in the middle of a hurricane without spilling a drop.

"Did you forget where you put everything?" Travis asked with a sexy smirk and raised brow.

I handed him a glass of wine and sat in the seat opposite him, realizing afterward what a mistake that was. I'd have to consciously avoid eye contact to keep from drooling all over myself. "No...I rented this place furnished, so most of what you see was already here. I should move things around, though. Seems like nothing's organized."

"Like what?"

I met his stare, immediately cursing myself when that beautiful combination of green and blue made me shift in my seat to ease the ache they'd caused. "These glasses, for one thing. The rest of the cups and mugs are right next to the fridge, whereas these were over there."

He followed the direction of my finger to the far end of the kitchen, all the while, visibly biting back his smirk. "Probably because that's where the wine cooler is. Putting stemware over there's a matter of convenience, rather than across the kitchen with the other cups."

"Wine cooler?"

"Yeah, right there," he said, pointing the same way I just did.

I was so confused. "The mini-fridge?"

His laughter bounced off the plain-white walls and enveloped me like a warm blanket. "I guess you could use it as one, but they're designed to keep wine chilled. They aren't supposed to be as cold as a refrigerator."

"Well, I'll be darned." I ignored the way he shook his head and laughed beneath his breath, obviously making fun of me. "Then where are the curved shelves that hold the bottles? There's literally nothing inside."

Travis got up and took about three strides with his long legs before kneeling in front of this supposed *wine cooler*. "Looks like the previous tenants removed them for some reason. If you don't find them, I'd call the landlord. They're good about taking care of things around here."

"Wait..." I stood as well, crossing my arms and leaning my hip into the glass edge of the tabletop. "How did you know what I have in my kitchen?"

"Because we live in a duplex...which means the inside of my place is exactly like yours but mirrored. I have the same thing."

Conceding to his reason, I nodded and took a sip of wine.

Apparently, I could be quite a vino snob, and the last thing I wanted to do was disrespect him by insulting his peace offering. However, I was pleasantly surprised. It didn't burn on the way down like the two-buck-chuck Piper habitually served.

I admired the bottle and said, "Wow, Travis. This wine is excellent."

"Thanks. My family owns a vineyard, so I always have a supply handy. You're welcome to peruse my fridge anytime." The vibrato of his tone caused my heart to skip beats.

"Seriously? Like, a *real* vineyard? Damn, I'm impressed." My eyebrows shot up as I took another sip. "I bet your family reunions are a blast. You literally have a never-ending flow of wine."

His shoulders jumped as he quietly chuckled to himself. "Yeah, they kinda are. And on top of that, my brother has a brewery, so we tend to have a few options at family dinners."

"I've never been a beer drinker."

"What about liquor?" His grin broadened, making my panties wet and my knees weak.

I actually giggled like a pre-teen trying to flirt for the first time. "I don't mind liquor, but I have to have a mixer. The few times I've tried to take shots... Let's say things didn't end well."

"My parents are looking into dipping their toes in the rum industry, but they haven't finalized any decisions yet." He sipped his wine and somehow managed to make even *that* erotic. The seductive glint in his eyes as he held the liquid in his mouth for a beat could've easily made me drool all over myself.

So.

Damn.

Sexy.

I gulped and tried to think of something to say before a puddle formed beneath me. The problem was that I couldn't recall anything he'd just said, so I was left with no option but to change the subject. "I bet owning a vineyard comes in handy with the ladies. You probably just walk outside to find dates, huh?"

"Eh, I wouldn't say that. Most of the women I come across are all the same, and honestly, I'm beyond tired and bored of their type. They're nothing but spoiled-rich trust-fund babies who have an unlimited supply of money yet no responsibilities."

Apparently, I wasn't odd after all. I'd simply been hanging out at the wrong places. Too bad no one ever told me that all I had to do was go to vineyards. This whole time, I could've been sipping wine with people just like me instead of enduring endless lectures about not having a job.

But I couldn't focus on that right now because he'd hit a major nerve.

Heat rose up my cheeks as irritation and humiliation swirled within me. This particular subject—about wealth and privilege—had been the bane of my existence throughout high school. The last thing I wanted to do was fight that battle again as an adult.

"I'm sorry, but I don't believe in generalizing people into categories."

He regarded me with confusion furrowing his brow. "What do you mean?"

"If you give any person a chance, they'd probably prove you wrong.

11

Writing someone off before taking the opportunity to learn anything about them is beyond cruel."

Travis held up one hand in surrender, surprise etching his brow in deep horizontal lines. "I'm so sorry... I didn't mean to offend you."

"No worries, you didn't." *Lie.* "I only wanted to make a point. You'd be surprised how many people out there don't give a shit about anyone other than themselves."

"Oh, I think I do. I see them every day at the vineyard."

I wanted to argue, but I decided to close my mouth before giving myself away.

The less he knew, the better.

AFTER HE LEFT, I topped off my glass and cut into the homemade fruit pie he'd given me. I could've easily shared it with seven other people, but fortunately for me, Travis had gone home and Piper never showed up. Plus, Gramps wasn't here to tell me I couldn't eat the entire thing by myself.

Which meant tonight's dinner would be apple pie.

I put a forkful of warm, gooey apples into my mouth and hummed. I'd never eaten anything more delicious in my life. Although, nearly reaching the point of starvation might've played a part in how amazing I believed it was.

However, the second and third bites were equally as good, and they gave me an idea...

I dialed Piper's number and waited for her to pick up.

"Um, hello?" Her voice almost sounded muffled.

"Were you asleep? At eight o'clock?"

"Nope. Just closing my eyes for a second while my phone charged."

"Oh, good...because I have an amazingly brilliant idea!"

"I don't think I have the wherewithal to listen to this," Piper complained with an elongated moan running through her words.

"Come on," I scoffed. "This is good. Probably the best idea I've ever had in my life."

"Like I haven't heard that ten thousand times before."

I could practically hear her eyes roll, which made me laugh. "I'm serious this time. My neighbor came over tonight—"

"The hot one with the smile?" She had a one-track mind.

"Yup. The one and only. And he brought over wine and a homemade pie to apologize for getting annoyed with me this morning."

"That was nice. Did he give you his digits?"

"No. But you have *got* to try this pie. It's seriously one of the best things I've ever eaten." I took another bite, and with a full mouth, I added, "I think this could be my thing."

"What thing? I'm so confused."

"My big endeavor." The sound of *duh* reverberated in tone. I couldn't believe she'd forgotten already. "The thing I use to prove to Gramps that I have my shit together. I could start a new business as a baker. I'd make bank! Trust me! This is delicious. And homemade, too. Which means they aren't sold in stores."

"Claire, I hate to point out the obvious and possibly crush your newly discovered life-long dream, but you have no capital to invest. And don't forget about your lack of experience in the business arena. Do you have any idea what a huge undertaking this is?"

"Yes. I understand completely." I found myself nodding with conviction. I'd never felt more confident about *anything*.

"Um, I think you need to take a step back and do some research first. How are you going to market this? What's your target audience? How are you going to package and display your items for sale? Do you plan to have a web-based business, or do you need a storefront?" Piper rattled off enough questions to make my head spin.

"Slow down. You're kinda jumping the gun a bit. The first order of action needs to be a plan to make these darn things. I don't even have the recipe," I admitted. "Which is why I need your help. You have to come over and help me figure out which ingredients were used."

"Are you high? You've never baked in your life." By Piper's laughter, I could tell she wasn't taking me seriously, but I would show her. This time I was serious.

"Just because I've never baked anything doesn't mean I can't. Imagine what would've happened if everyone had told Ariana Grande not to sing. She would've never found out she could. Talents are *discovered*, Pipes."

A long puff of air ran through the line and filled my ear. "How many rolls of Sweeties have you eaten?"

"Does this mean you won't help me?" I pouted, even though she couldn't see.

Piper groaned into the phone. "No, I'll help, but I can't tonight."

"Got a hot date?"

"Yeah," she replied sarcastically. "With my pillow. I'll see you tomorrow."

I was in the zone, so if she wouldn't come over and teach me how to bake, then I would have to watch a few episodes of *Nailed It!* That way, I could impress her when she finally got here.

Claire, the extraordinary baker!

Coming soon, to a bakery near you!

CHAPTER 2

TRAVIS

I SHIFTED my weight to my heels while lining up the ball with the hoop. This was for a three-pointer—the winning shot. If I made this, I'd have all the power.

"He shoots, *and he scores!*" I cupped my hands around my mouth to imitate the sound of a wild crowd screaming with excitement. In my head, everyone in the stadium rose to their feet and chanted my name...*Travis! Travis!*

"Travis!" Although that time, someone truly did call out my name, so I glanced at my brother. To my surprise, he flicked his gaze over my shoulder and offered a short, jerky nod, gesturing to something behind me.

Standing on the other side of the driveway was my sexy neighbor. A smile quickly crossed my face, but before I could utter a greeting, her irritated tone rang through the air.

"What is wrong with you?" Her light-brown hair stuck up in every direction, and she had some sort of jelly-like substance smeared on one side of her face.

I glanced over my shoulder and raised my brows at my brother Craig, but he only shrugged. So I turned back to the woman wearing the sexiest pajamas I'd ever seen—a tank top, which left very little to the imagination, and a pair of very small shorts that appeared to be made out of spandex.

Without trying, she proved lingerie was pointless.

She didn't need lace to make any man feel the need to readjust.

"Uh...nothing? What's wrong with you?"

Her dark eyes narrowed, and her mouth gaped. My response clearly stunned her. But after a few seconds, she broke free from the shocked trance and resumed her interrogation. "This is the second morning in a row you've woken me up before the sun."

She couldn't be serious.

"I'm sorry?" I hadn't meant for my words to come out as a question, but I was truly lost at what else to say. "It's after eight. The sun's been up for over an hour. And it's a Saturday." I bit back a laugh, not wanting to set her off any more than I already had.

She blinked toward the sky over the line of trees and growled. "That's neither here nor there. I was up working all night, and the only thing I want is a little bit of sleep. If this is what I have to look forward to every morning, just say so. That way, I can prepare myself in advance—or find somewhere else to live. I swear, you wait until I've hit REM before you start beating and banging and thumping around out here...or on my front door."

That genuinely made me feel terrible. I imagined her being a night nurse at the hospital or some other emergency care worker crawling into bed as everyone else in the world was getting ready to start their day.

"I'm so sorry..." I let my apology trail off and took a step toward her. "I wasn't aware you worked nights. What do you do?"

She pivoted her weight back and forth from foot to foot, becoming rather fidgety. "I'm a baker."

I stopped walking and narrowed my gaze. That was the complete opposite of what I imagined when she mentioned working overnight. Then again, if people demanded baked goods first thing in the morning, someone had to prepare them ahead of time.

"Well, again, I'm sorry. If I'd known you don't go to bed 'til late, I would've been more conscious of how much noise I make in the mornings."

"Thanks."

I couldn't do anything other than stare after her as she turned around and stomped back inside. Not even the soft bounce of her ass cheeks beneath the hem of her shorts was enough to draw my attention away from her departure.

Craig chuckled from behind me when she slammed her front door. That's when I finally cracked a smile. She intrigued me. Her whole argument was about how loud I was in the mornings, yet the echo of her dramatic exit could've been heard on the next street over.

"Damn, Travis...you didn't tell me you have a crazy person living next door."

I whipped my head around and stared at my little brother. We were the same height, but he was a bit scrawnier. Out of all four of us boys, we looked the most alike. We had a running joke in our family that our parents found Craig and me on the side of the road as kids, so they took us in and raised us as their own. Although, if I had to guess, I'd say Jake and Brenden were adopted because they didn't look like any of us.

"What? No she's not." I thought back to my visit with her last night. It'd been short, and we didn't talk about much, but I assumed I would've recognized crazy if it'd been there. Sure, she stormed out wearing next to nothing and screamed at me for waking her up, but if anything, I'd say she seemed stressed. Not insane.

"Say what you want, but that sort of behavior could be categorized as borderline psychotic. Then again, she's not my neighbor. I'm not the one who has to worry about the level of sound I make at noon."

I rolled my eyes at his ridiculousness.

"Oh, come on, Trav, don't tell me you've got a thing for her."

"I don't, okay?" I glanced back at her front door. Picturing her in that sheer tank top caused my lips to spread into a wide, goofy grin. It'd been a while since I'd been interested in anyone of the opposite sex. "Nothing wrong with a bit of harmless flirting. Might even be fun."

"Yeah, until she burns your house down."

With a sigh, I successfully shot one more basket before we made our way inside. We had to get ready since our parents had called a family meeting for this morning at ten. If any of us showed up even one minute late, it'd be mentioned at every family gathering for the next two years.

AN HOUR LATER, calmness enveloped me as I headed down the gravel road to the winery. There was something incredibly peaceful about driving between rows and rows of grapevines. And as I pulled into one of the many empty spaces in front of the giant barn-style building, I was reminded of the second-best thing about coming to the winery on my day off.

I opened the car door and was immediately met by two large, very excited dogs. This only happened on weekend mornings, though. Two or three extra dogs came with the workers during the rest of the week to sniff out diseases that could devastate a crop.

After I finished giving Rocky and Bullwinkle all the attention they sought, I headed inside to find my parents. I knew they were around here somewhere since Dad's pickup was out front, but considering the square footage of the winery, he wasn't always easily found.

Uncorked Vineyards covered about six acres of the family's overall fifteen-acre property. The land had been passed down for generations, but my parents were the first to produce a business other than farming. Shortly before my oldest brother was born, they sectioned off nearly a third of the property for harvesting grapes. But after five or six years of doing all the work for other people, they decided to open their own winery. And over time, they slowly increased their vine production while reducing the size of our family's generational farming business.

I pushed one of the heavy barn-style doors aside and left it open for Craig to follow behind once he finished with the pups. The giant front room never ceased to amaze me. My mom designed this entire building from top to bottom almost thirty years ago. We'd made a few minor modifications here and there as we grew, but overall, the style, décor, and layout stood the test of time...all thanks to the woman currently keeping inventory of our branded T-shirts.

"Hey, Mom," I called out as I headed to the front counter.

"Travis!" A warm smile brightened her face as she turned around and saw me walking toward her. She came out from around the giant oak counter and kissed my cheek. "You're early."

"Why do you sound so surprised? I'm not the one who's usually late— that's Brenden." Granted, I couldn't blame him for notoriously being tardy. After all, he had primary custody of his two kids, and even though I didn't have any, I'd been at his place enough times to understand how long they take to get ready.

Mom rolled her eyes in humor while waving me off. "I'm not. I'm just saying Craig is usually the first one here. Nothing against you."

Just then, my little brother strolled through the door. "Momma-Bear!"

"There he is," she said as if she'd been looking for him her whole life.

Mothers used different tones depending on their mood...but my mother had different tones for greeting each of her sons. And she made no secret of Craig being her favorite. She greeted each of us very lovingly and with an abundance of warmth, but there was no denying the syrupy weight to her voice every time he walked into the room.

"We drove together," I said as if still talking to my mom. And since she'd already walked away, I made my voice higher to sound more like her and replied with, "Oh, that's good to hear. It's nice to see you." Going back to playing myself, I smiled at the now vacant spot she stood in two seconds ago and added, "Same here. You should probably go hug Craig now. We wouldn't want him to feel left out."

"Talking to yourself again, son?" Dad came around the corner, likely from his office, his booming laughter echoing in the large, open space. His presence couldn't be missed. Standing over six feet tall, he was often compared to a linebacker—a position he played in high school.

"No..." I nodded toward the cooing over my shoulder. "Just finishing my conversation with Mom. She walked away to make sure Craig didn't have any scrapes or bruises, so I was left to complete our greeting."

His laugh grew deeper, more rumbly, which was how I could tell his amusement was genuine.

"Have you taken a look at those new label designs I sent you yesterday?"

He scrubbed one of his hands, which was the size of a bear's paw, over his mouth in an obvious attempt to wipe away his infectious grin. Nothing about my dad was small, especially his ability to change the tone of any room he was in based solely on his mood.

"No, I haven't." He turned toward the hallway that led to the offices and waved me on. "Let's do that now while we wait for the others to show up." Then he lowered his head and whispered, "Plus, this will give your mom a few minutes to boost your brother's ego."

While we sat in his office hovered around the computer, my other two brothers arrived. And by the grace of God, Brenden showed up with two minutes to spare. I wasn't complaining, though. I was quite thankful I didn't have to listen to fifteen minutes of my mom suggesting ways he could improve his time management.

"The longer we take to start this meeting, the longer we'll be here," my dad called out, hoping to make us stop talking and listen. He took the seat at the end of the large oval conference desk and crossed his arms on the wooden top.

This wasn't our typical family meeting.

Once we all quieted down, my parents got down to business. Dad started by reading out the updated progress on the vineyard, followed by Mom catching us up on where the winery stood in terms of sales. Both of which could've been included in an email. And in all honesty, I wished they had been because I struggled to pay attention to the meeting itself. Instead, I spent most of the time my parents talked thinking about my feisty neighbor and wondering when I'd see her again.

She intrigued me, though I couldn't pinpoint exactly what I found so appealing about her. Technically, she'd bitched me out the last two mornings, but she did so while wearing the tiniest pajamas ever made. So I didn't mind too much. I reckoned I could put up with a morning lashing every day of the week if she wore that outfit every time. Then I thought about last night when I took her a bottle of wine and one of my mom's pies. She was...normal. Definitely someone I could see myself being friends with.

"What do you think, Trav?" my dad asked, yanking me out of my thoughts.

There was no telling how long I'd been daydreaming, so I wasn't sure how much I'd missed. All I knew was that my dad wanted my opinion on whatever they were talking about. So I said the only thing I could think of. "I'll have to take a look and get back to you. Can you wait until Monday?"

The room was so quiet a pin drop could've been heard. As I glanced around the table, I began to think that maybe my response didn't fit the question I'd been asked. But before I could try to save myself, my dad shrugged and said, "Yeah, take your time. We don't have to have an answer quite yet."

I nearly released an audible sigh of relief.

"Okay, now that we have that somewhat settled, let's move on to the farm..." Mom glanced up from the piece of paper in her hand and settled her curious eyes on Brenden. "Why has our production of goat's milk been so low lately?"

This part of the meeting didn't concern me, considering I had absolutely nothing to do with the farm, but I found the question interesting enough to listen to my brother's excuse.

"Well, probably because the people who are responsible for doing the milking have been calling out at the last minute, leaving me with the impossible task of covering their shifts."

"That's what happens when you use volunteers from local youth groups," Craig said while snickering under his breath.

"Dude. I'm saving a ton of money that way. Do you have a better idea?" Brenden's stance changed; he puffed out his chest, and his eyes blazed.

"Slow your roll. I'm only saying if you spent money and hired a few *dependable* people, then you might have better results. You'd spend more upfront, but the higher milk production would even out the cost in the end. Not to mention, your stress level would be knocked down a few pegs. I mean, look at you. You're willing to fight me over spilled goat's milk. Nothing's that serious, bro," Craig reasoned.

Unfortunately, my oldest brother didn't quiet down. "Do you have any idea how hard my job is? Finding people who *want* to milk an animal, let alone a goat, is not easy. And those I do find don't stay long. I'd like to see you try to upsell that task."

"Easy-peasy," Jake spoke up with a harsh slap on the tabletop. "All you have to do is put a help-wanted ad out, asking if anyone wants to touch titties all day. If you say that, you might have a ton of high school boys volunteer, which would be a bonus because you wouldn't have to pay them."

"Jacob Spencer Cabrera," Mom growled. "Too far."

We all stopped laughing, including my dad. When Mom got serious and used our middle names, her tone alone was enough to scare the toughest of us.

To try and calm the mood in the room, I offered, "I can put the word out with some of my contacts. I can't make any promises, though."

"Sounds good." Dad closed his notepad and slapped his hands together. "Well, that about sums everything up. Brenden, I expect the scheduling mishap to be corrected next week, Friday at the latest. We're losing too much there, which I find completely unacceptable."

My brother groaned but complied with a nod, nonetheless.

"As for the brewhouse... Craig, I expect a full report regarding all bids from suppliers on my desk come Monday morning." He didn't wait for a reply before moving on to my second oldest brother, Jake. "The distillery got back with me this morning about available times we can tour their facility. I'll email them to you when we finish here, but I have to tell them something as soon as possible."

We didn't only have the winery and farm. We also owned a local brewhouse located off the property that Craig was in charge of. And over the last few months, Jake had decided to look into opening a distillery he could head up.

My parents had always been very business-minded people and extremely hard workers. Those traits were instilled in all of us, so I understood why my brother would want a venture of his own. So while each of us handled, managed, operated, and partly owned our own sector of the family businesses, we always kept everyone in the loop.

"And last but not least, Travis." Hopefully, he'd give me enough clues to help me figure out what they were talking about earlier—when I was too busy fantasizing over my neighbor to pay attention. "Give that a good think over the weekend, and we'll meet back up Monday morning. I'm looking forward to hearing your opinion."

Dammit.

While we all slowly made our way out of our seats, I contemplated asking one of my brothers to fill me in on what I'd missed, but as I ran through my options, I quickly changed my mind. My older brothers, Jake and Brenden, would never miss an opportunity to mock me.

Shitheads.

And if I asked Craig, he'd question me half to death about why I wasn't listening to begin with. He was pretty much a human lie detector, so lying to him wasn't an option. And if I told him the truth, not only would that ensure he *wouldn't* tell me, but he'd also never let me live it down.

My last hope was that my parents would forget.

This was doubtful, considering they were like elephants and never forgot anything.

CHAPTER 3

CLAIRE

MY NEIGHBOR HAD a way of making things go from bad to worse.

I'd spent all day on those wretched pies, and after many failed attempts, I finally believed I'd perfected the art of baking. So when I saw Travis's car out front, I figured now was a good time to take him one, hoping he'd share some insight.

So I stupidly decided to stroll across our driveways to his side of the duplex.

One minute, I was concentrating on not dropping the gorgeous pie, and the next, I was blind. Out of nowhere, water shot through the bushes near his front porch and soaked me. "Oh my God! What did I ever do to you?" I shrieked as I rubbed my eyes, trying to clear my vision.

"I'm so sorry!" a deep voice exclaimed, but I couldn't make out where he was.

Honestly, there had to be someone above laughing right about now. Every time I tried to have a decent conversation with this man, the universe had other plans. Or maybe my angels were sending a message—more like a warning in the form of multiple waving red flags.

"Are you okay?" he asked, though I now realized the voice belonged to Travis, and he was coming toward me. "I feel so awful. Here, come inside, and I'll grab you a towel."

"No, I'm all right. I'll just go home and dry off." I glanced down, noticing my sweater was also wet. "And change," I added beneath my breath, followed by a long sigh.

"I honestly had no idea you were there. I swear." The mortification painted on his face in the way of large, wide eyes, flaring nostrils, and loose jaw lessened my anger a little.

But only a little. "What were you doing anyway? Randomly spraying your driveway?"

"No," he said while shaking his head. His brows knitted together as he narrowed his gaze. "I came out to water the plants. I was turning on the hose when you walked up, so my back was to you."

Something about the sincerity in his eyes reminded me of my dad. And that one tiny reminder was all I needed to wring out the rest of my irritation. Now, if I could just wring out the water from my hair and sweater.

"I'm okay. This isn't the first time I've ever been wet," I reasoned.

Apparently, that was enough to calm him down because as soon as the words were out of my mouth, his expression softened. His lips even curled a little, causing a slight heat to color his cheeks.

"Anyway, the whole purpose in coming over was to apologize for this morning and bring you this." I held up the pie I'd spent hours baking from scratch; thankfully, it wasn't waterlogged.

"Did you bake this yourself?"

"Yeah, that's pretty much what I've been up to all day—doing nothing but trying to recreate the one you brought over last night. I still haven't figured out what you put in yours, but man, I've spent *hours* trying to come this close."

I prayed that would persuade him into sharing his recipe.

But instead of offering even a small suggestion, he took the dessert and nodded toward his front door. "Come in, and we'll share it...over a glass of wine," he added with a smirk, knowing the perfect way to entice me.

To my surprise, his place wasn't messy. Although I wouldn't say tidy, either; it had that lived-in feel. Regardless, this wasn't at all how I pictured a bachelor pad. And with his layout identical to mine, only reversed, I didn't have to pay attention to where I was going. Which meant I was able to inspect everything on my way to the kitchen. However, *not* paying attention meant I was caught off guard when he tossed me a hand towel.

Which smacked me right in the face.

I didn't bother trying to catch flying dish cloth. Instead, I watched it fall to the surprisingly clean tile floor, stared at the red-and-white striped rag for a second, and then blinked up at Travis, who stood behind the tiny kitchen island doing his best not to laugh.

"Thanks." Sarcasm filled my voice as I, too, fought against the smile tugging at my lips.

"Leave it; I'll grab you a new one," he said with humor swimming in his words. His shoulders continued to jump as he turned around and opened a drawer to retrieve a clean towel for me...again.

This time, I didn't let him toss it at me. Instead, I playfully snatched the colorful cloth from his hand before wiping off my arms and face.

"Do you want a dry shirt?" he asked, pointing to my wet sweater.

"Nah, I'm okay. I've got a tank on under this anyway."

"Well, feel free to take it off if you want." He released a short gasp and stared at me with surprised eyes. "The sweater, I mean. Not the tank." Embarrassment caused Travis to purse his lips and busy himself with popping the cork.

While he wasn't looking my way, I took the opportunity to pull the light-weight sweater over my head. The air felt cool against my chest without the wet fabric clinging to my skin, so I quickly dabbed myself with the cloth before his attention was on me again.

"Why don't you ha...*oly cow*!" Surprise interrupted whatever he was about to say and caused him to nearly drop the bottle of wine. But he closed his eyes, pulled in a deep breath, and regained control. "I was saying...why don't you take a seat while I grab us glasses and plates?"

I looked down but didn't see anything out of place, so I shrugged off his odd outburst and pulled out a chair from the kitchen table. This was very reminiscent of yesterday, though opposite. In every way possible—including the kitchen layout.

Travis set the opened bottle in the middle of the table and placed a tall wine glass in front of both settings. Then he went to the cabinet for two small dessert plates, grabbing utensils on his way to take his seat.

"Okay, so I want your honest opinion about the pie." The top was smooth and gorgeous, so I knew I didn't have anything to worry about. "Like I said, I loved the one you brought over last night so much that I was inspired to try my hand at it. I'm well aware yours is probably better, which is why I'd love your feedback."

A smile brightened his face, but as he pressed the knife against the top of the pie, his mouth slowly morphed into a frown. One side of his top lip curled, though I had hard time distinguishing his thoughts between disgust and confusion. But then the tip of his tongue peeked out, painting his expression with sexy determination. Within another couple of seconds, he pulled his bottom lip between his teeth. That, coupled with the deep lines etched into his brow, made him appear stumped, but I couldn't figure out why.

Until I glanced down.

Horrified at the sight, I took the knife and tried to cut the pastry myself. Except I couldn't slice through the crust. I tapped the blade against the now scratched-up top, which produced a hard, hollow sound.

"Well..." Travis surmised, "too bad I didn't soak this with the hose along with everything else; a bit of moisture might've helped."

"Very funny." I did my best to act unaffected by the moment.

In reality, red-hot humiliation coursed through me, urging me to leave as fast as I could. But I didn't run away anymore. I'd decided years ago that I would never be that person again—the one who ran from laughter aimed *at* her. Instead, I would own my humiliating actions or words, and if *anyone* laughed at me, I'd join in to show their teasing didn't affect me.

Except, this time proved to be much harder than my high school days.

The metaphorical weight of my situation settled on my chest, barely letting me breathe. If I failed at this, I had nothing to fall back on. I'd be left with two options: be completely penniless or disappoint my grandfather. Neither worked for me, so I had to figure this out.

"There must be something wrong with my oven."

He pushed the rock-hard dessert out of the way and picked up his glass. "That sucks. I was really curious to see if you're a better baker than my mom…considering you're a professional, and all."

"Oh, that was your mom's?" How I'd managed to speak without choking on my tongue was a mystery I'd never solve. The word *professional* caused my heart to practically cease all necessary, life-performing functions.

This won't possibly end well for me.

"Yeah, the recipe is super old, been our traditional family holiday dessert my entire life. Mom mostly uses apples now, but if I remember the story correctly, the original recipe called for blueberries. Somewhere along the way, my grandmother or great-grandmother tried other fruits and expanded the options."

"Aside from apples and berries, what else is used?" I began to wonder how much better mine would've been if I had used blueberries instead of apples. Hell, I probably would've had an easier time replicating the damn thing.

"Basically anything we have on the property—or whatever unused fruits our neighbors send over. Mom has used apples, peaches, cherries, strawberries, blackberries…" He settled his gaze on the wall over my head in thought. "She's used fruit from the store too, but they're never as good."

"Does she use any special ingredient that you're aware of?"

He picked up his phone and tapped on the screen in rapid succession. "Doubtful, but maybe. I've never made one—I don't bake, so I've never had any need for the recipe."

His eyes bounced around the room, and anytime he did look my way, he maintained brief but intense eye contact before glancing away again. Assuming he was either nervous or had some sort of tic, I brushed off his odd behavior and tried not to overthink it.

"Oh, darn…" I pushed out my bottom lip in a dramatic pout. "I guess I'll never figure out if I'm missing anything or using something I shouldn't. I'll just have to keep trying; regardless of how many years I'll waste in the process."

Travis laughed while studying his wine glass, spinning the stem between his fingers. "You're more than welcome to come out to the farm and grab some fruit. Maybe that's the key."

While I appreciated the offer, what I really needed was the recipe. Which I still didn't have.

His phone pinged with a message. I couldn't see the text from where I sat, but whatever conversation he was having must've required a response because he once again furiously tapped on the screen.

This went on a few more times, but whenever I asked if he needed to take care of something, he said no and encouraged me to stay. So I decided to at least finish my glass of wine before heading home.

"If you'll excuse me, I need to use the bathroom real quick." He pushed away from the table and stood, all without looking at me. His inability to do so, as well as being unable to wait until I left, made me assume he had to go number two and felt awkward.

He'd only been out of the room for a few seconds when another message alert sounded. I picked up his phone while simultaneously calling his name in case he hadn't reached the toilet yet. But I didn't utter more than the first syllable of *Travis* before his message thread caught my attention and stole my voice.

Right in front of me—*in my hand*—was a text thread between him and his mom. There were other messages in their conversation, though I ignored those. I didn't want to invade his privacy or anything. Instead, I focused on the attached file titled "Granny's pie recipe."

I pressed on the link, giddy when a document opened and filled the screen, and then tapped the icon in the top right corner. Excitement flooded my system; in my hand was the one thing that would make me a success.

I stared at the screen for a moment, contemplating what to do. Travis had clearly contacted his mother to get the recipe for me, which meant he'd probably send it to me once he returned from the bathroom. The angel on my shoulder told me to hold off for now. However, reality spoke up, reminding me that I couldn't afford to wait. I was already running out of time.

The desire to conquer my fears and make my grandfather proud made concentration difficult. The two voices in my head battled it out amid a storm of unorganized thoughts, but suddenly, everything became quiet. I went into survival mode as soon as I saw the option to Airdrop the document to my phone. My peripheral vision dimmed as my focus narrowed on the task at hand, waiting for the progress status to read *done*.

My cell buzzed in my back pocket, so I quickly exited out of the file, leaving his message app open the way he'd left it. Upon checking my lock screen for the Airdrop notification, I saw a message from Piper.

Piper: *leaving drive-thru now. B there soon.*

Her text had come in five minutes ago. Somehow, it'd gone unnoticed, but I didn't have time to concern myself with that at the moment. She would be at my house any minute, and if I weren't there, she'd leave. And considering she was coming over to teach me how to bake—something I recently learned was a hell of a lot harder than I thought—I couldn't afford to miss this opportunity.

I took no more than three steps before running into Travis. Being too focused on typing out a reply to Piper, I didn't see him turn the corner into the room. But one thing was made crystal clear based on the subtle hint of hours-old cologne—as well as how quickly he'd returned—I could confidently say he hadn't gone number two.

"Leaving already?"

"Oh, yeah...I'm sorry. I totally forgot my best friend is coming over tonight, and she just texted to say she's on her way. So I should probably head home before she gets there." That was the truth, yet for some reason, I felt like I had lied.

Probably because I'd just stolen a file from his phone.

"Doing anything fun?"

"Nah, just having dinner and a chill girls' night." Okay, so *that* was a lie. There would be *nothing* chill about baking. Piper had a reputation for becoming a Gestapo when teaching something.

"Oh, well, here...let me give you a bottle of wine to take with you."

"You don't have to do that."

Ignoring me, he continued toward the wine cooler beneath the counter. "This one hasn't hit the market yet. We experimented with a new grape last year, so you'll have to tell me what you think."

I certainly wasn't going to turn down an opportunity to be one of the first people to try a new flavor. So I accepted the wine with a smile, still noticing how he wouldn't meet my eyes. Instead, he regarded the bottle I cradled in the crook of my arm.

"Thank you so much, Travis. I'm sure our fast food will be extra fancy tonight," I added with a giggle.

"Well, maybe wait for a night when you cook a real meal."

I laughed under my breath and waved him off. "If I did that, it'd be vintage by the time anyone popped the cork."

"You don't cook?" He acted surprised.

My tangled web nearly tripped me up—I was a baker. I supposedly worked *in a kitchen*.

Doing my best to act unfazed, I shrugged and admitted, "I'm at the oven for long hours every day, so come dinnertime, the *last* thing I want to do is stand in front of one for a minute longer."

"Makes sense." He believed me, *thank God*. "That just means you'll have to come over one night and let me cook for you. I can't promise anything fancy, but at least you'll have a real home-cooked meal without any of the work."

For a split second, I wondered if this was his way of asking me on a date. But I took note of his body language and quickly rejected that idea. His friendly manner was just that, and when he spoke, certain syllables were laced with obvious friend-zone vibes.

Considering I had somewhat of an issue creating meaningful relationships with people—other than Piper—that should've reassured me. But it didn't...and I couldn't understand why. A tiny part of my ego felt bruised at realizing he wasn't interested in me in that way.

Eh. I assumed that was just one more of the narcissistic traits I must've picked up from my ex and moved on.

Nodding and smiling, I said, "That sounds amazing. I'll definitely hit you up for that sometime soon. But in the meantime, I really do need to go."

"Of course." He averted his gaze—again—and led me down the hallway.

I slipped past him as he held the door open and stepped onto the front porch. Taking one last glance at him, I smiled and said, "Thanks for the wine, Travis. Once my oven is fixed, I'll bake you something extraordinarily edible next time."

He chuckled with his chin tucked close to his chest. "I'll be looking forward to it, Claire."

Hearing my name in his voice caused my vagina to tense, but I didn't have time to think about my body's reaction to my neighbor. I could see Piper's headlights coming down the street, so I waved and hurried across the driveway before she caught me leaving his place.

No such luck.

"Where are *you* comin' from?" she asked as she climbed out of her car with McDonald's bags in hand. She'd be at this all night. That was exactly why I didn't want her to catch me.

I held open my front door and waited for Piper before heading inside. "I made a quick trip down skid row to barter for a pint of crack for your bong."

Using the wrong lingo had always been our thing. Drugs were something we'd never gotten into—or were ever interested in trying—which only made our exaggerated terminology that much funnier. Partly because we'd never been informed of the correct phrasing.

"Oh, good. I ran out this morning." She shoved past me and headed to the kitchen with our food. After setting the bags on the counter, she looked at me with a growing smirk. "You went next door looking like that?"

I quickly glanced down at myself. "No. Travis doused me with the hose, so I had to take off my sweater."

"I see that." Her smile continued to spread. "Were you aware your cami got wet, too? Or was that the look you were going for?"

Confused and a bit scared, I rushed to the bathroom. Then I screamed. Loudly.

Staring back at me from the giant mirror over the bathroom vanity were *both* of my nipples. Clear as day. Considering my tank top didn't feel soaked, only slightly damp, I didn't once contemplate the color of it.

White.

No wonder Travis kept looking everywhere *but* me.

I wanted to storm over there and scream at him for not telling me that my nips had been on full display. But I also never wanted to show my face again, which would've made confrontation a little difficult. I didn't even have his number, so I couldn't call to curse him out.

And that was how my neighbor had made things go from bad to worse.

THANKFULLY, I managed to calm down while we ate. I wasn't sure what helped the most—the Big Mac, vanilla milkshake, or the bottle of wine—but I no longer felt the need to murder my neighbor and scatter his body parts all over Tesorita.

"Okay, so let's see where you're at." Piper followed me into the kitchen to assess my baking skills.

I picked up the heavy pie I'd taken to Travis's and held it out for her to see.

"That's what you've been bragging about?" She held her fist to her smiling lips and bit back her laughter.

While this type of reaction would've upset me coming from anyone else, I'd never felt offended with Piper. She'd been there through all the laughing, the teasing, the ridiculing. There wasn't a bully she hadn't verbally beaten the tar out of on my behalf. So I knew this was innocent. However, my adoration for my best friend didn't stop me from playing the part of an insulted baker.

"That's actually not as bad as I was expecting."

"Hey!" I lowered my arm somewhat so she could focus on my obvious hurt feelings. "How bad were you expecting?"

"Well, to be honest..." That was never a good start to *any* conversation. Very few could handle Piper's style of brutal honesty. "I was kinda picturing something similar to the mud pies I used to make in second grade."

"Oh, come on, Piper…they're not *that* bad. I realize you weren't here last night to see the one Travis brought over, but I'm tellin' ya, this one is pretty darn close." Kind of. But not really. However, it was a *lot* closer than the first batch I'd tried baking.

Baby steps.

"I'm sure they taste better than they look." She shuffled to the kitchen table and took a seat, probably expecting me to follow with the pastry for her to sample.

I dropped my arm to my side, slumped my shoulders, and curled my chin toward my chest in utter defeat, mumbling, "You *can't* taste them."

"Why not?"

Letting her answer that question for herself made more sense than telling her that I'd managed to turn flour into rock, so I tossed the inedible dessert to her. First, there was a heavy thump. Then her arms went in the air. Followed by her legs as she fell backward off the chair and onto the tile floor.

"Oh my God! Piper!" I ran to her, shoving the kitchen chair out of my way to make room for both of us beneath the table. She wasn't speaking… Man, this was bad. Just my luck, I killed my best friend with my pie.

The only thing to make that headline better was if I were a *Florida Woman*.

But as soon as I straddled her waist and grabbed her shoulders, I realized she was okay. She was out of breath from laughing, not falling. However, she did have a pretty good welt on her forehead.

"I can't believe you threw a pie at me," she said, humor filling her breathless words so heavily I could barely understand her.

"*To* you, Piper. Not *at* you."

"Dude!" She worked on controlling her breathing so she could calm down enough to speak. Apparently, she thought this was hilarious because tears streamed down the sides of her face. "You literally chucked it at me."

"No, not *chucked*, more like an *underhand* toss," I defended. "Like a softball."

"Softball? Look at this!" Piper sat up and grabbed the dessert off the floor, holding the tragic excuse for a pie in my face. "You can't compare this with *anything* that contains the word *soft*. Okay?"

The crust hadn't even crumbled after hitting her *or* the floor. Crap.

"Regardless…who sits there while something's flying toward them? You didn't even try to block your face," I argued as I climbed off her to let her up.

"I wasn't looking. I was trying to rub out the spot of special sauce on my pants. I happened to look up a little too late to defend myself against your attack." She'd never let this go. "I hate to tell you this, Claire, but we've got *a lot* of work ahead of us if you plan to start earning a living from this in the next six months."

"I genuinely thought it'd be good," I whined. "Until I tried cutting into it."

"Have you felt the weight of this thing?" With the aluminum tin balancing on her palm, she lifted the pie up and down like a dumbbell. "Did you not once question the weight? Like...*hmmm, I wonder why my pies are so much heavier than literally any other pie in the entire world.*"

I shrugged. "Yeah, but I blamed the apples."

"Why would apples be so heavy?"

"Have you ever picked up a bag of them?" I stared at her, wondering what planet she was from.

Instead of replying right away, she smacked herself on the forehead and sighed. "Please tell me you didn't use whole apples."

"Of course not. I may be new to baking, but I at least grasp the important parts. I cut them in half."

"I'm gonna leave that for now since the fruit is clearly not what made this thing hard as a freakin' rock. Moving on...did you use the correct ingredients for the crust?"

"Yeah, I'm pretty sure I did. The dough tasted pretty good."

"Claire, I love you to pieces, but I've never heard of anyone tasting pie dough—it will make you sick. On top of that, raw dough shouldn't taste good whatsoever."

"Then why is cookie dough so delicious?" I really thought I had her there.

Until she said, "Not the same, Claire. One is a pie, and the other is a cookie."

This bit of information would've been helpful earlier...as well as saved me loads of time. I'd spent *hours* perfecting the crust. "Oh. Well anyway, mine did. I had to mix in sugar and vanilla, though."

"I'm gonna assume that's where you went wrong. Dough is supposed to be blandish; that way, when you take a bite, whatever's inside explodes in your mouth."

At this point, I doubted dynamite could've made my pie explode.

"Considering your level of baking skills, I think we should start small and work up to full-size desserts. Pies aren't something you learn overnight."

Unfortunately, I *needed* to learn how to perfect this overnight. I didn't have time to waste days on this. "Yeah, starting small is fine with me. Less work."

Piper laughed to herself as she started moving things around on the counter, organizing her workspace. "Well, what are you waiting for? Pull up the recipe, and let's give this a go."

I reached for my phone on the counter, suddenly remembering that I never actually got the file from Travis. I'd been too sidetracked with the new flavor of wine, the potential date and how I felt about that, coming up with a lie on the spot to explain why I could bake but not cook, and then there was the pool of desire in my panties from the way he said my name. I'd been too distracted to think about it before leaving his place.

Assuming he'd see his text and give it to me soon, I proceeded to unlock my phone. "I can't thank you enough, Pipes."

She shrugged, though her eyes were warm and comforting. "I don't have much of a choice, do I? You clearly can't do this on your own."

I leaned into her embrace, and as we pulled apart, I winced at the spot on her forehead. It'd turned from bright red to an almost a purplish color. "You should probably put some ice on that so people don't think you have a third eyeball."

CHAPTER 4

TRAVIS

KNOWING my parents wanted to "catch up" this morning regarding the part of our meeting I hadn't paid attention to, I specifically left for work a little later than normal. I needed to make a few stops on my way to the winery, and if I timed my drive right, Dad would be touring the distillery by the time I got there.

But as I turned the key to lock my front door, a whiff of smoke caught my attention. I glanced over my shoulder but didn't see any in the air, so I shrugged off my initial concern and headed down the driveway to my Jeep.

Then I saw it.

Light puffs of smoke billowed out of Claire's open front door.

I quickly dropped my leather planner on the hood of my Jeep and ran toward her place to make sure she was all right. The whole time, all I could think about was Craig's comment from the other day about her burning my place down. The coincidence made me want to laugh, but I needed to ensure my neighbor was okay first.

"Hey!" I called out from the doorway. "Are you all right?"

"Yeah," she yelled from the back of the house.

Even though she said she was fine, she didn't sound fine. Technically, her tone didn't lead me to believe she was in any danger, but I was able to detect a very intense emotion—similar to rage. And considering her house was practically filled with smoke, I became a bit worried.

So I ran inside to check on her more closely.

Standing in her kitchen with the window and back door wide open, she waved a dish towel in the air as if to move the grey haze outside. I could tell she'd never done this before because the only thing she managed to accomplish was dispersing the smokey air throughout the house.

"What happened?" I asked as I grabbed another towel off the counter to help wave the contaminated air outside.

"This stupid oven! That's what happened!" She began to beat the stovetop with her rag as if putting out a fire. "Piece of crap either burns shit or doesn't heat up at all."

I quickly compared the appliance to the one in my place, and from what I could see, they looked identical. "I'm not at all familiar with the inner workings of ovens, otherwise I'd happily take a look and see what's wrong. But if you call the landlord, they should send someone out this afternoon."

I began to wonder if this was the first place she'd ever rented. This was the second time I suggested she call the landlord in a handful of days.

"This is so infuriating. The stupid thing only seems to work in the middle of the night."

As I waved out the smoky air, I mentally began to run through a few things she'd told me. "You do all your baking here?"

"Yeah...where else would I do it?"

I took another moment to contemplate my response. "Well, why wouldn't you use one at the bakery?"

She suddenly stopped flapping her dishcloth in the air and began to smooth her bedhead with a wide-open palm. "Probably because I don't work for one. I work for myself."

"How do you sell your stuff?"

"Same as anyone else. People call and place an order. Voila."

"Where did you do all your baking before you moved into this place?" Something seemed off, though I couldn't put my finger on it. Or maybe she truly was a blonde trapped inside a brunette's body.

"At the house I used to live in."

She started to appear a little fidgety, so I tried to back off a bit by saying, "Oh, that sucks. I was going to suggest going there and using their oven until yours is fixed, but I'm going to assume that's not an option."

"Nope. All I have is this old thing."

I glanced around the kitchen and counted three trays of pastries on the counter. One contained about six cupcake-like treats, all of which seemed to have caved in. Another had four of the same, but whatever purple goop they'd been filled with had leaked out of the bottoms. And finally, the third tray—the one clearly responsible for the smoke—had five treats, all as black as coal. I wouldn't be surprised if they crumbled into a pile of ash if I touched one.

"Could you maybe have the temp set wrong?"

She practically glared at me. "I'm not an idiot, Travis. This isn't my first rodeo."

"Okay…so what kind of oven did you use before? Maybe you're simply used to a different brand or something."

She stumbled a bit, running her palms over her hair as if trying to tame the unruly strands. "I don't remember. A good one, though. New. But not brand-new. A few years old. Big…but not too big."

Unsure of how to respond, I slowly nodded and began to put one foot behind the other. "Well, I'm headed to the winery this morning, so I can ask my mom when I see her. Maybe she has insight into this. Will you be home tonight?"

"Yeah. I'm not going anywhere."

The doom and gloom written on her face left me feeling sorry for her, but not in a pitiful way. She was clearly having a bad day, and I simply wanted to make her feel better, so I leaned toward her and put my arm around her shoulders. "Hey, don't be discouraged. You'll have this all figured out in no time. Worst case scenario, the landlord buys you a new one. This isn't the only oven in town."

"Thanks." She leaned into me for a brief moment. "You should probably go to work. No need in us both having a shitty day."

There was something about her demeanor that made me want to stay. Kind of like a stray kitten who looked up at you with those eyes, silently begging for a saucer of milk. Okay, so I couldn't say that for sure because I'd never come across a stray kitten, but that was what I pictured when I looked into her golden-brown eyes.

"Right. I'll see you after work, then."

Her eyes shot open. "Why?"

"Umm…" I mentally ran through our conversation, ensuring I hadn't made this part up. And when I distinctly recalled the discussion about coming over later, I added, "To tell you what my mom said about your oven?"

"Oh, yeah. Sorry, my brain's a little fried at the moment."

That was understandable, so I didn't give her a hard time. Instead, I nodded and let myself out.

I DIDN'T EVEN REACH the end of the street before my phone rang, my mom's face flashing on the screen. "Hey, Trav…" Her soft, comforting tone filled the interior of the Jeep. "Are you coming in today?"

"Yeah, I'm on my way. Sorry, I got hung up next door. Speaking of which, while I've got you on the phone, can I pick your brain for a second?"

"Sure," she said, sounding a little hesitant.

I slipped on my sunglasses and tried to remember everything Claire had told me. "My neighbor is having issues with her oven."

"And you want me to let her borrow mine?"

Laughter rolled through my chest. "No, of course not. I was just wondering if you could offer tips or something. She said hers either burns everything or doesn't heat up all the way."

"I'm not sure what advice I can offer. Maybe she can't cook?"

"She's a baker. So I'm assuming she's perfectly capable of using an oven correctly."

Mom hesitated for a moment, the only sound coming through the speakers was her slightly heavy breathing. "She isn't the reason you asked about the pies last night, is she?"

"Well, kind of."

"Travis Matthew Cabrera." That was enough to make my butthole clench. "You didn't give her the recipe, did you? Because I was quite clear in my text that you are *not* to share the file with anyone outside of our family. So if you wanted to give—"

"My God, Mom. Chill. No, I didn't even show her. I only told her about the zest bit." I consciously lowered my tone now that she had stopped freaking out. "I understand the whole family recipe thing, but seriously, what's the big deal about anyone getting ahold of it? Is your pie *that* different than any other?"

She audibly pulled in a deep breath and slowly exhaled before explaining. "That recipe has been passed down from mother to daughter for generations, always with very strict instructions to never let it leave the family. And so far, that promise has never been broken."

"But what's the big deal?"

"People will change the ingredients, tweak the process, possibly make money by selling them...and that's not what my great-great-grandmother wanted. Those pies were meant to be the *one* thing we had all to ourselves."

"I don't understand."

"Think, Travis...all we have is the farm, right? Now the vineyard and winery—but before that, we only had the farm. And what happens to everything created from that land? Gets sold. Given away. We make it, and others enjoy it. The pie is the one thing we make that no one else can have—well, other than to eat."

She made a good point. "Oh, I've never thought about it like that. Then again, I've always been one of those who just enjoy eating them. Does this mean you never shared the secret with Brenden's ex when they were married?"

"No. The recipe has only ever been passed down to daughters, as they're the ones who grew up helping their mothers in the kitchen." She clucked her tongue and released a soft huff. Their divorce likely hurt my mom more than my brother. "That's neither here nor there. We've gotten off-topic. You were asking something about your neighbor's oven?"

"Oh, right." I shook my head. "So her oven practically caught on fire this morning. As I've explained, she's a baker, and she works from home, meaning she hasn't been able to do her job. I told her I'd ask if you knew what was wrong. I have no idea whether this is a common baking issue or not."

"Well, is her appliance new?"

"Doubtful. I'm pretty sure the owner put hers and mine in at the same time. I've had mine since I moved in, and I've been there nearly two years. All I can figure is that maybe the old tenants broke an element or something on hers."

"That could be the case, or maybe even something as simple as a difference in what she's used to. I've always had to tweak either the temp or the time when baking after getting a new oven. I'm sorry I can't be more helpful."

"Don't say that. You've been tons of help. She should be calling the landlord today, so hopefully, she'll be sorted and back to baking before I leave work."

"Oh, yeah?" Rhythmic tapping came through the line, giving me a mental image so clear I could've been in her office instead of driving there. For as long as I could remember, I'd seen her lift and drop her fingertips like the wave at a stadium, her nails clicking against the desk in rapid succession before repeating the action all over again. "Is there anything going on with this one?"

"For Christ's sake, Ma. No."

She didn't believe me, much like Craig hadn't when I told him the same thing. I wasn't interested in starting anything with Claire, so they didn't have anything to worry about.

"She just moved in. We've had a couple of run-ins with each other, but they've mostly been terrible. Even if I *was* interested in her, I can guarantee she's not into me in the slightest."

"Oh, don't say that, Trav. You're a catch!"

I rolled my eyes and huffed. "Whatever, Mom. I have a couple of stops to make in town before I'll be in. Okay?"

"Sounds good. See you soon."

Not too soon, though.

As I walked into the winery, I tried to focus on getting to my office before anyone stopped me. I hadn't seen Dad's pickup outside, but that didn't mean anything. He still could've been prowling the winery, waiting for me to show up so he could corner me about whatever we were meant to discuss this morning.

Somehow, I managed to reach my office without any interruption. This meant I could dive into work right away without spending hours getting pulled in every direction. We were at the start of harvest season, so I had a lot on my plate. As the distribution manager, my job was never done.

"Hey, son." My dad's gruff voice made me jump in my seat. I'd been so focused on the spreadsheet in front of me that I'd missed him walking into my office.

I glanced at the time in the corner of my computer screen—barely eleven. Which meant I'd only been at the winery for less than an hour. He was supposed to have been out until at least late afternoon—providing his schedule hadn't changed. "What are you doing here so early? I thought you were out with Jacob."

"I was, but the distillery called and asked if we could come in earlier. Worked out better if I'm honest, so we headed out there first thing this morning." *Dammit*. That meant I'd come in late for no reason. "How's your day going?"

"Busy." Hopefully, he'd take the hint and hold off on having this conversation until another day. Then again, one more day wouldn't magically clear the blank spot in my memory of Saturday morning's meeting. So technically, there was no point in stalling.

"That's great news." He nodded while leaning back in the chair across from my desk.

I often wondered how long that chair would last under his weight. He was pretty heavy—not overweight, just built like a stone wall. Everyone always said I reminded them of Dad. We had the same bone structure and strong jawline, and while I wasn't as big as he was, I wasn't far off. He had maybe two inches on me, which wasn't bad considering I was six-foot-one. But he always felt the need to point out how there was still time to grow up to be as big and strong as him.

"What's up, Pop?" I knew why he was here, but I decided to play dumb anyway.

"Not much."

"How was the tour of the distillery? You went to the one off Mavis Parkway, right?" I prayed he didn't ask how I knew that. If he did, I'd have to admit that I checked his schedule, which would prompt him to ask why since I had *never* checked his schedule in all the years I'd been at the winery.

Thankfully, he didn't catch on. "Very nice, actually. We were surprised. Based on the asking price and the company's history, we both expected the place to be in a pretty bad state of disrepair. But we were quite surprised at how well everything seemed to be taken care of."

"Then why the low selling price?"

"Apparently, they have family issues."

"What kind of family issues would make someone sell a perfectly functioning distillery for less than the appraisal price?" Go figure...now I was invested, which was the opposite of what I wanted. Being involved only meant I wouldn't resume my work anytime soon.

Dad shrugged and leaned forward with his elbows on his thighs. "Lots of reasons. Anything from divorce to simply needing to unload it quickly."

"Gotcha." I didn't, but I also didn't need to. "So what's the verdict? Has Jake made a decision? Or does he want to keep looking before staking his claim on one?"

"Well, I'm pretty sure he's gonna put in an offer." Dad leaned back again, though this time, he linked his fingers together behind his head. He was getting comfortable. *Great.* "He said he wants to sleep on it before doing anything. A business is a big purchase and shouldn't be made lightly, so I'm proud of him for not rushing into things."

Even though our parents technically owned the vineyard, winery, farm, and brewhouse, my brothers and I had invested our own money in each business. It'd started with Brenden; he'd visited a friend out of state and came home all excited about opening a brewhouse—a brewery with a bar and restaurant in the front that served their own label. Our parents told him they would put in the rest if he put up a percentage of the investment cost. However, after Brenden's divorce, he'd sold his share of the brewhouse to Craig.

"So? What do you think?"

My sight came into focus on my dad's raised brows. Damn, this was now the second time I'd spaced out only to be brought back to the conversation with a question aimed at me. At least this time, I couldn't blame it on being lost in fantasies starring my neighbor's ass. "I'm sorry, but what do I think about what?"

"What's gotten into you lately, son? You've been in the clouds more than ever. Is there something going on?"

I vehemently shook my head. "No, I just have so much on my plate right now with the harvest starting and all. I'm sorry, Pop."

"No worries. I understand. I used to do your job, and I'll be honest, you make everything look much easier than how I remember." Pride shone in his eyes and lined his smiling lips. "Well, I'm pretty sure I can guess what you're going to say, but I'll ask anyway... You've been talking for years about expanding the vineyard. With this new opportunity on the table, I think now would be the best time to make that happen. But if you're busy—"

"No, Dad. Not at all. I'm definitely not too busy to expand the vineyard."

I'd dreamt of this ever since I was old enough to understand the ins and outs of this place. We managed to supply quite a few shops and restaurants in town, as well as a small number of subscription packages, but I always thought we could do better, sell more bottles, reach more people. I wanted Uncorked wines to experience more growth than this town could offer. Hell, I wanted to go beyond this county.

"All right then." He leaned forward and beamed at me. "I'll start the ball rolling...as long as you're sure this is something you can handle."

I didn't understand why he thought I wouldn't be able to handle more work. I understood that things were hectic, but this was harvest season, meaning I had more than usual to juggle. That didn't mean I couldn't take on anything else. Plus, a few extra acres wouldn't be *that* much more. The whole property was only fifteen acres—nine for the farm and six for the vineyard. Which didn't leave me with much to expand on. So truthfully, I doubted the slightly heavier workload would even register to me.

He held up his hands in defense. "Hey, I'm only making sure you've taken all aspects into account—such as the time required for new vines to reach harvesting age. That's three to five years depending on the seasons, which means three to five years of no additional profit. You're okay with that?"

"Yes, Dad." I nearly huffed, but thankfully, I managed not to. "I'm well aware of everything that goes into expanding a vineyard. I've wanted this for years, so if the opportunity is here, I won't think twice."

"And you're sure you can take this on financially as well?"

I wasn't sure if his intention was to talk me out of it—and if so, why dangle the proverbial carrot in my face in the first place. Or maybe he just didn't have much faith in me. But that contradicted the look of pride in his eyes.

I waved off that thought and said, "I wouldn't have agreed if I had any doubts. You haven't raised idiots."

He needed to have more faith in me. We were only a talking about a few acres—probably three at the most. Grafting vines to plant new crops could be pricey, but not enough to break the bank. And if need be, I could handle getting a small loan.

"All right. If you say so. I'll make some calls."

I watched him leave my office, closing the door behind him...not once questioning what calls he needed to make. The entire property was ours, so we weren't required to inform anyone of our plans. Unless he meant Brenden. But still, the farm didn't utilize all nine acres, so in actuality, he didn't have an argument to make.

I couldn't spend my time obsessing over that, though. I had work to do, and at this rate, I'd be here all night. At least Claire stayed up late, so I wouldn't wake her when I got home.

I found it slightly concerning how easily she fit into my routine.

I tried to not overthink things.

But she had wormed her way into my predictable life.

CHAPTER 5

CLAIRE

"PLEASE, help me welcome back our contestant, Claire Hansen." Bob Archer beamed at me and asked, "How was your first blind date on *You Can't Buy Love*?" His grin never varied, appearing to be painted on. Strange, but at the same time, acceptable. Almost normal.

"Incredible. We had a romantic picnic next to a creek." My explanation astonished me, mostly because I couldn't remember living that moment, and I imagined something like that would definitely be a moment I'd want to remember.

"What else did you guys do?"

My mouth opened, and words came out, even though I had no clue what I was about to say ahead of time. "Well, we went swimming in the creek. We had so much fun."

"Sounds like you did! Let's see the footage." Bob pointed to a large screen along the back of the stage. Immediately, a video began to play. Two people splashed around in a nondescript creek, and somehow, I knew the girl in the video was meant to be me—or at least played the role of me. Then the camera panned out to show them—us—climbing out.

Her drenched hair dripped down her bare arms while they laughed and flirted with each other. But the worst part was when she turned to face the camera. She didn't have on a stitch of clothing. Quickly, I glanced down at myself, wondering why I suddenly felt wet, and to my horror, I was naked, too. On stage. Beneath intense lighting. In front of a live audience, who all laughed at me. I quickly crossed my arms over my chest, desperate for the nearest exit.

"Hey now, Claire. No need to worry. We've all seen your nipples before!" Bob chuckled, making the crowd hoot and holler even louder.

I wanted to run and hide, but there was no escape.

Suddenly, a loud ringing sound filled the stage. Not a phone. Just an elongated *ding*. Everyone quieted down, and the laughter stopped. I was almost thankful for the interruption until Bob announced, "That bell means we've reached the bonus round!" The audience went wild again.

I had no idea what the bonus round was, but I was about to find out. A heavy, velvet curtain along the side of the stage pulled away, revealing a shiny red convertible. I was so excited I practically jumped in my seat, no longer registering that I was naked.

"Now, to win this brand-new car, we'll ask you five questions about your date, things he told you during your evening together, and you must answer them all correctly. Answer one of them wrong, and you can kiss that prize goodbye."

I couldn't remember the date *or* the guy I was supposedly with. There was no way I'd be able to answer even one of these questions right, let alone all of them. But that didn't stop me from clasping my hands together in a prayer fashion—although I held them against one cheek instead of in front of my face. Odd, but not overly concerning.

"What is one thing he said he can't tolerate in a relationship: Stealing, lying, or being manipulated?"

I couldn't respond. All I could think about was how my relationship with this guy was doomed...because I'd done all three of those things. I'd stolen a file from his phone, I'd lied about who I was, and I couldn't recall a specific instance, but I was pretty sure I'd manipulated something in that short time.

Out of nowhere, the bell sounded again, although this time, it rang out twice. I hadn't even been given a chance to answer. "Well, folks, that's all we've got time for tonight. Until next time, remember... *You. Can't. Buy. Love!*" he shouted along with the audience.

I frantically waved my hands in front of him, trying to make him stop. He never gave me a chance to guess. No one told me whether I'd won the car or not. I tried to cry out for him to come back, but my voice wouldn't work. I screamed and screamed, but I couldn't produce anything more than a whisper, as if my voice had literally vanished.

Suddenly, I sat straight up, realizing I'd somehow been transported to my room. Thankfully, I wasn't naked. Then I realized what the sound in my dream was—someone was ringing my doorbell. No light came through any of my windows, which clearly indicated the late hour, so there was no telling who could've been at my house.

I shouldn't have been surprised when I opened the door and found Travis on my front step. No one needed an alarm clock with him as a neighbor. "Is everything okay?" I asked, worried that something might've been wrong at his place.

"Uh, yeah. Are *you* okay?" He stared at me as if I were the crazy one.

He couldn't have been serious. "I realize I've complained about you waking me up at the ass crack of dawn, but in case you misunderstood...I wasn't singling out the *dawn* part of that statement. I'm more concerned about you waking me up too early. So if I consider sunrise too early to wake up, you can bet your britches that I'd say the same about whatever ungodly hour this is."

Travis, silent and unmoving, held my stare for a second. Only shifting his eyes, he glanced to the right, back at me again, and then briefly to the left before meeting my eyes once more. He acted unsure, as if silently waiting for the punchline to my joke.

Then he cleared his throat and said, "It's eight."

"Eight what?"

"O'clock. As in...the time."

I flicked my gaze over his head to the dark sky behind him. "Impossible. The sun isn't up. I'm not falling for that one again."

This time, he laughed beneath his breath as he dropped his chin and held his fist to his mouth. "At night, Claire. Eight at night."

"What?" I had to have heard him wrong. "No way."

Travis glanced at his watch and nodded. "Technically, ten after. I told you I'd talk to my mom about your oven and asked if you'd be up tonight. You said yes. If I knew you were asleep, I wouldn't have bothered you. But I'm starting to think you don't keep a very regular schedule, do you?"

"I guess I've neglected sleep over the last couple of days trying to figure out this oven. Looks like it all caught up to me." I took a step back and opened the door wider. "Come in, and I'll grab us something to drink."

"What do you have?" He made no move to come inside, as if his acceptance of my offer hinged on what beverage I'd serve.

"Um, water. Milk. I can make instant coffee if you'd like. It's flavored."

"As wonderful as all those options sound, I've had a very long, tiring day, and to be honest, nothing less than beer will do. Please, don't take it personally."

"Do you have any at your place?" When he nodded, I said, "Grab a couple—along with a bottle of wine if you have one—and come back. I got a new oven that works, so I was able to bake a few pies. All of which are edible. I promise."

With a soft smirk, he said, "Sounds good. Give me about five minutes to change, and I'll be over."

Change. I hadn't considered my outfit before he mentioned his. Granted, he'd seen me in worse than baggy, ripped sweatpants and a stained T-shirt

I'd once worn to paint my old room. But that didn't mean I was okay with being a slob around him…or half-naked. I wanted to show him that I owned decent clothes that weren't see-through. So I decided to change as well.

I WATCHED as Travis brought the fork to his mouth. Any other time, I would've probably focused on his kissable lips or the way his tongue touched the bottom of the fork as he took his first bite. But not this time. I was too interested in his reaction to my pie to pay attention to much else.

"How is it?" I was too impatient to wait until he finished swallowing.

He hummed and nodded, studying the tiny dessert in front of him.

Piper had said to start small, and that's exactly what I did. Making an entire pie would take a lot more time and practice, so instead, I made tiny ones the size of cinnamon buns. And now that my oven was sorted, I was successfully able to make a few. I'd already tried one to make sure it was edible, so I knew it was good enough to share with Travis. Although, I still had a way to go before reaching the level of his mom's desserts.

"This is delicious, Claire," he practically moaned, which made me giddy. "Does this mean there was something wrong with the oven?"

I beamed with pride and nodded. I didn't care to delve into too much detail, so I decided to keep quiet on the oven topic—unsuspiciously.

"What was wrong with it?"

Well, that didn't go as intended. *Onto plan B.* "No idea. Just knackered."

He continued to eat his dessert, giving me a false sense of security that the conversation had moved on from the oven. Until he finished the pie and licked his fork clean. "They gave you a new one?"

Damn him and his obsession with my kitchen appliances. His inability to drop the subject prevented me from memorizing the way he licked his utensil. Or the way his tongue peeked out of the corner of his mouth as he licked a bit of jelly off his luscious bottom lip.

"Yeah. I got a new one."

"Wow," he said with bright, impressed eyes. "That's awesome. They're pretty good about keeping up with the place, but I didn't expect them to run out and buy a new one the same day."

"Well, the landlord didn't."

He turned to look at me, confusion set in his eyes. "What do you mean?"

"I called them, like you told me to, but they wouldn't be able to send anyone out before the end of the week at the earliest. And since I can't make money if I can't bake, I went out and got a new one. I couldn't wait."

His silence became worrying until he finally said, "You could've used mine while waiting until yours was fixed."

"Oh...I didn't think to ask. But it's okay. I found one on sale." Technically, my grandfather had, since he was the one who bought it for me after I cried about not being able to feed myself.

Travis laughed beneath his breath as he brought another forkful to his lips. I tried not to take his amusement personally, but it stung.

"Now, back to the pie. What did you think?" I swallowed the lump in my throat and kept the uncertainty at bay while I waited for his answer.

"Unbelievably amazing." He didn't bother to hide his surprise as he set the empty dessert plate on the coffee table. "I can't believe the difference between this and the one you brought over before."

I would've been perfectly happy if that disaster had never been mentioned again.

"Well, I'm sure my pie isn't anywhere near as good as the one you gave me, but it'll have to do...unless you want to share your mom's baking secrets with me?" I figured I would mention the recipe since he'd obviously forgotten to send it over. After all, there had been a lot going on between then and now.

Except instead of snapping his fingers in a show of remembering something, he dropped his chin and laughed to himself. "Sorry, Claire, but no can do. It's a family secret that's only ever been passed down from mother to daughter. My mom expressed *very* clearly that the recipe is not to be shared with anyone outside the family. Otherwise, I wouldn't think twice."

My chest tightened, and my stomach bottomed out. I felt like running to the toilet to expel the guilt that ransacked my entire body, but shock rooted me in place. If I'd known it was a secret recipe, I would've never taken it. I had stupidly assumed he'd gotten it from her to give to me.

Thankfully, he continued speaking, so I didn't have to respond. "I'm not sure what your weekend plans are, but if you're free and want a booth at the Tesorita town fair, I can reserve you one."

"For what?" My shame-ridden mind refused to move on.

Travis slowly blinked at me several times. When he realized I wasn't joking, he said, "To sell your baked goods."

"Oh!" I slapped my thigh for effect. "That kind of booth."

After waiting a few moments for my answer, he knitted his brow and asked, "So? What do you say? Should I have one saved for you?"

I wasn't sure how to respond. At this point, saying no wouldn't work without a plausible reason, and while admitting I'd stolen something from him would've sufficed, I'd only succeed at creating a whole new problem. So I did the only thing I could...I nodded and said, "Yeah, absolutely. I would love to do that."

"Give me your email address, and I'll send you the details."

"Thank you so much." Using his phone, I gave him my contact information, phone number included...in case he ever needed to reach me. Although, a small part of me hoped he would call or text for other reasons besides the festival.

"Well, since you'll need a lot of baked goods to fill your booth, you should come by the farm sometime this week and pick some fruit. With the fair being a local thing, it'd probably help sales if you advertise the use of local fruit."

"Sure. Yeah. Sounds great." Things just got worse and worse. I'd stolen his family recipe, and now he wanted me to use fruit from *his* family farm for the filling. I was doomed. *Doomed to hell!*

"Text me before you head up, and I'll make sure to be there. Trust me, you don't want to deal with my brother. He's been a basket case lately."

I forced myself to laugh, not knowing what he meant but not wanting him to question my disposition. I'd already come across as a fool around him —more than once. My main goal now was to lower the number of times I looked ridiculous.

My phone buzzed on the table and lit up with a text from Travis.

He glanced at me with a sexy smirk lining his lips, almost succeeding in calming me down. "There, now you have my number. The next time something catches on fire, call me. Well..." He held up a finger to make a point. "Call the fire department first. Then me."

In only a few days, I'd given him enough ammunition to tease me for the rest of the year. If I spent much more time with him, he'd have enough to taunt me until my dying day. This put me in somewhat of a pickle because I enjoyed his company...and wine. Avoiding him would be difficult.

I refused to admit the level of attractiveness I felt toward him. His appeal went beyond his appearance, too. He was kind and a true gentleman. He treated me better than anyone ever had.

I was definitely in trouble.

CHAPTER 6
TRAVIS

A LIGHT KNOCK RESOUNDED from my open office door. I could see someone out of the corner of my eye, but I was too busy concentrating on my phone call to glance up and see who it was. So I held up a finger, signaling the visitor—likely my mom—to wait a minute.

"Yes, sir. Absolutely," I said into the receiver, hoping to wrap up this call quickly. "I'll put those figures together and email them to you by tomorrow morning."

I set the phone on the cradle and dropped my head into my hands. A long exhale slipped through my parted lips as my eyes drifted closed. It'd been a long day, and I had a feeling it was only about to get longer.

Another light knock reminded me of my visitor—who couldn't have been there longer than sixty seconds. I quickly lifted my head, surprised to see my beautiful neighbor in the doorway. I'd completely forgotten I'd told Claire she could stop by to pick fruit.

"Is this a bad time?" she asked with raised brows.

This wasn't necessarily a *good* time, but I couldn't very well turn her away.

"No, no. It's totally fine. Here, come in." I stood and held out an open hand toward the seat in front of my desk. "I thought you were going to text me before driving out here."

She sat and smiled brightly, calming down some of my nervous irritation. "Yeah, but I was in the area, so I figured I'd pop in and see if you were free. Plus, I really wanted to see the place. I can't believe I've never thought to visit a winery," she said in awe as she glanced around my office.

"How'd you find the place?" I couldn't recall ever telling her where we were located, and unless you were familiar with the area, the vineyard was quite easily missed. After all, this didn't originate as commercial property. We'd added signs guiding the way to the winery, but our neighbors' farms went on for acres, as far as the eye could see, so getting turned around wasn't difficult to do.

She returned her attention to my face and narrowed her eyes slightly. "The name of the vineyard is on the bottles of wine you brought over. I did a simple Google search for the address, and my GPS did the rest."

I could understand now why she seemed so puzzled by my question. But in my defense, I didn't realize she'd paid any attention to the name on the label. I guess I hadn't given her enough credit. I mean, she'd portrayed a ditzy blonde for most of our interactions, so assuming she'd have a hard time finding her way out of a paper bag wasn't a stretch.

"If this is a bad time, I can come back another day. Like I said, I was in the area, so I figured I'd take advantage of the convenience. But I can just as easily make a trip to the market."

"No, you're totally fine." An idea hit me. "How about you take a tour of the vineyard while I finish up here, and then I'll meet you out at the grove and help you pick some fruit?"

"That sounds like a fabulous plan." Her eyes sparkled like gold in the sun. "I'd love to see a real-life vineyard."

"All right, I'll have one of the tour guides meet you at the entrance, and I'll join you at the farm when you've finished." I stood, but she didn't give me enough time to walk her out. She seemed a little too excited to wait for me.

So I remained at my desk and shot a text to Tony, one of our tour guides.

Do me a favor...pick up the brunette standing out front and take her through the vineyard to the farm please?

His response came almost immediately.

Tour Tony: The hot one?

I rolled my eyes, though a sharp flash of heat surged through me. I knew he was being Tony, the same guy who hit on all the single women during his tours, but for some reason, I took offense to hearing him call Claire hot.

Just do what I asked, please.

Not wanting to spend another second dissecting my reaction, I tossed the phone onto my desk and turned to my computer. The longer it took to type up that proposal, the longer it'd be before I could join Claire.

I hit the save button on the extensive spreadsheet that filled my screen and glanced at the clock on the wall. It'd taken longer than I hoped, but at least I was done. Granted, there were still loads more that needed my attention, but I could work on most of that from home. That was how I managed to stay caught up while avoiding spending twenty hours a day at my desk. So I turned everything off, grabbed my keys, and left the office.

I quickly checked the time. Claire had left my office roughly forty-five minutes ago. So I promptly drove to the farm on the other side of the property, hoping to catch her waiting out front.

But she wasn't there.

I parked my Jeep and walked toward the barn where I caught a few glimpses of movement. I scanned the area, figuring I'd spot her along the way.

Out of nowhere, I heard screeching. Alarmed, I immediately took off running, and when I reached the barn entrance, I was met with laughter. The sight in front of me made me stop so fast I nearly tripped over my own feet.

Claire sat on a stool in front of a goat, looking rather frazzled. At first, I wasn't sure what I walked in on...but then I spotted the bucket situated beneath the animal.

"Uh, Claire?" I seriously couldn't figure her out. As soon as I thought I had, she'd prove me wrong. I'd never met someone so skilled at keeping me on my toes.

Claire swiped away errant strands of hair from her forehead with the back of her hand. "Oh, hi!" She beamed at me with rosy cheeks. And just like that, every bit of impatient annoyance etched on her face vanished.

Not one part of this entire scene made sense. She was supposed to be finishing up the vineyard tour or waiting by the grove of fruit trees. Not milking a goat. "What are you doing?"

She stood up straight and arched her back, as if she'd been crouched in that position for hours. "Um...didn't we already have this conversation in your office? I'm here to pick fruit."

She was kooky and slightly strange, but in a way that made me want to spend more time with her. I was quickly becoming addicted to her antics and found her quite entertaining. I thoroughly enjoyed myself whenever she was around.

"No, I don't mean *here*. I mean *there*." I pointed at the tiny stool she vacated a second ago. "Why are you milking a goat, Claire?"

"I was told to." She must not have successfully removed all the hair from her brow because she pulled her bottom lip to one side and blew the rest out of her eye. "That guy over there said you told him I would."

I followed her finger, finding my brother Brenden standing near the tack room.

"I don't mind, but I would've preferred to have been told ahead of time that you'd offered up my services. I would've worn different clothes."

A lightbulb practically flickered on over my head.

I turned back to Claire, who for some reason never questioned the request to milk a freaking goat. "Do you do everything you're told?"

She shrugged but answered anyway. "I assumed this was my end of the bargain. Like, my way of paying for the fruit. I told him you sent me, and he acted like he knew why. So what reason would I have to question him?"

There were so many reasons she should've been able to come up with, but this wasn't the time to deal with that. "How long have you been in here?"

She stared upward and squinted, making me wonder if she was thinking or literally timing herself based on the sun's position in the sky. "Well, how long ago was I in your office?"

I glanced at my watch and did mental calculations. "Roughly forty-five minutes ago."

"Okay, so I've been here for forty."

My eyes practically bulged out of my head. "Are you kidding me?"

But I didn't wait for her response. Instead, I grabbed my phone from my pocket and immediately tapped out a message to Tony.

You didn't take her on a tour of the vineyard before bringing her to the barn???

I hesitated for a moment before typing "her," unsure of how to refer to Claire.

Tour Tony: No. You didn't tell me to.

I scrolled up a couple of lines to our earlier messages, ready to react to the one where I'd specifically asked him to take...

I read and reread my text a few times to myself. *Take her through the vineyard to the farm.* I assumed it would be obvious what I'd meant, especially since his frickin' job was to give tours, but I could see where the miscommunication might've come from.

Rather than respond, I shoved my phone deep into my pocket and returned my attention to Claire. "You can use the ladies' room right over there to clean yourself up. I'll meet you in front of the gate to the orchard."

As soon as she left, I stormed over to Brenden, not caring in the slightest that he was getting ready to head home. I stopped in front of him with my hands on my hips. "What the hell, Brenden?"

"Good to see you too, nerd."

I was too bothered by the Claire situation to concern myself what whatever childish name he chose to call me. "Seriously. I send my...*friend*...over here, and you make her milk your goats? What the hell is wrong with you?"

"Hold up." He put his large hand in front of my face. If there was one thing he got from our dad, it was his pair of oversized hands. "How was I supposed to know she was your friend? Tony brought her over, and she told me you'd sent her, so I assumed she was someone you found to fill the job."

"When did I ever say I found anyone?"

"At the meeting, you said you'd find me someone."

I couldn't believe what I was hearing. He was the oldest—he should've been the smartest, yet he wasn't. "I said I would *ask around*."

"Okay? Again, how was I supposed to know? For heaven's sake, she didn't argue one bit. I mean, she appeared a little disgusted by the thought when I first explained what to do, but she never put up a fight or even complained."

"Whatever."

"I'm sorry, but you should be smart enough by now not to bring over anyone you're dating. I can't be held responsible." He acted cool, though I could tell he struggled not to crack a smile.

"Dude. She's my *neighbor*. She came to pick some fruit, and *you* made her touch goats in ways they shouldn't be until at least the third date."

I didn't wait for a response—mostly because I could tell he was dangerously close to losing his composure. And while I could find the humor in this ordeal, I wasn't ready to give him the satisfaction. After the day I had, I just wanted to be done with this place and go home, so I walked away, ignoring the snickers coming from behind me.

I reached the grove, surprised to find Claire already there and waiting.

"Listen, I'm sorry about my brother," I said after pointing out which trees she could pick from. "Let me make it up to you. Since it's so late—and you don't cook—why don't you come over for dinner?"

"Tonight?" She sounded surprised.

"Well, I've got the slow cooker on, and I'll have more than enough for one person."

Claire glanced over her shoulder at me as she plucked apples from the tree. She appeared hesitant, which somehow left me panicked that she wouldn't accept my offer. The anxiety riddling my nervous system made no sense; this was a last-minute suggestion, so I couldn't understand why I'd be worried about her turning down my offer.

"I'll head home and change. Just come over once you finish putting away your fruit and doing whatever else you have to do." I paused for a moment, thinking of something I could use to help me convince her. Suddenly, I remembered what she said the other day. "I've got wine."

Her eyes lit up, and her brows arched. "Sounds good. Should I bring anything?"

"Just yourself."

As I walked back to my car, I questioned if I'd made a royal mistake by inviting her over. I probably wouldn't be the best company. Not to mention, she'd be at my house for however many hours, which meant I wouldn't be able to do much—if any—work. But considering how concerned I became at the thought of her turning me down, I figured it was out of my hands.

I tried not to overthink it, which was hard when she was all I wanted to think about.

"THIS IS the best thing I've ever eaten," Claire mumbled around a mouthful of food. "How did you learn to make this?"

"I think I found the recipe online. Super easy to make, too; you simply mix a few condiments together and then pour the sauce over the meat. I prefer to use a slow cooker because you just put the lid on and go. You should look into getting one. They're a lifesaver."

"So you don't have to do any of the work?"

"Well…" I slowly chewed my bite, needing a moment to consider my response. "Sometimes you have to prepare things first, like brown your meat, but overall, it does everything for you."

"If that thing can make food taste this amazing, I'm getting one tomorrow."

I laughed, although I couldn't tell whether she was serious or joking. With her, there was no telling, especially after the whole oven debacle. "Do you seriously never make dinner?"

She shrugged while staring at her plate. "I wasn't ever taught how, and the few times I've attempted have been utter disasters."

Her response was so unexpected my head began to spin. The last time we'd discussed this topic, she excused it as a consequence of standing in front of an oven all day. Which made sense. Yet now, she claimed she didn't possess any culinary skills. I wanted to ask for clarification, but I was stopped in my tracks when she began to elaborate without any prodding.

"My mom was an amazing cook. But unfortunately, she died when I was fifteen, so she never got the chance to teach me…nor did she leave behind any written recipes I could've learned from. I guess I was destined to eat fast food for the rest of my adult life."

This was the first personal thing she'd ever divulged, and I wasn't sure how to respond. I knew I needed to say *something* after hearing she'd lost her mother at such a vulnerable age, but her body language kept me from understanding what kind of response was warranted. She didn't appear fazed, although I couldn't imagine that was true.

After a few seconds of mulling over what to say, I opened my mouth and let whatever came to me flow out. "What about your dad? Was he in the picture?"

"They died together…skiing accident." Again, she sounded like she was telling me about a movie rather than her life. She didn't even stop eating to speak; she simply talked around her food. The whole thing made no sense, and to be honest, I wasn't sure how to react.

I ultimately decided to continue our conversation instead of focusing on her lack of visible emotion. "Who raised you after that? Well, I guess three years wouldn't technically be considered *raising*, huh?"

"No, I wouldn't say so," she said with a giggle flowing through her words. "But to answer your question, my grandfather moved in and took care of me. That's actually where I was living until I came here."

That surprised me so much I nearly choked. I wasn't personally aware of a single person who'd lived at home after high school, so the concept of her waiting so long to move out was hard to fathom. Granted, I wasn't sure how old she was. While she appeared to be in her twenties, it was entirely possible she simply looked older than she was.

"How old are you?" I asked.

"Twenty-three. Why, how old are you?"

I hesitated a moment, trying to decipher if this was her way of changing the subject or simply returning the question. "Twenty-six." And to give her the benefit of the doubt, I very quickly added, "Did you live at home so long because you were still in school?"

"Unfortunately, no. I enrolled in the local community college after graduation, but I very quickly realized that school just isn't for me. Not everyone can learn by sitting in a classroom—at least I certainly can't. I have to actually do something to grasp the full concept."

That made sense. I wasn't one of those people, but I knew plenty who were.

"So why did you wait so long to move out on your own? I fled the nest the first chance I could. Although, I had saved most of the money I earned from working the farm over the years, so I probably had a bit of an advantage that most don't. But, yeah, I don't think I could've stayed until I was twenty-three."

"You worked the farm too? For some reason, I assumed you've always been at the winery."

"Yeah, kind of, but when we were kids…" My words slowed as I realized what she'd done. She managed to turn the conversation around to avoid my question completely. Assuming she'd done so on purpose, I decided to let her out of the hot seat for a bit. "When we were kids, we helped on the farm. It was something we all did as soon as we were old enough."

"You said you have brothers, right?"

"I sure do. Three. Two older and one younger—he's the one you met last weekend."

Her brow raised, and her mouth slowly dropped open. "That was your brother?"

"Sure was. Craig. He's the baby. Honestly, he's the one I'm closest with. I used to idolize Brenden—the oldest—but he changed after he opened the brewery."

Claire appeared comfortable again. Not that she necessarily seemed *un*comfortable before, but while I asked questions about her parents, she tensed up somewhat. Apparently, she preferred to listen about my life more than talking about her own.

"I remember you telling me they make beer. I guess I didn't realize you meant an actual business. I assumed they did it for fun."

I smiled as I chewed my now room-temperature dinner. The more I talked and less I ate, the colder my food became. But I didn't mind because I found myself greatly enjoying her company. "Yes, the brewhouse is a real business. I love going there, actually. The restaurant, which is located in the front, has the best wings in town. And with a brewery in the back serving one-of-a-kind drinks, you really don't have any reason to go anywhere else. You should check it out sometime. I understand you don't like beer, but theirs is different. I think you might enjoy their label."

"Sounds like fun. So…your oldest brother is the one who brews beer, right?"

"Uh, no. Not anymore. He sold his share to Craig a couple of years back." I took in her creased brow and narrowed gaze and decided to elaborate. "We basically co-own our businesses with our parents. So he was never the sole owner, just like I share ownership of the vineyard and winery with my mom and dad. So when he needed to let the business go, he simply sold his part to Craig."

"What does he do now?"

"Who, Brenden? He's the asshole at the barn today who made you milk the goats."

She giggled and held the napkin up to her mouth. "Well, he technically didn't make me *do* anything. I was a willing participant who stupidly didn't question him."

"That seriously didn't bother you? Because it pissed me off."

"What did? That he put me to work?"

I bit my tongue for a moment, wondering why she wasn't as irritated as I was about the situation. "Well, yeah. First of all, most people wouldn't enjoy doing something like that. And secondly, you were there as my guest to pick fruit."

She ran one hand over her hair, something I'd seen her do a few times but not sure of the motive—unconscious or not. "If I wasn't upset, why were you?"

Her question left me pondering the answer before I finally admitted, "I guess I feel guilty or something. He's my brother, and I'm the one who sent you over there, so strictly speaking, the whole thing's my fault."

Her laughter filled the room, and I suddenly didn't want any other sound echoing against the walls in my kitchen. "Technically…milking a goat would be all my fault. But I don't care, because at least now, I can add *squeezing goat udders* to my list of things I enjoyed but would never do again. Seriously, though, there are bigger things to be upset about in the game of life."

Claire continued to amaze me. Well, more like puzzle me. I'd seen this woman flip out over being woken up at eight in the morning, so she hadn't given me the impression of being the go-with-the-flow type. Yet when it came to something she had every right to be pissed about, she wasn't. I started to think I would probably never figure her out.

"I appreciate your desire to defend me, though. That's not something I'm used to."

Now, *that* caught my attention. "What do you mean? Surely you've had boyfriends come to your defense."

She lifted one shoulder and pursed her lips. "Nope. But I also haven't dated much."

"Any particular reason?" There was no telling how long I had before she changed the subject again, so I wanted to find out as much as I could before the opportunity was lost.

She sipped her wine before continuing. "Well, most of the guys I start dating end up showing their true colors rather quickly. So those don't count because they never lasted long enough to be considered an *actual* boyfriend. And the last guy I was with—Oswald—dumped me, saying he needed more than I could offer. Which is ridiculous because we were together for two years. How much more could he have possibly needed from me?"

I continued to eat while listening, trying to act as if I wasn't as enthralled with her story as I actually was. I couldn't be sure, but something about the way she spoke of personal issues led me to believe she had a very high wall built up around her. It wasn't necessarily *what* she said, but more of *how* she said it—almost emotionless.

"What about you? Do you date much?" Once again, she changed the subject right as we were finally getting somewhere.

But like last time, I didn't argue or try to steer the conversation back to her. "Not really. I'm kinda like you; I haven't dated much. Mostly because I stay pretty busy with the winery, and the women I've been with couldn't handle coming second to my job. Didn't matter how much time and attention I gave them when I wasn't at the office…apparently, giving up the occasional day or two while I got caught up with work was too much to ask for."

"For real?" She tilted her head to the side and squinted, as if she were having trouble seeing me. "I realize I haven't been your neighbor for long, but I certainly wouldn't consider you too busy for a relationship. I think I've seen you every day this week. And most of the time, we've actually hung out."

She'd probably feel differently if she knew how much work I'd sacrificed to spend that time with her. But I couldn't think about that without confusion and anxiety overwhelming me. I didn't have a clue why I'd make time for her when I'd never done so before.

"Then again, I *do* live next door, so hanging out with your neighbor is probably more convenient than with someone who lives miles away." Claire pointed to the counter and asked, "Do you mind if I have a little more?"

"Oh, absolutely." The tables had turned. Now I was the one relieved to have gotten off the topic of my life while she managed to escape by supplying limited information.

Before I could grab her plate, she scooted away from the table to help herself. I was happy that she enjoyed dinner, but most of all, I was thrilled at how easy things were. She'd only been inside a couple of times, yet she acted at home here.

"So, how's the wine business?" she asked as she resumed her seat at the table. "Any news about the new flavor you let me have the other day?"

I laughed to myself while swallowing a bite of food. "Funny you should ask. My dad just brought up the topic of expanding the vineyard, which would give us more room to add different grapes. The bottle I gave you was from grapes we acquired from another vineyard. That was kinda my way of testing the waters. So I'm really eager to launch that new prospect on our own land."

"Oh…" Her eyes lit up, filled with enthusiasm. "That sounds exciting."

I set down my fork and leaned back in my chair, taking the opportunity to reverse the conversation like she'd done to me. "What about you? How long have you been a baker?"

She swallowed her bite and immediately began to cough uncontrollably.

"Are you okay?" I leaned forward, ready to help if needed.

"I'm fine." She waved me back. "Wrong pipe." She coughed once more before taking a hefty sip of wine.

"Let me grab you some water."

Again, she waved me off. "No, really, I'm good now," she said, her eyes glistening as she blinked.

I waited a moment to ensure she was all right, and when her breathing returned to normal, I picked up where we left off. "Have you always wanted to be a baker?"

"Um, not really. Baking was something I sorta *fell* into."

"How long have you been doing it?"

She flattened her hair and hummed to herself for a moment. "I can't say for sure, but most of the time, I feel like my career started only yesterday. You know what they say…time flies when you're doing something you love."

Not wanting to give her the chance to change the subject, I asked, "Do you think you'll be ready for the fair?"

"Definitely. I have my new oven and fresh-picked fruit, so I'm ready to go. My best friend, Piper, is coming over next Saturday to help with packaging. I want to keep things simple, but she has all these extravagant ideas. Thankfully, the pies are small, which means the packaging can't be too elaborate."

"I couldn't agree more."

"But if I'm honest, I'm a little nervous."

That surprised me to hear. "About the fair?"

"Yeah. I've never done anything like this before."

I had to have misunderstood something because I couldn't wrap my mind around a baker who'd never sold their own product. "You've never done what before? Sold your pastries?"

"Of course I have." Her mouth curled into a knowing grin. "But this is completely different than any platform I'm used to."

That made sense.

"Well, don't worry. I'll be there to help you every step of the way. You won't be alone."

CHAPTER 7
CLAIRE

I MISSED my parents every day, but there were times when I missed them more than others.

Until today, my high school graduation had been the worst. It was so bad that I skipped all the parties and stayed in bed for the entire weekend. And since then, I'd kept a ten-foot-high steel wall around me, protecting me from having to experience that level of pain ever again. It'd been impenetrable...until now.

The annual Tesorita Town Fair was today, which I'd looked forward to for the last week and a half since tweaking the recipe. Piper came over yesterday to help me finalize everything, and she would've been with me today too, but I assured her that I'd be fine. I guess I felt like I had something to prove.

Except the only thing I'd managed to prove was how wrong I'd been.

About everything.

The entire day from beginning to end had been bad, but as the minutes and hours ticked by, it only became worse. I'd gone from anxiously excited to just plain anxious, then stressed, and right before the fair ended, I felt alone.

Which was how I ended up on my kitchen floor surrounded by boxes of pies when Piper walked in.

"Claire?" she called out from the front door. She knew I was home. I was so upset that I hadn't even bothered to pull my car into the garage. Instead, I'd parked half in the driveway and half in the grass. She probably thought I was drunk. "Claire? Where are you?"

The front door closed, and the soft pitter-patter of her feet moved in my direction.

She came to a complete stop at the entrance to the kitchen and stared at me with furrowed brows. "What in God's creation happened?"

"Nothing," I mumbled before shoving another bite of fruit filling into my mouth. I couldn't even manage to eat it without images of mugshots and black-and-white striped jumpsuits filling my thoughts.

She slowly walked closer, kicking a few empty pie tins out of the way. "Well, *something* clearly happened. Your kitchen looks like a bomb went off in a bakery, and you're on the floor eating all the evidence."

I set the half-eaten dessert on the floor and shoved it out of the way. "I'm a failure, and my life is headed down the crapper with a one-way ticket to shitsville."

"Well, let's take one thing at a time," she said in her soothing voice—the one she used when talking me off a ledge—and sat in front of me with her feet tucked beneath her. "First of all, why do you have so many pies left?"

I glanced up and eyed what I could see of my countertops. Small boxes were stacked everywhere. This was exactly how my kitchen looked yesterday after Piper had helped me package everything in preparation for today. "I only sold two."

"Are you kidding me? Why? What happened?"

I knew what happened…Karma happened. This was my punishment for stealing the recipe and proclaiming to be a baker. But I couldn't admit that. I trusted Piper to stand behind me through almost everything, but that didn't mean she wouldn't have *many* choice words for me regarding my lack of good decision making. So instead of telling her why I thought I'd only sold two, I simply offered a pathetic shrug.

"*Okay…*" She obviously had to bite her tongue. Piper didn't deserve my attitude, but thankfully, she knew me better than anyone, so she knew my mood wasn't directed at her. "Let's start at the beginning, shall we?"

"The very beginning?"

"Yup. Start with leaving the house this morning."

I dropped my head back against the cabinet door behind me. "Well, I was able to fit everything in the car just fine, but since I don't have any experience traveling with a back seat full of pies, there were a few casualties on the way to the fairground."

"Why did you put them in the back seat?"

"Where else would I have put them, Piper?"

"Um, the trunk?" She made that option sound so logical.

Unfortunately, I didn't possess logic. "I put all the display stuff back there."

Piper rolled her eyes and waved me on.

"Anyway, when I got there, I went to check in so I could find my table, except my name wasn't on the roster. So I called Travis to come help since he's the one who got me the booth to begin with. Come to find out, I was listed as *My Neighbor Claire*."

Travis swore up and down he didn't put that as my name, but I couldn't imagine why else it would've been listed that way.

"I'm sorry, but that's the funniest thing I've heard all day," Piper said, squealing with laughter. "How did you not crack up?"

Normally, I would have, but considering the day I'd had, I couldn't even find the strength to smile. "Probably because I'd lost half a dozen pies thanks to the sharp corner turning into the place."

"Oh, yeah. Sorry."

I took a deep breath and waited for her giggles to end before I continued. "This entire week, Travis swore he'd help me at the fair. Except once we got the whole name debacle figured out, he was nowhere to be found. So I had to do everything myself."

"Back up...do *what* by yourself?"

"Bring all the pies from my car to the booth and assemble everything."

Piper held up one finger. "You couldn't drive to the booth, or at least the gate, to unload?"

"I could have...if I'd been aware of that option beforehand. I got everything to my table before someone kindly pointed out that convenience. But by then, I was already bathed in sweat. It was rather unattractive."

"And from the sounds of it," Piper interjected, "unhygienic."

"Yeah, that too." Which had probably been one of the many factors leading to my dismal sales. But that was neither here nor there. "I didn't see Travis again until the entire booth was already set up. He was absolutely *no* help whatsoever."

"Maybe he was busy."

"He probably was, but it doesn't change the fact that he promised he'd help, only to show up and be stuck doing everything on my own."

"You're right. Not helping when he said he would was a shitty thing for him to do." She only wanted to pacify me long enough to move on with the story. "But I doubt his lack of assistance has any bearing on why you only sold two pies."

My shoulders slumped as I recalled the details from my pathetic day. "People stopped to ask about them, but they didn't buy any. And I had quite a few comments about how cute they are...and then they'd walk away. I don't know what I'm doing wrong, Pipes. I honestly don't. But today was enough to prove that I can't do this."

"Can't do what? Make it on your own?"

The backs of my eyes burned, but I refused to cry again. I had already allowed myself a moment of complete self-pity when I left the fairground. Piper didn't need to see an encore. "How am I supposed to prove to Gramps

I can be responsible? I've pretty much blown my entire allowance on these pies. What am I going to do now?"

Sympathy softened her expression as she leaned forward and grabbed my hand. "We'll figure it out together. Like we always do."

I didn't want to imagine where I'd be in life if without my best friend. "I appreciate you so much, Pipes. More than you'll ever realize. You somehow always know exactly when I need you, even if I don't admit it. You, like, sense my tears and come running."

"That's what best friends are for."

Honestly, she was more like the sister I always wanted. "Thanks for coming over."

"You're welcome...but this isn't goodbye."

"What do you mean?"

Her lips curled into a smile right as her eyes twinkled in the kitchen lights. "You don't seriously think I'm gonna leave after hunting down your ass and finding you crumpled on the floor, do you?"

"Umm...no?" Technically, that was exactly what I thought. Or hoped.

"Good, now stand your ass up and go take a shower while I deal with this mess."

I scanned the kitchen, realizing how much of a mess I'd made. "You don't have to do that; I'll clean up later. You have work tomorrow, and it's getting late."

Piper shook her head. "I'm a big girl. Let me worry about work. In the meantime, you need to take a shower. A nice, long, hot shower."

"I don't need one," I countered.

Her expression remained soft, yet her gaze narrowed on me when she said, "I love you, Claire, but you really, *really* do. You admitted to sweating your ass off this morning, but even if you hadn't told me, I can smell you. Not to mention, you have pie filling covering the front of your shirt."

I glanced down and saw a blob of what looked like cherry jam smeared across my chest.

"Fine." I gave in because I knew I couldn't argue with her *and* win. Plus, a hot shower sounded like heaven.

THERE WAS no telling how long I'd spent beneath the hot spray, but by the time I reemerged, my body felt nearly healed from the day's torment. My mind not so much, but the shower had helped me relax enough to accept that I only needed to focus on one thing at a time.

Piper, the thoughtful friend that she was, had laid out a set of pajamas with a pair of white fuzzy slippers. The fact that she'd picked out the red flannel set with the button-up top and matching shorts didn't go unnoticed. She knew those were my favorite, and she knew why—they reminded me of the ones my mom used to sleep in. And the slippers...which my parents had given to me on our last Christmas together.

I quietly slipped out of my room, expecting Piper to have already gone home. The night sky was completely dark through my window, and considering how early she got up for work, I wouldn't be surprised if she was already asleep in her own bed by now.

But she wasn't.

Instead, she jumped out of the living room right in front of me with her hands in the air. "Geez, Piper, you scared me half to death. What are you still doing here? And what's with the jazz hands?"

She immediately dropped her arms to her sides and gave the most pathetic frown, as if I had personally wounded her soul. She'd been my best friend for almost half my life, and I'd never, not once, seen her feelings actually hurt.

"I have a surprise for you and don't want you to see before I do the unveiling. Now, close your eyes." She held her hands over my face and directed me around the corner into the living room before releasing me. "Surprise!"

I scanned the room, wondering what the hell had gotten into her. Seriously, the floor looked like red roses had exploded everywhere. "If this is your way of confessing your love for me, now isn't the best time, Pipes. I have too much on my plate to consider—"

"No, you moron. Although, if that *was* what I was doing, I'd be pretty heartbroken right now." She crossed her arms over her chest and fell into the oversized loveseat.

"So what's with all this?" I gestured to the overly romantic setting in front of me. She had my large fleece spread out in the middle of the floor surrounded by flower petals and lit candles along a couple of shelves on the wall. She also had wine displayed on the coffee table with two glasses filled to the brim.

"Well, I was going for a nice gesture." She continued to pout—badly. This girl could fool nearly anyone. Except me. I'd lost track of how many times she'd gotten her way by pretending to cry or feigning insult. Unfortunately, her antics didn't work on me.

I stepped into the room more and smiled at my best friend. "You're right, this is a very nice gesture. That's not what I meant, though. I was more or less asking where everything came from. I didn't see you walk in with anything other than your purse, and I couldn't have been in the shower long enough for you to have robbed a florist, come back, *and* set everything up."

"Correct. I didn't do any of that. I collected all the candles from around your house for ambiance, and your neighbor brought over the wine. All I gotta say is damn, girl, you weren't lyin' when you said he was hot. He almost burnt my retinas from looking at him. How do you manage to keep your hands to yourself? I would've been all over him by now."

I dropped onto the cushion in shock, unable to do anything other than stare at her. "Travis?"

"Unless you have another hot-as-balls neighbor you've been keeping to yourself."

I rolled my eyes, not fazed in the slightest about what she thought of his good looks—his sex appeal was rather undeniable, so I couldn't blame her for recognizing it. What I cared about was him stopping by while I was in the shower. "Did he say anything?"

"Not really. Someone knocked on the door; I answered. He asked if you were here, I said you were unavailable, so he handed me the bottle and asked if I would give it to you."

"*That was it?*"

"Pretty much. Does he deliver booze often?"

I shrugged, thinking back on the times he'd reached out over the last several weeks, wanting to make amends for one misunderstanding or another. "Only when he wants to apologize for something. Which means he's probably feeling bad about today. Should I text him?"

Piper sat up straight and held onto my shoulders with both hands. "Listen to me, Claire...whatever you do, do *not* text him. Let him sweat for the night. Let him come crawling to you tomorrow and apologize face to face. You're a rather forgiving person, but he needs to realize that he'll have to do more than bring you a bottle of wine—which he probably gets for free —to win you over. Don't. Text. Him."

"What if he thinks—"

"*No.*" She shook me forcefully, nearly giving me whiplash. "It doesn't matter what he thinks. If you want to forgive him in the morning when he texts or calls or comes knocking, that's your prerogative. But right now, your bestie is over here cheering you up after your shitty day—which he was a part of. He can wait until tomorrow."

Piper was right. Tonight, I would enjoy his peace offering while spending time with my best friend.

"Did he bring over the rose petals, too?" I asked, pointing to the ones scattered around my living room.

"Oh, no. Those were mine. They've been in my car since Valentine's Day. After I lit the candles and poured the wine, I thought they'd be a nice touch, so I rummaged through my trunk and found them."

I shook my head, stifling the first laugh of the day. "Valentine's Day was six months ago."

Piper dismissed me with an eye roll and humorous huff before passing me a glass of wine. "Here, drink this and shut up."

"Who's that for?" I pointed to the second glass which was now in her hand. "You *never* drink if you have to drive."

"Good thing I'm not driving, huh?"

Confused, I stared at her as if I could read her mind. "But it's a Sunday night. You have work in the morning."

"And your point is? I don't plan on getting sloshed, so I won't have to worry about a hangover. I'll just leave early to allow myself time to go home before work. My bestie needs me—nothing else matters." Piper Dodson was by far the best human being to ever walk the earth. Much, *much* better than me, considering she would've never stolen someone's super-secret family recipe—accident or otherwise.

God, I had a one-way ticket straight to hell.

I set down my glass to wrap both arms around her shoulders. I hadn't cried since getting into my car after the fair, but I could feel the tears making their way to my eyes as she squeezed me back. I didn't want to get emotional again, so I released her and pulled away from the embrace.

However, I was apparently destined to cry anyway. When I reached for my glass, I found that she had covered the coffee table with my mother's favorite tablecloth. It was pale blue and decorated with tiny embroidered daisies.

My mom had only ever put it out for special occasions—their final Christmas being the last time. It'd still been draped over our dining room table when I returned home after the accident. I had grabbed ahold of the soft, blue fabric and pulled it with me as I crumpled onto the floor in a flood of tears. That was the first time I truly understood my parents were never coming back. Since then, I'd kept it in a secure lockbox along with all my important documents and keepsakes.

"I figured you needed a piece of home with you tonight."

I wiped my eyes and brought the corner of the fabric to my nose. Even though I was fully aware their scent wouldn't be detectable, I sucked in a lungful of air anyway. However, to my surprise, I could smell my mom's perfume. I pulled away and stared unblinkingly at Piper. The expressive smirk on her face said everything.

"How...? Where...?"

She slid off the couch cushion to the floor right next to me and tucked my wet hair behind my ear. "I found a bottle in the box with the tablecloth. I know how you are with scents, so I thought you could use a reminder."

Maybe it was because Piper had been there before I became an orphan, or because she was there with me when I'd received news of their death. Or maybe it was as simple as her being her...but whatever the reason, she was the only person I could be vulnerable with. She was literally the only person I didn't keep at arm's length. While I kept everyone—including my grandfather—on the outside of my protective wall, Piper owned a permanent spot inside.

She was more than my best friend.

"I forgot what she smelled like." I held the fabric to my face again, consumed with memories and the kind of comfort I'd never find anywhere else.

Their scent in the house and on their clothes hadn't lasted long after they died. I always believed that it disappeared because I'd gone around sniffing everything until I'd lost the ability to smell them at all. I never knew what perfume my mom had worn or what aftershave my dad used to wear, so I couldn't even buy a bottle of my own.

The security their scent had always provided was gone.

Until now.

One whiff and it all came back. The happiness, the love, and yes, the tears. The pain. The grey cloud of despair that hung around the edges of my peripheral vision, reminding me that its destruction was never far away.

"I know," Piper whispered as she pulled me into her. My head fell naturally into the crook of her neck, and the longer she gently rubbed my back in soothing strokes, the more I began to let go. Eventually, I stopped caring about the pool of tears that soaked her shirt. I simply cried and let my best friend witness what no one else on earth ever got to see.

My pain.

My grief.

"You're the best, Piper," I said once the sorrow began to wane—at least enough to do anything other than sob on her shoulder. "I'd hate to think about where I'd be right now if I didn't have you in my life."

"Thank God you don't have to think about that, huh?" She passed me my glass and took her own, neither of us moving from our spot on the floor. "You already said I'm the best, but to prove your point even more, I got us some sweets to snack on. Just in case the heroin I spiked our drinks with gives us the munchies."

I slapped my hand over my mouth to stop myself from spewing wine everywhere. Somehow, I managed to swallow without much more than a few dribbles down my chin. "You're really making this a party, huh? Should we put on strobe lights and techno music?"

"Duh. What else do people do when they're high?"

Laughter rolled through us until we were both clenching our stomachs with tears cascading down our cheeks. Finally, Piper grabbed a dinner tray from the side table between the two sofas and held it out for me to see. In front of me were six giant rolls of Sweeties.

"Aw, Pipes. You brought me my favorite candies?" I prepared myself to hear her tell me they'd been in her car since Valentine's Day too, along with the satin rose petals.

"No, I stole them from your nightstand. I hope you don't mind. I would've stopped and picked some up, but I wasn't aware what I'd walk in on. And let's be real...there was no way I could've possibly been prepared for what I saw when I got here."

I dismissed her with a wave. I doubted I was *that* frantic when she showed up.

"Would you like to brainstorm on either the pies or possibly another employment option?"

I put my hand on her knee and looked her in the eyes. "I love you, and I appreciate you being there for me through everything, but can we just chill tonight? I miss watching TV with you, and after the day I've had, I would much rather sit and do nothing with my best friend than fall into the black hole of depression all over again."

"I'm good with that."

And like every other horrible time in my life, Piper was there to make everything better.

I WAS NOT surprised to see the other side of my bed empty when I woke up the next morning. If Piper was even two minutes late to work, someone would be on the phone with the authorities reporting a missing person.

However, what did surprise me was the heavy knocks coming from my front door.

Then again, I should've been used to being woken up by knocking or banging, thanks to Travis and his impeccable ability to interrupt my sleep.

Regardless, I rolled out of bed, grumbling with every step from my room to the entryway. I fully expected it to be Travis, coming to see if I'd gotten the wine, so imagine my surprise when I opened the door and found my grandfather on the porch.

Before saying anything, I glanced over his shoulder, ensuring that he didn't bring the homewrecker with him. He must've picked up on what I was doing because he chuckled and said, "She's at the garden center, Claire. I came alone."

I smiled, invited him in, and kissed his cheek as he passed.

He cradled a beautiful bouquet of flowers in the crook of his arm, but before I could ask about them, he checked his watch and said, "Did you just wake up?"

"Yes, I was catching up from the lack of sleep I got all last week."

"Why? What happened last week?"

"I'll tell you everything in a second, but right now, I desperately need to pee and brush my teeth. So make yourself at home, and I'll be right back." I pointed to the living room and then quickly turned around and headed straight to the bathroom.

I ignored the notifications on my phone as I checked the time. It wasn't *that* late, only eleven o'clock. There had been many days when I still lived at home that I wouldn't roll out of bed until after lunch. So I wasn't sure what point he was trying to make.

He probably thinks I don't have a job, I smugly thought to myself.

Although, I kind of didn't. Especially after my utter failure yesterday.

I pushed that thought aside and pulled up Piper's texts from earlier this morning while brushing my teeth.

The first one came shortly after seven, likely as she left her house for work.

Piper: I hope you don't mind, but I took your copy of your parents' will this morning. I found it last night in the lockbox and thought there might be something in there that could help you. I'll go over it at work between tasks and let you know if I find anything.

The next came almost an hour later.

Piper: How much do you miss Waldo???

And then, less than thirty minutes ago…

Piper: Never mind. It won't work.

I immediately responded, hoping she wasn't too busy to see her phone.

What is it? And why won't it work?

Thank God she didn't make me wait for a reply.

Piper: It's a marriage clause. It says that your trust fund will be released to you either on your twenty-fifth birthday or when a legal marriage certificate is established, whichever comes first. Too bad we didn't know all of this when you were dating Waldo!

My head spun…or maybe it was the room. All I know is the letters on my keypad blurred as I frantically tapped the phone screen.

Why won't it work? I'm pretty sure I can convince him to marry me. Especially if he got paid for it!

I hit send and immediately began typing again.

And his name is Oswald. Not Waldo.

Excitement filled me, hope of a second chance.

But with one text, my optimism vanished, leaving me empty and even more disappointed.

Piper: According to Insta, he's engaged to someone else. But don't worry, I'll keep looking. In the meantime, don't do anything. Okay? We'll discuss it when I get out of work. I'll call you on my way home.

There must be a solution. I just need to find someone to be the groom.

I rinsed my mouth and then shuffled my way to the living room. As soon as I rounded the corner, I was reminded of the mess we'd left behind. Our movie had ended late, and we were both falling asleep, so we decided to head to bed and leave the clean-up for me in the morning. At the time, that seemed like a pretty decent idea; unfortunately, I wasn't aware my grandfather would show up before I had a chance to do anything with the mess.

Thankfully, I didn't have to witness his inspection of the living room. Instead, I found him in the kitchen filling a vase with water. I took a seat at the kitchen table and dropped my head into my hands. My phone buzzed twice, calling my attention to the messages on the screen.

Piper: Okay??

Piper: Claire! I need you to respond so I know you're not plotting anything stupid.

"Who's Travis?" I heard, breaking my concentration on Piper's texts.

My head jerked back. "Huh? Why?"

Gramps smiled as he stuck each flower into the vase, one stem at a time. "Because your living room looks like Cupid threw up a rose bush while sitting on your couch, and whoever this Travis guy is sent you a rather expensive-looking bouquet."

He passed me the card that had been stuck in the flowers. I originally assumed they were from my grandfather, a house-warming gift of sorts. But they weren't. The card had been signed by my oh-so handsome neighbor.

Claire, I feel horrible about yesterday. Let me make it up to you with dinner tonight.

My face remained stoic as I tried to comprehend his message. There was no need for the flowers after sending over wine last night. I mean, it was complete overkill. Which meant he must've felt horrible for practically ignoring me all day.

My attention bounced back and forth between Piper's texts and the message with Travis's name typed below. But once again, Gramps yanked me from my thoughts when he asked, "Who is this fella? You didn't tell me you were seeing anyone."

The only thing I could focus on was Piper's text, informing me of the supposed marriage clause. I glanced at my phone one more time before turning my attention to Gramps. His demeanor seemed to change as he waited for my answer; the longer I took, the more tense things became.

I read Piper's text one more time, then replied, "Surprise! I'm getting married!"

CHAPTER 8

TRAVIS

IT'D BEEN an hour since receiving email confirmation of the flower delivery, yet there was still no word from Claire.

There was a lot of work left to finish, but I had trouble concentrating on a single task. Images of Claire crying in her car after the fair randomly flashed in my mind, interrupting whatever I was in the middle of doing. I couldn't seem to forget the sight of her practically crumpled against her steering wheel with her face in her hands. I needed to right my part in her pain, but until then, I had to focus on my tasks here at the winery.

A knock on my office door startled me, despite the fact that I'd been waiting for Enrique, our vinter—commonly referred to as the winemaker. We'd set up a meeting for today to discuss the progress of this season's wine production. Hopefully, this would be good news. I wasn't sure I could handle hearing anything serious.

"Hey, Boss. While I'm here, do you mind if we also discuss your plans for the expansion?" he asked as he took the seat opposite my desk.

"Of course not. We can discuss anything you want, my friend." Since he oversaw every aspect of the harvesting process through to the final product, his input on adding more land was crucial. "What's up?"

"So, I've spoken to a few other vinters in the business, and they all have the same reservations I do."

"With what? The expansion?"

He nodded and took a deep breath before elaborating. "If I'm honest— and this seems to be the opinions of the others as well—it's a rather big task to jump into without the sort of advanced preparation needed."

"What do you mean?" I leaned forward, propping my forearms on the edge of the desk and clasped my hands together. "This is something I've been talking about for years—long before I was ever this involved with the winery. Why all of a sudden is it being made to sound like an impulsive move?"

"I wouldn't say impulsive. Not well thought-out, maybe. Trust me, Travis, I understand how long you've wanted to do something like this. My concern is merely that—*concern*. Not judgment or criticism." Enrique had always been soft-spoken, which made unpleasant information easier to hear.

"That's what I'm not understanding, though. What concerns do you— and your friends, who are not involved in this decision *or* this vineyard— have?" My mind immediately jumped to conspiracy theories, excusing the opinions of the other vinters as selfishly motivated. The only reason they would get involved was if they saw Uncorked Vineyards as a threat and wanted to keep our product reach as small as possible.

He drummed his fingers on a file folder in his lap. "It's a pretty risky gamble, that's all."

"In what way?" I trusted Enrique more than any other employee, so as much as I wanted to dismiss his concern, I knew it was essential to hear him out. What I did with his opinion in the end was on me, but I needed to listen to what he had to say first. "How is this any more of a gamble than the brewery, or this distillery my parents are looking at with Jake?"

"I'm not saying that. Those other ventures have nothing to do with me, and honestly, this one doesn't either, other than giving me an increased workload." He shook his head and waved his hands in the air between us. "Never mind. Forget I said anything. I shouldn't be getting involved."

I took a deep breath and calmed myself enough to continue without any perceived attitude or defiance. His opinion was important, and for that, he deserved to be heard. "No. You obviously see a potential issue I don't, so please, help me understand. I won't be able to make an informed decision without your insight."

"Okay," he said, relaxing in his seat. "I can't deny that in the long term, already owning the property makes more sense than waiting, and the land may not be available when you're ready. But in the short term, you have to admit that expanding so quickly *is* a huge gamble."

He might as well have been talking in Spanish because not a single word registered. If he'd been my mom or dad, I would've assumed I had drifted off again, but not with Enrique. This man knew his business; he'd been a winemaker for as long as I'd been alive, so I usually paid attention to every syllable he spoke. Except right now, he was making as much sense as baby babble.

"This addition will more than double your current acreage. Which, like I said, is a huge plus for future expansion options. But in the present—"

"Back up…more than *double* the acreage?" Maybe he'd been the one confused, not me.

"Well, yes. As of now, you have six acres of vines. We maintain them quite well with scheduled grafting spread out so we don't have any regular underproducing seasons."

"Yes, yes…I'm with you on all that. And I understand that cropping an entire expansion at once runs the risk of those vines slowing down at the same time, causing the chance of underproduction. But—and correct me if I'm wrong—we have done an amazing job at staying ten steps ahead of issues like that."

"You're absolutely correct. But we also only have six acres to look after. Being able to continue that level of care for an additional ten acres would require more manpower, which leads to a higher payroll. All of which should be taken into account when considering the time and money you'll already be losing before the new vines produce anything of value."

I had so many questions bouncing around my head like pinballs, yet I couldn't focus on just one in order to ask anything. Instead, I stared at a pen mark on the top of my desk and repeated *an additional ten acres* over and over in my mind.

"Listen, I understand this isn't my place," Enrique spoke up, sliding closer to the edge of his seat as he leaned forward. "I have absolutely *no* say in this decision, other than if I'm up to the challenge of more work. Which I am. I've already told your father that, and we've already discussed the option of bringing on another vinter to split the crops. I'm only here because I'm concerned about how this could potentially devastate your parents. I've seen my fair share of vineyards expanding too rapidly without the necessary means to do so. And considering you guys are like family to me, I couldn't live with myself if I didn't speak up when given the chance to keep anything bad from happening."

I felt like I was in the twilight zone, and the harder I fought to make sense of this, the more confused I became. So I decided to take a breath and slow things down. "Explain what you mean by potentially devastating my parents."

He narrowed his dark eyes, as if he thought the answer was obvious. "I'm not familiar with the private details of your family's business ventures, and I'm even less informed about your family's financial situation. However, I trust that if you go through with this and fail, your parents can bail you out without losing everything they've worked so hard for. Don't misunderstand me; that doesn't mean I want to see this expansion fail. I only worry because I imagine their future includes a smaller workload while you boys continually take on more and more until they eventually retire. And that won't happen if they have to bail out this project."

Enrique was genuinely a good man. He'd been with our family since before my balls had dropped, which practically made him an honorary Cabrera. He cared about my parents—and the four of us kids—so I couldn't blame him for having concerns.

"Thank you, Enrique. Have you mentioned any of this to my dad?"

He shook his head. "Not really. When he first sent out the email, we had a chat, but he was very clear that he trusts you and your ability to take this winery further than he ever could. Which was why I decided to come to you before any concrete plans have been made."

I didn't hear anything past his first sentence. "What email?"

His expression morphed into confusion. "The one from a couple of weeks ago when the possibility of expansion was first proposed. He included attachments with graphs and charts from the seller. We were all CC'd on it."

Everything suddenly made sense. Dad had mentioned the prospect in the meeting two weeks ago, assuming I'd already gone through the information, when in reality, I wasn't aware a proposal even existed. So when he'd asked my opinion, I assumed he'd meant reallocating our own property. Not buying more.

Shit.

I'd really jumped to the wrong conclusion this time.

It was imperative that I talked with my dad about all this, but first, I needed to fully understand the entire situation. This was much bigger than the two or three acres I assumed would be transferred from the farm to the vineyard. *Ten acres...* I didn't have a clue where that amount of land would've come from.

Rather than give me a full briefing on the harvest so far, Enrique left me with a file folder with all the numbers I needed to ensure my production and distribution goals were up to date. I could go through those figures later. Right now, I needed to search my inbox for that missing email.

FOR THE FIRST time in my career at the winery, I'd called an early day and left shortly before noon.

After meticulously going through every Google folder possible, I'd finally asked Enrique to forward me the email. And once it was in my inbox, everything started to make sense. Come to find out, I hadn't been copied on the proposal—no doubt an accidental oversight on my dad's part. Which explained why I hadn't been aware of any land for sale. And I couldn't say anything to my dad without giving away that I didn't have a clue what he was talking about, even though I'd pretended otherwise.

I'd told my parents to go for it, that we wouldn't have an issue with the expansion. I'd dismissed their concerns regarding finances and increased manpower, saying I understood what was involved in growing our crops... all because I'd assumed this meant we'd convert a few acres we already owned. In that scenario, I'd only be monetarily responsible for the new plants and tilling the land. But now that I'd seen the full proposal, anxiety riddled my nervous system. I wasn't sure how I'd make this work...or *if* I could.

I struggled to comprehend anything, and I quickly found that I couldn't focus at the office. There were too many interruptions to concentrate, so I headed home. At least there, I would have some peace and quiet to formulate a plan and look into every option.

Or so I thought.

As I approached my house, I saw a car on my side of the driveway, right next to Claire's. And when I came to a complete stop, I observed Claire and an older man standing between the two vehicles. This was the first time Claire crossed my mind since Enrique flipped my world upside down. And the second I saw her, all the anxiety and pessimistic thoughts over the vineyard vanished.

Granted, that might've had something to do with the way she stared at me.

Her brows were arched unusually high, mouth gaping, shoulders slowly moving up and down in time with her deep, terror-filled breaths. Fear colored every aspect of her expression from the worry etched along her brow to the hollowness of her cheeks.

I completely forgot my worry about the vineyard or the bank. My only concern was ensuring that Claire was all right. I wasn't familiar with who she was talking to, but from my vantage point, she didn't want him there. So I quickly pulled the handbrake and turned off the ignition, flinging open the door and removing my keys at the same time. All the while, my eyes never left hers.

Blood pumped through my ears as I neared the two, muffling the sounds around me while anger darkened my vision. However, I still managed to catch the sight of Claire trying to push the old man into his car—the driver's side door already open. The more he protested, the angrier I became.

"Everything all right over here?" I couldn't be sure, considering my hearing wasn't up to par at the moment, but I believed I'd sounded like my dad—deep, booming voice with a little bit of threatening grit.

"Oh...yes, yes. All good." Claire nodded frantically, her words coming much faster than usual. "You were just leaving, weren't you, Gramps?"

The old man, whom I now assumed was her grandfather, turned and greeted me with a welcoming grin. He opened his mouth and started to move his arm as if readying himself to hold out his hand, but before he could say or do anything, Claire stepped around him to stand between the two of us.

"Thanks again for the visit." With her hands flat on his chest, she gently directed her grandfather between the open door and the driver's seat. "You should call ahead next time, though. Tell what's-her-face I said hi. See you soon. Love you."

At least I wasn't the only one who picked up on Claire's odd behavior. Her grandfather squinted at her and grinned before returning his attention to me. With soft, dismissive laughter in his tone, he asked, "Is this Travis?"

I wasn't sure who the question was directed to because his choice of words sounded like it was meant for Claire, although his gaze was set on me. Either way, I wasn't given a chance to respond before Claire, still very highly strung, went back to nodding and shoving.

"Yes. Yes, this is Travis. Too bad you don't have time for a proper introduction. I'm sure Travis only came home for lunch, and the longer we're held up out here chitchatting, the less time he'll have to eat. Such a shame. But next time, yeah?" Still, she failed at getting him into his car.

Everything was happening so fast I didn't have enough time to contemplate how or why her grandfather knew who I was. Or why she wanted him to leave so quickly.

"Home? You live here, too?" His eyes widened, giving me the first—and so far, *only*—reminder of Claire.

I lifted my finger to point at my side of the duplex right as Claire announced, "Yup, he sure does. I'll explain everything later, Gramps. Love you."

"Wait, wait, wait…" He finally pushed back a little, creating more space for himself in the conversation Claire seemed desperate to end. "I understand that you are both adults, responsible of making your own decisions, but I'm not sure how I feel about you two living together. How long have you even known each other?"

Stunned by his assumption, I couldn't do much more than open and close my mouth. And for the first time since walking up, I found myself desperate for Claire to interject. Except she didn't. Instead, she laughed. Slow and soft to start, then a little louder, until she sounded like a cackling hyena.

"Uh, no, sir," I finally managed, considering *someone* needed to say something, and that clearly wasn't going to be Claire. I pointed to the right side of our duplex and added, "I live over there."

"Oh…" He nodded while staring at the front of my house. "Is that how you met Claire?"

I found his choice of questions a bit strange. Then again, he was Claire's grandfather. She wasn't the most ordinary person I'd ever met—and thank the Lord for that! I preferred quirky and different. At least now I could see that her oddities ran in her family and wasn't only her.

"Yes, actually. We met the morning after she moved in when I woke her up because her U-Haul was blocking my side of the driveway. It's been an exciting ride ever since."

After Claire's over-the-top laughter finally settled down, she crossed her arms and shuffled her feet along the driveway, appearing beyond uncomfortable. "Yup. Definitely been a whirlwind."

"Well, I don't want to take up your entire lunchbreak, so I should probably head home for some food myself." He held out his hand and shook mine as he said, "It was nice to meet you, Travis. Look after my granddaughter for me, please."

"Absolutely." I released his hand and headed to my Jeep to retrieve the proposal documents I'd printed before leaving the office. Not only did I need them to formulate a plan moving forward, but I figured they deserved a little privacy to say goodbye.

By the time I had everything and started to make my way up the front lawn, her grandfather backed out of the driveway, waving at me through the window. Nice guy, though I still wasn't sure of his interest in me. Granted, Claire was young and lived alone, so maybe my presence gave him some contentment knowing someone was close by in case she needed anything.

"What was that all about?" I asked as I approached Claire, who was now leaning against the side of her shiny Audi SUV with her arms crossed over her chest. Normally, I hated flashy things, cars included, but for some reason, I wasn't bothered by hers. If anything, I was impressed. The price tag proved she was successful at her job.

She shrugged, her attitude appearing to have made a complete one-eighty since I first arrived. No longer did she appear wound tighter than an antique clock. Instead, she acted like she'd narrowly escaped death—subdued with overwhelming relief. "I guess he was in the area and wanted to stop by to check on me."

Something didn't add up, but I didn't have enough information about their relationship to question anything or make an assumption. But I could sense that her day seemed to be going as well as mine.

"Since misery loves company, and noon is a little too early to start drinking, wanna grab something to eat?" My invitation surprised me considering all I had to do today, but I excused it as needing a break before worrying about work.

She lifted her chin and narrowed her gaze in interest. "Where?"

"Anywhere. They just opened a Salad Plantation down the street."

Claire ran her hands over her hair as she contemplated my offer. "Instead of dinner tonight?" She must've picked up on my confusion because she added, "The flowers... You said you wanted to have dinner."

With everything that happened at work this morning, the bouquet, the note, the apology, as well as yesterday had all slipped my mind. I wouldn't be surprised if she thought *I* was the crazy one. "We can do both if you want."

Again, she fidgeted with her hair as if contemplating what to say. Finally, she dropped her arms to her sides, lifted one shoulder, and said, "Yeah, sure...why not. Let me change real fast, and I'll come over when I'm ready. Give me, like, five minutes?"

"Sounds good."

The expansion documents practically burned a hole in my palm as I held the folder to my chest. I had so much work to do—not just figuring out my plan of action for the vineyard, but also my regular daily workload that I hadn't even looked at. Having lunch shouldn't have been an option, yet for some reason, I felt at peace. I felt as though this was what I needed to calm my mind enough to rationally come up with a resolution.

I only hoped I hadn't convinced myself of that so I'd have an excuse to spend time with Claire.

CHAPTER 9
CLAIRE

I was ecstatic to learn there was a new Salad Plantation in town. It was more than a salad bar. They offered soups, pastas, sandwiches, pizzas...and of course, salads. And the best part was it was all you could eat. Well, not quite. Piper and I stayed nearly all day once, but when the staff caught on, they asked us to leave after our second meal.

Before this one opened, the closest had been on the other side of town, near Piper's office. I used to meet her for lunch on the first Wednesday of every month. Unfortunately, we hadn't been since I'd moved.

"They have the best chicken noodle soup," I said with my mouth full.

Travis laughed, though he waited until he swallowed his food before speaking. "I'm not sure how you can possibly make that claim considering you're missing the chicken *and* the soup."

I glanced down at my bowl, not understanding what the problem was. "So? The noodles are the best part. The rest only gets in the way."

He laughed again, though this time, I couldn't help but join in.

"Since you won't tell me why you came home at noon, can I guess?" I'd spent the last ten minutes trying to find out why Travis had left work early. He'd mentioned his day wasn't going so well, though he wouldn't offer anything more. Truth be told, I only kept at it to keep him from asking about the awkward exchange with my grandfather.

"This should be interesting. Go on, why do you think I took a half-day?"

I tapped my warm spoon on my bottom lip while creating a mental list of all the plausible reasons one would come home early on a weekday. "Because you felt horrible for ignoring me yesterday, so you wanted to come home and beg for my forgiveness."

He slapped his hand over his mouth, likely preventing himself from spewing soda all over the table. "While I do feel bad about yesterday, and I would feel so much better if you accepted my apology...that's not why I left early."

"Okay..." I went back to tapping my lip with my spoon, which was now cold. "You accidentally knocked over all the barrels and had to drink the wine off the floor with a straw to hide the evidence. But your mom caught you and sent you home for drinking on the job."

His smile widened, nearly blinding me with his perfect teeth. "Nope. Try again."

"Umm...because you won the lotto, and since you don't need the paycheck, you quit?"

"I wish I won the lotto, but no. Not even close."

"Then why did you leave so early?" I asked, practically whining.

Travis put the last piece of pizza in his mouth and leaned back in the booth as if stretching. After swallowing, he took a deep breath and said, "Okay, fine. You win. But first, I want to talk about yesterday."

I dropped my spoon and groaned. While I appreciated his desire to make things right, I really didn't want to relive such a horrible day. Then again, discussing how he'd abandoned me in the middle of a bunch of strangers was much better than being asked about the scene in our driveway he'd come home to.

"I ended up being a lot busier than expected." He leaned forward and met my stare, ensuring I was listening. "Not only did I have an insane number of customers want to sign up for subscriptions or buy cases of wine, but I'd also been volunteered for fair duty. And to make the whole thing worse, I had to do everything by myself since my brothers never showed up. But none of that matters because, at the end of the day, I gave my word I would be there for you, and I wasn't. Honestly, Claire, I can't tell you how sorry I am."

His apology was heartfelt and sincere. The only problem was I'd already forgiven him. I knew in my gut he wouldn't intentionally hang me out to dry. So I had no intention of putting that on his plate. "It's okay, Travis. I was bummed at the time, but I understand."

"Are you sure? Because I have to be honest...I saw you leave the fair, and you looked quite upset. Don't act like it wasn't a big deal now because you just want to drop the whole thing and move on. We can do that, but only after you understand how bad I feel and how sorry I am."

Hearing that he'd seen me upset made my heart race and chest constrict. I had completely broken down once I reached the safety of my car, so if he saw me then, he'd witnessed more than anyone in my life—aside from Piper.

"I do understand, and that's not what I'm doing. You were only a tiny reason for how I felt when I left yesterday."

"Yeah?" Concern furrowed his brow. "What else happened?"

I didn't want to go there with him, but I figured there was no point in keeping it a secret. My failures were public information for anyone walking past my booth. "I just had a horrible day all around. I only sold two pies."

The deep creases in his brow eased a little, turning his concern into confusion. "Really? Did you have samples for people to try?"

"Samples?" To my own ears, I sounded offended, which wasn't the case at all. More than anything, I was surprised. "No, I didn't think to offer any. I'd spent so much on the little tins and boxes for the packaging that I guess the thought of losing money by giving away free slices never clicked in my brain."

"Well, first of all, you'll never lose money that way. Cutting up ten pies to use as tasters could turn into fifty sales. Trust me, I gain a ton of business by giving people a chance to try my wine. I believe in my product, so I'm not afraid of giving a little away."

This conversation would've been more helpful on Saturday.

"And my second suggestion would be to rethink your packaging. You're still making the single-serving pies, right?" When I nodded, he added, "Okay, so rather than waste time and money worrying about tins and boxes, do away with them."

"And do what? Sell them out of my hands?"

He dropped his chin and shook his head, laughing to himself. "No, Claire. Haven't you seen the ones shaped like a crescent moon or look like they were folded in half? You hold them as you eat instead of using a fork or a plate."

"Like the ones they have at gas stations and grocery stores?"

"Yeah. Exactly like those. If you did that, you wouldn't have to worry about the tins, and if you wrapped them in cellophane instead of using boxes, you could cut your expenses *way* down." As if suddenly thinking of something, he knitted his brows and asked, "Have you always packaged your products like that?"

Oh shit. Back to the charade of being a professional baker versus someone who had literally just learned that raw dough wasn't supposed to taste good. If I kept this up, I'd eventually get caught, but for the time being, I decided to keep it going.

"Well, the bakery always handled the packaging." That technically wasn't a lie; I never said the desserts sold at the bakery were mine. "I haven't been on my own for very long, so this side of things is sorta new to me."

That wasn't a lie, either.

He nodded slowly. "Gotcha. So what's your business name?"

I couldn't tell him I didn't have one, so I came up with one on the spot. "Pies by Claire." And then I practically rolled my eyes at myself.

"Not bad, but you might want to come up with something a little catchier."

I shrugged, feeling somewhat deflated. I was grateful for the suggestions, but they wouldn't do me any good now. We were past the time for coming up with helpful ideas. "I couldn't think of anything else."

Travis, deep in thought, hummed to himself while mindlessly rubbing his chin. "What else do you offer?"

"Right now, just pies. I figured I should probably focus on one thing rather than overwhelm myself by trying to do everything."

"Makes sense. Well, if they're all small like the one you gave me, then what about Cutie Pies?"

I literally felt the excitement pump through my veins. "That's brilliant! There were a few people who stopped to tell me how cute they were, so that's a freakin' perfect name!"

He beamed at me from across the table, clearly satisfied with himself.

Until this very moment, I'd accepted that my new venture was dead in the water. And I was okay with that, especially after learning the history of the recipe I'd stolen. Part of me was relieved I never made any money off the pies. I doubted I'd be able to sleep at night if I had, let alone live with myself. But now, with this new plan, everything changed. I could reinvent myself and actually have a chance at succeeding. But if I accepted his suggestions and moved forward with these new ideas, I'd have to do so with a different recipe.

Or at the very least, a severely revised one.

"Damn, Travis. I bet you sell the crap out of your wine, huh? This new expansion of yours is gonna put you on the map. I have a good feeling. In a few years, everyone will be drinking your brand around dinner tables all across the state."

The pride radiating off him mere seconds ago dimmed before completely vanishing into thin air. I wasn't sure what I'd said to make him go from excited to disheartened. It couldn't have been the compliment, so I was at a loss for words.

Finally, after wiping his mouth, he wadded up his napkin and tossed it on the table. "I'm not sure what's going on with the expansion anymore. I found out a few things today which kinda puts a monkey wrench in my plans."

That was surprising to hear. It also explained his earlier comment about his day not going well. "Is that why you came home early?"

Travis nodded and then cleared his throat to continue with his explanation. "Yeah, I need to figure out a few things, and I couldn't do that at the office."

Laughter bubbled past my lips no matter how hard I tried to stifle it. "I'm sorry, but if you left early to work from home, why are we out having lunch? Shouldn't you be dealing with whatever the issue is?"

"Technically, yes. But to be honest, I had so much going on in my head I think I needed a bit of a breather before diving into it."

"I do the same thing sometimes, but for me, I'm straight up procrastinating. I get so overwhelmed I don't even want to think about whatever the issue is, so I put it off. But trust me…doing that only makes everything worse. Because eventually, you can't put it off any longer, and by then, your options are extremely limited."

His lips curled the slightest bit, offering a reassuring grin. "I know, and I promise, that's not what I'm doing. I thought I had everything figured out until this morning. And the worst part is I can't discuss any of this with my family."

"Why not? Don't you guys make all your business decisions together?"

"Yeah, which is exactly why I can't go to them about this. We've already agreed on the expansion; I've already told them to go ahead with it. If I tell them I had all the details wrong and am completely in way over my head, they'll call the whole thing off. I don't want to bail on the project. I only need a minute to find a solution."

"Well, why don't you try talking to me? Maybe talking out loud will help you see a way around the problem. I might not be able to offer much, but I can listen. And maybe, if I ask enough questions, you'll be able to find the answers. I think a lot of times when we find ourselves at a crossroads, we tend to overthink the solution because the problem is so big or complicated. When in reality, the answer is right there." There were moments when I came up with some amazing pieces of advice…too bad I never figured out how to apply them to my own life.

Travis finished his soda and rattled the ice for a moment as he grew lost in his thoughts. But then he set his cup down and appeared to settle more in his seat. "Are you sure?"

"I wouldn't have suggested it otherwise."

"Okay…" He mindlessly twisted an empty straw wrapper around his finger as he spoke. "I'm not sure why or how, but I was under the impression the expansion would take place on property we already owned. When I initially agreed, I imagined a few extra acres and told my parents I had everything taken care of and to move forward. But this morning, I found out it's more extensive than that. Our neighbor has offered to sell us a ten-acre plot of land at a discount before listing it publicly."

I didn't understand where the issue was, but I tended to interrupt and start asking questions which may very well be answered if I simply kept my mouth shut. So I leaned against the edge of the table with my elbows and kept quiet, waiting for him to give me all the details before unleashing my interrogation.

"Based on what I've seen in the proposal, the offer is all or nothing. Which means, I can't turn around and say I only want half the land. I have to take all ten acres or nothing. If I don't, then I have no idea when we'll have another opportunity to expand the vineyard. But purchasing the entire lot now, when I don't have the means, is a huge risk."

"Why don't you have the means?" That didn't take long before I hit him with a question.

"We'll be going from six acres to sixteen, which means we'll need more hands in the fields. That's more money in payroll. We'll need more vines for the additional land—we're talking about grafting and planting, and that doesn't even cover the attention they need to develop properly. Then there are other things to consider such as new machinery, which is never cheap. So while I'm pretty sure I could find a way to get approved for another loan to cover my part of the sale, I would still need to find a way to cover the added expenses of everything else."

"Okay...but doesn't increasing your stock mean increased income? You can't possibly add ten acres of grapes and not make your money back tenfold in wine sales."

For the first time since opening up about his situation, his expression softened. A faint smile crept onto his lips, and his gorgeous Caribbean eyes danced in the light. Humor brightened his complexion, even if it was likely caused by my ignorance.

"Eventually, but new crops take time to mature. Which is where the entire issue is. If there were already grapes on the new land, this wouldn't be a problem—although the lot would be way more expensive to purchase. But since we have to start from scratch, there's a lot of overhead we'll need to cover ourselves. It's definitely not impossible, but I don't see it being very easy without a bank giving me a substantial loan to cover the land *plus* five years of unreturned expenses."

His situation made me more determined than ever to regain access to my funds. And it'd be a lie if I said at least part of my motivation wasn't fueled by the guilt I still felt for taking something from him. Even if he never learned of what I'd done, I knew, and I needed to make it right.

It also helped to justify the little white lie I'd told Gramps about being engaged.

An idea slowly formed, but rather than tell him my thoughts, I placed my hand over his and said, "I'm sure everything will all work out, Travis. As long as whatever you do, you don't give up this opportunity. Okay? Secure the main loan to cover the land and worry about the rest later."

"I can't do that."

"Yes, you can. As long as you have the property, you're fine. You don't have to start expanding right away, do you?"

He slowly shook his head, a calm understanding enveloping him.

"Okay then…you're good. Sounds to me like the most important aspect of your dilemma is the risk of losing out on the chance to expand if you pass on this sale. This way, you won't have to turn it down, nor will you have to worry about going broke."

I was rather proud of myself when he smiled, clearly impressed with my suggestion.

This turned out to be a productive lunch—he'd helped with a marketing strategy for my pies, and I had helped him remove a few of the monkey wrenches from his situation. Now, if only I could figure out how to get out of my newest problem while still gaining access to my money.

"Welcome back to a brand-new episode of *You Can't Buy Love*," Bob Archer announced, and the crowd chimed in at the end like they always did. "This week is family week. Are you ready to get to know our contestant, Claire Hansen, a little better?"

Excitement coursed through me as I glanced around the studio, looking for my parents. But my enthusiasm quickly diminished when I didn't see them come out from behind any curtains. That was when I remembered my parents were dead. I didn't have anyone coming to this week's episode because I had no one.

The clapping in the audience slowly faded as Bob came to stand next to me. "Since you don't have any family, we've found the next best thing. Someone who knows you inside and out. Please welcome to the stage…"

My heart pounded as I waited for Piper to show herself. No one else on Earth knew me better than Piper Dodson. So imagine my surprise when she didn't show up, either.

Instead, Bob Archer had other plans. "Waldo!"

"It's *Oswald*," I argued, trying in vain to rip the long, skinny microphone from his hand. I didn't understand why no one could accurately remember his name.

"Have a seat, Waldo." Bob held out a hand, directing my ex to sit between me and my date. Although, I still couldn't remember his name, other than it started with a *T*. But I couldn't concentrate on that at the moment because Bob's booming voice filled the room once more when he said, "In your own words, please tell the audience why you two broke up."

"Oh, that's easy," Oswald answered with a laugh, as if this were a trivia show and he was just given the simplest question in the world. "Because Claire only cares about herself."

"What? That's not true!" I stood and turned toward my ex, ready to smack the smirk right off his face.

Unfortunately, he stood as well, though he kept up with his cheerful disposition despite anger rolling off me like plumes of smoke. "You never did anything I wanted. Everything was always your way or the highway— what movie we watched, which songs we listened to in the car, where we ate for dinner. Hell, you can't even get my name right."

That threw me off. "Your name? It's Oswald."

"No, that's just what you've always called me. My name is Waldo."

I took a step back and eyed him head to toe, surprised to see him suddenly wearing a red-and-white striped collared shirt and sporting round, black-rimmed glasses. "Since when?"

"Since always, Claire. You've never noticed because you're always stuck in your own world. Admit it…you only care about yourself. When you found out that this guy over here"—he hooked his thumb over his shoulder to my date—"might lose his dream of growing corn fields, you were excited."

"I was not." I was beyond angry, but I couldn't do anything more than cross my arms over my chest and square off with him. For some reason, I couldn't form words to defend myself; the only thing I could think of was to inform Oswald that T had a vineyard, not a corn field. But after discovering I'd been calling him by the wrong name all these years, I began to question everything.

Maybe Oswald was right…

Maybe I did only care about myself.

Which was further proven when he said, "You thought about helping him out, so I'll give you *some* credit. But you can't deny that you saw his situation as a way of getting your money sooner. You don't care about his financial bind, only how his situation could propel you into getting what you want. Money. That's what it always comes down to with you, isn't it? You're a little rich girl who can't live without her American Express card."

The audience erupted into laughter. I peered over my shoulder and caught several of the guests clutching their stomachs and leaning forward in their seats, the hilarity too much to sit up straight. Others were slapping their knees as they dropped their heads back and howled with amusement surging through them.

"*That's not true!*" I argued, trying to make the crowd stop laughing and listen. But they wouldn't stop. No matter how close I got to them, how fast I waved my arms to gain their attention, or how loud I yelled…they wouldn't quiet down. They wouldn't stop laughing at me.

Oswald came over and, with his lips so close to my ear I could feel the heat of his breath, he whispered, "Wake up, Claire. You're gonna be alone for the rest of your life if you don't wake up."

Blinking my eyes open, I yelped, startled to find Piper practically in my face. I ignored her laughter as the weighted fog of sleep dissipated, allowing me a few seconds to gather myself. Piper had come over for an early dinner, and after we finished eating, we sat down to watch a true crime marathon together. We were still on the couch, but rather than documentaries about killer neighbors playing out on the TV, *The Price is Right* was on. At least that would explain the clapping and audience laughter.

"I had the worst dream," I admitted while rubbing the sleep out of my eyes. "I was on a game show, and Oswald was there. He kept telling me how I only care about myself, and I never pay attention to other people. He even said his name is Waldo, not Oswald…as if I could've spent two years with him and *not* know his real name."

Piper, biting back a smile, shrugged. "Both names suck."

"Do you think he's right, though?" I asked after a few seconds of contemplating my dream.

"Do I think who's right?"

"Oswald…when he said I was selfish."

"Oh, so you're asking if I agree with the dream-version of Douche-wald?" She rolled her eyes, but at least she continued with a real answer. "Not really. I mean, we all have moments when we put ourselves first, but I wouldn't call you a selfish person."

"He said that's the reason we broke up."

Piper laughed while shaking her head. "You're ridiculous. You already know why he broke up with you—because you kept your entire relationship on the surface rather than truly let him in. I'm no Dr. Phil, but I wouldn't say that's selfish. It's merely the way you've decided to protect yourself and cope with the loss of your parents."

I sat up straight and glared at her. "That's not what I do."

"Are you saying your inability to make real connections with people isn't a coping mechanism?"

"That's exactly what I'm saying, because it's not."

"Then why do you keep everyone at arm's length, Claire?" she countered, leaning closer as if readying herself to witness my psychological breakthrough. But that wasn't going to happen because there was nothing to break through. Out of everyone, she should've been the *last* person I needed to explain this to.

"I don't know what the professional word is, but I'm pretty certain it originated from years of making friends only to be stabbed in the back. Repeatedly. All those times I'd tell someone a secret, only for it to spread like wildfire around school, making me the laughingstock. None of which has anything to do with my parents."

Piper held up her hands in surrender, but before she got a chance to respond, her phone rang. She grabbed her cell off the table next to her and mumbled to herself, "Why is he calling me?" She listened for a moment and then pressed the screen to her chest, mouthing, "I'll be right back."

She didn't even give me a chance to ask who it was because a split second later, she hightailed it into my room and practically slammed the door behind her.

I was left on the couch, silenced by bewilderment. Piper wasn't one to run off like that; something had to be wrong. So I pushed off the sofa, determined to find out. Some guy called her, and then she ran off. I needed answers.

Except, before I stepped foot out of the living room, someone knocked on my front door.

Travis stood on my porch, looking as hot as ever. It'd been a busy week, so aside from a friendly wave here and there, I hadn't seen much of him since our lunch date five days ago. Not that I kept count or anything.

My breathing hitched as I took in his pale-yellow shirt unbuttoned just enough to show a hint of his white undershirt. It should be illegal to look that good. And I refused to recognize how much I'd missed seeing him and all his sexiness.

"Hey, Travis. What do you have there?" I pointed to the cardboard box in his arms.

"There were workers at the farm today, mainly picking all the ripe fruit, so I immediately thought of you because I figured you could put these to good use."

"Oh, wow!" I exclaimed as I took a look at what was in the box. The fact that he'd thought of me meant a lot. Another thing I would never admit. Maybe Piper was on to something with her earlier comments. "Thank you."

"No problemo. Where would you like it?"

I held out my arms, surprised when he took a step toward me, inviting himself in.

"It's heavy. Just tell me where."

"The kitchen would probably be best." I put one foot behind the other to allow him to pass and then closed the door behind him. "Would you like something to drink? I made a fresh pitcher of sweet tea a couple of hours ago."

"As amazing as that sounds, I should head home. I've had a *long* day."

"You haven't been home yet?" Damn, it should be criminal to look so fresh and edible after a long day.

A soft smile lilted his lips as he said, "No, I came straight here."

I was speechless. Travis had literally stolen my ability to form words.

But luckily, I didn't have to come up with anything to say because Piper called out, "*Claire Elizabeth Hansen!*" from the other side of the house. Unfortunately, I wasn't as lucky as I thought because her following words didn't save me from a damn thing. "Did you seriously tell your grandfather that you're marrying your next-door neighbor? What in the *absolute hell* were you thinking?"

Travis looked at me, complete terror filling his wide eyes. "We're getting married?"

Piper, finally finding me in the kitchen, came to an abrupt stop when she realized Travis was in the room. My eyes jumped back and forth between Piper and Travis like I was watching a tennis match. But while my best friend stared at Travis in surprise, clearly not expecting him to be here, he stared at me with the same anxiety I felt gurgling in my stomach.

My mind spun so fast I couldn't fully comprehend the situation in front of me. Piper had completely thrown me under the bus.

No...not a bus.

She threw me in front of an eighteen-wheeler. I bounced off the front only to slam into a cement truck. Finally, a paving truck flattened me like a pancake.

I was in a lose-lose situation, but I had to do something. So I launched myself at Piper, pushing her down the hallway to have a private word with her, leaving my neighbor standing in my kitchen alone. It wasn't the best solution, but at the time, I didn't have another option.

"What the hell, Piper?" I whisper-shouted, not wanting Travis to hear anything else.

"Funny, I was about to ask you the same thing. Why in the world would you tell him you're marrying Travis?"

"How'd you even find out about that in the first place?"

Likely miffed as to why *I* was interrogating *her*, she dramatically blinked at me, rolling her eyes at the same time—the look she reserved for people she thought were ridiculously stupid. "Because he just told me."

Realization smacked me in the forehead. "Wait...that was my *grandfather* who called you?"

"Yeah. He wants my help with a surprise engagement party he and Maureen are throwing for the *happy couple* next weekend."

"*Next* weekend?"

Piper leaned against the wall behind her, her shoulders drooping as if she was the doomed one in this situation. "I thought we agreed to hold off on doing anything until we could come up with a *logical* plan."

We'd talked a lot since Monday, but rather than figure out a loophole in the will, I'd kept her busy with helping me develop a business plan for Cutie Pies. And once I fully explained my idea of asking for access to my account so I could start up a business, she'd pretty much dropped the will altogether. Crisis adverted...until now.

"Bring what up? Our engagement?" Travis came out of the kitchen and stood several yards away with his arms crossed over his chest. "Because if that's what's up for discussion, I think I should be involved. Don't you?"

Piper glanced to the side at Travis and then back to me, and without another word, she quietly walked to the living room where she'd dropped her stuff upon arrival. A few seconds later, she stood with her sandals on her feet and her purse in her hand. "You two need to talk."

"You're leaving me?" I asked incredulously.

She slowly stalked toward me, a mixture of disappointment and pity in her gaze. With a gentle hand on my shoulder, she lowered her voice to a whisper so Travis couldn't overhear. "We're not in high school anymore. Nothing you tell him will lead to anyone pointing and laughing at you while whispering to their friends."

"I can't." Fear gripped me and refused to let go.

She tilted her head and pulled her lips to one side, offering the kind of honest compassion I could only get from my best friend. "What do you have to lose?"

"Everything," I argued under my breath.

"Babe...look around." She rolled her head from one shoulder to the other, gesturing my house. "You've already lost everything. It's time you start rebuilding. Take a chance and be honest with him. You never know, he might surprise you."

I rolled my eyes, highly disbelieving that, but I quickly stoned my expression when she stepped away, no longer hiding Travis from my view—or me from his.

"I'll let you two sort this out alone. Call me later, Claire." She walked out and closed the front door behind her, leaving me all alone with my neighbor —who'd just discovered I had told my grandfather we were engaged.

Oh.

Shit.

CHAPTER 10

TRAVIS

MAYBE CRAIG WAS RIGHT when he said Claire was crazy.

Being a thoughtful and kind neighbor, I'd taken a box of fruit next door. And what followed couldn't have been considered anything less than crazy. It was completely coocoo. Off-the-rails insane.

"Claire, why does your grandfather think you and I are getting married?" I figured that was a good place to start. Now that her friend had left, we were able to deal with this together.

Claire stood frozen in the hallway outside her bedroom doorway. The only expression she wore was one of complete fear. Prior to her friend stomping off, her words had been desperate and pleading. But now that we were alone, her entire body seemed weighted down with hopelessness.

"Because he's old and senile?" She attempted a smile, but it was unconvincing at best.

If I truly wanted an answer, there was only one thing left to do. Call her out. "That's okay, I'll find his number so I can call and explain the truth to him."

"Wait." Panic widened her eyes, darkening the gold hue I'd grown used to. "I'll tell you, but I need a minute."

I was out of options, so I gave in and let her have her way. "Fine. Come over when you're ready to explain it to me. And I want the complete truth, so don't bother unless you're ready to be honest. I don't want my time wasted."

I didn't say anything else before leaving her place and heading to mine. My gut told me there was so much more to this than her being crazy or her grandfather being senile.

It didn't take long for Claire to ring the doorbell.

As she took a seat on the couch, she didn't appear tipsy or buzzed, so I didn't have a clue why she needed a minute. But hopefully, whatever she did before coming over was enough to make her open up and tell me what the hell was going on.

"I've told you my parents died when I was in high school," she started, grabbing my attention from the start. "And I told you my grandfather was the one who moved here to take care of me."

"Yes." I kept my reply short and concise so she wouldn't have an excuse for a detour.

"Well, what I didn't tell you is that my parents started a company when I was little, and at the time of their death, they had accumulated a rather substantial net worth. Their business partner bought out their share, so that money, plus the cash from their stocks and investments, all went into a trust. As their only child, their estate was all left to me."

I wasn't sure what this had to do with the engagement confusion, so I continued to sit silently and wait for more information. But if she thought she'd gain sympathy by telling me how rich she was, she was dead wrong.

"Except there's a caveat. I can't access any of the money until I turn twenty-five, which is in two more years. As of right now, my grandfather is in charge of the entire estate." She dropped her chin and took a deep breath while focusing on her wringing fingers in her lap. "About two months ago, he decided to teach me all about responsibility, so he kicked me out of the house and put me on a pretty tight allowance. Much tighter than I've ever been accustomed to."

"But don't you work?"

Claire held up one finger, refusing to look at me. "I'll get to that in a second."

I sat back, letting her have the space to finish explaining. Staying patient was nearly impossible because, so far, everything she'd said made things more complicated instead of clearing anything up.

"Anyway, I've been trying to find ways to prove to him that I'm responsible so I can get my life back." Finally, she glanced up. The humiliation in her eyes was almost too much to bear. "I lied to you, Travis."

"I think we've already covered that part."

"No, I'm not talking about the whole engagement thing with my grandfather." She wrung her hands until her knuckles turned white. "I'm not an actual baker."

"What do you mean?" Shock coursed through me. She had baked pies. I'd seen them, so I didn't understand what she meant.

"I was impressed with the one you brought over, so I decided to try my hand at it. My parents had started their own company from scratch; I figured I could, too. That kinda stuff runs in the family, right?"

Suddenly, things started to come together and make sense. But I knew she wasn't looking for a response, nor was I ready to give one, so I simply shrugged and let her continue.

"I spent every waking hour teaching myself how to bake, and when I finally got it, I thought I was on my way to something good. Everything seemed to fall into place, especially after you suggested selling them at the town fair. I was so excited, Travis. After blowing through almost my entire month's allowance in a few days, I thought this was my chance to earn some of that back. You've eaten my pies; you know they're good enough to sell."

Technically, I only had one, and prior to that, I'd seen mishap after disastrous mishap, so I couldn't guarantee the ones she had at the fair were any good. But I didn't want to bring that up right now. Instead, I nodded my agreement and let her carry on.

"So when I only sold a measly two, I began to spiral. Not only was I pretty much out of options, but I also didn't have any money coming in. I'd wasted it all on a chance, only to have it blow up in my face. I was frantically trying to find a way out of the corner I'd backed myself into...and that's when my grandfather showed up."

"I'm sorry, but I still don't see the connection, Claire."

Again, she held up a finger, though she didn't pause before explaining it to me. "Piper came over the night of the fair to console me. While she was there, she found a copy of my parents' will. She looked over the terms the next morning and told me about a marriage clause she discovered. Basically, I gain complete access to my trust fund on my twenty-fifth birthday *or* when I get married, whichever comes first. Literally five minutes after I found out about that, my grandfather showed up and saw the flowers you sent me."

I scrubbed my hands down my face, trying to understand how a bouquet would have led anyone to assume we were getting married. "Why would he automatically think we were engaged? I could see if he thought we were dating, but getting married seems like a pretty big leap. For heaven's sake, you moved in less than a month ago."

She released a long, harsh huff, her shoulders drooping even more. "He asked who you were, and the only thing on my mind was the marriage clause. If I'd actually given myself a second to think it through, I wouldn't have said anything, but I was still a mess from the day before, and to be honest, I was desperate to have my life back. I said whatever I could think of to make my grandfather give in."

The more she explained, the further away she seemed. As if she sank deeper into the couch cushions as she confessed. I understood she was most likely humiliated, but I'd never seen anyone literally grow smaller before my

91

very eyes. I forced myself to mentally block out any sympathy that bubbled up. Regardless of how bad I felt about her situation, the fact still remained that she had lied…repeatedly.

"So you told him we're engaged." It wasn't a question, more of a statement left for her to confirm. When she nodded, I took several deep breaths. This had never happened to me—or anyone I knew—so I didn't have the faintest idea how to deal with it. "How exactly did you see this playing out?"

Claire was a shell of her normal self when she said, "I don't know."

Her demeanor almost broke me. This had been a woman so full of life. Since meeting her for the first time, she'd hijacked my daydreams and refused to leave. Appearance aside, she was funny, entertaining, intriguing, and yeah, maybe a little crazy. I enjoyed spending time with her, actually looked forward to her company on shitty days, so I had a hard time comparing what I knew about her with this new information. I wasn't keen on liars, although that gut feeling continued to hang around, telling me there was more I needed to hear.

"You can't tell someone you're getting married and never discuss it again. Not to mention, you have to actually *be* married to gain access to your money, right? Not only engaged? So why bother with the lie in the first place? I'm sure you weren't planning on drugging me and then dragging me down an aisle."

Out of nowhere, an image of Claire in a wedding dress floated through my mind. I had to quickly shake that thought loose before it completely altered my reaction to this situation.

"*Trust me*, Travis. I know. But like I said, I wasn't thinking. I was desperate. And desperate people do foolish things. I guess I hoped that if he *thought* I was getting married, he might ease up a little."

I warred with myself about whether or not I should pry, but at this point, I figured I didn't have anything to lose. "How much money are we talking about?"

"Two hundred thousand, tops."

For some reason, I was still amazed at the perception younger people had with money. "That's all? You're doing this for something that might only last for the next few years?"

"That's all I need it for."

Confused, I leaned forward and narrowed my gaze. "You lost me. Why would you want your money to only last a few years?"

"Because I'll have full access to the rest after that."

I felt as though I was missing a large piece of information. "Let me see if I understand… You're not trying to access the whole thing, only a piece?"

"Exactly."

"Okay, so how much is in the *actual* trust fund—*no*." I shook my head and held up both hands to keep her from responding. "Never mind. Don't tell me."

At the end of the day, her money was none of my business. It hadn't slipped my mind how I'd whined to her a few days ago about not having what I needed to expand my vineyard. And it didn't go unnoticed that, while knowing I was in a financial dilemma myself, she had the audacity to complain about needing enough *spending* money to last until her twenty-fifth birthday.

I was torn between understanding her dilemma and being pissed at her inconsiderateness.

"I realize it was stupid and makes no sense. Obviously, I wouldn't have let it go too far. I would've told him we'd broken up before anything crazy happened. And I certainly would've never expected you to have any part in it, so there was never a possibility of you being dragged down an aisle."

Again, an image of her in a white dress flashed through my mind.

And my heart settled a little.

"Listen…" She scooted a few inches closer and stopped, as if suddenly remembering her embarrassment. "I'm beyond sorry about everything. And I fully understand how this looks. I wouldn't blame you if you avoid me from now on, and to be honest, I deserve it. I only ask that you don't turn this into a big deal. Whether you think it is or not, I would appreciate it if this stayed between us."

Humiliation continued to weigh her down, but now, there was something else in her eyes. Genuine fear. And the only thing I could assume had caused it was the mention of other people finding out.

Her demeanor made picturing her as a small child easy.

"Your friendship means a lot to me," she said with a sniffle. "And I would miss our little meetups…or whatever they are. But I understand if losing that is the price I have to pay for lying."

"I wouldn't cut you out of my life for something this silly. I understand—well, no, I really don't. But regardless, I don't have to understand everything everyone does." I shrugged. "We're neighbors, okay?"

She dropped her gaze and nodded somberly. "I appreciate it, Travis."

"Hey, don't worry about it." Honestly, I was just happy to find out she wasn't telling the whole town or making up a relationship with me in her head. I still thought what she did was ridiculous, but in the grand scheme of things…it wasn't a big deal. It could've been a lot worse.

Realistically, she only embarrassed herself.

"Would some wine make you feel better?" I enjoyed the way her eyes lit up anytime I mentioned Uncorked vino. The level of pride I felt was incredible.

"You're making a habit of using wine as a peace offering."

"Hey, you do what works..." I winked and excused myself to pour her a glass and grab a can of beer for myself.

I'D SEEN Claire nearly every day for the last week, ever since the whole faux-gagement confession. And I had to be honest...the more time that went by, the less the whole engagement lie bothered me. So by the end of the week, I wasn't fazed whatsoever.

However, just because her deceit didn't bother me didn't mean I hadn't come up with a list of questions I wanted to ask. My growing curiosity probably stemmed from the fact that the entire subject had been avoided every time we'd seen each other. But there was only so long I could go before demanding answers, so I decided to compile all my questions and confront her after work on Friday.

I should've been nervous as I knocked on Claire's door and waited for her to answer, but I wasn't in the slightest. If anything, I had to keep myself from laughing. I'd been in this exact spot several times, only to be greeted by an angry woman who'd just been woken up. The sun was still up, so there was hope she wouldn't scream at me.

Then again, there was no telling when it came to Claire Hansen. She kept me on my toes.

"Hey." Claire's bright smile outshined the sun. "What are you doing here?"

"I wanted to discuss something with you, if you don't mind."

"Sure..." She seemed hesitant yet opened the door wider anyway.

I followed her to the living room and took a seat next to her on the couch. I'd made a mental list of everything I wanted to ask, but I never thought of coming up with a lead-in, so I decided to just jump in. "Have you told your grandfather about us not being engaged?"

Her pupils grew large. "Uh, no. I've been waiting for him to mention the party, but he hasn't yet, so I've kinda ignored it in the hopes everyone forgets."

I laughed at her. "That's not going to happen, Claire. They aren't simply going to forget something that big. And didn't your friend—"

"Piper," she interjected. "Her name's Piper."

"Okay, didn't *Piper* say he's planning a surprise party?"

She nodded and then quickly shrugged.

"Exactly, so of course he's not going to say anything."

"I know, I know." Claire dropped her head back, practically sinking into the sofa. "I'll make it right, I promise. I just haven't been able to yet, and I can't explain why."

I didn't need to hear her explanation. I was well aware of the reasons she hadn't come clean to her grandfather yet. And to be honest, I couldn't exactly blame her. Afterall, I still hadn't told my parents the truth about the confusion regarding the expansion.

"What I don't understand is why you'd go to such extreme lengths for a small slice of your inheritance instead of waiting. We're talking, what...a couple more years?"

Claire blinked a few times, likely unsure of how to answer. "Well, technically, the money I was thinking of isn't part of my trust fund. A savings account was created for my grandfather when he took guardianship of me. Trusts come with a ton of red tape to wade through when you make a withdrawal. So it's customary to put an allotment for living expenses into a savings account to allow the guardian easier access."

"Well, if you don't tell him...how long do you think before he backs off and gives you what you want?" I asked, taking both of us by surprise. "Like, if you played up a long engagement, do you think he'd wait it out? Or would he concede once he felt you were established enough in life to take care of yourself?"

That hadn't been on my mental list of questions to ask, but for some reason, my mouth opened and out it came. The strangest part, though, was the lack of regret I felt for asking. It was a genuine question, one I truly wanted the answer to, yet that wasn't the real reason I'd asked.

"I doubt he'd wait until an actual wedding takes place. Like I said, backing off the savings account is all on him. There are no legal clauses or hoops to jump through. What he chooses to do with those funds is literally his decision, and his alone."

"But what I don't understand is...how can he keep that money from you?" I didn't have a clue about how trust funds worked, and until now, I hadn't given two shits about finding out, either. In my opinion, they were meant to prevent kids who were born with silver spoons in their mouths from squandering all their parents' hard-earned money on drugs and booze and crap no one would ever need.

"My parents funded a separate account for him to subsidize the cost of raising me. So while he has complete control over everything in that account, my grandfather would never misappropriate funds or withhold what I'm owed. This is merely his way of forcing me to grow up."

"Last question..." I didn't think twice before I asked, "What does one wear to an engagement party?"

Her eyes narrowed and then flashed wide. She was obviously afraid to express any emotion without a full understanding of my question.

So I explained further. "You and I both need money for two completely different reasons, but being in my situation, I can't consciously stand in the way of you gaining what's due to you. If I had an opportunity to attain the funds needed to pursue my dreams, I wouldn't bat an eye. So I understand the reasoning behind what you did. I don't fully agree, and I don't condone what you did, but I can't blame you, either."

"Does this mean...?"

"Yes, Claire. That's exactly what this means. I'll play the part of devoted fiancé, as long as you promise this will end long before any march down an aisle. *Long* engagement, remember?"

I was aware there was a chance I could grow to regret this decision, but I also knew there was a chance I wouldn't.

Her face lit up and she practically lunged at me, wrapping her arms around my neck in an extremely appreciative embrace. And without a single thought or second of hesitation, I put mine around her waist, returning the hug. I realized in that moment that I hadn't felt a woman's touch in a long time. I didn't fathom how much I missed it until I got a taste.

"If he lets me have that money, I'll totally give you some for doing this for me."

I adamantly shook my head. "No, Claire. I don't want your money. I don't want any of it."

"Then why are you doing it?"

I couldn't explain my reason for agreeing to be a part of this charade because I didn't fully understand myself. But I believed if I stood in the way of someone else achieving their dreams, Karma would get in my way. And at this point, I couldn't afford that.

Especially not after the continuous rejections I'd received from banks.

"Because...we're friends."

A DAY and a half did not give us time to come up with a story before the "surprise" engagement party.

Needless to say, my anxiety was through the roof the second we arrived.

And my nerves only worsened.

After acting surprised, we made our way around the room. Jerry, her grandfather, introduced us to everyone, and it quickly became clear that Claire didn't have any friends in attendance. She only knew a handful of the guests, but other than that, she wasn't familiar with them outside of being her grandfather's close friends. At least Piper was here, though.

We hadn't been here more than fifteen minutes before someone stepped into the middle of the large living room and carefully tapped a silver utensil against the side of her glass. I couldn't be certain, as I'd met a lot of people, but I thought she might've been Jerry's girlfriend—which sounded weird considering their ages.

Everyone quieted down, allowing her to take the floor to speak. "I just wanted to say how happy I am that you all are here with us, celebrating this very special occasion. I know it was a last-minute invite, but hey…their announcement was a surprise to us as well."

Claire moved closer to me as snickers came from all around the room. She had already informed me of her feelings toward this woman, which had obviously been colored by her sense of betrayal over being cut off financially. However, her sudden closeness didn't come off as disdain for this woman. If anything, it felt more like fear. Or humiliation. Except I couldn't figure out the cause of either emotion. Feeling the need to offer her a sense of comfort, I dropped my hand to my side and laced my fingers with hers.

Strangely enough, her reaction was immediate. Her body, now slightly leaning against mine, softened. And the sigh that crossed her parted lips might've been quiet, but I heard it all the same. As much as I wanted to believe holding her hand was enough to calm her down, I knew that couldn't be the case. This was all a farce. None of it was real.

"And I know some of you aren't familiar with Jerry's granddaughter outside of his numerous tales of her childhood," she continued from the center of the room, everyone now in a circle around her. "But whether you know her well or have only heard how amazing she is, we want to thank you for being part of this special day."

Some clapped while others drank whatever they had in their hand. But a few tapped silverware on the sides of their glasses, the universal suggestion for a couple to kiss. And of course, that caused Claire's shoulders to curve in and her body to tense up all over again. I squeezed her hand in reassurance, which helped somewhat.

Without releasing my hold on Claire, I turned to face her. Anxiety darkened her irises and made her nostrils flare slightly, but at least she held my stare. I smiled, hoping she could see it in my eyes, and whispered so only she could hear, "I won't bite…I promise."

As soon as her expression relaxed, I knew I had succeeded in calming her nerves. I reached up and lightly cupped her cheek while she still clasped my other hand in a death grip. I didn't need to urge her closer as I bent down and pressed my lips to hers. They were so warm and soft. The kiss was light, but everything changed when she took a breath. Rather than pull air in through her nose, she parted her mouth, and my lips naturally followed her lead.

Claire laid her free hand on my chest where she fisted my shirt as the kiss deepened. Our lips joined intensely, but with a sense of comfort. Her body molded to mine like the missing piece I'd been endlessly searching for. The warmth of her mouth as my tongue subtly licked her bottom lip intoxicated my senses, bringing them to life. In that moment, only the two us is existed. I increased the tempo and pulled her closer, then slipped my tongue between her parted lips. Heat wrapped around me made my body ache for more as—

People cheered and hollered.

My brain slowly came back into focus as realization of where we stood hit me. We were in front of all Claire's grandfather's friends.

As soon as I pulled away, I began to crave the soft warmth her lips offered.

Claire's cheeks glowed pink, making me fear what my complexion looked like. I was relieved to know the kiss was equally intense for her, because I would hate to be the only one affected. I couldn't stop thinking of future opportunities to taste her lips again. That thought, though, was enough to keep the heat between us on simmer and allow us both to catch our breaths.

We continued to stand close to one another, and thankfully, we had our backs to the wall.

Because the very next second, Claire grabbed my ass.

CHAPTER 11
CLAIRE

I COULDN'T BELIEVE I did that. I'd gotten caught up in the moment, that was all.

"Well, it's obvious these two have chemistry!" Maureen announced as she finished her speech. "We have cake and desserts located on the patio. Thanks again for helping us celebrate this very special day."

"What the hell was that?" Piper whispered in my ear.

"What was what?" I quickly looked over to make sure Travis hadn't heard her. He seemed involved in a conversation with the guy next to him, although he'd kept his arm firmly wrapped around me. It was all part of the game. At least that's what I'd tell myself tonight when I relived that toe-curling kiss over and over again.

"Dude. I never even saw you kiss Waldo like that." She shoulder-bumped me. "That was hot...with a double *T*."

"It seems you've forgotten this is all for show," I said through gritted teeth.

"There was enough heat in your lip-lock to light your kitchen on fire. Oh, sorry. I forgot, you've already done that." Piper giggled to herself, ignoring my annoyed glare.

"There was no fire. Only smoke." It'd been long enough that I could now laugh at my humiliating moment, but I didn't care to give in to Piper's teasing right now. I was still too overheated by the memory of Travis's lips on mine.

"My cup's empty." She rattled the ice around the bottom of her glass. "I'd ask if you'll be okay without me for a minute while I refill my drink, but I think it's safe to say you will. Just whatever you do, don't molest him in front of everyone…well, if you do, at least wait 'til I come back."

I waved her off while glancing around, making sure no one overheard her vulgarity.

"Come with me a sec," Travis whispered and pulled me to follow him.

"Where are we going?" I'd grown up in this house, so I was aware of every crevice, but I had no clue where he was taking me.

With my hand firmly in his, he pulled me down a long hallway with closed doors on either side. "I wanted to find somewhere quiet so we could talk."

"That's the study. We should be left alone in there." I pointed to the second door on the left.

"Perfect." He smoothly slipped us both inside the quiet room.

"What did you want to discuss—"

His lips met mine, and as if they had a mind of their own, they quickly resumed where we'd left things moments ago. I moaned and wrapped my arms around his waist, which helped me pull his warm body closer. My lips automatically opened to allow his tongue entry. He plunged it deep; his assertiveness was a far cry from the careful smooch we'd demonstrated earlier.

Piper hadn't been far off about how I'd never been kissed like this before. I'd taken part in my fair share of make-out sessions throughout the years, but none could hold a candle to this level of passion. I kept thinking I was just making more out of it than there was, but no. This lip-lock soared high on the passion meter.

He anticipated my advances, expanding on my moves in such a relaxed manner. The comfort contradicted the intensity of the moment; it was as if we'd been dancing together for an eternity. His movements were fluid with mine. He provided exactly what I needed, even before I knew what I wanted.

I brazenly wrapped my leg around his to pull his hips impossibly closer. He urged me to the edge of the desk and lifted me into a sitting position. He held my face so tenderly that had I not been so engrossed in the sensualness, I would've melted into a puddle. Even in this passion-filled moment, his kindness was evident. He made me feel as if I mattered.

Travis positioned himself between my legs, and his bulge was in the exact spot I needed. I moaned and started bucking my hips, rolling myself into his hardness. With each move, I began to climb higher and higher, so close to coming apart without any intimate touch.

Dry humping never felt so good.

"Claire?" Gramps's voice came from the hallway, and it grew nearer every time he said my name. I knew we only had a matter of seconds before he checked this room, so I quickly pushed against Travis's chest, tragically ending the *hottest* kiss I'd ever had. Thankfully, he heard Gramps too, so I didn't have to push much because he'd already started to move away.

I slid off the desk, realizing just how unsteady I was. My legs felt like they were made of rubber and ready to give out on me at any minute. So I was happy that while Travis had moved away, he hadn't gone far. He was still by my side.

"Oh, there you are." Gramps poked his head into the room almost as soon as my feet touched the floor. "I'm not interrupting anything, am I?"

"No...not at all." Our voices were nearly unison—they were also both deep and scratchy from almost being caught red-handed. I prayed my grandfather didn't pick up on the heaviness in our tones, or the way we both sounded out of breath. If he did, I doubted I'd ever be able to look him in the eyes again.

"Oh, good." He stepped into the room, not at all appearing to have suspected anything. Thank God. But he didn't come all the way in like I had expected. Instead, he stood next to the door, clasping the handle, and turned his attention to Travis. "Do you mind if Claire and I have a moment?"

"No, sir. Not at all." He cupped my elbow and met my gaze. "I'll wait for you in the living room."

I nodded, remaining silent as I watched him leave the room.

"Have a seat." Gramps gestured to a set of chairs in front of my dad's old, heavy oak desk.

My heart pounded as I sat. There was no telling what he wanted to talk about—honestly, by this point, his options were endless. My brain wasn't fully functioning yet, and the only thing I could think about was Travis's hard body between my thighs.

"I wanted to discuss this with you." Gramps took the empty seat next to me, and I finally recognized the white pages he gripped between his fingers. It was the proposal I'd spend all week typing up. I was excited because I knew I'd done a thorough job, but the nerves were still prevalent.

"Right now?" Apprehension hit me like a freight train. The last hour had been a jumble of emotions, and now I suddenly felt like I wasn't ready to discuss my business plan with him. The thought of him criticizing my hard work made me nauseous.

I tried to occupy myself with comforting thoughts. I'd learned my multiplication facts in this room while Dad worked on his computer. The meaning of this space alone made me feel melancholy and proud. After all, this was where my parents had built their empire.

They were masters at business, which added to the pressure I put on myself as I readied to attempt the same thing. Well, not quite the same thing. They had probably been a lot more serious about their ventures. But that wasn't the point. Here I was, about to propose a business plan that would accomplish two things. And one of them was not negotiable.

"Well, no, I guess we can talk about something else first." He must've picked up on my nervousness and felt this was a better way to ease me into the conversation. But then he said, "Please don't tell me you're rushing into this because you're pregnant, Claire. I don't think I can handle that, too."

I was pretty sure I stopped breathing as I stared at him with utter shock running through me. "Heavens, no. Why in the world would you ask me that?"

He shrugged, as if the answer was obvious. "You got engaged extremely fast, and based on the intimate display you two put on out there, almost anyone would make that assumption. You can't blame people for questioning it." He hid a smile, which made me relax some. I was grateful for his attempt to try and lighten the mood.

"No, Gramps. You don't have to worry about babies. I promise. We plan on having a *long* engagement." I hoped he didn't want to ask a bunch of questions, because there was a chance I'd give the complete opposite answers as Travis. We hadn't prepped for any of this.

"Phew, I'm really happy to hear that."

Discussing the business plan no longer seemed scary; not to mention, it was a hell of a lot better than coming up with believable answers regarding my non-existent personal relationship. So I gestured at the pages he still held in his lap. "I see you received my email."

"Yes, I did. Why don't you start off by telling me what this is about?"

I didn't understand why I needed to explain when he could've read the proposal for himself. I certainly didn't spend so much time typing it up only to turn around and repeat the whole thing. But considering I needed the money, I gave him what he wanted. "Do you remember the pie I gave you a couple of weeks ago when you dropped by the house?"

He hummed while flipping through the papers.

"Well, I've enjoyed baking them, and I thought it would be a terrific idea to turn it into a business. I want to start my own company called Cutie Pies. Have you taken a look at any of the proposal?"

Gramps stopped on a page and hesitated for a second. "I have; however, I found one part of this concerning. These numbers appear a tad high. Are you planning to take this to a bank?"

My stomach dropped as I sank into the chair, no longer prim and proper on the edge of my seat. If he was already under the impression that my numbers were too high, my plan was dead in the water. "No. I was hoping you could help me with that part so I wouldn't have to take out a business loan."

Rather than address the fact that I had just suggested he give me the money, he tapped on the page in front of him and asked, "How did you come up with these figures?"

"Piper and I worked on it together." She'd spent most evenings last week at my place helping me write up a well-thought-out plan that would kill two birds with one stone. Technically, she only knew about one of those birds, but that was beside the point.

"Okay. Well, this is your chance. Pitch me your idea. Put this proposal into action and walk me through the next steps."

My grandfather sure knew how to put me on the spot.

Now it was my time to shine and try to pull this new prospect out of my ass.

CHAPTER 12
TRAVIS

I was so relieved to have Piper with me. Without her, I wouldn't have had anyone to keep me company while Claire was off in another part of the house with Jerry, talking about something private.

"You truly are one in a million, Travis," Piper admitted.

While the guests mingled, Piper and I hunkered down on one side of an extravagantly large living room. I'd probably spent an obscene amount of time gawking at the incredible—and most likely custom—architecture around me. The ceiling alone was worth a solid five minutes of observation. The peak was at least twenty feet high.

But what amazed me the most was how comfortable everything else felt. While the house itself was large and clearly worth a mint, the belongings inside set a different tone. It was homey. I could practically feel the love in every room. There were little personal touches everywhere that likely only held sentimental value.

"Thanks, but why do you say that?" I turned my head to the side and asked.

She shrugged, continuing to gaze out into the crowd before us. "I don't know of another human being who would've agreed to this. Yet here you are, playing along with Claire's impulsive ideas. You deserve a medal."

"Um, thank you?" I said with whispered laughter in my words.

She glanced my way with a raised brow. "I'm not entirely sure it's a compliment."

"Why not?"

"Claire needs...*guidance*. She's like a puppy. If you let her off her leash, she'll run off, wanting to go here and there and everywhere all at once with absolutely no direction. I swear, she has the focus of a crackhead with untreated ADD in a house of mirrors."

I held a closed fist against my lips to keep myself from spewing soda everywhere.

"I'm serious. She gets these crazy, over-the-top ideas, and without thinking, she goes for it. She never stops to think about how she's gonna make it happen. She just dives into the deep end. And when it falls apart, like all her ideas tend to do, she can't understand why it didn't work."

I mulled over her words and tried to see Claire through her eyes. They'd been friends for over ten years, so if anyone understood her, it'd be Piper. Theoretically, I should listen to her, take everything in.

They were best friends, so I doubted Piper would've said anything with so much as an ounce of malicious intent. However, I happened to see Claire differently. I realized I hadn't known her long, but I genuinely felt as though I had a pretty solid understanding of who she was, which, in my head, didn't match up with what Piper was saying.

"I don't know..." I scanned the room, though I wasn't looking at anything or anyone in particular. "I recently made a business deal without securing a way to make it happen, and one of the guys I work with— someone I actually look up to—called the decision impulsive. So I can't exactly say much about her choices."

Piper giggled to herself. "I'm starting to think maybe the two of you need a chaperone when you're together. Going along with her crazy ideas is one thing…it's another to encourage her."

"Hey, now. I never said I encourage any of this. Trust me, *this* is not my idea of fun." I lowered my voice and made sure I didn't mention anything about faking the engagement. I didn't agree to help Claire only to sabotage it by being overheard admitting that we were a fraud. However, the kiss had been a definite perk to the whole sham. One I hoped to repeat once we were alone again.

Before Piper could respond, an older woman stopped to chat. "You're a very handsome young man. You and Claire make such a good-looking couple. I wanted to tell you that. I wasn't sure if anyone else has said anything, but it's been talked about a lot today."

"Yeah? Everyone's talking about how handsome I am?" I teased with a smile so wide it caused my cheeks to ache. "And thank you. Yes, I agree with you—Claire and I look quite good together; although, I think that's because she's so beautiful."

She pulled her hand to her chest and sighed softly. "I am so happy she's finally found someone. We all worried she'd never find a good man to marry. And after the good Lord took her family away, we all wanted her to have a family of her own to love as much as her mama and daddy loved her."

Her words multiplied the guilt I harbored for deceiving all these people. I hadn't once thought about how they would feel after we confessed the truth. People like this woman, who must've had a special place in her heart for Claire, would be heartbroken.

After a soft pat on my bicep, she walked away, leaving me quite curious about several things. So I turned to Piper for a little clarification. "Who was she?"

"A neighbor. She's known Claire most of her life and was always friendly with her parents. I think she came by a lot after Mr. and Mrs. Hansen died to check on things. Her grandfather said she was one of the only people who actually tried to help him after he moved in."

"That's really sweet. I bet Claire's happy to see her here."

"Not quite." She paused to take a swallow of her soda, fully aware that I needed more explanation. "Claire avoids all motherly-type figures. She used to come to my house *all* the time when we were younger, but after she lost her mom, she stopped. Instead, I had to come here to spend time with her outside of school. And of course, she started visiting me again after I moved out and got my own place."

"Okay, but why doesn't she like mothers?"

"It's not that she doesn't *like* them. I just don't think she's ever dealt with the fact that she doesn't have hers, so she's kinda avoided all mom-types. Don't ever say that to her, though. She'll argue to her death that her coping mechanisms have nothing to do with her parents dying."

The more she told me, the more I wanted to know. "Where are all her friends?"

"They're here."

"Where? I haven't met any of them."

Piper turned to me with arched brows. "Just me and you, buddy."

That couldn't be right. "She doesn't have any other friends?"

Piper shook her head slowly.

"Why not?"

"Claire doesn't trust anyone."

I stared at her, hoping to convince her to explain more without having to ask. I felt that asking would be prying, and I didn't want to put Piper in a position of betraying Claire's trust. But I justified to myself that if she offered the information, it wouldn't constitute as prying.

"I already know she told you about her money, so I guess it wouldn't hurt to tell you this." She released a long exhale as sorrow dimmed her expression. "After the accident, she had family coming out of the woodwork offering to be her guardian. I'm talking about relatives she never heard of before, let alone met. On *both* sides of her family, too. One even took her

106

grandfather to court to convince a judge he was too old to properly care for a fifteen-year-old."

"Because they wanted the money?"

Piper pulled her bottom lip between her teeth and nodded. "Her grandfather is the only one who's ever had her best interests at heart. So that right there laid the groundwork for her trust issues. The rest came from high school. Right after she lost her parents, she kinda shut down."

"Which is completely understandable," I added.

"Well, at the time, she had these two best friends who we'd gone to middle school with, Stefanie and Kristina. They had already created some drama because they didn't like her spending so much time with me. But once Claire started to pull away, they talked about her behind her back and ditched her. They said I was toxic and basically accused her of being a bad friend for not going to *them* with her problems since they were friends before I came into the picture."

"Are you freakin' kidding me?" I was fuming. I realized it'd all happened years ago with two girls I didn't know—and who'd more than likely grown into mature adults since—but it didn't calm the anger boiling in my chest. I couldn't think of a single reason anyone would turn their back on their supposed "best" friend after her entire world flipped upside down.

"Oh, but it gets worse."

I sighed, sightly regretting asking for this information.

"Claire's always had a huge heart, and she tended to be quite generous with everyone in her life. So some of the girls in school befriended her and let her pay for things. They were usually small things to keep her from catching on that she was being used. And then after, when Claire pretty much stopped buying everything they wanted, they turned on her. Anything she'd ever confessed about herself or her family became public knowledge. She became defenseless, because anytime she'd try to stand up for herself, they'd all laugh at her. It messed with her head. To this day, she gets uncomfortable when people laugh at her."

That explained Claire's reaction when the guests sniggered beneath their breath during Maureen's speech. I couldn't complain, though, because it led to her leaning on me and holding my hand.

"And she's never made friends since?"

"Where would she meet these people, Travis?"

"Work?"

She huffed a single laugh, though it was devoid of actual humor. "She's confessed to you about the whole baker thing, but has she ever by chance mentioned any previous employment?" When I shook my head, she elaborated. "Probably because she's never had a job. Well, a couple of years ago, she worked in the mall for about a week and a half, but other than that... nothing. She's not a loner, so don't think that's what I'm saying."

"Oh, I know she's not."

"Good. She enjoys her own company, but I think that's because she keeps herself entertained with her whacky ideas. She's always up to something new. Which is why I only push back when I know something will end disastrously. Like this, for example. But when it comes to things like her plan to start baking, I figured they won't hurt."

That bothered me. "She's your best friend. Why would you root for her to fail?"

"I don't. At all."

"You just said you didn't think the baking thing would go anywhere."

Regret flashed in her eyes. "That's not what I meant. Of course I want her to succeed and make something of herself—more than anything. But after being by her side for as many years as I have, you start to assume certain things won't go as far as others. Prior to eating your pie, she'd never baked anything. In fact, I doubt she had ever used an oven before then."

I couldn't understand why I felt this intense desire to protect her—even to her own friend, who was clearly on her side. I had no idea what had gotten into me, but it wasn't something I was used to. Testosterone raged in our house growing up, so no one ever needed to be defended.

"Well, I think Cutie Pies could definitely take off." I didn't have to stand up for Claire, yet I felt the need to voice my support anyway.

"Oh, I do as well. She told me about some of your ideas, and I think they're genius, so we spent most of the week coming up with a business plan for her to take to her grandfather. She emailed it to him a couple days ago. I think they're discussing it right now, actually."

I wondered why Claire never told me about this. I would've loved to take a look at her business plan if she'd only given me the chance. Who knows, I might've been able to suggest a thing or two to really sell her grandfather on it. It also hit me that if her grandfather funded her project, I'd be off the hook.

Which, for unclear reasons, didn't offer the relief I expected.

I didn't want to pretend to be her fiancé forever, but for some reason, I wasn't ready to give up my role quite yet. I was enjoying getting to know Claire better, and if she called off our faux-gagement, that would all come to an abrupt halt.

And I didn't want that to happen.

THINGS HAD BEEN tense between Claire and me ever since she returned from her private meeting with her grandfather. I expected some kind of affection after the kisses we shared, but she portrayed the complete opposite. She was quiet, and it was obvious she'd forced every smile that graced her face. I'd asked several times if she was okay, but all I got in return was a disingenuous nod. I tried not to take her mood personally, but it was hard. Thankfully, Piper managed to pull her away to talk, and when she came back, she appeared in better spirits.

However, by then, I was the one faking grins and desperate to leave.

While Claire was gone with Piper, Jerry had called me to another room to chat. At first, I thought he wanted to have the typical *you better take care of her, or I'll kill you with my bare hands* talk, but I quickly learned that wasn't the case. In fact, it was quite the opposite.

He'd given me a diamond ring. Not just any ring, though…her mom's engagement ring. Apparently, Jerry had saved it all this time for this very occasion. And considering how I'd admitted earlier that I hadn't found the perfect stone for her—the only thing I could come up with to explain why she didn't have one—I'd lacked an excuse to turn down the offer.

And now, as I drove home, the simple yet elegant diamond burned a hole into my thigh, a constant reminder of what a pile of shit I was. I couldn't give it to her, especially after Piper's confession about how Claire hadn't dealt with the loss of her mom. Doing so would more than likely cause more harm than good. But if I didn't, there would be questions. Lots of them. Questions I wouldn't be able to answer. It would also mean I'd have to go back to Jerry to return it…after our supposed break-up.

There was literally no winning in this entire situation.

"Are you sure you're okay with this whole charade?" Claire shifted in the passenger seat to face me.

I couldn't look at her without feeling worse about having her mom's engagement ring in my pocket, so instead, I pretended to focus on the road. "Yeah, I'm good with it. Why?"

"You've been quiet, which isn't like you at all."

Since I couldn't tell her the real reason I was distant, I went with a believable—and honest—excuse. "I guess I'm just a little thrown off by your mood changes today. Everything was fine until you met with your grandfather. And to make matters worse, you refuse to tell me what happened. Then you leave with Piper, and suddenly, everything's hunky-dory again."

I realized I sounded a bit like a real fiancé who was jealous that she'd confided in her best friend instead of me. When in all actuality, I was fully aware why she would've gone to Piper about her issues. I didn't blame her one bit.

"I'm sorry, but only Piper knows about it."

"Knows about what, your business proposal?"

I didn't need to see her to picture her eyes blinking rapidly and her mouth going slack.

"Granted, I don't know anything else about it other than you and Piper spent the better part of the week putting it together, and you included some of the things I suggested at lunch a couple of weeks ago. I'm pretty sure you discussed it with your grandfather, and then you returned in a foul mood. I could make assumptions, but I would prefer if you told me what happened."

She appeared to calm down some and settled in the seat next to me. "I was going to explain every detail to you, but I wanted to wait until I had the money. Except Gramps said no. So there went my plan."

"He did?" I didn't know the man, but it still seemed odd that he'd turn her down.

"Well, he didn't technically say no. He told me he wanted to see more effort on my part before giving me start-up funds. He said a month isn't long enough to spend on something before deciding if it's worth investing in."

"Has he had any of your pies?"

"I gave him one when he stopped by the house a couple of weeks ago. Apparently, Maureen tried it and said it was delicious. But that was the first time he even heard about them, and considering I was ready to give up, I didn't bother to tell him they were a new business venture. I don't think his decision has anything to do with the product, though. I'm pretty sure his issue has to do with the lack of time I've spent baking, along with my inability to prove a reasonable demand for them. He said the business proposal was good, but the risk factor was too high at the moment. Which is why he said to wait longer. But I don't have time."

"I'm sorry." I pulled into my side of the driveway and turned to face her. "I'm sure everything will work out. I understand what he's saying, though, and at least you weren't rejected. Trust me, being flat-out denied is a total kick in the teeth. Thankfully, you still have hope. You only have to prove yourself first, and I doubt you'll have a problem doing that."

Her gaze narrowed. "Have you gotten your loan for the expansion?"

I dropped my head against the headrest. "No. The bank holding the note for my original loan said they could give me a line of credit to purchase the lot, but they won't go above that to cover future expenses."

"Does this mean you can't move forward?"

"No, just means I can't utilize the land until I have enough saved to cover a few years' worth of loss." I tried not to let the disappointment show. This was about Claire, and while I understood her knack for flipping the subject, I wanted to keep the focus on her for now. "So have you thought about what you're going to do?"

She shrugged and leaned back in her seat. "I guess I should probably start by making pies, huh? I like your idea of cutting out the tins, but I haven't tried that yet."

"Well, what are you waiting for?"

"Confidence, I guess."

I removed my key from the ignition and nudged my head in the direction of her side of the duplex. "We still have time before the day's over. Wanna give it a try?"

"You know how to make them?"

I laughed and shook my head. "Hell no, but between the two of us, I'm sure we can at least figure out what *not* to do."

Claire hesitated for a second. Then she dropped her gaze to my chest, smiled, and asked, "Do you have any wine?"

"I've got as many bottles as you want."

Appearing pleased, she nodded and opened her door. "Yeah, let's give it a try. At the very least, it'll be entertaining."

CHAPTER 13
CLAIRE

"CHEERS TO BERRY PIE." I held up my third glass of wine and waited for the light tap from his before I took a sip. "Let's hope this works."

We'd finished creating the new crescent-shaped desserts, but they were still baking. I'd made them with a drastically revised version of the recipe this time. I'd spent days researching and combing through famous cookbooks and online techniques until I finally found a way to make the filling my own without the risk of completely ruining them.

Well, *minimal* risk.

Now we just had to wait until they were done to make sure these pastries were successful. Since they were smaller and without tins, I had to keep an eye on their progress, assuming they'd need less time to cook. Except, I wasn't entirely sure what I was looking out *for*. Smoke, maybe? Regardless, if they didn't turn out right, at least I enjoyed collaborating with Travis and bouncing my ideas off him. After all, this was all experimentation.

"Stop stalking your pies," Travis said with laughter lacing his words.

I'd turned into an overprotective nutcase and refused to leave the little window on the oven door. I didn't want anything to happen to the delicate pastries we'd slaved over. A lot was riding on this, and the more time it took to perfect it, the longer it would take to reclaim my money. Thankfully, though, Travis had brought over a few bottles of wine. Which was enough to keep most of my anxiety at bay.

"I can't help myself. It's like I'm watching a ticking timebomb. Like they could explode or deflate at any moment." I'd learned so much about baking over the last few weeks, but I still had so much more to learn. Instead of spending my days surfing online shops for things I didn't need, I now browsed blogs for baking tips and tricks while covered in flour.

Pulling myself away from the oven window, I decided to sample the berry filling one more time because the flavor was so damn good. So I swiped my finger around the inside of the bowl to scoop up as much as I could. *Most* of the filling made it in my mouth… I looked down at the deep-purple blob on my T-shirt and whined, "Oh, shoot!"

"Good thing you changed your clothes when we got back because that's probably going to stain." He smirked and turned to refill his wine.

There had been plenty of innuendos and subtle touches exchanged during the baking process, yet we never addressed the kisses we shared earlier. My reason for losing my nerve was simply because I hadn't been intimate with anyone in quite a while. I was definitely rusty, which brought about massive amounts of self-doubt.

I glanced down at my top again and said to myself…*screw it*. Now was as good a time as any to throw caution to the wind and go for what I wanted. So, before I lost my nerve, I pulled my shirt over my head and flung the stained fabric in his direction, hitting him in the back of the head.

"Thanks for the towel—" As he turned toward me, his mouth opened, his sentence ending on the spot. He didn't move. Or blink. His breathing intensified, which only served to embolden me even more.

"This filling is so good. Have you tried it?" I swiped my finger along the inside of the bowl again and smeared the berry mixture down my chest from my collarbone to the top of my cleavage.

He stood so still he looked like he'd soon need mouth-to-mouth, which I was completely willing to do.

"I need help cleaning this off." I dipped my chin and pursed my lips, enticing him to move.

Travis finally woke up and stalked toward me. He tentatively wiped the schmear with his finger, but before he pulled his arm away, I grabbed his wrist and brought his hand to my mouth. I slowly wrapped my lips around his finger and sucked on it like a freezer pop, all while staring directly into his eyes.

"Oh, but now I'm going to be sticky. I need something wet to clean myself off."

The intense heat in his gaze burned clearly as he bit his lower lip. He took a page out of my book and moved slowly. It was my turn to wait, and I tried to be patient. But the anticipation was too difficult to bear, so I arched my back against the countertop to try and force him to move quicker.

When his mouth finally met my skin, I moaned.

He continued to move up my neck, and by the time he reached my lips, I had already started to grind against him. His impressive erection proved he wanted me as I wanted him, and the expectation of what was to come made my clit ache. Desperation took over my senses, and I contemplated rubbing myself on his thigh to help ease the mounting pressure.

He pulled away just enough to expose the purplish fingerprints I'd left on the front of his white shirt from where I had fisted it. At first, all I could think about was how happy I was that he'd taken off his nice button-up before we started baking. At least I'd only ruined his undershirt.

"Oh, no. Now this is dirty." He lifted his gaze to look right at me, added a seductive grin, and pulled his shirt over his head.

The overbearing hormones running rampant in my body didn't allow me to wait for permission. I immediately reached out to touch him, unable to keep my hands off his bare chest. Oh, and what a chest it was. Aside from a small patch of light hair in the center between his beautiful pecs—which I happily ran my fingers through—his skin was completely smooth.

I needed him *now*, so I reached down and began to tamper with his belt.

But before I could fully release the buckle, Travis lifted me onto the counter. He made no secret of what he wanted as he pulled my cotton shorts down my legs. Thank God he didn't make me wait long before lowering himself between my thighs and hooking my knees over his shoulders.

His breath was cool, and his wet tongue was warm. The two sensations at once felt so good. I dropped my head back and closed my eyes. No longer in control of my actions, I used my heels to pull him closer as heat ignited in my body. As the fire continued to build in my lower stomach, I grabbed his hair, needing to grind myself against his mouth. His teeth grazed my clit, which made me come undone.

Losing all control, I gave in and came on his tongue.

Once the waves of euphoria finished rolling through me, he peppered kisses along my inner thighs and began his slow climb up my body. I thought he'd stop once he got to my neck, but he didn't. Instead, he did something I'd only ever read about in books. He leaned closer and kissed me. Tasting myself on his lips nearly made me come all over again.

I'd never experienced anything hotter.

I pushed off the counter and reached for his belt again. Thankfully, he didn't stop me this time, but if he'd tried, I wouldn't have budged. It was *my* turn. With my mind set on returning the favor, I successfully dropped his pants to his ankles. But he grabbed my waist, preventing me from kneeling, and turned me so my back was flush with his warm skin.

Part of him had become harder, and it was *very* noticeable, which made me beam with excited pride. Turning someone on like that was a feeling like no other. I was in the middle of relishing the erotic sensation of being skin-to-skin when he abruptly bent me over. No sooner than I got my bearings straight, he sent my head spinning again by sliding his cock between my legs and along my outer lips, lubing himself with my juices.

I was embarrassingly wet, but I didn't have time to worry about that because I had grown beyond impatient. I wiggled my hips, hoping to entice him to move it along; however, that seemed to have the opposite effect because he swatted my ass. This, in turn, caused me to become frantic with impatience. Still, he continued to tease me.

By this point, I'd had enough. It was time to take charge.

He might've been enjoying himself as he moved through my folds, but I needed him inside me. *Pronto*. So, to help guide his erection where I needed it the most, I reached between my legs and cupped my hand at the apex of my thighs, creating a tunnel that directed him to my entrance. Nowhere else.

That did the trick.

He immediately grabbed my hips and pushed in, not giving me a chance to adjust to his size—which was something I could've definitely benefited from. And not only because it'd been a while, either. But because this boy had girth!

Every time he pushed all the way in, he'd hit a spot inside, a magical spot, bringing me closer and closer to orgasm with every punishing thrust. And the further up Mount St. Bliss I climbed, the harder it became to hold myself up. I worried I was about to collapse onto the floor as my leg kept sliding along the tile like a one-legged split. But finally, he moved his foot to the outside of mine, preventing it from slipping any more.

My hero.

As I focused on holding myself up with my elbows locked and my head dangling between my arms, I opened my eyes and lifted my gaze, only to realize my vision was in line with the oven rack through the small window.

"Mmm...pies."

I didn't have a clue where those words came from. But before I had time to contemplate it, Travis turned us around. We were now propped against the kitchen island, the oven behind us. I practically draped myself across the cool countertop when he grabbed my thigh and held up my leg, which opened me wider *and* allowed him to thrust deeper.

His breathing became faster...as well as his plunges. In my experience, his exertion meant he was about to come. And to my surprise, the mere thought of Travis getting off shoved me to the verge of another orgasm, so I concentrated on the mental image of him coming inside me. And after half a second, I exploded in a second orgasm. Tingly heat radiated throughout my entire body as my legs shook.

When I finally came back down, with even less energy now, I realized he was still pushing forward, meaning he hadn't gotten off. In the past, I would've been over it by now, ready to pull up my pants and carry on with my day. But not with Travis. His body felt so good against mine that I'd be perfectly happy going all night long just like this. He managed to hit all the right places, so even if it didn't finish me off, it still felt incredible.

"Oh my God," I moaned, which caused him to push deeper inside me. The sharp edge of the counter bit into my forearm, tempting me to take control and change positions. Not to mention, I frantically wanted to see his face. I thought about how he'd moved me away from the oven a few minutes ago after I mentioned the pies. Wondering if he'd do it again, I decided to test my theory. So I quickly moaned, "Those pies smell so good."

As I expected, he pulled out and turned me around, my back now pressed against the cold granite. But he didn't slide between my legs again, and I began to worry that I had killed the moment. Instead, he propped himself up with his hands against the countertop on either side of me and leaned over enough to kiss my neck.

It was intoxicating, yet it didn't stop me from noticing he was doing something with his legs, though I couldn't figure it out. And to be honest, I didn't care. I was too wrapped up in what his lips and tongue were doing to my neck to give a shit about the frantic motion of his lower body.

Then he pulled away slightly, grabbed the backs of my thighs, and lifted me off the floor. My legs instinctively wrapped around his bare waist as he carried me to the kitchen table. Now I understood what he'd been busy doing—kicking off his pants. He'd left them in a heap on the tile floor, right next to my shorts.

He set me on top of the table, the glass top shockingly cold against my bare ass cheeks. My body felt overheated, but I wasn't sure what I needed or wanted. Just more. His hands moved up my back until he reached my bra clasp. Usually, I was the one to unhook my bra. Men always seemed to have such a hard time with them…until now. The fabric became slack in less than a second, no longer offering the support it had moments ago. It was like he touched the clasp, and the whole thing magically fell off.

In this position—propped up on the table with my arms outstretched behind me, Travis between my thighs—I was finally able to take him in. His chest expanded with every breath, emphasizing his defined pecs. His biceps flexed as he clutched behind my knees. And as he lifted my legs, holding them up in the shape of a *V*, he proved once again he was more than a pretty face. One look at his dick as he realigned himself to enter me again, and I thought my eyes would pop out of their sockets. He appeared to be slightly longer than average, but the thickness… *Holy hell.*

The girth gods had blessed him.

And as he slid back into me, I felt blessed as well.

I dropped my head back and closed my eyes, but only for a second. I finally had him in front of me, and I wanted to take advantage of watching him. I didn't want to miss anything, so I lifted my head enough to watch. Just in time, too.

He closed his eyes and bit down on his bottom lip as he continued his unhurried strokes. They were so slow they were almost torturous. He'd practically pull all the way out so the head was only partially inside, and then leisurely slide all the way back in until the tip lightly kissed my cervix.

I needed more.

Needed him harder.

Needed him faster.

My conflicting emotions were involved in a battle: I wished for an end to this torture while, at the same time, never wanting this moment to end.

With my legs in the air, I couldn't control the pace, so I did the only thing that came to mind. I dropped to my elbows, laying myself a little flatter on the tabletop, and began to vocalize my desires. Every time he pulled back, I hummed in pleasure. And when he slid in, reaching my cervix, I released a slight gasp.

But rather than encouraging him to increase the pace, my moans must've persuaded him to rub my clit instead. He licked his thumb and pressed the warm pad against my tight ball of nerves. Even his circular motion was too slow. I became convinced this guy was an assassin set out to kill me.

When I couldn't take any more and was close to screaming or losing my sanity, I decided to give up the fight for control. I completely dropped to the table, pressing my bare back against the cool glass, my ass perched on the ledge with my legs spread in the air.

He eventually moved his thumb faster, and to my surprise, the heat began to build in my lower stomach all over again. I was climbing higher and higher, and right as I was about to come, he slammed into me. I didn't just fall over the edge into the pool of ecstasy. No. He shoved me into it.

I cried out in pleasure. Had I been aware of what I was doing, I would've felt insecure about letting go like that. I'd never been one to make *any* noise in the bedroom, let alone the carnal wail that just tore through my throat. But in all fairness, I'd never reached orgasm that many times in one sitting. The only explanation I could come up with was that I'd simply had the wrong partners, because Travis made me whimper and groan and mewl like a cat in heat.

After I came down from my third orgasm, I expected Travis to let up again. But he didn't. His harsh, punishing thrusts continued at the same desperate pace he used when getting me off. His head fell back a little more, his eyes now firmly closed.

I could've watched this all night. The look of pleasure on his face did things to me I hadn't known were possible. But then it happened. His grip on my thighs tightened, his knuckles so white they bordered on translucent. He dropped his chin a little, and his mouth went slack, releasing his bottom lip from the death grip between his teeth. His brow relaxed, his eyes were at half-mast, and a long, guttural bellow filled the air.

He slowed his thrusts but never stopped. With a coy smirk on his face, he continued to slowly slide himself back and forth, his cock continuing to pulsate with his waning orgasm.

Watching Travis come was the sexiest thing I'd ever seen in my life.

Which meant we'd be doing a lot more of this for as long as we continued to be neighbors.

Travis bent down and kissed me softly, then pulled away to bring me a damp cloth to clean myself with. He got one for himself, and soundlessly, we both got our clothes from the strewn pile on the kitchen floor.

As soon as he lifted his khaki pants, the oven dinged.

"Oh! The pies are ready!" My excitement diminished slightly when something flew out of his pocket, catching my attention. We both heard the clanging of something hard yet small bouncing off the tile. But while I curiously glanced around the space, he frantically dropped to his hands and knees and began to scour the area as if searching for the most sacred item.

Whatever had been in his pocket, he certainly didn't want me to find. Which made me all the more curious as to what it could be. His suspicious attitude also made it obvious that I needed to find it first.

I turned around to grab the rest of our clothes in case it'd landed near the pile. And as soon as I lifted my shirt, I saw something shiny. My heart stopped, but only because I couldn't fathom why he'd have a diamond ring. We were only pretending to be engaged after all. Then I thought he might've gotten it for show and forgot to give it to me. Before he realized I'd found his secret, I grabbed the piece of jewelry for a closer look.

I managed one very brief glance before Travis snatched the gem out of my hand. But that was all I needed because this wasn't the first time I'd seen that ring. If I closed my eyes, I'd see the silver band with two small pear-shaped emeralds on either side of a brilliant half-carat diamond. I'd stored the image away in my memory to see whenever I felt nostalgic.

But the real question had yet to be answered…

Why did Travis have my mom's ring?

CHAPTER 14
TRAVIS

OH. Shit.

Claire stood frozen with her T-shirt clutched to her chest. She stared without blinking while I desperately tried to come up with something to say. My thoughts raced as I tried to determine if she recognized it, or if she'd simply misunderstood the situation. There was a chance she hadn't gotten a very good look, and here I was, on my knee with a diamond in my hand. That could quite easily explain her panicked reaction.

It was crazy how quickly things changed. Moments ago, the kitchen had been filled with moans and the scent of sex, and now…anxiety flooded the room with a hint of apprehension and fear.

"It's not what it looks like," I muttered and then cursed myself for not being able to come up with anything better. After all, that's what one would usually say when they were caught cheating. So I shook my head, took a deep breath, and tried again. "I can explain."

Yeah, because that was an improvement, dipshit.

I wouldn't be surprised if I'd actually rolled my eyes at myself. But to be fair, my blood hadn't fully returned to the appropriate places yet, and my thoughts were still consumed with the memory of being inside her. I hated that this situation might ruin what we'd just shared.

"Well, I sure hope so." Her tone was normal, but her expression remained robotic.

I stood, fully aware that neither of us wore a stitch of clothing, and clenched my fist, feeling the prongs pinch my palm. "Earlier today, at your grandfather's house—"

"That house is technically mine…but go ahead."

My mouth opened and closed a few times as I tried to gather my bearings. I wasn't sure which direction to go in: explain why I had the ring or ask about the house. My curiosity won out in the end. "*Your* house?"

"Yeah, I'll explain later. *After* you tell me why you have that." She pointed to my closed hand.

"Oh, yeah…" I shook my head, annoyed at myself for my inability to say anything intelligent. "Like I was saying, earlier today at the party, your grandfather pulled me aside. He didn't tell me why at first, but then he gave me this."

I opened my hand for her to see the ring.

She picked up the band between two fingers and stared at the glittering jewels. Familiarity flashed in her eyes, but to my surprise, her expression remained nearly emotionless. I didn't understand. After what Piper said about how Claire hadn't dealt with the loss of her parents, I half-expected her to at least display some sort of emotion. But there was nothing, not even the faintest hint of a tear.

"I couldn't say no without a realistic reason, and I didn't have one, so…"

"When were you planning to tell me?"

"I'm not sure. I've struggled with that ever since he gave it to me. I didn't want to upset you by forcing you wear it, so I decided to wait until I had time to sort everything out."

She tilted her head and looked at me quizzically. "Why would I be upset?"

I shrugged, further confused by her lack of emotion. "Because it was your mom's?"

"Yeah, but shouldn't that make me happy?" She slipped the ring on her finger and gently pushed the band over her knuckle. "When I was little, I used to ask to try it on. I'd hold out my hand and admire it as if it was *my* engagement ring."

Claire parodied her story. With her wrist bent and fingers spread, she stretched out her arm to regard the diamond shining in the kitchen light. She seemed lost in her memories, but surprisingly enough, there still weren't any tears.

"She always told me it would be mine one day. Although, it went without saying that it wouldn't be mine until after she died because she would've never given it up before then. And I knew she wouldn't die for a long, long time…until she did." Her voice cracked the tiniest bit, finally hinting at some sort of emotion.

I narrowed my concentration, wanting to soak up every word of what she had to say. Hopefully, she'd offer a clue as to why she always acted so detached when speaking of her deceased parents.

"Dad used to buy her lots of jewelry after they started making more money. Over the years, the diamonds got bigger, but the one thing she would never trade up was her ring." Claire's giggle as a memory came to her vaporized that tiny hint of sadness from a second ago. "She'd have these big ol' earrings—each stone was easily two carats—and some fancy necklace with its matching tennis bracelet, and then you'd look at her hand and find this."

Normally, I couldn't stand to listen to people talk about money, but this was different. These were her memories, not bragging rights. So, rather than become annoyed, I continued to study her, waiting for the first indication of the grief Piper had mentioned earlier. "Wearing it doesn't bother you? Even given the circumstances?"

"Not at all." She held out her hand again and winked. "To be honest, Gramps probably never would've given me this ring if it hadn't been for our fake engagement."

"I highly doubt that. Your grandfather would give it to whoever asks for your hand in marriage."

"Exactly, Travis. Except I'm pretty certain no one will ever propose to me."

"Why do you say that?" I leaned closer, no longer caring that we were still stark naked.

But rather than respond, she waved me off, slipped her hand into an oven mitt, and opened the oven door to retrieve her desserts. Between her interest in the pies while we were having sex, and her obsession with them now, I was ready to smash every last pastry if it meant I'd have her full attention...*and* answers to my questions.

While she set the trays on the stove, I proceeded to grab my clothes off the floor. My irritation continued to build, and the last thing I wanted to do was pick a fight moments after sharing such an intimate moment. So to keep myself occupied, I pulled my pants up my legs and fastened them at my waist.

"I just don't see myself getting married, Travis. It's no big deal." She stretched the neck hole of her T-shirt and slipped it over her head, not worrying about her bra, which was probably still somewhere around the kitchen table. "This will more than likely be my only engagement, and if that means the ring I've always wanted is now mine, then so be it. Don't apologize."

"Okay then, I won't. I guess I'm only sorry I didn't tell you sooner."

"It's fine." Still only wearing a T-shirt and panties, she slid a small, crescent-shaped pastry onto a dessert plate and set it in front of me. "You try it first. I'm too nervous."

I wasn't about to let her avoid yet another conversation about herself. If she didn't want to open up about the ring or her parents, fine, but I wouldn't back off as I had in the past. "I answered your question. Now answer mine. What did you mean about the house being yours?"

"It's exactly what it sounds like."

On the brink of losing my patience, I shoved the plate away and took a step back. "All right, Claire. If you don't want to talk about anything remotely close to personal, fine. I can't force you. But I have to be honest... I've literally done everything possible to help you out. Even going as far as pretending to be your fiancé. Everything I've done has benefitted you, and you alone. The least you could do is have a genuine conversation with me instead of acting like I'm drudging up your deepest, darkest secrets."

I rounded the corner of the island to retrieve my shoes, but Claire grabbed my arms before I had a chance to pick them up. She held my stare, and the emotion in her eyes looked vaguely familiar—something resembling resignation, maybe. Except I couldn't recall a time I would've seen her resigned about anything.

Her shoulders rose and fell dramatically as her breathing intensified. And even though her lips were parted, she didn't make any move to speak. Just as I wondered if this was nothing more than a waste of time, she closed her eyes, dropped her chin, and released a heavy sigh.

Suddenly, I remembered where I'd seen this side of her before—last week when she confessed to telling her grandfather we were engaged. If so, that meant she would eventually open up with a little more time.

"Travis..." she croaked out and shook her head. After clearing her throat, she met my gaze once again and offered a slight nod, conceding to my wishes. "You're absolutely right, and I am truly sorry. At the risk of sounding completely ridiculous, I'm pretty sure I'm allergic to talking about myself. Whenever I think I've said too much, I practically break out in hives."

I knew she wasn't serious about getting a rash, but I understood what she meant. So to calm her nerves a little, I settled my hand on her hip, trying my best to ignore the warmth of her bare skin beneath my palm. "It's okay, Claire. Like I said, I can't make you share anything. If you're too uncomfortable then—"

"That's not it." She shook her head and closed her eyes for a second, as if collecting her thoughts before speaking again. "I mean, kind of, but not the way you're thinking. I'm uncomfortable talking about myself in general, which has nothing to do with you directly."

Seeing the sheer pain written all over her face, I resigned myself to blurt out what her best friend had mentioned earlier. I released a long sigh and leaned against the edge of the counter. "It's okay, Claire. After those stupid girls in high school betrayed your trust, your hesitation to confide in anyone is completely understandable."

Her gaze narrowed, and eventually, she glared silently at the center of my chest with her jaw clenched. It wasn't clear if she was angry or simply searching for the right way to respond until she lifted her chin and whispered, "Who told you?"

"Does it matter?"

Claire shrugged and took a step back, pulling away from my hold on her hip. "I guess not."

Much like the other night on my couch, she appeared to shrink in size. As irritating as it was that she refused to divulge anything about her life, I never wanted to cause her pain. I'd rather go the rest of my life without knowing anything about her than to see her fold in on herself like this.

I reached for her forearm to keep her from retreating even more. "Don't shut me out, Claire. I'm not judging you. My adverse opinions are solely reserved for anyone who's ever hurt you. I swear, I don't think of you any differently today than I did yesterday."

That wasn't necessarily true, but I figured this wasn't the time to point out all the different thoughts I now had about her—more precisely, about being buried deep inside her. I could confess those things later, after she calmed down and stopped trying to run away in her own house.

"I guess I just don't understand the need to play twenty questions for anyone to figure things out about me. I personally believe if you don't know something, then you aren't paying attention." She'd clearly convinced herself of that lie.

"I beg to differ. You like to sleep in late, and instead of reaching for something chocolate to satisfy your sweet tooth, you go for a roll of Sweeties. But —and this is a total assumption—only the big ones. You prefer white wine over red, yet you won't turn down any bottle if offered. You're a homebody, although I suspect that's because of your need for self-preservation."

She stared without blinking as I ran through the list of things I'd observed about her.

"You would rather listen to others talk about themselves, even when you're not interested in what they have to say. Most of the time, you keep the spotlight on other people to avoid it landing on you. And whenever it does, you effortlessly turn it right back around—a talent you've obviously developed over the years to avoid intimacy."

Finally, she did something other than stare. She rolled her eyes, which meant I was getting somewhere. Defensiveness was much easier to work with than the withdrawn demeanor she'd exhibited seconds ago.

"And even though you miss your parents, you refuse to allow yourself the freedom to *feel* it. You push down the anger, dismiss the pain, ignore the sadness, and whether you want to admit it or not, you pity yourself—well, the fifteen-year-old version of yourself, anyway."

"You have no idea what you're talking about," she argued with her arms crossed over her chest in a defensive stance. Disbelief flashed in the golden flecks of her eyes, as if she were offended by my assessment. She could deny it until she was blue in the face, but we both knew I'd hit a bullseye with my last statement.

"Oh, Claire…I think you'll find that I do. I know exactly what I'm talking about. You just got done saying that if people wanted to learn things about you, they should do so without asking questions. That's what I've done. I've paid attention, but there are still parts of your life I'd love to discover. You can't possibly understand someone's motives for being who they are by simply observing them. Those are the things that need to be shared. Hence the reason for questions."

She dropped her arms and busied herself with stepping into her shorts. Evidently, she felt bare and wanted to hide as much as possible. This was proven when she moved to the other side of the island, conveniently putting distance and an unmovable object between us.

To my surprise, though, she responded. "I've been called out so many times over the last six or seven years for avoiding deep conversations, and not once has it ever bothered me. My ex used to complain about it all the time. He said he knew my mailman better than he knew me, and I'd dismiss that ridiculous claim with a laugh, thinking he was being dramatic."

I felt the need to interject before she got too far into her story. "Wait a minute. Are you saying you honestly believe you were open with him?"

"Yeah. It's not like I flat-out refused to share my life with him. We were dating, for crying out loud. I'd told him lots of things over the years, so yeah, every time he brought it up, I assumed he was being overly sensitive or melodramatic."

"What about with me? Do you think you've been open with me?"

Claire paused and took a deep breath, then exhaled slowly, likely to buy herself a little time. "You're different. And before you ask why, I can't explain it, because I haven't been able to figure it out yet."

"Okay, I won't ask why. But can you at least tell me *what* makes me different?"

She didn't seem to notice, but I'd been gradually making my way around the island, closing the distance between us. I hadn't quite reached her yet, but it wouldn't be long before I stood next to her again.

She licked her lips before answering. "Well, for starters, I'm fully aware that I purposely avoid telling you anything personal about myself. Except I can't understand why because when you tell me things about your life, a small part of me begs to join in and share my own experiences. But I never allow myself."

"Maybe that's because I'm not just someone you have occasional run-ins with. I'm your neighbor, and considering you've convinced yourself that anyone with personal information about you will use it against you, you're worried it could create a bad home environment for you."

She nodded and closed her eyes. "Yeah, maybe."

I took the opportunity and moved across the tile until I stood less than two feet away. When she opened her eyes again, rather than freak out or walk off, she laughed breathlessly to herself.

As much as I wanted to prod more about her grandfather's house belonging to her, I wanted to savor her laughter even more. So I posted a mental sticky note in my thoughts to remember to touch on that subject later. For now, though, I decided to enjoy my time with Claire while filling up on the most amazing pies I'd ever eaten.

"WHAT'S GOT you in such a good mood?" my mom asked as I entered the winery the next morning.

I stopped and glanced around the mostly empty shop, feigning confusion. "I have no idea what you're talking about, Ma." Truthfully, I did, but I wasn't about to tell her that I was still riding the high from having sex with my neighbor yesterday.

"You're just so…giddy. Is there a girl?"

"It doesn't always have to be about a girl." Luckily, I managed to dodge that bullet without telling an actual lie.

Hoping to avoid more questions, I quickly moved through the shop on my way to my office. But my mom stopped me seconds before rounding the corner to the hallway.

"I've got good news…we officially have a contract on the land for the vineyard expansion. Your father and I signed the papers this morning. And we also agreed on a closing date—two weeks from tomorrow. So you might want to mark your calendar."

I needed to do more than mark my calendar. I needed to secure the loan before it was too late. At this point in the game, I had to accept that I likely wouldn't be able to obtain the additional finances needed to *actually* expand the vineyard. But I couldn't worry about that. I had to take everything one step at a time, and the first step was acquiring the land. I'd have to figure out the rest later.

"Sounds good, Ma." Once again, I tried to make an exit.

And once again, she stopped me. Although this time, she needed my advice. "I have this entire corner over here, and I can't decide what to fill it with."

"What did you have there before?"

"Crates. It looked good, but I figured having this entire area blocked off by decorations was a waste of space I could be using for merchandise."

I scratched my head, wondering why in the world she needed my help. "Well, what are my options?"

"Anything."

"Yeah?" I laughed and placed my hand on her shoulder. "Then I think you should fill it with crates. They'd look perfect there."

Mom huffed and smacked my stomach with the back of her hand. "I'm serious, Travis."

Deciding to give her question some real thought—for my mom's sake—I glanced around the shop, taking inventory of product we could move around. There were T-shirts and hoodies behind the large counter in the back of the room. Along one wall were displays filled with various limited-edition bottles of Uncorked wines, and on either side of that were shelves stocked with two different sizes of personalized wine glasses. One with a fancy stem, and one without, both with *Uncorked Vineyards*, along with our logo of a grapevine, etched into the front of the glass.

Decorative inspirational signs lined the opposite wall. Those had been something Mom added to our inventory. We all assumed they'd be a waste of money, but had quickly been proven wrong. To our surprise, they were one of our biggest sellers.

She'd found a place to have them specially made using her wine-isms, meaning they couldn't be found anywhere else. That might've been part of the appeal, but I believed their success had more to do with the phrasing my mom used. They said things like *I need to re-wine my life* and *Be quiet, it's time to wine down.*

"Well, Mom, unless you want to move all the shirts and hoodies out from behind the counter, I don't have a clue what to tell ya to put here."

"You're no help." She groaned to herself then asked, "Would you mind helping me haul the crates back out here?"

"I don't have to set them all back up again, do I?"

Mom laughed and waved me off. "No, you don't have to worry about that."

"Okay, then...yeah, I can do that for you." I didn't want to, but none of us could tell our mom no. We didn't have it in us. So while I might've griped to myself the entire time I dragged crate after crate back to the same spot they'd been in the day before, at least I did so with a smile on my face.

Two hours later, I was at my desk, thoroughly enjoying one of the pies Claire and I had made yesterday. I only packed myself one for the day, though. They were so addictive that I would've eaten them all in one sitting if I'd brought more.

As I licked the berry filling off my fingers, I was quickly reminded of how sweet Claire's arousal was on my tongue yesterday. I couldn't prove it, but I was willing to bet that no one tasted as amazing as Claire; she was one of a kind. Suddenly, an idea came to me. Without bothering to clean anything up, I pushed away from my desk and hurried to the front of the winery.

Thankfully, my mom was still there, taking her time restacking the crates.

"I have an idea for the corner," I called out as I made my way to her.

She glanced over her shoulder and eyed me with a hesitant grin lining her pink lips. "What is it?"

Instead of explaining, I decided to show her my vision. I quickly moved around a few wooden crates, turning them from a decorative display into a marketing production. "Pies. I told you about my neighbor, the baker, right? Anyway, she makes these amazing little personal-sized desserts. I think they would fit in perfectly here."

"You want me to use space in the winery to allow someone else to make a profit?"

"Well, when you put it like that, it sounds bad. But just listen to me for a second... Most of the fruit she uses comes from the farm, so it's kinda attached to us anyway. And I'm sure we can figure something out as far as compensation is concerned, whether she rents the space or gives you a cut of each sale. What if it becomes really popular? You could rent out shelf space to other small businesses in the area. You could call it *Rent-A-Corner* or some-thing. Anyway, she could really use a hand with getting her pastries out there. I swear, Ma, they are amazing. I'd let you try one, but I just finished devouring the only one I brought with me."

"Of course you did," she teased with laughter rolling in her words. "Fine, I'll consider it. Have her stop by to discuss the details, and we'll go from there. Don't tell her it's a done deal, though. I haven't made up my mind on anything other than talking about it."

She didn't need to tell me twice. I ran back to my office to grab my phone. When I texted Claire, I didn't want to make her nervous, so I didn't mention the possible opportunity. Instead, I told her that I'd eaten my only pie and asked if she'd bring me more.

Thankfully, she didn't have any plans for the day.

CHAPTER 15

CLAIRE

I LAUGHED at myself as I pulled up in front of the winery. When did I become the girl who went running as soon as a guy called? That had never been me. And truthfully, it still wasn't, but it didn't stop me from dropping everything to bring Travis more pies.

Granted, it was a nice boost to my ego.

I had to admit, I'd accidentally stumbled upon this new recipe variation last week. Normally, I soaked the fruit in apple juice for half a day, but when I'd gone into the kitchen to prepare some apples and berries, I realized I'd run out of juice. Instead, I'd used one of the bottles of Uncorked wine Travis had brought over. I'd also indulged in a little vino myself, so I'd forgotten about the soaking fruit until the next morning.

Apparently, that was the meal ticket.

After sending Travis a text to tell him I'd arrived, I tossed my phone into my purse and slid out of the driver's seat. He never mentioned how many pies he wanted, so I brought four—two blueberry and two apple.

Travis greeted me in the shop at the front of the winery as soon as I walked in. I was certain the smile on my face gave away my thoughts, which was *I can't believe I had sex with this gorgeous man*. Then again, I doubted it mattered, considering the grin curling his lips. It made his eyes burn with the same heat I felt in my lower stomach.

"Good timing," he said with a waggle of his brows. "I just finished my inventory check of the barrel room."

I handed him the small paper bag containing his pastries. "You seriously have a barrel room? I thought those were just something they used in movies…or in those super fancy vineyards in France."

128

"I sincerely hope you hadn't meant that as the insult it sounded like." His teasing tone contradicted the offense lining his expression.

Flattening my hair with my palms, I scoured my brain for the alleged insult he'd mentioned, but I couldn't find it. "What did I say?"

"You assumed we didn't have a barrel room because we aren't one of those *super fancy vineyards*," he mocked. The corners of his mouth twitched as he slowly lost control over his feigned hurt feelings. "I'll have you know, we are super-*duper* fancy. The south of France has nothing on Uncorked Vineyards."

"Oh, you must've misunderstood... I only meant I assumed you would've had an entire barrel warehouse instead of a *room*."

Travis gave up on his forced frown as breathless laughter rushed past his smiling lips. "Would you like to see it?"

Excitement coursed through me, and I fought the need to jump on the balls of my feet like a child at a birthday party. "I'd love to."

He grabbed my hand and escorted me into the back, down a wide hall-way, and finally, into what had to be the most magnificent room I'd ever stood in. The wooden ceiling was high and arched, and the way the lights hit it made it glow like the sky during sunset. It caused me to study the lighting closer. They were built into the fitted molding that decorated the tops of the walls as well as the rafters running the length of the room. It reminded me a lot of a swanky event ballroom at an upscale hotel.

"Wow, Travis. This is amazing." I didn't care if I sounded like an impressed idiot. I literally stood in the middle of heaven. Heavy wooden shelves decorated three walls, all stacked with large oak barrels. They were all arranged so perfectly that they gave the impression of a staged scene.

While his expression didn't change, pride brightened his eyes. "One of these days, I'll convince my parents to open up this space for weddings. I've already drawn it up—we could extend the shelves up to the ceiling to fit these." He waved his hand at the rows of neatly stacked barrels in the center of the room. "It would give us plenty of space for banquet-style tables."

I took in a slow, exaggerated breath and hummed. "The combination of a white dress, candles, flowers, and the scent of wood screams romance. It almost makes me want to tie the knot just to have that experience."

Travis was quiet for a second, and when I turned on my heel to face him, I found a deep hunger in his stare. It replicated what I'd seen last night in my kitchen, right before he'd bent me over the countertop. "I agree...it offers a very intimate atmosphere."

"Have you ever had sex in here?" I asked, the throbbing between my legs making me desperate and slightly more brazen than normal. But mostly desperate.

"No." He flicked his eyes up to the corners of the ceiling. "We have cameras in here."

I stepped closer until I stood right in front of him, close enough to cup his bulge without it being obvious to the cameras. "What a shame, because the thought of being bent over a barrel of wine with your hard body behind me *severely* turns me on."

His breathing grew heavier, each exhale bathing my face in heat that went straight to the apex of my thighs. I had to pivot my weight from one foot to the other in the hopes of alleviating an ounce of the ache he created between my legs.

"There aren't any cameras in my office," he suggested, appearing as eager as I felt. We were both seconds away from saying *screw it* and ripping each other's clothes off. Or maybe that was just me.

"Yes, you should take me to your office. Right now."

He didn't hesitate. Instead, he grabbed my hand and practically dragged me out of the room and down the hallway. My feet were heavy and refused to function properly; they were too eager to be wrapped about his waist. Once we made it to the shop, he whipped me past the vacant front counter to another hallway lined with offices.

My body hummed with unfettered desire, making this short trek seem more like a mile-long hike. But as soon as he approached an open door and slowed down, I knew the wait was over. I followed him into the brightly lit room, only to practically slam into the back of him when he abruptly stopped right inside the doorway. Thankfully, he moved to the side before I could say anything.

A woman sat perched in a chair in front of Travis's slightly disorganized desk. She wore her hair pinned back without a strand out of place, and her attire was quite tidy. I wasn't entirely sure who she was, but I felt confident in my assumption that this woman was his mother. They had the same eyes, though hers appeared older. Wiser, even.

"Hey, Ma. What are you doing here?"

The building heat in my lower stomach had been extinguished at the realization of someone else in his office. However, finding out that our very own clam-jammer was Travis's mother eliminated every ounce of warmth in my entire body, like tossing a cold bucket of water over my head.

"Is everything okay?" Travis asked as he maneuvered around her to sit behind his desk. He'd left me standing in the doorway alone, which bothered me a little at first. But my irritation quickly vanished when it dawned on me that, after getting so worked up in the barrel room, there was a chance he needed to sit.

"Yeah, I'm fine. They're painting my office, so I decided to do some work in yours. The fumes were making me lightheaded." Without closing her laptop, she set it on the edge of the desk with the screen facing her. "I hope you don't mind."

"Of course not, Mom. You're always welcome." He finally gestured to me, as if suddenly remembering I was still here. "This is my neighbor, Claire. Claire, this is my mom, Carla."

"It's nice to meet you, Mrs. Cabrera."

"Likewise. Here, have a seat." She slid the other chair out from beneath the desk so I could sit next to her. And as soon as I did, she pointed to my hand and said, "What an absolutely beautiful ring. Is it antique?"

Not understanding what she was talking about at first, I glanced down. But when I caught a flash of sparkle from my mom's diamond, it made sense. I smiled, fighting the desire to look at Travis, and said, "Oh, thank you. I just got it yesterday. It's old, but I don't think it's considered antique."

"Engagement?"

My cheeks ignited in flames. I couldn't take my eyes off the brilliant diamond between two glowing emeralds as I racked my brain for an appropriate answer. I was wedged between a rock and a hard place.

Thankfully, Travis came to my rescue. He cleared his throat and loudly asked, "Why didn't you take your computer to the front and do your work at the counter?"

"I needed to sit in a proper chair. Thanks to moving those crates a hundred times, my back's been bothering me today."

He nodded slowly, clearly unhappy over the interruption of our desk romp. "Well, I was just up there. No one's watching the shop. What if someone comes in?"

She tilted her head the tiniest bit and said, "I'm watching it from my laptop."

Travis appeared visibly anxious, and after a quick glance at her computer screen, I understood why. His mom had the security footage pulled up, meaning she likely saw us in the barrel room.

While I became riddled with anxiety, he managed to pull himself together enough to offer his mom the paper bag I'd given him. "Claire brought some more pies. You should try one."

My chest constricted so much I worried my ribs would snap, and my erratically palpitating heart made me believe I was on the verge of heart failure. Panic consumed me as I stressed about his mom recognizing the pie. But then I reminded myself how much I had modified it, so it couldn't possibly be considered their recipe anymore.

I managed to snap out of my racing thoughts when she waved her hand and said, "I'll have one later."

"If I haven't eaten them all by then. You've been warned." He laughed and shook his head. "Anyway, I got Claire here, so are you ready to talk business?"

I'd gone from nervous to panicked to relieved in three seconds, and now I was confused. I wasn't sure if I could handle anything else and wondered how long I had to be here. He'd only asked me to bring him more pies since he'd eaten his. And now he was talking about business.

"Have you explained your idea to Claire?"

They spoke as if I weren't in the room, and while it annoyed me, I was also grateful because it meant I didn't have to say anything. At this point, I doubted I had the wherewithal to string four words together, let alone four words that actually made sense.

"Not yet. I figured we could do that together." He offered his mom a short nod and then turned his attention to me. "Mom was talking about doing something with an unused corner in the shop. Right now, it's filled with a bunch of wooden crates stacked on top of each other in some sorta farm-style decoration. But I had an idea..."

I sat silent, unable to blink, and held my breath as I waited for him to continue. Instead, though, he just stared at me like I could read his mind. At this point, I couldn't even read my own, so I couldn't begin to guess what he wanted from me.

After a long moment, he grinned and waggled his brows, which somewhat calmed me. But only somewhat. There was no chance in hell I'd be able to completely settle until he admitted the real reason I was here.

"Since you mostly use the farm's fruit, I thought it might be a good idea to utilize the corner to sell your pies. What do you think?"

I hated how he'd put me on the spot. While this was obviously an amazing opportunity, I still felt that it would be wrong. Even though I no longer used his mom's recipe, the guilt of taking it in the first place wouldn't allow me to jump on his offer the way I should have. I recognized my reasoning was probably ridiculous, but even so, I couldn't rid my mind of the shame that cloaked me every time I thought about what I'd done.

The longer I remained mute, the more pressure I felt from his aquatic stare. It was enough to compel me to say something, if only to kill the suspense. "I'm not sure, Travis. How would we even do that? I can't work here if that's what you're suggesting."

"No, nothing like that. And this is why you're here, so we can all discuss the logistics. I figured we have an empty corner and nothing to put in it, and you have desserts and nowhere to sell them. This could be your chance to convince your grandfather that there *is* a market out there for Cutie Pies."

"That's the name of them?" his mom asked, her brow raised in awe. "I *love* it."

"See? I'm tellin' ya, Ma...you'll have people stopping by just for her baked goods. It'll increase foot traffic. And once they're here, they'll find something else to buy too. This can be good for both of you, as well as beneficial for the winery." He shoved his chair back and stood. "Come on, I'll show you what I'm talking about. Once you see it, you won't be able to say no."

I didn't want to follow him, but after his mom stood, I realized I didn't have a choice and silently complied.

With every step I took between his office and the shop, I contemplated ways to pay him back for this—retributively, not monetarily. It was a very kind and generous offer, but he could've warned a bitch ahead of time.

SUNDAY MORNING ARRIVED TOO QUICKLY.

It'd be a lie if I said this new opportunity didn't completely freak me out. Oddly enough, though, my nerves had nothing to do with my guilt. Instead, I was worried I would replicate the failure I'd experienced at the fair. Except this would be on a much bigger scale with much more to lose. But I'd agreed to give it a go—on a trial basis to start—so I needed to push those fears aside and move ahead as planned.

I'd spent the entire week in my kitchen preparing for the unveiling of my corner at the winery. Travis even came over a few times to help me "bake." That was now our code word for sex. He didn't help me with squat when it came to the pies, but he did, however, help me tremendously by lowering my stress. Which was why I chose to relive those hot-and-heavy moments in my head as I drove my first carload of pies to the winery…to keep me calm, cool, and collected.

Thankfully, replaying every detail of sex with Travis kept me from driving across the border and running away; however, not even the thought of his magnificent cock could completely calm me down. Having him in the actual flesh might've been able to, but not simply a mental image. So the closer I got to the winery, the worse my anxiety became. And by the time I pulled into the parking lot, my heart had found a new home in my throat, effectively choking me.

I suspected this would end up being a major moment in my life, and not having my parents here only increased the hysteria running through me. But I refused to let my grief win, so I put on my big girl panties and gave myself a pep talk. I sat in the driver's seat with my forehead against the steering wheel, trying to convince myself that I was more than capable of doing this on my own.

A knock on my window snapped me out of my mental chat. I sat back, finding Carla standing on the other side of my car door. I foolishly rolled down the window. I knew why she was there and what she needed, yet my brain didn't reach those conclusions before I had the window down.

"Need a hand?" Light-pink lipstick painted a welcoming smile across her face.

"I'll take all the hands I can find." I opened my car door, careful not to hit her in the process, and led her to the back gate of my SUV. "I think I'm still out of breath from loading everything up this morning."

"You should've made Travis do that for you."

I shrugged and then grabbed a box. "I'm sure he would've if I asked, but I didn't want to bother him on a Sunday morning."

Honestly, I hadn't asked him because I didn't want to risk him coming with me. I had enough stress to deal with; I didn't need to make it worse by adding his looming presence to the mix. There was still a chance he'd show up, but I refused to concentrate on that at the moment.

We carried the boxes inside and set them on the floor next to the stack of crates in "my" corner. Until I had a better idea of which fruit filling sold best, I'd decided just to bring them all. However, now that I had them inside the winery, I realized I might've made too many.

"You must have a good feeling about this," Carla teased as she set down the last box.

I took a step back and regarded the corner, taking in the empty wooden crates and useable space. "Well, I figured you'd probably want samples with it being a new product and all, so I accounted for that. And it's always better to have extras than empty shelves *if* they do well. I would need at least two days to make them, so this way, I'll have time to restock if they're as popular as Travis claims they'll be."

"Travis isn't the only one who thinks so." She caught my attention. "I had two of them—apple and blueberry, I think. And Travis came to work a few times this week with new ones he let me try. If I remember correctly, they were peach, raspberry, mixed berry, and…apricot, maybe?"

"Yeah, it was apricot. I did it as a tribute to my mom." That thought flowed effortlessly through my smiling lips. It wasn't until she asked why that I realized what I'd said. I *never* mentioned my mom, not because I didn't want to talk about her or was ashamed of her, but because I knew from experience that it only led to curiosity. And I hated being asked question after question about my parents. But since I'd brought her up, I had to answer, so I casually said, "She loved apricots."

"That's so nice of you. I'd like to think at least one of my boys would create something in my memory after I'm gone, but the chances of that happening are slim to none." She didn't stop working as she spoke, as if we were discussing the weather, not my dead mom.

While she unpacked the boxes, keeping the pies organized by their filling,

I arranged the crates into a functioning display that would give each fruit its own space. "I haven't exactly met your other boys, but I wouldn't be surprised if Travis dedicated a special type of wine to you. At the very least, I imagine he'd name one after you."

"You two are pretty close, I take it?"

While I was happy to be off the subject of my mom, chatting about Travis wasn't any better. "Well, I mean, we're neighbors. We hang out from time to time when we're both home."

"He mentioned something the other day about going with you to a party at your grandparent's house last weekend?" Based on the inflection at the end of her sentence, it sounded like a question. Yet its purpose was a little unclear, unless she was simply looking for confirmation.

"Um, yeah?" Apparently, the interrogative lilt was infectious. "I mean, yes…he did."

"That was really nice of you to invite him. Other than here at work and the occasional family meeting, I don't see him often, so I worry about him. Ever since his last relationship ended, he hasn't had much of a social life." Carla playfully rolled her eyes while laughing to herself. "It's a mother's job to worry about her kids. I'm sure yours are in heaven worrying about everything you do."

I was quiet for a moment, wondering if that were true—although I hoped not because I didn't want to think about my mom watching *everything* I did. For reasons I'll never understand, I opened my mouth and asked, "Do you think people in heaven can see what's going on?"

"I'd like to think so. The idea of our loved ones watching over us is… comforting. When you imagine your parents are with you, doesn't that offer a little reassurance? For instance, now. With these pies. Doesn't it help to imagine they're right next to you, supporting your every move?"

I hesitated, unsure of what to say. For the first few months after their death, I'd imagine my parents were still around, offering moral support and encouragement. However, doing so only led to greater sadness. While pretending they were with me had offered a semblance of peace, that calming comfort only lasted a brief moment. Because as soon as I'd open my eyes, I had to, once again, accept that they were dead. So eventually, I stopped. Instead, I'd remind myself that my parents were gone; they weren't with me, and they weren't coming back. I only had myself, and I had to be okay with that.

"Yeah, I guess it does," was all I could muster.

While organizing the cellophane-wrapped pastries in their respective crates, the backs of my eyes burned. I focused on my breathing to keep from letting on that she'd unleashed an emotion I fought desperately to keep buried.

This was why I didn't like talking about my parents.

It was a hell of a lot easier to overlook the pain when the subject was ignored.

Somehow, Carla must've recognized how badly I needed the subject changed because she said, "I'm so glad we could utilize these crates. They're perfect for displaying the pies, and at the end of each day, when I have to put them in the cooler, I don't have to worry about loading and unloading anything. I can just carry them back there and put them in as-is."

"I guess it was meant to be."

She offered a gentle smile I felt in my soul. "I'll go set up the printer so we can make you some signs."

While she busied herself behind the front desk, I finished organizing the pastries and tucking in the fabric we used to line the crates. We only needed to set everything up and take pictures so Carla could refer to them when putting it all back together in the morning.

"Oh, shoot," she said with a harsh stomp of her boot on the wooden floor. "The printer isn't working. We'll have to run to the house and use the one in our home office."

"*We?*" Agreeing to this much interaction with his mom was already beyond my comfort level. Going to her house could very well paralyze me. "You...you need me to go with you?"

"It'd be best. That way, you can tell me what to put on the signs."

"Easy. *Shove this pie in your hole.* Here, I can handwrite it. Got a piece of paper?"

Carla laughed and waved me off. Little did she know, I wasn't joking. "Come on, it won't take but five minutes. I'll even drive to save time."

If you're watching, Mom, please don't let me hyperventilate in front of Mrs. Cabrera. Or pass out. Or cry. And if you could keep me from screaming and running away, that'd be great too. Thanks.

CHAPTER 16

TRAVIS

THERE WAS NO WORSE time to have someone ring your doorbell than as soon as you've stepped out of the shower. Any other time, it's easier to ignore. On the toilet? Oh well, nothing you can do. *Actually* in the shower? The doorbell would likely go unnoticed. But as soon as you step out, dripping wet, is—in my opinion—the absolute worst time for someone to show up at your house.

With my towel wrapped around my waist, I made my way to the front door, careful not to slip on the tile. Considering it was five o'clock on a Saturday, it was a tossup between Craig or Claire, and it wasn't like they'd never seen my bare chest. In fact, ever since our faux-gagement party six weeks ago, Claire had seen it *a lot*.

Not even bothering to hide myself, I swung open the door. And just as I suspected, I found Claire on the front step, a shit-eating grin quickly stretching across her face.

"Did you install cameras in my house?" I asked as I let her in.

She furrowed her brow in confusion—though it didn't go without notice that her eyes never left my chest. "No, why?"

"It never fails, you either text or show up when I'm naked." I turned on my heel and carefully made my way back to my bedroom to change.

Not surprisingly, she followed. "What can I say? I have impeccable timing."

"Can't argue with you there." I grabbed my clothes and disappeared into my bathroom. If I'd dropped my towel in front of her, it would be at least thirty minutes before I finally got dressed. Before Claire, I didn't think it was possible to have as much sexual chemistry as we did. "What's up?"

"Thought I'd come over to see if you have dinner plans."

"Why, are you asking me out on a date?" I teased.

Silence filled the air for a moment, which told me I'd freaked her out. I had to admit I enjoyed making her swallow her tongue, so every time an opportunity presented itself, I took full advantage. I found it amazing how she seemed more comfortable physically naked than metaphorically. She could ride me all day long, but the second I made a joke about being in an actual relationship, she'd all but shut down.

Much like every other time this happened, she completely ignored my question as if I hadn't asked one. "I turned on my slow cooker this morning, but I forgot to plug it in. And I didn't notice until I went to scoop some into a bowl. So I'm hungry and thought I'd see if you were, too."

Claire had almost become a different person in the last six weeks since the unveiling of her pie corner at the winery. The biggest difference was by far her confidence, especially in the kitchen. She made dinner nearly every night, and most of the time, it was a new recipe she'd found online. I ate at her place almost every weeknight, and she never served the same meal twice. However, even with all the changes, she was still a blonde at heart.

And truthfully, I hoped that never changed.

"I could eat. What do you have in mind?" I hung up my towel and left the bathroom, finding her perched on the end of my bed.

"At this point, I don't care. As long as it's not still alive, I'll eat it. I'm starving."

"You didn't have lunch?"

She followed me into the living room and immediately claimed her spot on the couch. By now, it was automatic. Everything about us had become so natural and effortless, as if we'd been together for years. "No. I baked the entire day."

"Without me?" I loved watching heat rush to her cheeks anytime *baking* was mentioned. It was something I didn't think I'd ever grow tired of.

It'd only taken two weeks for word to spread about her pies. They'd become so popular she was stuck in front of her oven every day of the week just to keep up with the demand. She'd originally thought about adding other pastries, but once the pies took off, she wasn't left with a single second in her schedule—or room in her oven—to make anything else.

"Are you saying you were in the kitchen all day and not once realized the slow cooker wasn't on? Doesn't it have a light on the front to tell you whether it's on or not?"

"Yeah, it does, but..." She smacked her forehead with an open hand and mumbled, "I don't want to tell you because you'll laugh at me."

That was enough to fill my chest with amusement, so there was no point in even attempting to claim I wouldn't. "Oh, come on. You can tell me."

"I put the slow cooker in the living room because I needed every inch of counter space for my trays. So I didn't see it." She lifted up her head enough to look at me, probably ensuring I wasn't making fun of her. Which I would never do anyway.

At least not out loud.

I bit my lip and fought like hell to keep the humor that filled my chest from creeping out. "Well, looks like you're in luck, little lady, because I didn't pull anything out for dinner and was just about to call for pizza."

The happiness sparkling in her eyes was totally worth lying to her.

I had a steak in the fridge; it'd been marinating since last night.

THERE WAS ALWAYS something new to learn about Claire. Such as her love of pizza crust smothered in ranch dressing. She only ate one actual slice, letting me eat the rest as long as I gave her my crusts.

The other thing I'd learned over the last two hours was if someone told her they were stressed, she refused to talk about anything else. It might not have been a big deal for some people, but for me, it could potentially drive me to drink. If something stressed me out, the *last* thing I wanted to do was talk about it incessantly.

"I'm sorry, Claire, but can we please discuss anything other than the vineyard expansion? As much as I appreciate all your support and ideas, I can't do anything this late on a Saturday." I covered my face with a couch pillow, not wanting to see her expression in case I had upset her.

We'd closed on the property a little over three weeks ago, and ever since the papers were signed, my parents had done nothing but talk about the next steps. Except I still couldn't procure the finances to cover what was supposed to come next. At this moment in time, my only option was to confess.

While it wouldn't kill the project completely, it would put an extended hold on it. But that wasn't the worst of it. The worst of it was letting my parents down by admitting how I'd been lying to them from the start. That was the part I didn't want to face. It was also the part that continued to cause the most stress.

I was pretty sure I'd developed a stomach ulcer, and unfortunately, that unbearable pain refused to go away no matter what I did.

"I'm sorry. I just want to help."

I tossed the pillow to the floor and sat up straight. "I understand, Claire. And I can't tell you how much I appreciate all you've done, but really, there isn't anything you can do at this point. I'm gonna have to come clean to my parents. So if you want to do something, you can keep my mind distracted for the rest of the weekend."

She wagged her brows, more than likely thinking about all the ways she could keep me busy for the next thirty-six hours. "I can do that. But first, I'm going to need you to change your clothes."

I glanced down at my grey sweats and band tee. "Why?"

"Because I want to take you somewhere, and what you're wearing isn't appropriate attire."

"So what should I wear?"

She furrowed her brow and tapped her chin in thought. "Jeans and a decent shirt. But not what you wear to work. Short sleeve would be best, but one with a collar."

I smiled and asked, "You want to take me on a date, don't you?"

Again, she froze, but only for a split second. I was pretty sure she was onto me by now.

She rolled her eyes and waved me off with a quick flip of her wrist. "Don't even start with me, Travis. Just put on something decent and meet me at my place."

I wasn't left with any room to argue. When Claire said something, nothing would change her mind, so I did as I was told and put on an outfit she would approve of. The entire time, I tried to figure out what she had planned.

By the time I made it next door, Claire was walking out. And holy shit. I had to quickly adjust myself to keep my impromptu semi from becoming noticeable. She was hot as hell—not that I was surprised; she was always extremely attractive, regardless of her attire. But tonight, she wore a short black skirt and a white top that showed off her belly button. Her heels made her almost as tall as me, but I still had a few inches or so on her.

"I couldn't have taken *that* long to change." I stood in awe of her, swaying as if I had already started drinking. Which wasn't the case. "You didn't possibly have enough time to do all that..."

Claire held out her arms, a small black purse in one hand, and glanced down at herself. My God, the way her calf muscles flexed in heels nearly did me in. And the most amazing part was she didn't have a clue how sexy she was. She might've been aware of how gorgeous she was, but if she did, she never acted like it. It made me wonder what she saw when she looked in a mirror, because when I looked at her, I saw a goddess.

"Well, getting dressed doesn't take but a minute or two, and I showered earlier today after baking, so I didn't need to worry about that. My makeup probably took the longest."

She was right about not wearing much, but she couldn't have been more wrong about not doing anything special. Her dark eyes were lined in black, her lashes so thick they could've been fake, and she wore a light-pink gloss on her lips, which made me want to suck it off.

I circled my finger in front of her head. "What about your hair? I've dated before…I've witnessed how long that takes."

As if completely oblivious to the things she did to me—specifically, in my pants—she ran her fingers through the top of her shiny locks. When she dropped her arm to her side, the soft strands fell into place, framing her face like each piece had been strategically put there by a photographer looking for the perfect shot.

"All I did was take out the braid." She acted as if most women looked this amazing after two minutes in the bathroom. It was clear she didn't have many friends, because if she did, she would've known better. "It was wet when I tied it back, and it dried in the braid, so it's kind of a cheater's way of curling it without a curler."

I barely heard a word she said. It was nearly impossible to pay attention to anything when she stood in front of me, especially when she was all dolled up. My thoughts were evenly split between my complete appreciation of her and flashes of memories of all the times I'd made her cry out in plea- sure. Seriously, making her come had to be on the top of the list of my most favorite things in the world.

"You look nice," she said while running her hand down the front of my shirt as if smoothing it out, even though we both knew there wasn't a single wrinkle in the fabric. "Are you about ready to go?"

That was enough to shake me out of my very perverted thoughts of all the things I wanted to do to her while she wore those heels. "Oh, yeah. Where are we going?"

"Someplace to have fun and take your mind off your problems." She winked and sauntered toward the road. "Piper will be here any minute to pick us up. I hope you don't mind, but I figured we could use a designated driver."

"I take it there will be drinks involved?"

She peered at me from over her shoulder with a naughty glint in her eye. "Correct. And tonight is my treat, got it? I won't put up with any arguing over the tab."

That would be impossible, and she knew it, too. I found it emasculating to have a woman pay for things if we were out together. Taking care of the bill at restaurants or the tab at bars was my responsibility. This was why I didn't agree with her demands. I'd let it go until the time came to pay the bill.

"You still haven't answered me. Where are we going?"

Her smile caused my dick to twitch when she said, "You'll just have to wait and see."

Piper showed up a minute later, and together, all three of us headed downtown. We spent the entire drive talking about whatever came to mind, so it took me a second to realize that we'd pulled into the parking lot of my brother's brewhouse, Deja Brew.

"I didn't think you liked beer?" I asked, surprised she'd want to take me here.

"Well, I don't, but you told me I might like what they have to offer since it's not like the regular, store-bought stuff. Not to mention, Piper's been before and said they have a full-service bar, so I'm pretty sure if I'm not crazy about their beer, they'll have *something* I like."

We got out of the car, and I was a bit annoyed to find out Piper would be tagging along. I couldn't complain, though, especially since she'd volunteered to be the sober driver, letting Claire and me drink without the worry of getting home safely. But that didn't mean I wasn't disappointed.

Around Piper, Claire wasn't as affectionate as she was when it was just the two of us. Which meant I couldn't hold her hand as we walked inside, touch her thigh while we sat at the bar, or steal kisses after she had a few drinks in her system.

Coming out tonight was meant to take my mind off my stress.

Being this close to her when she looked so damn sexy yet not able to touch her did nothing but *add* to my stress.

"Hey, Trav!" Bailey, the woman behind the bar, called out with an excited grin curling her ruby red lips. "Does Craig know you're here?"

I'd played a bit of hoops with my brother earlier today, so I knew he was around, but I didn't want to announce I was here. If he saw who I was with, he'd never let me live it down. So I shook my head and said, "I doubt it. I came with these two," referring to the brunette next to me and the raven-haired woman next to her.

"Want me to tell him you're here?"

Again, I shook my head, though I tried to act unaffected by the possibility of my brother seeing me. "Nah, I'm sure he's busy. Plus, I don't want to run the risk of him trying to take one of these pretty ladies away from me."

Bailey giggled and set a cocktail napkin in front of each of us.

She already knew what I wanted, considering I rarely switched it up, so I went ahead and picked out something for Claire to try…and Piper ordered sparkling water. But before Bailey could come back with our drinks, a large palm landed heavily with a smack on the back of my shoulder.

I didn't need to turn around to find out who it was, nor did I care to see the amusement on his face. So I didn't move. I simply said, "Hey, Craig," without looking his way.

Unfortunately, there was a vacant stool to my left, which he happily took. "Hey, bro. What brings you in tonight?"

"Same thing that brings me here every time I come by—alcohol." As soon as the words left my mouth, I grabbed the stein of Deja Brew orange lager from Bailey's hand before she had a chance to put it down in front of me. I couldn't have timed it more perfectly if I had tried.

Craig must've watched Bailey serve the other two drinks to my guests, because he leaned forward and quietly asked, "Who's the chick?"

I knew who he was asking about, but to keep it from being obvious, I hitched my thumb to my right and said, "Craig, you remember my neighbor, Claire." Then I pointed to her right. "And this is her best friend, Piper. Piper, this is my brother, Craig."

"Oh, hey!" Between his cheerful tone and familiar grin, I assumed they knew each other. After all, Claire had mentioned that Piper's been here before, so maybe they'd already met. But I didn't get a chance to ask because he quickly slipped off the stool and moved to stand next to Piper without another word.

For the first time since getting out of the car, I thought things could very well turn around for me. If he kept her entertained for the rest of the night, I wouldn't have to worry about keeping my hands to myself.

Before long, they fired up the karaoke machine. Every Saturday night, they had some sort of entertainment, whether it be a local band, a traveling comedian, or like tonight, the patrons belting tunes out of key to a room full of drunks. It worked out perfectly, though, because it pulled Piper to the stage in the corner, causing my brother to follow her like a puppy dog. It made me wonder if he had a thing for her.

However, I couldn't give that thought much attention because as soon as they were gone, Claire brought her lips close to my ear. In a sexy whisper loud enough for me to hear, she asked, "Which part of my body is your most favorite to touch?"

Just as I had hoped, the longer we hung out in the back corner with Bailey efficiently refilling our drinks, the more relaxed she became. Claire's true emotions emerged without her inhibition holding her back. This was the side of her that could guarantee to keep my mind off everything *except* her.

I cupped her chin and turned her head, making it easy to lick and suck her earlobe. Then I answered by huskily muttering, "Why don't I show you." It wasn't a question. It was a statement, and based on the gasp that escaped her lips, followed by a quick nod, it was obvious she understood.

Before she could respond, I slipped my hand under the hem of her very short skirt, my palm flat against her bare inner thigh. The heat of her skin created an inferno in the pit of my stomach. Between where we sat—on the side of the bar—and the way we were turned in toward one another, no one could see where my hand was or what we were doing. But it didn't stop the excitement of how risky it was. Especially considering it being Craig's bar. I doubted he'd ever forgive me if someone caught us.

Piper was in the middle of belting out another song, and with Craig sitting in front of the stage like a pathetic groupie, I figured they'd be occupied for at least the next several minutes.

Claire dropped her head back, closed her eyes, and let out a moan. It vibrated through her into me and set my entire system ablaze. I needed her, but I couldn't fathom being able to find a place with any semblance of privacy. The bathrooms were off-limits. Craig would kick us out and never let us come back.

Her reactions to my touch held me hostage and everything else faded. I somehow missed her hand on my thigh until she maneuvered it to cup my hardening bulge. If I didn't rein this in soon, there was no way I'd be able to hide the evidence of what she did to me. But I couldn't pull my hand away from the heat between her legs. It was as if a magnet kept me touching her.

With a sharp gasp, she parted her legs the tiniest bit, enough to move her panties to the side and slip one finger into her tight heat. There was no doubt in my mind that I had her very turned on.

So wet.

So warm.

I continued to tease her until she bucked her hips. It was only a matter of time before she'd come apart right here on this barstool. Even though I would've given anything to watch the ecstasy color her cheeks and feel her muscles tighten with pleasure, I couldn't risk it. She tended to be a bit loud when she came, so there was no way in hell we'd get away with it.

Slowly, I pulled my hand away and made her watch as I sucked her juices off my finger.

To my surprise, she pushed me away. Not just away, but off the stool. I wasn't sure what was going on until she grabbed my hand and announced, "Let's go bake a pie."

"Where?" Truthfully, I didn't care. I was only trying to see if she had a plan.

"Parking lot," she said, dragging me to the front door.

On our way out, I glanced over my shoulder to make sure Craig or Piper hadn't spotted us leaving. But they were too busy looking at the song list to care.

Claire didn't release me until we made it to Piper's car, which was parked in a secluded area away from the main entrance. Thank God, because I wanted to be the only one to witness her bent over the trunk. I moved behind her and squeezed her hips right before flipping up the back of her skirt and sliding her panties down her legs. The heels she wore made her tall enough to align the curve of her ass perfectly with my pelvis.

The outline of her skin in the moonlight almost did me in. My desire for her was so strong it consumed me. And I decided right then and there that I definitely needed to have her wear these heels again at home.

My balls ached and my dick strained against my pants, so I lowered my zipper and freed myself. I didn't even have to worry about entering her slowly because her readiness was evident, so I slammed into her. Without waiting for her to adjust, I dove in, over and over again, unable to control the pace. Frenzy took over and I lost all restraint. I pushed into her deeper than I ever had, thanks to the height of her heels.

I couldn't focus on my surroundings, which was dangerous, yet it fueled the passion. I plunged into her, and Claire's growing moans somewhat pulled me back to reality. If this continued much longer, someone would undoubtedly catch us. Then again, being with her felt so good I didn't care if the whole world saw us.

I reached around to rub Claire's clit. In less than thirty seconds, she began to buck, and I was finally able to let go of everything I'd held onto all night long. I grunted and voiced my approval as we both came together.

I laid on top of her for a moment and shut my eyes before blaring honking noises commenced.

"What the—"

I zipped my fly in record time before helping Claire pull her panties up her quivering legs. She seemed unsteady on her feet as she remained practically collapsed on the trunk of Piper's car, despite the car alarm blaring.

Claire used my arm for support as we rushed to escape the loud beeping without gaining unwanted attention. When we made it to the front door, I grabbed her arm, needing to wait a second before we went back inside. She stopped and turned to look at me, calm confusion lightly creasing her brow —she was too satisfied to show much concern or care about why I had stopped. But what little bit of bewilderment she had in her eyes quickly vanished with a sharp gasp once I gently cupped her cheek and lowered my face to hers.

This obviously wasn't our first kiss, but something about Claire made every time feel like the first. Maybe it was the way she took in a sharp breath right before our lips met, as if she'd been waiting her whole life for this. Or perhaps it was the way my entire world calmed at the sensation of her tongue on mine. Whatever it was, I never wanted this feeling to end.

"What was that for?" she whispered with her eyes still closed.

I laughed to myself and grazed the tip of her nose with mine. I wasn't sure when that had started or why, but I seemed to do it every time after sex without any forethought. It wasn't something I set out to do; it just happened, and it felt right.

"I needed to taste you."

Her lips slowly curled into a coy smile. "Well, good. Because I needed to taste you, too."

THE SHRILL RING of a phone pulled me out of my drunken sleep.

With one eye barely open, I couldn't see enough to figure out where I was. But as soon as I heard someone groan and felt a body shift next to me, recognition set in, making my memory a tad clearer. After Piper dropped us off last night, I'd walked Claire to her front door. We were both pretty intoxicated, so I wanted to ensure she got inside safely. I hadn't planned to stay, but she'd made it clear that her intentions were different. As soon as she had the door open, she grabbed my shirt and yanked me inside.

The phone stopped ringing, only to start all over again. I could tell by the ringtone it wasn't mine, so I mumbled, "Are you gonna answer that?"

She slapped her nightstand a few times, blindly searching for the source of the noise. Once she found it, she grumbled to herself and answered the call, putting it on speaker and closing her eyes again.

"Claire?" a deep voice came from the device sitting on her chest.

A sharp pang of jealousy cut me deep until she said, "Hey, Gramps."

He was quiet for a second, probably wondering if Claire was all right. Finally, he cleared his throat and asked, "I was calling to see if you had time today to come by the house. I want to go over a few things with you, and Maureen has some wedding ideas she wants to discuss."

"Yeah, sounds good." She held one hand over her eyes while the other gripped the phone, her voice extremely monotone.

By this point, I was wide awake. There was no way I could've gone back to sleep after this. Not only did her grandfather mention the wedding, which I specifically stated would never reach the planning stage, but Claire acted like there was nothing wrong with them organizing things for a wedding that would never take place.

I didn't speak up, though. I couldn't even if I wanted to. So I remained quiet, both eyes now fixated on the ceiling while I forced myself to breathe.

"Do you think you can make it for lunch?"

She hummed to herself for a moment. "What time is it now?"

"Almost ten."

"Probably not. But I can be there as soon as I roll out of bed and take a shower."

His laughter boomed through the speaker. "Should I set out an extra plate for dinner instead?"

"Yeah, sounds good."

How her grandfather didn't pick up on the repeated robotic responses was beyond me. If he did, he didn't say anything about it. Instead, he softened his tone and said, "All right, Claire-bear. Sleep well and call me when you're heading over. I love you."

She mumbled something resembling *love you too* before disconnecting the call. Part of me wondered if she'd still been asleep.

"Um, Claire?" I propped myself up with my elbow and practically burned a hole in her head with my panicked stare. "Why is your grandfather planning your wedding? Didn't you tell him we wanted a very long engagement?"

"Don't worry about it, Travis. This is his version of playing chicken…and I don't intend to squawk first."

"How can you be so cavalier about this? What if you're wrong, and he actually *is* getting things together for a wedding you promised we wouldn't have?" My chest constricted, anxiety taking hold of me in its unrelenting talons.

She rolled onto her other side and squinted at me. "We got engaged so fast, and then I asked for money, like, a second later. He's only making sure I'm not up to something. Seriously, don't sweat it. It'll be fine."

"How can you be so sure of that?" All of a sudden, a very problematic image crossed my mind. It was of a chapel, and we showed up only to find out they had everything set up for us to exchange vows that day. "How long do you plan to let this façade go on before we call it off?"

The corners of her lips curled, and her eyes fluttered closed. "Depends."

I waited for more, but when she didn't elaborate, I pressed, "Depends on what, Claire?"

Her eyes popped open, and her smile widened into something more flirtatious. "On how familiar you are with annulments."

My mouth fell open, and I was pretty sure my breathing stopped altogether. Her giggle proved she was only teasing, but I refused to trust that until I heard her admit it. Until then, I couldn't relax, fearful that, in the process of being a caring and helpful person, I'd gotten myself into an inescapable situation.

"Relax, Travis. Nothing's going to happen. I doubt they've even glanced at a wedding magazine. If anything, they've made a list of ideas and want to run them by me. I'll simply remind them that we are looking at an extremely long engagement. We've got a good excuse with the vineyard, anyway."

There was no way in hell I could calm down. Not only did I have the wedding issue to worry about, but while trying to reassure me, Claire inadvertently reminded me of another major point of stress in my life.

"What excuse would that be?"

With her eyes once again closed, she hummed to herself, much like she'd done on the phone with her grandfather. "You have a lot going on with the expansion, so it's not the time to make any plans."

I couldn't manage to do anything other than watch her as she fell back asleep. Even though I wanted to stay and enjoy the fact that I actually woke up next to her—which had never happened before—I needed to be alone so I could pull my hair out without any witnesses.

She was supposed to make my stress go away.

Not pile more on top of it.

CHAPTER 17

CLAIRE

I'D BEEN BAMBOOZLED, and it was all Travis's fault.

If he hadn't *thoroughly* worn me out until who knows what time in the morning, I wouldn't have been in such a bliss-fueled coma when Gramps called this morning. So thanks to Travis and his incredible ability to reset my brain like one would reboot a computer system, I was stuck going to see Gramps and his live-in hussy.

At some point, I'd have to let go of my hatred for Maureen, but not today. Probably not tomorrow, either. But one of these days, in the very distant future, I'd have to give in and learn to like her for my grandfather's sake. I couldn't deny how happy she made him, so realistically speaking, I didn't have a tangible reason to dislike her.

It also didn't help that she was so damn nice. Before I could slip out of my car, she had the front door open, a simple smile stretched across her aging lips while waving as if I couldn't see her standing in the doorway.

"If it isn't little miss Betty Crocker." She beamed with rosy cheeks.

I decided at that moment I would accept her as part of my life as soon as she stopped talking to me like I was ten. It wasn't like this woman didn't have grandkids of her own. She knew how this worked—just because I was a grandchild didn't mean I was an *actual* child.

"Hey, Maureen. Where's Gramps?"

She stepped back to let me into the house and pointed down the hallway. "He's on the computer in the office."

Without waiting for permission I didn't need, I went to the study and rapped my knuckle on the door a couple of times before walking in. As soon as Gramps saw it was me, his eyes lit up, brightening his entire expression. There was no denying he enjoyed it when I visited.

"This is a little unusual, you asking me over out of the blue. I hope everything's okay."

As I moved his way to hug him, I thought about the last time I'd sat in this room. It was the day he rejected my business proposal—which had been nearly a month and a half ago. At the time, I was hurt, but I'd gotten over it since then, especially since my pie sales continued to grow at the winery.

In fact, I'd gotten over a lot of things.

Since moving out, I felt content with my life for the first time. If Gramps hadn't forced me to spread my wings, I likely would've never discovered my love of baking. And I truly did love it; it was no longer a desperate means to a desperate end. Baking became the first thing to give me purpose since my parents died eight years ago. Not to mention, if I'd never moved out, I wouldn't have met Travis. And without him, the opportunity at the winery would've never existed.

As my dad used to say...*every storm cloud has a silver lining*.

"Of course everything's okay. Can't an old man miss his girl every once in a while? I never see you anymore." He kissed my cheek before pointing to the chair on the other side of the desk.

"Listen," I said, sitting on the edge of the seat with my spine ramrod straight and my shoulders pulled back. "You mentioned something about Maureen coming up with several wedding ideas, but I have to stop you there. To be honest with you, Gramps, we aren't quite at the planning stage yet."

"That's perfectly fine, Claire. Maureen got a list of contacts in the wedding business from a friend whose daughter recently got married. But I didn't ask you over to discuss your nuptials."

The atmosphere had just taken a drastic turn from light and airy to shady and stuffy. And considering I was a fraud who'd lied to him about being engaged, my guilty conscience refused to let me remain calm as I waited for him to spit it out.

"When you were here for your engagement party, we discussed Cutie Pies. I told you that you needed to put more time into it before I could even consider offering you the type of funding you were asking for."

With my breath held in my chest and my ass cheeks tightly clenched, I was unable to speak. So I simply nodded and waited to see where he was going with this.

"Honestly, Claire...I expected it to take *months* to see which way it would go. I would've guessed no less than six, and that's being quite generous to be fair. But at least by then, we should have an idea of how this business venture would pan out. So imagine my surprise when Maureen came home the other day with one of your pies."

Surprise lifted my brow and turned my mouth into the shape of an O.

"One of the women at the garden center gave her one, and she said it was the best pie she'd ever eaten. Once she found out it was one of *yours*, she went to the winery to check it out and discovered how well they've been doing."

I held up my hand to stop him long enough to ask, "How did she find that out?"

"About how well they're selling?" When I nodded, his expression brightened, and his eyes softened. "She asked the woman who owns the winery. She said they're always fresh because she can't keep them in stock, and they're usually sold out by three or four in the afternoon."

Everything after his explanation of Maureen talking to Mrs. Cabrera went in one ear and out the other. This was the first time I realized how easily I could be caught in my lie. Carla was Travis's mom, and Travis, according to Gramps and Maureen, was my fiancé. Whereas, according to Carla, Travis and I were nothing more than neighbors.

Dammit…this could go south fast. I needed to come clean, which was much easier said than done. My grandfather meant everything to me. I never wanted to disappoint him. Envisioning the look on his face after confessing my deepest, darkest secret was enough to keep me from opening my mouth.

"I'm so proud of you, Claire." The conviction in his tone calmed me somewhat.

I doubted he could say anything to settle my nerves completely, but at least I was able to breathe again. And unclench my ass cheeks. The tension literally started to melt away, although I still had a lot more to shed. And I would own up to it soon. Very soon.

But not right now.

"Thank you, Gramps. That means a lot."

He pulled out a folder from one of his desk drawers and set it in front of him. Crossing his arms over the top, he settled his attention on me. "How are your profits? Are you making enough in sales to cover the next batch as well as earn an income?"

I hesitated for a moment, trying to recall the colorful charts Piper and Travis had made for me. "Uh, yeah. I'm making headway, though not as much as I could if I had the ability to produce more. Right now, my kitchen is too small to bake more than I already do. But I'm working on it."

"Are you making enough to cover the business as well as living expenses?"

"Not yet, but I have a plan. Since I still have an allowance for the next three months to help cover the difference, my strategy is to reinvest every penny back into the business for now. My hope is to be able to fully support myself *and* Cutie Pies on my own by the time your monthly checks stop."

He nodded while mindlessly picking at the corner of the folder. "Do you have a bank account started solely for your business?"

"Yes, sir. I opened one as soon as I was offered the corner at the winery."

"Good. You'll want to deposit this straight away." He opened the folder and tore off a check that had already been written out. "Now, this isn't for the full amount you asked for in your proposal, and I'll tell you why. I went over those numbers, and I truly don't think you need that much. Especially with as well as you're already doing."

I took the check with a shaky hand and looked at the front. When he said it was less than I'd asked for, I became nervous it wouldn't be as much as I needed. But I was relieved and pleasantly surprised to read the amount, knowing it was more than enough for what I planned to do with it.

It could cover Travis's entire part of the expansion with a little left over to invest in my pies. I couldn't fully recall the original amount I'd asked for, so I didn't have a clue how much he'd taken off, but it wasn't important. At the end of the day, this was more than I expected—mainly because I'd given up on ever getting it.

"Wow, Gramps. I can't begin to thank you for—"

"Yes, you can," he interjected softly. "You can thank me by carrying on the Hansen name and succeeding in whatever you choose to do."

The backs of my eyes burned, so before the first tear could show itself, I slid off the chair and practically lunged at my grandfather, wrapping my arms tightly around his neck. It had been so long since I'd felt worthy of something.

Apparently, pretending life had stopped after losing my parents didn't do me any favors. But at the time, I couldn't imagine living without them. They were the two most important people in my life. I couldn't fathom being truly happy if they weren't here, like it would be a dishonor of some kind to carry on with life as if they were still alive. It never felt attainable, so I didn't even bother to try.

Until now.

Until I was forced to.

Piper had mentioned something about tough love once, and I still couldn't comprehend it all, but I believed my grandfather had done the right thing. I may have gone through it kicking and screaming, but I had to admit...I wouldn't change any of it for the world.

There was still so much to learn. I wasn't even close to being as mature or stable as I should've been at my age. But at least I'd become woman enough to recognize my shortfalls and brave enough not to stop until I got there.

"I also wanted to talk to you about this house," Gramps said, giving me a chance to resume my seat before he continued. "Your lease is for a year, correct?"

"Yeah, why?"

"Well, as I'm sure you're aware, this house is yours. It won't be solely in your name until you're twenty-five, but it doesn't change the fact that it belongs to you. Not me. I need to make sure you don't think I'm taking it from you. You'll have it back when your lease is up—unless you end up getting married before then."

The old me would've blurted out the first thing that came to mind to gain what I wanted. But I wasn't that impulsive person anymore.

Well, that was a lie.

When it came to Travis, I couldn't seem to keep my hands off him, so anytime he turned me on, I was more impulsive than I used to be. But when it came to saying anything to have my way, I'd learned to stop and think it through. I had way too much to lose by this point to be tempted down that rabbit hole.

I definitely didn't need any additional wrongs I'd have to right.

So instead of saying something I wouldn't be able to back up or follow through with, I asked, "If it's mine, why did you kick me out? And why did you move Maureen in?"

He huffed and glanced around the room. I'd never seen him so nervous, which didn't help my own apprehension. But then he released a long breath, and everything seemed to settle. "For starters, I worried about you living here alone. It's a big house, Claire. You've never had any major responsibilities before. You've never had to pay the bills and buy the groceries and cook the meals—and clean up after yourself—before. So I thought if you lived on your own, you'd be better equipped to handle a place of this magnitude by yourself."

It made sense, but I was still a little leery. After all, he had yet to explain why Maureen lived there if the plan all along was to give the house back to me.

Thankfully, he continued with his explanation. "As far as Maureen goes, we wanted to live together, and since it'd be another year before I can establish my own place, it made more sense for her to move in. I'm no spring chicken." He chuckled. "We don't have years to be engaged or wait until we're married. Our clocks have been ticking for quite a while."

I trusted him; after all, he was the only one who'd stepped up to the plate to care for me without any hidden agenda. He didn't have a reason to lie to me. But I had a hard time letting go of my preconceived notions about why he kicked me out in the first place. It was much easier to have my guard up and not let anyone in.

Suddenly, my heart tightened at a thought. "What if I don't want the house?"

"Well, it's yours to do what you want with it. Keep it, sell it, rent it out...I don't care."

I didn't want to sell it; it was the last place I'd seen my parents alive. I couldn't get rid of that. And I hated the thought of renting it out. I couldn't chance having people come in and destroy the things that reminded me of my parents the most.

However, I wasn't sure if I could live in it alone, either. It was one thing to be there with Gramps, but if he left, I'd be in this big house all by myself. That thought scared the shit out of me.

"Calm down, Claire-bear." Gramps reached out and placed his hand over mine. His gentle eyes soothed my soul enough so I could take in a full breath without hyperventilating. "You don't have to make any decisions now. The house isn't going anywhere, and as of this minute, neither am I. But I won't be able to stay here much longer. I'm getting older, and I need a smaller place. Preferably one without stairs."

A burst of unexpected laughter escaped at the thought of how he had to waddle up the stairs as it was. Given a few more years, he'd probably have to install one of those seat lifts to carry him up.

I moved around the desk to give him a proper hug and kiss. I'd wasted so much time being angry—at him, at my parents, at God. This was the first time in as long as I could remember that I wasn't mad. I was grateful and appreciative. And I was able to experience those emotions without the onslaught of guilt.

Things were definitely looking up.

I COULDN'T WAIT to surprise Travis with the good news that he wouldn't have to disappoint his parents after all. In fact, I was so eager to see him that I used my fork and spoon as shovels, stuffing my mouth before finishing the previous bite. How I didn't choke on dinner was beyond me.

I just wanted to get home.

And when I got there, I didn't bother going to my place first.

It would've been a waste of time.

"Travis!" I pounded the side of my fist on his front door. "Travis, it's me. Open up!"

Finally, after what felt like a million minutes, he opened the door wearing a pleased smile on his face. The sheer look of happiness to see me was something I'd grown rather fond of. Although, I continued to ignore what it meant. I wasn't ready for that yet.

"Can I come in? I have something exciting for you."

He rolled his eyes but stepped aside to let me in. "What is it...a wedding date? Or did they reserve a church? At this point, I'm ready to say just tell me when and where, and I'll be there."

Stunned, I asked, "You realize we're not *actually* getting married, right?"

"Yeah, but I'm kinda scared what'll happen if I don't go along with whatever you and your grandfather are planning. I may end up finding myself drugged and tied to a pole like a scarecrow at the altar."

I couldn't help but laugh at his ridiculousness. But as strange as it sounded, if I had to marry someone, I'd choose Travis. He made me feel safe. Not to mention, he also had the most amazing penis I'd ever seen, and he knew how to use it to bring me unbelievable pleasure. There were other reasons I'd pick him, but those were the most important ones.

He waited until I took my spot on his couch before sitting down. Concern lined his face as he studied me, and part of me wanted to drag this out for the fun of it. If he got to pick at me about going on dates, then I should be able to use this to my advantage.

Except, I was too excited to share the news to prolong the announcement.

"I found a way to move forward with the vineyard expansion without having to tell your parents about the issues with the loan." I watched his expression change. It was the slightest difference, yet I was still able to pick up on it. "My grandfather gave me the check I'd asked him for back at the engagement party when I presented my business plan."

"That's really awesome news, Claire...but what does it have to do with me? It's for Cutie Pies, not Uncorked Vineyards." He sounded like he was holding his breath.

"I don't need it all. I've been doing quite well—mainly thanks to you—so I only need a tiny portion of it."

Travis shook his head and stared at his feet. "I fail to see how that has anything to do with me. I'd never take your money. Especially after everything you've gone through to get it. Don't give it away. You'll regret it."

"No I won't. And as I recall, not too long ago, you told me that if you had a way to get the money to make your dreams come true, you'd take it. Well, buddy...here it is."

Annoyance flashed across his eyes, though it was likely caused by having his own words thrown back in his face. "You're not listening to me, Claire. This money was given to you to invest in baking."

"Oh my *God*, Travis. Cutie Pies is doing fine."

"One thing I've learned from owning my own business is you can always use the extra cushion, regardless of how well you're doing. You can never predict what might happen or what opportunities might come up."

I couldn't denounce his argument, considering he wasn't wrong. Having funds in the bank would never be a bad thing. However, I'd come to learn there are things in life more important than a large savings account. When I'd come up with the plan to ask my grandfather for money, Travis had been the main reason. I wanted to help him as much as he'd helped me.

"I've listened to you stress over the vineyard and letting your parents down for weeks. Meanwhile, I've been rather stress-free. A lot of it thanks to you. So if this helps you, then I don't care if I never see a penny from the check."

"Don't be ridiculous. You can't live without money, Claire."

"I never said I could. However, I do believe I could live perfectly fine on the income I'm making with my pies at the winery." It'd be difficult, but I was confident I could succeed on my own without this money. I covered his hand with mine and leaned toward him, silently begging him to give in. I'd never felt this desperate to help someone before Travis. "Please, let me do this for you."

Finally, he shifted in his seat to face me, his shoulders practically squared with mine. "I can't accept your money, and you know it."

I managed to swallow my groan, but I hadn't been as successful with hiding my eye roll. "At the end of the day, it's my decision what I want to do with my grandfather's check. And if I say I don't need it, then I don't need it. Okay?"

He dropped his gaze, ran his tongue over his bottom lip, and sighed.

I'd been told in the past that I always unapologetically got my way. And for the most part, that was true. This time, however, getting my way meant helping someone else, and for that, I refused to apologize.

And to be honest, it felt damn good.

CHAPTER 18
TRAVIS

I took a deep breath, needing the moment to formulate an acceptable response. This was the *last* thing I expected Claire to say, so I was at a loss for the right words to use. Finally, I sighed and met her stare, making sure I had her full attention when I said, "You're absolutely right—it is your decision. But you can't force someone to take it, so technically, I have a say in it, too."

She didn't speak for a moment, proving she'd anticipated a different response. "Are you seriously telling me you would rather tell your parents you don't have the funds to expand on the land you just purchased than take my money?"

"That's exactly what I'm saying."

"I don't understand, Travis…you'd take a loan from a bank, but not from me?"

She wasn't going to make this easy. "That's entirely different, Claire. One is a bank—handing out loans is a service they provide. And the other is you…" My cheeks flamed with heat as I thought about what she was to me, but I quickly shook it off and continued. "You're my neighbor and friend. Getting my mail if I'm not home, signing for a package if I need you to, and giving me a cup of sugar if I run out are parts of your job description, *not* financing my vineyard."

"Okay, but if I have the means to be both your neighbor *and* your banker, why turn me down? It would be one thing if I needed it, but I don't. You, my friend, need it." Her motivation remained unclear, yet I trusted wholeheartedly that it came from a good place.

There were only a couple of reasons I would ever accept money from someone outside my family, whether as a gift or a loan. And if I did, it would

157

have to be the absolute *last* resort. Regardless of how tough it would be to confess to my parents or how hard she pushed, I wouldn't take a penny from her.

"You say you don't need it, but you're not looking at the big picture," I started with a soft tone so I wouldn't offend her while simultaneously rejecting her offer. "You may be doing quite well for yourself now, but without capital, you can't advance. And isn't that the ultimate goal of starting your own business: growing your brand?"

Every time I gave a reason why I couldn't accept her help, she seemed relieved, as if already prepared with a rebuttal at the tip of her tongue. And this time was no different. Her shoulders relaxed, and a spark of hope brightened her eyes. "I can do both."

"How?"

"I can put aside a portion of the check for Cutie Pies while I work toward making enough profit to cover both my business *and* personal expenses. But I don't need much, which leaves the rest sitting in a bank. It makes more sense if it gets put to good use. And who better to use it than you?"

"This is what I mean, Claire. You can't increase your profits without expanding your inventory, and you can't do that without a proper kitchen. I've heard you complain about yours many times—about how you don't have enough room and how much easier things would be with a second oven. To have that, you need to lease space...*which costs money.*"

Again, the corners of her mouth curled, telling me she had another answer prepared. "I'm not sure if you saw the kitchen at my grandfather's house while we were there for the party, but it's perfect for what I need, and he said I can use it anytime I want. So I don't need to rent anything."

"Okay, but you can't borrow your family's kitchen forever."

"I won't have to. Gramps told me tonight that when my lease is up, he'll give me back the house." She'd mentioned something before about the house being hers, except she'd never clarified what she meant. "They'll move out, which will give me the entire place to myself."

"You still haven't explained the house situation," I said, prodding her to spill more information without making her close herself off like the last time we'd broached this subject.

Thankfully, she seemed to keep her walls down...somewhat. "It's part of the trust, so it's not technically mine until I turn twenty-five, but Gramps said he's really proud of how far I've come since moving out, so as long as I continue along the same path, he's okay giving it back sooner."

"Then why did you leave to begin with?"

Claire rolled her eyes and flicked her wrist, as if waving off my question, yet she answered anyway. "He said it was to teach me responsibility."

"You don't believe him?"

She flattened her hair with both palms and stared at the floor for a moment. "I believe him, but I think it was an unnecessary, harsh, and extreme way to do it. In my opinion, he could've taught me these things himself while we were both under the same roof. A mother bird doesn't shove her babies out of the nest without teaching them first how to fly."

I figured this wasn't the right time to inform her that fledglings are, in fact, kicked out of the nest and forced to learn how to fly on their own. Instead, I decided to stay on topic. "Don't you still have, like, nine months left on your lease? I'm sorry, but I don't see you going to your grandfather's house every day until you move back."

"You're not hearing me, Travis. I've already made up my mind, and I plan to put some of the money aside for myself. So if I need help getting through the next nine months, I'll have access to it. But I don't need it all."

I grabbed her hand and held her eager gaze. "I understand what you're saying, but it doesn't change anything—I still can't accept your overly generous offer. I wouldn't be able to look at myself in the mirror if I did. But your gesture means more to me than you'll ever know."

"What if I told you I asked for extra to begin with, knowing I wanted to share with you? And that was before I started doing so well, which means I now have *way* more than I would ever need. Taking it wouldn't leave me stranded in the slightest."

As much as I wanted to accept it and put an end to the stress I'd been buried in for the last couple of months, I couldn't. Claire meant more to me than money, so if I had to give up my dreams to prove that her worth didn't have a dollar sign in front of it, then so be it.

I shook my head. "It doesn't change my mind, Claire."

With a stiff smile, she said, "It's okay. I get it. However, if you change your mind, it's yours. No questions asked. No strings attached."

"Thanks, Claire." I squeezed her hand. Feeling the need to change the subject, I asked, "Would you like a glass of wine?"

"As long as it's a big glass. And I'm talking, like, a *large* glass."

IT'D BEEN a week since Claire offered to help me pay for the expansion, and she had continued to reiterate her offer every day since.

I knew I was running out of time to confess to my parents that I didn't have the funds to expand on the new land. Getting that off my chest would not only remove a lot of my stress, but it would also stop Claire from continually trying to shove her money down my throat. The longer this dragged on, the harder it would be in the end for everyone.

So I decided to put an end to it. Now.

First thing Monday morning, I walked into the winery and headed straight to my dad's office. I didn't bother dropping off my leather planner and lunch on my desk. This needed to be dealt with immediately. I'd put it off long enough.

"Hey, Pop. Do you have a minute?"

Dad looked up from an open folder with a glint of pride in his eyes at the sight of me, which only made this harder. "I have all the time in the world for you, son," he said, gesturing for me to take a seat across from him. "What's going on?"

"Well, I wanted to discuss the plans for the new property."

He beamed with bright, excited eyes. "Your timing is perfect. I received this offer last night, and I think it's nothing short of an answered prayer."

I took the folder and began to flip through the pages. There were too many things flying through my head to pay attention to the words, so I set it on the desk and asked, "What is this?"

"A couple of months ago, Enrique put out feelers with a few local nurseries regarding the cost of ready-to-plant vines."

I held up a finger, making him pause so I could ask, "Why? We've never entertained that option because it's too expensive. What's the difference now?"

He released a heavy breath and leaned closer with his hands folded on top of his desk. "With the purchase of the distillery, we decided to consider all avenues that would produce earnings quicker."

"I understand, but this would cost a lot more upfront. Grafting is seventy-five percent cheaper than replanting. Not to mention, we still have to pay to have the land irrigated, which isn't cheap." The more I said, the faster the words came out, and the more muffled my hearing became. My anxiety had grown increasingly harder to control over the last couple of months, but this topped the charts.

Thankfully, my dad remained calm. He was a true leader, one who kept a sedated attitude, even while surrounded by chaos. "We haven't forgotten the cost of getting the land ready. Like I said, this might be more at the start, but it also ensures we'll begin turning a profit *years* earlier than we would with grafting. And don't forget, son…the success rate of grafting is only about sixty percent on the first pass, which would mean more out-of-pocket expenses down the road. It's a gamble either way, but with this option, paying a little extra upfront could increase our profit more than projected."

I tried to calm down by taking deep breaths while doing my best not to give myself away. This could change everything. I didn't have the funds to cover my share of the cheap route, let alone practically doubling the price to utilize the land sooner. Panic consumed me at the thought of coming clean now, even though that had been my plan until about two seconds ago.

But then a light bulb flickered above my head. I closed the folder in my lap and set it on my dad's desk. "Listen, Pop, this all sounds great, but did you forget you have a third person involved in this project? How do you expect me to finance the expansion if we take this route?"

"No, Travis, we didn't forget about you. Your mother and I talked about it many times while we were waiting to close on the property. This land was an opportunity we couldn't pass up, especially once you were on board. And don't forget, we tried to discuss the financial side with you, but you shut us down time and time again, saying you had it covered."

I couldn't argue because he was right. Had his email about our neighbor's offer actually made it to my inbox, I never would've dismissed the type of in-depth conversation we needed to have about it. But again, that wasn't something I could tell him, so rather than speak up and defend my side, I suffered in silence and continued to listen.

"Like I mentioned, our family is investing in more than the vineyard right now. We also have the distillery, and we decided not to let either purchase affect the other. We refuse to favor one son over another. And much like this venture, the distillery also won't turn a profit right away. We wanted to look into ways to minimize the length of time before we start seeing a return on our investments, so we asked Enrique to put some feelers out, and he found this place." He tapped the front of the folder without dropping his gaze.

"I fully understand everything you're saying, and I agree. But if we can't afford it, then there isn't anything we can do about it. It's not like I can run back to the bank and see if they can increase my loan *again*." I nearly slipped and confessed right then and there, which would've taken this conversation in an entirely different direction. "I barely got approved this last time."

If this was what he wanted to do, I figured I could go along with it yet suggest we hold off a bit. This way, I could buy myself a little more time to come up with the money without having to tell my dad how I'd wasted his on land we couldn't use.

"However..." I tilted my head and gave him what I intended to be a let's-make-a-deal stare. There was no way to ensure if I had executed it correctly, but based on the tension along my forehead and between my brows, I felt rather confident I at least came close. "If you could hold off on doing anything until after next season—including preparing the land—then it would give me time to save, and then maybe I could afford this option."

Soft laughter bubbled up from my dad's chest. "You haven't let me finish."

This made me nervous and firmly rooted my ass in my seat.

"This nursery has offered us a drastic discount if we order all our vines through them, which wouldn't be a problem considering they have nearly every variety under the sun. It would bring our total cost down and a lot closer to what it *would be* with grafting. But this would have to be something we act on now. It's a one-time offer with a firm expiration date." He turned his wrist to look at his watch and then added, "A decision needs to be made ASAP because we're running out of time to prepare the land for spring planting."

My heart pumped so fast my entire body felt on the verge of overheating. "Then I guess we have to say no. I'm sorry, Pop, but I don't have that kind of money."

"That's okay, son. When your mother and I first came up with this idea, we considered your financial share of this project, and we're willing to cover your portion of the additional cost. We would never consider doing something so drastic like this and expect you to pull cash out of thin air."

I was right—this *literally* changed everything.

It put my plan to come clean to my dad on the back burner for now.

He wasn't wrong about this being an incredible opportunity. I doubted something like this would ever come around again. We'd be fools to turn it down, but this plan would fail without the funds. I didn't see another option.

If I didn't do something, I would've made my parents purchase the land for nothing. I would've wasted everyone's time and money. My gut twisted as guilt and regret ate at me—I should've been honest from the start. I still would've upset my parents and killed my dream of expanding the vineyard, but at least I wouldn't have put my entire family's legacy in jeopardy.

I needed to come up with the money.

There were no ifs, ands, or buts.

"Well, I assume you guys will want to make that back first. So come up with a strategy for me to pay you guys off quickly, one that won't leaving me penniless, and I'll give you my decision no later than tomorrow. Does that work?"

"They want an answer within two days, so getting back to me tomorrow would be perfect." He jotted down something on a small notebook next to his computer and then returned his attention to me. "You came in here for something. What was it you wanted to talk about? Something to do with the land?"

I grabbed my leather binder and lunch bag and scooted to the end of the seat, readying myself to stand and leave. "It doesn't matter anymore, Pop. It was about the expansion project, but the replanting idea solved it for me."

My stomach soured after talking to my dad, as if I'd chugged a gallon of expired milk. And it only grew persistently worse for the rest of the day. Rather than do any of my regular daily tasks, I'd spent hours on end making phone call after phone call. Even the places that charged insane interest rates and prided themselves on accepting every applicant turned me down for a loan. I'd been prepared to come clean this morning, but now, just thinking about the irreversible damage I'd cause by confessing the truth made my nervous system go haywire.

I'd found myself in a lose-lose situation.

My only option was to pick the one with the least amount of destruction.

I PACED BACK and forth in front of my window, waiting for Claire to get home. Normally, she was already there by the time I returned from work, but not today. And the longer it took for her to show up, the closer I was to dying from either this ulcer perforating the lining of my stomach or a massive heart attack.

About two hours later, Claire finally pulled into the driveway, and I couldn't have been happier to see her fancy SUV. Granted, the only reason I was so desperate to see her was to get this metaphorical castration over with. At the end of the day, nothing would've made me feel better, but at least the anticipation would be gone.

When she saw me stalk toward her, her eyes lit up and brightened her face. As much as I wanted to bathe in that sight, the burning tightness in my chest wouldn't let me.

"Did you come to help?" she asked, walking around to the back of the vehicle.

"Where were—" My question died on my tongue once she lifted the back gate, revealing boxes of pastries. "Oh, did you use your grandfather's kitchen?"

She gaped at me with knitted brows. "Yeah, I told you last night I'm going to start going over there at least three times a week to bake."

Truthfully, I couldn't recall what she'd told me. I'd been so stressed lately I struggled to find my way out of my own head long enough to comprehend what people around me were saying. I hated it because I never wanted her to think I wasn't listening, so I shuffled past that by saying, "Oh, yeah. I remember now."

"Can you grab a couple of these for me?" She pointed to the boxes before walking off to open the fridge she kept in her garage.

I did as she asked and helped her put away all four boxes. "Why didn't you drop these off at the winery? Seems like double the work to load them into the car, unload them here, load them back up tomorrow, only to unload them once more when you deliver them to my mom."

"I'd planned on it, but when I called her, she said they weren't home, and the winery was already locked up. So I was kinda hoping you would be able to take them with you tomorrow morning." She raised her brows and gave me the smile she used when she wanted me to agree to something.

Regardless of needing a huge favor, I still would've done it. I probably would've done almost anything she asked of me. "Of course. Only if you're awake when I'm ready to leave, though. I think I'm still traumatized from waking you up at *the ass crack of dawn*," I said, mimicking the attitude she'd given me a few times after she first moved in.

"Don't worry, I'll definitely be up. I have to go back to Gramps's house to bake some more. I got so much done today, but I still have so much more to do. I plan to only be in the kitchen three days a week, so I can at least have a couple of days to focus on other business matters."

I could only laugh to myself. The supply she gave the winery on a daily basis never made it to the end of the day, so baking extra would only mean they'd last until five o'clock. She could probably spend seven days a week in front of the oven and still sell out. Her pastries were *that* amazing, and I was beyond proud of her. Nearly everyone in and around Tesorita had heard about them.

"Did you come over to help me with the boxes, or did you want to hang out?"

I took a deep breath, struggling to bring up the money situation. Considering she'd asked me about it every damn day, I figured if I waited a bit longer, she'd bring it up herself, which would keep me from having to grovel. "I wasn't aware there were boxes to unload, so clearly, I'm here for something to eat."

She rolled her eyes in amusement and invited me in.

Rather than have a slow-cooker meal ready for dinner, she'd left chicken in a homemade marinade all day. I was impressed. It seemed impossible to compare this woman to the one who moved in three months ago. Even though I didn't really know her back then, I felt like she'd experienced more growth than I could only imagine.

I completely understood why her grandfather was proud of her—I certainly was.

We'd managed to make it through forty-five minutes of cooking, maybe half an hour of eating, then fifteen to twenty minutes of cleaning up without the money being mentioned. For the last seven days, she'd practically begged me to take it within five minutes of saying *hi*. And then the one time I was prepared to accept, she didn't once mention it. Which meant I'd have to bring it up, and to be honest, I was terrified. Taking it from her was bad enough, but outright asking for it made me feel like a complete pile of shit.

I reminded myself of my decision to choose the lesser of two evils and took a deep breath.

"So, I wasn't entirely truthful earlier," I said after we moved to her couch to let our food settle. "While I enjoyed dinner—like I always do—that wasn't why I stopped by. I wanted to talk to you about your offer."

She narrowed her gaze and knitted her brows as if slightly confused. Finally, after several drawn-out seconds, understanding lit her eyes. "The money?" When I nodded, she adamantly shook her hand and waved both hands in front of her face. "You don't have to worry about that anymore. I got the hint. I won't say another word."

"No, it's okay, Claire. I'm not upset about it at all."

"Oh, good. Listen, I'm so sorry. I never meant to be pushy."

"I know, and it's all right. I promise."

Claire dropped her hand to my thigh, and in that one move, she managed to change so much about this conversation. First was the apprehension that filled me at the start of our evening. It had completely vanished. Not only vanished, but her touch covered me in a wave of warm contentment. And the second thing it changed was my attention span; the heat of her palm had a way of disrupting my focus.

Then again, it might've also been the fact that she continued to talk. "I'm just glad it didn't come between us. Money has a way of ruining relationships, and I wouldn't be able to forgive myself if I'd let that happen with us."

"Hold up…are you saying we're in a relationship?" I teased, loving the way her cheeks glowed like brake lights on a desolate road at midnight. "I mean, I'm fine with it; I just want a heads-up before you take my last name."

Her mouth opened and closed, though she never removed her hand from my thigh. She pulled in a deep breath, her chest rising with the long inhale and deflating with the rushed exhale, and then she returned her eyes to mine. "You're fine with us being in a relationship?"

Either she was calling my bluff, or she'd finally given up on trying to deny it. Oddly enough, though, the latter didn't bother me. It kind of made my heart pump harder, and not in a bad way. "Claire…we eat together most nights, and correct me if I'm wrong, but neither of us is sleeping with anyone else. What would you call that?"

"Fantastic neighbors?"

Laughter ripped through my chest, causing me to take a moment to calm down so I could continue our conversation. "Okay, Claire. If that's what you want to call it."

"Is this how it happens?" Fear colored her expression. "One day, you're baking pies, and the next, you're an old married couple?"

I waited for the smirk to tug one side of her mouth before I replied. "Yeah, but it's all right because I foresee us baking pies for a very long time."

Desire burned in her stare; it was a look I'd seen often. And because I was so familiar with that glint in her eye, I felt confident we'd end up tossing this conversation aside, along with our clothes, if I didn't steer things back to the issue at hand.

"Hold on, Claire. We got off track a bit. Forget the relationship status for a moment because I do need to discuss your offer." I reached forward to touch her leg in a move to keep her from interrupting, but I thought better of it at the last second, and instead, I grabbed her hand. "I need you to be clear about something real quick…are you saying it's now off the table?"

"No, not at all. I only meant you don't have to worry about me bringing it up all the time. I talked to Piper about it today, and she thinks I'm putting you on the spot, and that's the last thing I want to do."

"I honestly appreciate that, but I need you to ask me one more time. Please." I held my breath, hoping she followed my hint. If not, I'd have to be more obvious, and I would do almost anything not to have to do that. This was embarrassing enough.

"You want me to offer you the money again?"

I nodded and said, "Just one more time."

"*Oh-kay…*" She clearly wasn't picking up what I was putting down. "Have you changed your mind about it? Do you want to borrow it now?"

This wasn't how I saw it going, but beggars can't be choosers. And at this moment, I was the epitome of a beggar. "As long as the offer's still on the table."

"Of course it is." Enthusiasm brightened her face as if she'd won a prize.

Not wanting to excite her too much, I held up one finger and waited until I had her undivided attention. "But before I officially accept, I need to make one thing clear."

Worry darkened her expression as she nodded, waiting for me to continue.

"Listen, I realize I told you to forget the relationship subject for a moment, but it needs to be mentioned now. Before I take a cent from you, I need you to understand something. I need *both* of us to be on the same page regarding it. Okay?"

"Regarding what?" The worry on her face melded with confusion. "Our relationship?"

"Yeah."

Claire shook her head and waved me off, hijacking my opportunity to put all my cards on the table. "Don't worry about it, Travis. We're not only neighbors, we're also friends. Extremely good friends if I say so myself."

"Okay, but—"

"There are no buts. I fully understand we aren't *together* like that. We have sex—and as you've pointed out, only with each other—and we spend a lot of time together, but I'm not foolish enough to confuse the situation." Technically, she was confused about the situation because that wasn't at all what I was trying to say.

"You're not hearing me, Claire. I—"

"Yes, I am." She leaned closer and lowered her voice, putting one hand high on my thigh. The twinkle in her eye implied one thing, but her words said something very different when she added, "And what I'm trying to tell you is that you have nothing to worry about. We aren't in a romantic relationship. We're friends—end of story. Borrowing money won't blur those lines."

It wasn't like I'd gone into this with some sort of fantasy of her jumping into my arms once I made my feelings for her known. And it wasn't like I had any plans to establish an official relationship, either. All I wanted was to make it clear that money was the absolute *last* thing I wanted from her. And if I had to choose between the loan or her, I'd pick her every single time. So I couldn't understand why it felt like she just dropped an atomic bomb on my expectations, leaving my hopes and dreams in a disintegrating pile of ash and soot.

"So, now that's out of the way…are you going to let me help you?" While she beamed at me with hopeful, animated eyes, I couldn't do more than offer a simple nod. Lucky for me, though, she appeared too excited to pick up on any amount of dejection in my response. Which she proved when she asked, "Seriously? Does this mean you're going ahead with the expansion?"

"Yeah, I guess I am."

"What changed?"

Emptiness continued to consume me the entire time I described the change in plans for the new land. But at least it allowed me time to settle my emotions and come to terms with where we stood.

"Have I ever told you how erotic it is when you use that sexy vineyard lingo? Because it's super hot. Like, it's a total turn-on." She shifted on the couch until she straddled my lap. "In fact, listening to you has me so wet I may need you to irrigate my crop."

Rather than explain how that made no sense, I grabbed her from behind the knees and stood, disregarding the voice in my head telling me this would only make things worse in the end. After all, this was the kind of relationship she wanted from me, and while somewhere inside I knew I wanted more, I rationalized to myself that this was better than nothing at all.

I playfully tossed her onto her bed and crawled on top of her, my fists digging into the mattress on either side of her head. When she wrapped her legs around me and tried to pull me closer, I grazed the side of her neck with the tip of my nose and whispered, "Why do I feel like this makes me a prostitute?"

She gasped and slowly rolled her hips, grinding against me. Finally, with a subtle moan, she said, "No idea, but I really like that thought. It does things to me. It also means I can cross *sleeping with a hooker* off my bucket list."

I pulled away enough to look at her, questioning her seriousness for a moment. But the second she wagged her brows, I was willing to pretend to be anything she wanted me to be. "Well, good, because now I can cross off *getting paid for sex* from mine."

I couldn't bury myself inside her fast enough.

There was something about this woman that drove me crazier than anyone else ever had...as long as I ignored the reality that she was also capable of hurting me deeper than anyone else ever had.

CHAPTER 19
CLAIRE

"OH, THANK GOD YOU'RE HERE!" I abandoned my position in front of the cooling rack and ran to Piper, practically mauling her as I grabbed her in a tight, desperate embrace.

"I came as fast as I could. What's going on?" Her voice sounded muffled thanks to my hair covering her face.

I'd called Piper this morning amid a mental breakdown and begged her to come to my grandfather's house to help me fulfill the Thanksgiving orders I'd received from the winery. "It's utterly ridiculous how many people in the area want apple pies for the holiday."

Travis's mom, Carla, had thought it would be a brilliant idea to take special requests for Thanksgiving. Neither of us ever expected the turnout. She'd stopped accepting orders a week ago...and I *still* had to spend the entire week in front of the oven to fill them all.

"Seriously, whatever happened to pumpkin?" I continued to complain. "Based on how many I have to bake, it's safe to assume *no one* in a two-hundred-mile radius is having pumpkin pie at Thanksgiving."

Piper waved me off and set her purse on the floor next to the kitchen table—which was completely covered with trays of treats waiting to go into one of the ovens—and came to stand next to me. "How long have you been at this?"

"Today? Or in total?"

She raised her brows and laughed beneath her breath. "That long, huh? Well, I'm here now, so utilize me. We can use this time to catch up, too. I feel like I don't have a clue what's going on in your life these days."

"Tell me about it. I don't think *I* know what's going on in my life these

169

days, either. I wake up, bake, go to sleep, and start all over again the next morning." I held out my hands as if to showcase the countless trays and racks lining every bit of counterspace available. "I've pretty much been at this for the last forty-eight hours. I slept here last night so I didn't have to waste time driving back and forth."

"Ah, so now you know what it's like for the rest of us poor souls who have to work for a living. Is it all you thought it would be?"

I glanced around and took in the scene before me. Until this very second, I'd almost been on autopilot, not once taking a step back and looking at it through the lens of my old self. I'd busted my ass to prove to Gramps I could be responsible, yet I hadn't taken a moment to admire my accomplishments. And for the first time—in probably my entire life—I felt proud of myself.

"You know what, Pipes? No, it's not at all what I thought it would be."

She slapped a hand over her mouth to contain her laughter. "Why not?"

"Well, I thought I'd bake a few pies and make a ton of money. I guess I skipped the startup side of things and jumped straight to having employees to do all the work for me. I'm exhausted, Piper. Like, dead-on-my-feet exhausted." I bit my tongue, not wanting my whining to be mistaken for complaining, because that wasn't how I felt at all. "But I can't put into words how accomplished I feel."

For the first month and a half of having my corner at the winery, I'd sold out of pies every day by four o'clock. Then Gramps had let me use his kitchen so I could increase my inventory. In the last six weeks, I'd not only increased my production, but I'd also been able to branch out and try new things. And still, we somehow managed to sell out before the end of the day —but at this point, I didn't see a way to keep that from happening.

I genuinely had *nothing* to complain about.

Piper grabbed an apron off the hook next to the fridge and sidled up next to me, playfully bumping my hip with hers in the process. "Welcome to adulthood, my friend. Enjoy this stage in life while it lasts, because in the blink of an eye, you'll be getting married and having babies, and then you'll *really* be exhausted. It'll make these last few months seem like free time."

"First of all, how would you know? You're neither married nor a mother. And secondly…don't be ridiculous; I'm never getting married."

She twisted at her hips and stretched her neck, dramatically peering toward the kitchen door. With a thumb hooked over her shoulder and two deep creases in her brow, she lowered her voice and asked, "Does this mean you've told them about Travis?"

At first, I didn't have the faintest idea what she meant, but then she pointed to her left ring finger, and it all came rushing back to me. Travis and I had been beyond busy this past month, so our non-engagement didn't come to mind much. Gramps and Maureen asked about him frequently, but he'd become a significant part of my life, so I hadn't thought much of it.

"You mean, like, have I told them the truth?" Now I was the one peering around the pantry to keep an eye on the closed door. "No, not yet."

"Why not?"

I shrugged. "Umm...it hasn't come up?"

She glared at me with those perceptive eyes piercing mine, forcing me to look away. "I see what this is. You don't want to give up the idea of being with him, and *that's* why you haven't said anything. As soon as you told me about your hot neighbor, I knew this would happen. Well, not the engagement part—I doubt anyone could've seen that coming. But you falling for Travis...yup, I called it. Granted, I never thought it'd be much deeper than a wham-bam-thank-you-ma'am kind of thing."

I wanted to act offended, I truly did, but I simply didn't have it in me. If anything, I was shocked, though I couldn't put my finger on why. So instead of acting appalled by her assumption, I decided to occupy myself with the pies that were ready to be bagged in cellophane. "You're delusional."

"If you say so." She began separating the plastic bags for me, obviously not prepared to give it up. "So, tell me...how is Travis doing these days?"

"Busy." Short answers were best when dealing with a meddling best friend.

"How are things between you two?"

"Good."

"Uh-oh. What does that mean?" Apparently, one-word responses wouldn't work.

I finished bagging the rack of pies and stepped back with a shrug, abandoning my short-lived plan of remaining vague. "I have no idea, Pipes. I still see him quite a bit, and we're still having amazing, off-the-charts sex, but with everything he's responsible for with the expansion on top of his normal tasks at the winery, he's been...*off.*"

Piper tilted her head in confusion. "I'm gonna need more information."

I had to think about it for a moment because I had a hard time understanding it myself, let alone explaining it to someone else. There seemed to be a lot of changes in him, but they were all small, and they could all be excused by being busy at work. Which was something I understood more than most.

"Well, for one, he doesn't stay the night much anymore. He does on the weekends, but it's less frequent than before. And there are times he doesn't come over for dinner, either. I can see he's home, but he doesn't bother to stop by."

"You said he has a lot going on at the vineyard, though. Right?"

I nodded and tossed the gloves into the trash before taking a seat at the long kitchen table. "Yeah, this time of year is always chaotic for him, and now, he's got the expansion to worry about, too. He just has a lot on his plate at the moment."

She pulled out the chair next to me and took a seat. "You sound bothered by the fact that he's not around as much. Are you still trying to convince yourself you don't care? Because you're not convincing me of shit right now."

I rolled my eyes. There was no way I'd make it out of this unscathed, but it was hard—no, *impossible*—to tell her how I felt about Travis when I couldn't figure it out for myself. At this moment in time, I was too tied to my fears to delve into all the feelings I had surrounding not only him, but the thought of an *us* as well.

So rather than take that route, I decided to go with a different approach. "I understand he's busy, but the whole thing makes me a little self-conscious. Like, what if he's not interested in continuing this thing with me, but he can't say anything because he borrowed money? And I'm over here making him have sex with me when he doesn't want to."

Piper couldn't hold in her amusement and barked out a harsh laugh. "Now you're being an idiot. He wouldn't sleep with you if he didn't want to. He already has the money, so it wouldn't make sense for that to be a motivating factor for him."

"How can you be so sure?" I sounded paranoid, but I couldn't help myself. Ever since he caved and accepted my offer, things had changed. They were little things here and there, but in the end, they added up to major differences, and it was hard for me *not* to think I'd caused them.

"I'm not even gonna justify that with a response." Which she didn't. Instead, she grabbed a pie off one of the cooling racks and took a bite.

And as she sat there breathing heavily out of her gaping mouth to cool off her burning tongue, I laughed. "That's what you deserve for dismissing me so easily. I'll recognize your scorched tastebuds if you validate my fears."

"Nope," she said around the bite of piping-hot apple pie. When she finally swallowed it, she acted like it was no big deal—*bitch*. "You only validate things you can confirm or prove are real. I can't do either for your feelings because they're irrational."

I slouched in my seat and huffed in frustration. "I can't explain it, Piper, but something is going on with him. I can *feel* it. There has definitely been a shift in the way he is around me, but it's not something I can describe with words."

"Have you asked him?"

"Of course I have. Except he says everything's fine; he's just preoccupied with the vineyard. Which is true. I've seen the work they've been doing to the new land over the last month, so I don't doubt that a lot of his time and energy and focus has been spent there."

"You just told me why he's acting different, so what's the problem?"

I pulled in a deep breath, hoping this conversation would end soon. As much as I loved talking to my best friend about everything, discussing my feelings had always been difficult for me—even with Piper. And not being taken seriously only made it that much harder. "It doesn't matter what he says…it's more than him being busy at the vineyard. There has to be more to it than that. And since he's already taken *and* used the money, he can't come out and be honest about what's going on."

The timer on the oven saved me from having to sit in the hot seat any longer. I got up and busied myself with swapping out the trays and setting the hot ones to the side to cool enough for the next step in my process. There was probably an easier way to do this, but considering I wasn't aware of it, my way would have to do for now.

I made sure to slow down my movements to prolong my return to the table. I knew Piper well enough to guarantee she wasn't done with this topic. And when she was determined to find answers, she was like a dog with a bone—relentless. There wasn't much I could do to stave off that conversation.

However, as if she were my guardian angel in disguise, Maureen chose that exact moment to join us in the kitchen. Her presence would buy me at least another five or ten minutes, long enough to hopefully redirect Piper's attention.

"I love it when you're here, Claire," Maureen cooed as she opened the refrigerator for something to drink. "The whole house always smells like a bakery. I'm going to be sad when I don't have that anymore. Well, we both will, your Gramps included, but I'm willing to say I'll miss you the most."

"Looks like you'll have to come hang out and keep me company when I'm baking so you won't have to go without it."

She giggled to herself while rummaging in the fridge. "Would either of you like something to drink? I have fresh-squeezed orange juice or tea. And I think I have a few sodas out in the garage."

Before I could answer, Piper slapped her hand on the table, narrowed her gaze on me, and said, "That's so thoughtful of you, Maureen. Thank you. It's nice to be offered a beverage when going to someone else's house. I'll take a glass of tea."

I returned my best friend's teasing glare. "First of all, this isn't my house…yet. So it's technically not my job to ask if you're thirsty. Second of all, you've been here a gazillion times; you're perfectly capable of either helping yourself or asking me. And lastly, you've got two legs…go make it yourself."

I was joking, and Piper knew it too, but Maureen didn't. Which became obvious by her sharp gasp and frail hand flat against her chest. She couldn't seem to do anything other than stare at me with round, baffled eyes.

Thankfully, my best friend threw a bucket of cold water on the situation —figuratively speaking, of course. She stood and swiftly shuffled her way to me. "It's okay, Ms. Gilfreid. I'm used to her being rude. If she's nice, I start to wonder what I've done wrong."

Maureen visibly relaxed, though she glanced at me for confirmation, so I offered a quick smile to reassure her everything was fine. Oddly enough, her uncomfortable response warmed my heart. It was yet another stepping-stone in our growing relationship.

Ever since I started baking at Gramps's house, I'd grown a lot closer to his *lady friend*. Somehow, I was able to put aside my unfounded issues so I could become more acquainted with her. And I couldn't have been happier.

As I accepted the cold glass of tea Maureen offered Piper and me, I regarded her warmly and ensured my gratitude was heavy with syrupy sweetness. "You make the best tea, Maureen. I think we should make a deal…my pastries for your tea."

She giggled and said, "Sounds amazing. But I think we should add a foot-note: both have to be fresh."

"Of course. How about I give you my baking schedule, you provide the pitcher, and I'll supply the lemon and dessert?"

"I'll hold you to that." Her cheeks warmed as she moved closer to the kitchen door with her glass in hand. "It looks like you need every inch of space available, so I'll leave you two alone. Holler if you need anything."

Piper craned her neck and waited until the door softly closed before swinging her head my way. "Am I in the twilight zone?"

I fought against the desire to celebrate the successful subject change. Instead, I shrugged and returned to what I was doing, knowing that would make her question me harder. Which, in turn, meant the previous conversation was gone for good.

"What the hell, Claire?" *Bingo.* "You get along with her now?"

We had only discussed Maureen once over the last few months, which was when I first started to use this kitchen for baking. Piper had asked how it was to be around her all the time, and I told the truth—Maureen wasn't home much, so I didn't see her often. Which wasn't a lie; not to mention, that was before I'd decided to lose my hatred of the woman who made my grand-father quite happy. I just hadn't caught Piper up on it all yet.

I peered over my shoulder and shrugged again. "I guess, if that's what you want to call it."

"What do *you* call it?" she asked, still in shock.

"I realized I didn't have a reason not to like her, and once I gave her a chance, I discovered she's a really nice person. She's actually super sweet once you get to know her." I'd already returned my attention to the next batch of pies I was preparing to put in the oven, so I was startled by the soft slap against the back of my head.

When I turned to find out what Piper had hit me with, I found her standing behind me with an oven mitt in hand and a deeply furrowed brow. It was the typical expression she used when thinking to herself, *are you freaking kidding me?*

For the first time all day, I actually felt bad for not having told her any of this earlier. It wasn't like it was dire information, but she was my best friend, and I did miss talking to her every day, even if there was nothing exciting to share.

"I'm sorry, Pipes…should I go back to despising her?"

"No, of course not. I'm just surprised. I didn't think you'd ever come around and see what we've all known from the beginning." Piper wasn't the only one, either. My grandfather was probably the most shocked—and grateful—for the switch in my attitude, although Travis wasn't far behind.

"To be honest, a lot changed when Gramps told me his reason for kicking me out. I'd assumed she had something to do with it, but she didn't. I'd say the majority of my disdain came from the idea that she played a part in it all just to have my family's house all to herself. I realize now how completely wrong my assumptions were, so yeah…I have absolutely no reason to hate the woman anymore."

Piper was quiet for a moment, her mouth pulled to one side. I'd seen this face enough times to presume she was contemplating how blunt and honest she should be…or considering how to word a question so I wouldn't immediately shut it down. Which one it was would come down to what came next. A deep breath would point to brutal honesty, whereas a soft sigh would be a question.

Then it happened. She sighed.

Oh, joyous.

"So what's the reason for the rest of your hatred for her?"

"Huh?" Here I was preparing for something hard-hitting, and she gave me that. Granted, I didn't have a clue what she was talking about, so there was a chance it might've actually been a tough one.

"You said the false image in your head about her taking your house was the *majority* of your disdain. So what was the rest?"

Yup. I was right. It was something I didn't want to answer. I liked it better when I was confused and didn't understand what she was asking. Unfortunately, I made her clarify her question, and now, I was stuck having to answer. Without a doubt, I would've been able to offer something vague if only I had kept her in the loop over the last couple of months.

It was my turn to take a deep breath as I once again returned to my baking sheets. I knew she would see straight through any lie I could come up with on the spot, so I resigned myself to giving her the truth. "She might've only temporarily taken my house, but she's taking my grandfather from me permanently."

I couldn't look her way while she silently moved to my side, and my chin practically dropped to my chest at the warmth of her reassuring touch on my shoulder. I had never been able to figure out how to handle so many contradicting emotions swirling within me. On the one hand, I was immensely appreciative of her support, but on the other hand, I realized how ridiculous I sounded, so her sympathy made me feel stupid. Either way, I didn't lean into her embrace, nor did I shrug her off. I simply continued to line tins with prepared sheets of dough.

"I thought you only sold the personal-sized pies," she said with a curious inflection in her tone. "Isn't that what you're known for?"

I couldn't have been happier for her swift subject change. This was now twice in one day. However, I became slightly paranoid at the possibility of my luck running out, so I had to make sure that we stayed on this side of serious topics from now on.

"Yeah, but Carla suggested we make whole ones for Thanksgiving …but only for the people who pre-ordered. I won't be doing this all the time."

"Who's Carla?" Yet another reminder of how little we'd talked lately.

"Travis's mom."

Again, she grew quiet for a moment before asking, "How's that going?"

"How's what going? The corner at the winery? Umm…" I eyed the endless trays of pastries covering every inch of surface in the kitchen. "I thought we already established that business was good."

She laughed, though I wasn't sure at what. Then, once she calmed down enough to speak, she said, "No, I meant with his mom. Do you have to deal with her often?"

"Well, I mean, I see her nearly every day, but I wouldn't say I *have* to *deal* with her. I actually enjoy her company, and she's brilliant at coming up with new business strategies. As long as I have that corner, I can learn so much from her. She's the one who came up with the idea to use a different shape for each fruit filling to make it easier to differentiate between the flavors."

Piper was so quiet I had to look her way, worried I might've said something wrong. And based on her utterly blank expression, I replayed my words in my head to verify that I, in fact, hadn't stuck my foot in my mouth inadvertently.

"What? Why are you staring at me?"

That was enough to snap her out of whatever trance she was in. She shook her head and released what sounded like a long-held breath. "Sorry, I wasn't expecting that. It really took me by surprise."

No matter how hard I tried to understand why she'd be surprised, I couldn't. And the longer I thought about it, the more confused I became. "Why? What were you expecting?"

"I'm not sure, but I can tell you it was *not* that."

I waited for her to elaborate or answer my first question at least, but as the seconds ticked by, it became obvious I was waiting for nothing. "Okay, but *why*? I'm so lost."

"Well, mainly because she's Travis's mom."

I started to believe that I'd never make sense of what she was trying to say. So I waved it off, glanced over my shoulder to make sure the kitchen door was still closed, and went back to lining the tins with dough. "It's not like she thinks we're together or anything, so that has no bearing on my relationship with her."

"Yeah, okay...but that's not what I meant." She paused and settled against the counter next to me, leaning over it to look at my face while she spoke. "You've always avoided mothers, regardless of who they were. So it surprises me that you seem so close with Travis's mom."

If her reason for leaning against the counter was to prevent me from having to stop working to look at her, then she utterly failed. My hands immediately froze in the middle of what I was doing, and my attention went straight to her face. I wasn't sure if I wanted to laugh or roll my eyes at the absurdity of it all.

"Are you kidding me? Seriously, Piper, has our lack of communication over the last couple of months made you forget who I am? I've never had a problem with *anyone's* mom."

"Not a *problem* per se, but ever since your parents died, you've completely avoided motherly figures." She held me in place with her piercing stare, thoroughly studying my expression as if cramming for a final exam.

"And let me guess...it's because my mom's gone?"

She shrugged. "Who knows why, Claire. All I'm saying is you have, and the fact that you have a good relationship with Travis's, not to mention your turnabout regarding Maureen, is a pretty big deal."

I laughed dismissively at her. "You always try to psychoanalyze me, looking *far* too much into the smallest, most innocent things and turning them into something crazy. I have *never* avoided *anyone* because of what happened to my parents."

"Then why did you stop coming to my house before I moved out on my own?"

"What are you talking about? I didn't do that."

177

Her jaw dropped as she gaped at me in disbelief. "Yes, you did. As soon as your grandfather came to live here, you completely stopped coming to see me. I always had to come here if we wanted to see each other outside of school."

I opened my mouth to argue but quickly closed it as I began to think about how things were back then. I remembered spending a lot of time with her, especially over summer breaks, but I couldn't for the life of me recall *where* we had hung out. It didn't seem possible that we would've spent all our time here, except I couldn't come up with a specific instance when we were at her house. Nor could I remember the last time I'd seen Piper's mom.

Needless to say, I didn't have anything to argue because I couldn't convincingly reject her claim. So I decided to put that thought to one side and continued preparing the pies for the apple filling.

"Even if you're right—which I'm not saying you are—it wasn't a conscious move on my part. I don't recall ever thinking to myself, *I don't want to go to Piper's house because being around her mom makes me think of mine.*"

"I never said it was intentional. Much like most of the coping mechanisms you developed after they died, I think you did it without a single thought as to why. You were simply protecting yourself. So it's a shock to find out that you're finally working through some of those things...and I mean that in a good way. I'm really proud of you."

A sharp, incredulous laugh tore through my throat and blew past my lips without giving me a second to stop it. "You're proud of me for talking to a woman because of some unconscious fear I had about mothers reminding me that mine's dead? Do you even listen to yourself when you say these things?"

She'd started to grow annoyed with me; it was obvious in the way she rolled her eyes. It wasn't the flippant, sarcastic kind of roll. It was somewhere between that and an angry eye roll, which told me I was dangerously close to hurting her feelings.

I pulled off one glove and touched her arm, making her meet my gaze so she could see the truth in my eyes. "Thank you for telling me you're proud of me. I may not understand why, but I appreciate it all the same."

"I'm pretty sure if you took a second to think about what I said—not only right now, but things I've mentioned in the past—you'd understand why I'm proud of you. And I'm willing to bet you'd agree with me."

"Can you at least give me a hint?" I phrased it as a teasing question... although there was a fair amount of seriousness in it as well. I didn't doubt what she was telling me; after all, no one knew me better than Piper Dodson. But I needed help seeing it all through her eyes. Apparently, I couldn't trust the view from my own.

At least her irritation with me had vanished. "You have never dealt with the loss of your parents. You say you have, but I've been right there with you for the last eight years, day in and day out. I've seen you go through the motions, but you never fooled me. I saw right through that wall you put up to keep others out. I noticed your reactions when other kids at school would talk about their families, and the way you'd shut down at any mention of an accident—of any kind. You might be able to trick everyone else, including yourself, into believing you've worked through all the stages of grief, but not me."

Damn her.

If we hadn't already been best friends at the time of the accident, I doubt she would've picked up on any of that crap. Granted, I couldn't deny any of what she said. Even though I didn't specifically remember doing any of that, it all sounded rather familiar. And if she was right about these things, there was a good chance she'd been right all along with everything else she'd claimed were *coping mechanisms*.

The time had come to pull back the curtain and accept all the ugly things I'd been avoiding for the last eight years.

I tossed my gloves in the trash and moved to the sink to wash my hands. "I probably don't wanna ask what you think is the reason for my break-through, do I?"

"Not unless you want an answer you'll flat-out deny...even if we both know it's true," she added with a giggle. "I think it's probably best if I let you consider everything I've told you and come to your own conclusions. But only as long as you don't put those rose-colored glasses back on."

I sucked my teeth and popped my hip, feigning annoyance over not being able to lie to myself any longer. "Fine, but in case you were wondering...you're no fun."

"I guess it's a good thing I'm not here for fun. I'm here to help. So put me to work."

I glanced around the kitchen, figuring out what needed to be done first. There were many things I needed her help with, but every task followed another. Finally, I pointed toward the front of the house and said, "I need the pies from the outside fridge loaded into boxes. I won't have any room for these until we move those out of the way. And when I put the last batch in the oven, would you mind taking the boxes to the winery for me? I'll tell Travis you're coming so he can keep an eye out for you."

"No problem."

Piper Dodson was hands-down the greatest person in the whole universe. There wasn't even an extraterrestrial being cooler than my best friend. She always had my back, and I would live until my last breath showing her how much I appreciated and loved her.

CHAPTER 20
TRAVIS

CLAIRE HAD CALLED A WHILE AGO, asking if I would be at the winery to let Piper in. Assuming she was on her way, I'd decided to hang back and wait for her. Apparently, I had assumed wrong, considering it only took twenty minutes to drive here from her grandfather's house, and so far, it'd been an hour and ten minutes.

Correction—an hour and eleven minutes.

Headlights shone through the front windows and flooded the shop, pulling my attention away from the second and minute hands of the clock on the wall. The same clock I'd been staring at for the last fifty-one minutes.

"I am so sorry," Piper started as soon as I opened the front door. "I got halfway here and turned around when I realized I forgot my phone. Then I got lost. I really hope I didn't keep you long. I got worried when I pulled up and all the lights were off."

It was kind of hard to stay mad at someone while they profusely apologized to you. Not to mention, she clearly felt horrible, so there was no point in making it worse. Instead of telling her everything I'd thought of over the last...fifty-two minutes, I decided to go easy on her.

I flipped on half of the shop's fluorescent bulbs and said, "Nah, there are plenty of things to do around here; my work is never done this time of year. Not to mention, Thanksgiving is a busy time for Uncorked Vineyards."

"You guys will be closed on Thursday, right?"

I followed her outside to help carry the boxes of pies from her trunk to the front of the shop. "Yeah, which is why I'm here today. I don't normally work on Sundays. But we aren't open on major holidays, and I have too much to do to take an extra day off this week."

"That sucks you have to be here on a weekend. I can't believe Thanksgiving is in four days, though. This year has flown by."

"Tell me about it."

There was something about keeping lies from your family that made time disappear. Granted, I'd spent a couple of months with a constant ticking sound playing in my head, warning me of the clock running out on the vineyard deal. Maybe the pressure of that might've played a part in it, too. Either way, it didn't matter anymore. We were well on our way to having new crops planted in the spring, so it was all behind me. The only worry I had now was about Claire, and I didn't see an end to that anytime soon.

"So you spent all day with Claire?" I followed Piper out to grab the last two boxes. Seeing how many she'd baked today blew my mind. "How stressed was she?"

"You'd be surprised at how calm she was. In a good mood, too."

I gawked at her while she set down her box to close the trunk.

"Shocker, right?" She followed me in and placed the last banana box on top of the stack right inside the front door. "I can't begin to explain to you how much you've done for her in such a relatively short amount of time. You've known her for, what...four months? There are people who've been in her life ten times as long and never got through to her the way you have."

That took me by surprise. "What do you mean?"

Piper glanced around the large room, likely deciding what she could tell me without betraying her best friend's trust. When she figured it out, she met my stare and smiled. "Let's say you've opened doors for her that I'd convinced myself would stay locked and boarded up forever."

"You mean like her corner?" I pointed to the neatly stacked crates beneath the hand-painted sign that read *Claire's Cutie Pies*. It was silly, but I loved that sign. Claire and my mom had worked on it together in the first two weeks of having Claire's pies here, when they realized what a success it would be.

"Well, yeah. That's one door—and let's be honest, it's a *big* door. It's truly helped her grow into an amazing adult."

I laughed and shook my head, amused at how Piper talked about Claire as though she were an infant at the start of this. "Honestly, it's no big deal. It was an empty corner my mom wasn't utilizing; not to mention, it's not like she had any reason to say no."

"Wow, you've gotta have the most generous and thoughtful family ever."

"Why do you say that?" I cocked my head and narrowed my gaze, not understanding what she meant. While it wasn't unusual to receive compliments about my family and the products we provided throughout our businesses, this didn't seem like typical praise.

"I haven't met many people—make that *anybody*—who'd let someone come into their place of business to sell something of theirs. It's unheard of."

"I don't understand why, though." I expected her to say something about my mom offering the space to Claire rather than utilize it for something more profitable for the winery.

But she didn't. Instead, she gave a half-answer, half-question. "Umm... because they're her pies?"

"Exactly. So why would my mom care if she sold them here?"

"Because she could sell them herself and keep all the money."

Confusion continued to plague me, leaving me silent and motionless. I could only stand there and stare at her, blinking more than usual while waiting for her to spell it out for me.

And that's *exactly* what she did.

She said, "It's your mom's recipe, so she could make them herself and keep the profit."

I had wanted her to spell it out, but that was before I knew it'd be: Y-O-U G-O-T S-C-R-E-W-E-D.

Unfortunately, she continued before I was able to wrap my head around what she'd just disclosed. "It's truly incredible that she'd let Claire not only take the credit but also keep the money. Granted, I'm sure your mom is super busy with this place, so it's probably a relief to have someone else do all the manual labor. Saves her time and money while still earning something from each sale."

I shook my head and held my hands between us in a stop motion. Something wasn't right here, and I needed to get to the bottom of it. Finally, I stood straight with my shoulders pulled back and crossed my arms, ready for answers. "What makes you say she's using my mom's recipe?"

Her brows knitted together, causing a deep crease to line her forehead. "Uh, because Claire told me it was. She said you gave it to her because she liked the one you brought over so much."

Pieces of what she said were accurate while others weren't, making it difficult to maneuver through her words and depict the truth. I *had* given Claire a pie right after she moved in, and she *did* say how much she'd enjoyed it. But I'd never given her the recipe.

"Claire worked really hard to replicate the one I gave her. I remember her talking about how she was up all night baking, trying to figure it out. She came over the next day for tips on how my mom had done it so she could try it again. I texted my mom, so maybe that's what she meant."

She looked uncertain as she pulled her lips to the side and shook her head. "You know what? You're probably right. She told me a few stories about you and the infamous dessert when I initially came over to teach her how to bake. So I more than likely meshed them all together until my brain assumed the recipe had come from you. That must be it. Forget what I said."

Words formed into knots in my throat as I watched her push the door open, staring at me with one foot in and one foot out. There was no way I could simply forget what she said. And she knew it too, which was why she was in such a hurry to leave.

Regret covered her face like a mask as she released a long, slow, quiet sigh through her downturned lips. "Honestly, Travis...ignore everything I said. You've been with her way more than I have ever since she moved into that duplex, so seriously, you'd know better than I would. Not to mention, I'm pretty sure you're familiar with your mom's pies."

I offered a short nod right before she slipped outside. The headlights to her car blasted through the large windows next to the door, but only for a brief moment. Piper didn't wait around, and to be honest, I didn't blame her. She just threw her best friend under the bus. She then backed over her a couple of times. If I were her, I'd be on the phone with Claire in a nanosecond. In fact, I wouldn't be surprised if she'd dialed her number before reversing out of her parking spot.

The room began to spin as I desperately rifled through my memory for a time she could've gotten her hands on the recipe. But I couldn't come up with a single way she could've possibly gotten it. I didn't even have a copy lying around, as far as I was aware.

However, regardless of Piper's request to ignore everything she'd said, I couldn't. She had reminded me that Claire couldn't even bake when she first moved in, so there was no way she would've been able to recreate *anything* by taste.

The more I thought about it, the angrier I became until I forced myself to take a seat on my mom's wooden stool behind the front counter. It only took a second before I found myself with my head in my hands, my hair between my fingers, the roots taut at my scalp. My mind was broken, all my thoughts scattered. Not a single thing made sense.

Dread filled me and left me unable to form a plan of action.

As much as I wanted to confront Claire, I needed to calm down first. Except I couldn't calm down until I figured out what the hell was going on, which I couldn't do without speaking to Claire. It was an endless cycle that only made the room spin faster.

There were too many questions and not nearly enough answers to sit around and take a breather. But I knew that the deeper, darker emotions currently flooding my system would spin out of control if I didn't. So I decided to work off some of the anger by taking the pies to the storage cooler in the back.

Once the last box was on the shelf dedicated for Claire's pastries, I froze, unable to pull my eyes away. The large openings on the top of her banana boxes made it easy to grab one of the cellophane bags without disturbing the others. So I did. I stole one, not caring what fruit was inside, and took it back to the front desk.

I'd already packed up for the day, only waiting around because Claire had asked me to let Piper in to drop off tomorrow's inventory. Truthfully, I should've been on my way home by now, not sulking behind a stack of T-shirts with an opened, uneaten pastry in front of me. Honestly, I wasn't even sure what purpose it would serve, considering I pretty much already knew the truth. Although, *how* was the real question, and I wouldn't find the answer inside this pie.

That didn't stop me, though.

I took a smaller bite than normal and allowed the flavor to settle over my tastebuds. It was hard not to devour it, but I needed to see if I could tell the difference, so I closed my eyes and took another bite, really delving into the essence and texture.

Once I finished it, I sat there and stared at the empty cellophane, angrier than before because I still didn't have answers. I'd thought it would've hit me as soon as I took a few bites. I would've been able to tell if it was like my mom's, except I obviously lacked that kind of palate. I could name and pick out almost anything when it came to wine, but unfortunately, this was a pie. Not wine.

Feeling like the only solution was to eat more, I went back to the cooler and grabbed a few others. I made sure to pick out a variety of fillings this time in case the other was inconclusive because it wasn't apple—which was what my mom made most of the time. I took two of those for good measure. I didn't need to make a third trip.

I'd finished the blueberry, the peach, and the cherry. The only thing I could determine after each one was how good they were. Now, only the ones with apple filling were left, which I was grateful for, considering I still couldn't definitively say whether it was my family's recipe or not. If I couldn't figure it out after these two, I'd have to try something else.

One bite. Two bites. Three and four. It didn't take long for the first apple pie to vanish. Without wasting time, I unwrapped the last one. Unfortunately, it didn't last as long as the others. But it was fine because at least I had come to a conclusion by the time I finished.

Well, a few of them.

The first was that Claire's desserts were incredible; they were without a doubt the best I'd ever had. The second was that she was one hell of a baker, regardless of not knowing her elbow from a rolling pin four months ago. And finally, the third conclusion I came to was that, even though it'd been a while since I'd had any of my mom's baked goods, I genuinely believed these were different. I couldn't put my finger on it, but they weren't the same as the pies I'd grown up eating at home.

The jingling of keys from outside startled me, but not nearly as bad as when the door opened. All I could do was sit on the stool and peer over the stack of merchandise that likely kept me hidden from view.

"*Hello?*" Claire called out with only her head peeking through the open front door.

I suddenly realized I'd forgotten to lock up after Piper left. Not wanting Claire to mistake me for an attacker, I jumped up from my seat and moved to stand at the end of the counter, mostly so she wouldn't see the empty cellophane wrappers cluttering the space.

Clearly, I didn't think that through because my movements ended up scaring her anyway. Surprise lit her eyes, which were almost as bright as her smile once she realized it was me. As if I wasn't confused enough, I was unsure why she'd be happy to see me. Unless she hadn't spoken to Piper, in which case, she wouldn't have come here with a lie prepared. At least that eased my nerves a bit.

"Claire?" I waited for her to calm down and fully step inside the shop. "What are you doing here?"

"I was about to ask you the same." She hitched her thumb over her shoulder. "I came to drop off pies like I always do. What about you?"

I knew my mom had given her a key so she wouldn't have to wait for Claire at the end of the day. This way, she could let herself in, which she'd done many times over the last couple of months. I simply wasn't expecting to see her here tonight. "I thought Piper dropped them off for you."

"She only brought the first half. I knew they wouldn't all fit in my car, and it beat making two trips. She left while I finished cleaning up, which is why I couldn't let her in." She cocked her head and furrowed her brow. "Why are you still here?"

As if suspicious of me, she moved closer, head still tilted, and peered around me to see the backside of the counter. When she gasped, I turned to see what surprised her. It was obvious my mind was all over the place because, in less than a minute, I'd already forgotten about the empty wrappers on the countertop.

"I should've told Piper not to leave before you to ensure you didn't help yourself to all my merchandise." She tsked jovially. Her happiness threw me off. It was difficult to remain focused when she was like this, which had usually been one of the things I liked most about her—how infectious her attitude was.

Maybe her positivity was what annoyed me. I didn't want to joke around or laugh and tease each other. I needed answers, but her bubbly personality made that almost impossible.

"How many did you have?" She walked around me and picked up the pieces of cellophane, which only contained crumbs by this point.

I forced myself to steer away from that rabbit hole. We had enough to talk about without adding her opinion of my impulsivity regarding her baked goods. So I shook my head and refocused myself. "I take it you haven't heard from Piper?"

She stilled and looked my way. Apprehension darkened her eyes, making my stomach do flip-flops. "Not since she left the house to come here. Why?"

My expression must've been disturbing because the longer I hesitated to answer, the more paranoid she appeared. I didn't want to drag it out, but I knew there was at least a fifty percent chance that whatever we had between us would end after this conversation. And I didn't want that. In fact, I couldn't fathom my life without Claire in it.

Without realizing it, I had completely fallen for her despite our decision to keep things casual. We'd never discussed it, but there seemed to be an unspoken agreement that, for right now, casual worked for us. But for whatever reason, I believed we'd have the opportunity to explore our relationship a little bit more once things settled down.

Although the idea of dating her made me so anxious I could vomit.

"Travis? What aren't you telling me?" She dropped to the stool I'd vacated with nervous anticipation evident in her expression.

I now regretted not following her down that rabbit hole and talking about how many pies I had eaten…instead of this. But I couldn't go back now, so I gripped the edge of the wooden countertop to steady myself and said, "I wasn't sure if she told you anything about her visit."

Her bottom lip quivered, which made my heart threaten to give up. I couldn't stand to see her upset, but this was one of those situations where I couldn't avoid it. A horrible feeling settled in the pit of my stomach, telling me that by the end of this, we'd both be destroyed.

And I'd be the one who destroyed her.

That was a hard pill to swallow.

"Listen, if you have a thing for her, come out and say it. Don't beat around the bush. I can handle it." She didn't believe a word of what she said. Her voice broke as she spoke, so I wasn't sure who she was trying to convince, but it wasn't me.

I had wanted to cut her off as soon as I realized where her head was at. But for some reason, the words weren't coming. It was like my brain was as shocked as I was, too busy gawking at her in surprise to function properly. In fact, speaking wasn't the only thing I couldn't do. It seemed my brain was too stunned to tell my lungs to work.

Finally, I was able to gather myself enough to explain. It probably wasn't nearly as long as it felt, but considering she was done speaking, I'd say it took far too long. "No, Claire. Nothing like that, I swear."

The relief that saturated her left me torn. It made me contemplate bagging this entire idea and just going on with life, never to think of Piper's words ever again. Except I couldn't do that. Claire had lied to me before, and even though I'd been able to move past it, it wasn't something I could easily forget. If I found out that Piper was right about the recipe, I doubted I'd ever be able to look at Claire the same. Not only would she have lied—again—but it would also mean she'd betrayed me.

"So what is it?" She might've been relieved, but it didn't mean she wasn't still worried.

I took a deep breath and dropped my gaze to the floor. I was having a hard enough time getting this out; there was no way I could do it while looking into her chocolate eyes. "Um, we were talking about Cutie Pies and how far you've come…" This would take forever, so I pulled my head back, stared at the ceiling, and blurted, "Where did you get your recipe?"

She was quiet for a moment, causing me to drop my chin and look at her. Then it was her turn to inhale deeply and drop her eyes to my feet. "I kinda made it up as I went. I would run out of something, so I'd have to substitute it with whatever I found in the fridge, and if it turned out better, then I continued to do it that way."

It was completely believable, and for a split second, I was the one dripping with relief. Until she lifted her gaze. There was an emotion in her eyes I'd only seen once. Which was the night Piper had inadvertently spilled the beans about the engagement. *Guilt.* It colored her face in shades of pain, outlined with regret. Aside from happiness, it was the one emotion she displayed with conviction. The one she couldn't hide.

I knew right then and there that any remaining doubt was gone.

"What about the original recipe?"

"Why?"

Her one question was enough to ignite my anger. "Because I want to know. So answer me, where did the *original* recipe come from? The one you used before you started making changes. The one you used with Piper when she taught you how to bake?"

Tears came from nowhere and silently slipped down her face. As one plummeted off her chin, another appeared from the other eye. All the while, she remained completely still. She didn't stand, drop her head, wipe her face. Nothing.

"I assume your silence is the answer to my question." Unfortunately, I couldn't leave it there. After getting this much from her, I needed more. "How did you get it? At least give me that."

Finally, she dropped her chin and swiped beneath both eyes. With a sniffle, she lifted her gaze, except she didn't look at my face. She stared off at something over my shoulder, as if looking through me. "When your mom sent it to you, I copied the file onto my phone."

That actually shocked me. In all the different ways I'd come up with how she had gotten her hands on it, not one involved her going through my phone. Aside from being a major invasion of my privacy, I didn't see how it could've been possible, so I never considered it.

"Okay, but *how*?" I decided to leave the betrayal aspect for later, focusing instead on the logistics. "My phone is password protected." I gasped at a thought and took a step back. "Do you have my password?"

She quickly stood in defense. "No, no…it wasn't anything like that."

"Then tell me what it was like."

"You went to the bathroom and left your phone on the kitchen table —*unlocked*. You got a call or a text or something—I can't remember which one—so I picked it up to take it to you because you had literally *just* left the room."

"How do you go from bringing me my phone to rifling through it?"

"I didn't rifle through it. I swear, Travis. It was on the screen. I didn't read any of your texts with your mom or do anything else on your phone. I glanced at the screen to… I don't remember why, but I saw the attachment. I sent it to my phone and put yours back." She was undoubtedly telling me the truth. The way she explained it was likely the exact way it had happened, but it didn't change the fact that she'd stolen something personal from me.

My jaw hurt from clenching it so hard, and my palm stung from my harsh grip on the edge of the counter. But after hearing it all, a wrecking ball could've slammed into me, and it still wouldn't come close to how badly my heart hurt in this moment.

"Why?" It didn't matter, but I couldn't ignore the desperate need to ask.

She shrugged to begin with but quickly decided to speak. "I needed a job, but I didn't have anything to put on a résumé. No previous employment, no schooling, no experience or talent. So I figured maybe I could start my own business. Except I didn't have any known skills."

I started to question if she intended to garner my sympathy again, like she had when she lied about us being engaged. It might've worked then, but it wouldn't this time. This was one too many betrayals to fall for that tactic again.

But before I could object, she continued. "I was working on my résumé right before you came over with the pie from your mom. It was so good I just knew it could be a huge seller. I tried all night and most of the next day, but I couldn't do it. I felt defeated, and that's when you got the recipe from your mom. I thought you asked her for it so you could give it to me. In my head, I was simply speeding it along. But I swear, I had no clue it was top-secret until two days later when you came over after work and told me. And once I found that out, I changed the entire thing. I never made a penny off yours. I swear. In fact, I'd spent an entire month's allowance on it, only to lose it all. It wasn't until I changed most of the ingredients and almost all of the preparation that I actually had any success."

"I believe you." I watched as her shoulders fell in sync with her sigh. But I'd practically grown numb by this point, so it didn't affect me the way it normally would have. "Except it doesn't change anything."

Her eyes grew wide as she sucked her sigh right back in as a gasp. "What do you mean?"

"Don't you see? You stole from me, Claire. You took something from me. Invaded my privacy. What's worse is you've lied to me for months now, and it's not like this is the first time, either. You took it one lie too far."

"W-what does this mean for us?" she asked after what felt like an eternity.

I might've been pissed and betrayed and mostly numb, but over the last several months, despite it all, Claire had snuck her way into my chest and made a home in my heart. Seeing her hurt held the potential to ruin me regardless of everything else. So I stared at the rubber mat behind the counter and said, "There is no us."

"Is this why you've been acting weird?"

Surprised, I narrowed my gaze and asked, "When have I been weird?"

"Well, maybe not *weird*, but you haven't been normal. You haven't been yourself. It's more than work, but I can't figure it out. Have you been looking for a reason to cut things off with me, and now you have one?"

My short nails bit into my palms as I fisted my hands by my sides, trying my best to restrain the anger running rampant through my entire body. If only she understood how utterly absurd her theory was... Over the last couple of months, I'd wanted *more* with her. Not less. Granted, I couldn't blame her for not knowing how I felt considering I'd never told her.

"Are you kidding me? If I wanted to end things, I wouldn't need an excuse."

Claire swallowed harshly. "Well, it was after I gave you the loan, so I thought maybe you weren't into it anymore yet felt obligated because of the money."

"Not at all. I was with you because I wanted to be, not out of any silly obligation. And if I *did* feel obligated, the loan wouldn't have been why."

"So why have you been weird with me?"

I wanted to tell her it was nothing more than stress from work, but she would've seen right through that. She'd seen me stressed, so she was aware of its effects on me. I wasn't stupid enough to think I could make something up; however, after all this, there was no way in hell I would've been able to tell her the truth. "If you thought something was off, why haven't you asked? Why haven't you said anything?"

"Because I didn't want to open that door for you."

"So you would've continued our relationship—or whatever you want to call it—even if you thought I didn't wanna be there?" My anger quickly fell away. I didn't need to ask her why she'd stay because I could see the answer in her eyes. She had feelings for me, possibly similar to those I felt for her.

Suddenly, I hated the universe for its timing. Then again, if I'd been aware of how she felt before tonight, before the revelation about the recipe, it would've made everything so much worse.

So maybe the timing was a blessing in disguise after all.

She nodded, and the movement must've knocked another tear loose because one slipped out and slid down her cheek like a figure skater on ice. Every fiber of my being wanted to catch it before it fell to her shirt, which was smeared with evidence of her baking. However, the thought of never touching her again stung so badly I actually stepped away instead of toward her.

"I should head out," I said, mustering enough courage and determination to leave despite the level of pain I was in. It ran so deep no one could convince me it wasn't physical. I would've rather my arm been ripped off by a pack of wolves than to have gone through this. "But first, I need you to listen to me, Claire. Are you listening?"

She nodded and stared at me with sheer desperation in her dark eyes.

"Nothing—and I mean absolutely *nothing*—will keep me from paying off the loan. I don't care whether you move away, or I move away, or if we never say another word to each other for the rest of our lives. I will pay back every penny I borrowed from you. Got it?"

Complete defeat crippled her as she shrugged in response. "I don't give a shit about the money. I didn't then, I don't now, and I sure as hell won't in the future. I offered it to you because I wanted to help."

"Let me ask you this…did your guilt over stealing my mom's recipe have anything to do with your decision to offer me the money?"

"Not at all." Her answer was immediate. "I found out about the recipe's history and devised the plan to get money from Gramps almost simultaneously. At the time, I felt I needed to do something to make up for my actions, but at the end of the day, I would've offered it with or without the guilt. I felt bad, but I wanted to help because I care about you. End of story. That was my only motive."

To be honest, I knew the answer before I even uttered the question, but I needed it to come from her mouth. Without a doubt, I believed what we had together was real and not born out of regret or shame. Claire was a girl who had it all, and for some reason, she wanted to share some of it with me. I was beyond grateful, but it didn't stop my own guilt from eating at me. Even though it wasn't true, I couldn't help but feel as though I'd gotten something from her and then split.

Truth be told, I'd felt shitty for the last couple of months. I wasn't lying when I said I had fallen for Claire Hansen. I'd fallen hard, head over heels. And I struggled with handling those feelings without making her think they were in any way connected to money. I never, not in a million years, wanted her to think she'd bought my love.

But I guess none of that mattered now.

"I really do need to head home," I said as I pushed open the front door.

Shock riddled her face. "You're just gonna leave me here?"

"You have a key, so I'll leave you to lock up." The words *see you at home* almost slipped off my tongue. It'd become so natural to say it to each other over the last several months, and this was only a reminder that we would never say those things to each other again.

I realized I could change this. I was the one walking away, which meant I could be the one to stop and work things out. My pain was, in a way, self-inflicted. However, after already looking past her deception once, doing it again would only set the standard...and there was no way I would ever be okay with a life of lies.

Claire stayed silent. She stood in front of the stool and nodded. Her eyes were closed, and she had her chin tilted down, but it didn't keep me from seeing her inward sobs.

Or the rivers flooding her cheeks.

Even though I knew this wasn't the last time we'd see each other, it didn't stop me from feeling like it was. Then again, this was the last time I would ever see her as anything more than a neighbor I owed money to.

CHAPTER 21

CLAIRE

"How was I supposed to know?" Piper's high-pitched voice pierced my ear through the phone. "As far as I was aware, he gave you the recipe. If you don't want me to say something, you have to tell me so."

As soon as I'd gotten home, I put my phone on charge so I could call my best friend. I never, not once, thought she ratted me out on purpose. And it wasn't lost on me how I was the only one to blame—for everything. But I was heartbroken, and she was the only person I could call and cry to about it.

If I wasn't already aware of how badly I'd screwed things up, this would be when I realized it. What I had assumed were innocent lies, ones that wouldn't hurt anyone, ended up costing me one of the three most important people in my life. And once Gramps learned of my other lie, I'd likely lose him, too. My selfishness and inability to see past my own wants and needs landed me here. Too bad the fallout happened *after* I'd learned to think of others first.

"I don't blame you, Piper. I promise. I lied to everyone. It's all my fault."

"Stop," she scolded, taking me by surprise. "Don't play the victim, especially when this could've all been avoided. Now listen, I'm here for you. And I always will be. No matter what pile of shit you put yourself in, I will *never* turn my back on you. However, I can't sit here and listen to you pity yourself."

I opened my mouth to argue, but I quickly snapped it shut when I realized I didn't have a leg to stand on. She was right...I *was* pitying myself, and even though I couldn't figure out how to be any other way, she didn't deserve to deal with that.

"Now, what are you going to do about Travis?"

I paused for a second and played back her words in my head, ensuring I had heard her correctly. "You've gotta be high on bath bombs because I can't do anything about Travis."

She giggled softly, as if she tried to stop herself yet failed. "I'm sorry, I just got a mental image of someone scraping off some bath bomb powder and sniffing it." She laughed louder. "And all I can think about is it fizzing up in the back of their nose like it does in the bath."

Somehow, Piper managed to hit the reset button on my emotions. That one random comment acted like a small paper bag, relieving me of the dread that threatened to suffocate me. Granted, it would all immediately return to hysterical levels once the moment passed, but at least I was able to rewind them for a second.

It was better than nothing.

"You can't let him walk away, Claire." Piper sounded as if she truly believed I had a choice. "You've never been this way with anyone before. If you let him go, it'll end up being the biggest mistake of your life. Do you seriously want to lay on your death bed regretting this?"

"No, I don't. But what choice do I have? I can't change things." It was obvious she hadn't seen the look of betrayal in his eyes; otherwise, she'd have agreed with me. "Trust me, if going back in time was an option, I'd take it in a New York minute."

"You're right; you can't change anything, but it doesn't mean you can't fight."

I rolled onto my back and huffed out a long breath while staring hopelessly at the ceiling fan in my room. "I think it's too late, Pipes. As much as I wish I could do something about it, I can't. I've lost all his trust, thanks to my stupid, impulsive ideas."

"To be honest, I think he's more hurt that you kept it from him. I imagine if you came clean back when he told you about the recipe being a secret, he might not have taken the news so badly. So chalk this up to a lesson learned —from now on, be open and honest, no matter what you think the outcome might be. Because at least you'll have a chance of it ending in your favor, whereas getting caught in a lie will almost certainly resort to this."

"I hate it when you do that." I added a short, pathetic laugh to assure her I wasn't too serious. I mean, I did hate it when she lectured me as if she were my mom, but I couldn't be angry at her for it, especially considering I clearly needed a healthy dose of tough love. "Yes, I've learned my lesson. I'm aware of what to do next time, but I'm not crying about next time right now. Fingers crossed there won't be one. Let's stay focused on the present, shall we?"

193

She groaned, making her frustrations clear as if they were somehow muddled. "I've already told you what to do, Claire. But you're not listening to me. You have to fight, and I don't mean start an argument. Make it obvious that you're serious about him."

"What if he's not serious about me? I mean, like, even before tonight. I asked him if this was why he's been acting differently toward me...if he was looking for an excuse to cut things off with me."

"You didn't tell me that. What'd he say?" It was never hard to make her excited about juicy details.

I rolled my eyes, despite the fact she couldn't see me. If she could grunt, I could roll my eyes. "All he said was he wouldn't need a reason to stop hanging out with me. If he didn't want to spend time with me, he simply wouldn't. But he never explained his change in attitude."

"Well, at least he told you what it wasn't. That's something."

"Yeah, but whatever it is, it's not helpful."

"Let him have a breather. Try talking to him tomorrow."

"And what if he doesn't want to talk to me?"

Piper tsked through the phone, acting as if the answer was obvious. "Then you wait until the next day and try again. He'll eventually cave and at least hear you out. Trust me, I have firsthand knowledge of exactly how persuasive you can be when you put your mind to it."

She wasn't wrong. I did have a knack for wearing people down, but this wasn't a simple *want* for me. Making things right with Travis was more of a *necessity*. And when it came to something this important, I tended to choke and mess it up one way or another.

"You could both do with a night to think about everything."

I sighed, hating how Piper was always right. "Good idea. I should go to bed anyway."

"Okay, but you better call me if you talk to him," she demanded. As if it needed to be said. Not only was she my best friend, and therefore, the first person I went to with everything, but she was also the only person left in my life.

Until she realized what a horrible person I was and decided to split, too.

I definitely wouldn't be able to handle that.

"WELCOME back to a brand-new episode of *You Can't Buy Love!*" The crowd grew louder as claps and cheers filled the studio. "This is going to be an intense show tonight! Please help me welcome Claire's date...come on out, T!"

The spotlight shifted away from me to the red curtain behind the stage. The same handsome man with Caribbean eyes and panty-dropping smile from before came out to take the seat next to me. Except this time, instead of being perfectly styled, his hair was all over the place, and there were holes in both his shirt and pants.

In fact, his entire wardrobe looked like the leftovers from a donation box.

Everyone quieted down once he took his seat, allowing Bob Archer to begin this segment. "You're looking rough, T. Do you care to fill us all in on what's been going on since the last time we saw you?"

T dropped his gaze and stared at his wringing fingers in his lap, which was where his focus stayed the entire time he answered Bob's question. "Well, let's see... I've moved since the last time I was here. Now I live in a homeless shelter downtown."

That news surprised us all as gasps rang out through the studio.

"What horrible news. Tell us what happened. How'd you lose everything?"

"Claire happened."

Everyone's eyes were on me. They were like hundreds of burning needles scorching my flesh. I frantically glanced around, hoping to find at least one person to come to my defense.

But there was no one.

Only myself.

"What do you mean *I* happened? What did I do?"

T narrowed his gaze, his betrayal-filled eyes piercing my soul. "You stole everything from me. You took it all and left me with nothing. I lost my job, and without an income, I eventually lost my house. I can't even find a new job because I don't have decent clothes to wear, a bed to get proper sleep required for a full day of work, or even a car to take me back and forth."

I covered my mouth with my cold, trembling fingertips as I desperately scoured my brain for something to say. I felt horrible, but unfortunately, expressing that wouldn't change anything. So finally, I dropped my hand to my lap and said, "I'm so sorry...I didn't think—"

"Exactly," he interrupted, although not with anger. Defeat clung to his voice when he added, "That's your problem, Claire. You never think. Well, unless it's about you."

"You're lying." I didn't have a right to be angry, especially with him, but I couldn't hold myself back. No one else was here to stand up on my behalf, so I had to. "I'll admit yes, when we first met, I was selfish. There were plenty of times when I only thought about myself. But I've changed. I'm not the same person anymore."

T shrugged. "Doesn't matter though, does it? The damage had already been done. You can't steal a person's entire life and get away with it because you're a better person when the fallout takes place."

He was right. I didn't have anything to say because it was the truth.

"Well, let's approach this from a different angle, shall we?" Bob, still using his game show voice, moved to stand between T and me. "Is there anything Claire can do now to make this right with you?"

I held my breath, praying for a reasonable response.

"No. She can't do anything about it now. Too late."

A loud pop filled the air, the audible manifestation of the sound my optimism made when it was popped like a balloon. Things couldn't get worse.

That was a lie…things could *always* get worse.

"Okay, what about before you lost everything? Could she have done anything—aside from not stealing from you to begin with? Anything at all she could've done to prevent your tragic, downward spiral?"

Again, I held my breath and hung onto his every word, hoping he might offer me a crumb.

T glanced up at the stage lights and took several deep breaths. "She could've told me about it; at least then, I would've been prepared."

Another pop rang out, silencing the entire studio. It was just one more bubble of hope exploding.

Bob cleared his throat into the long, skinny microphone apparently glued to his hand. "Tell me, T…why share this grim news with us on *You Can't Buy Love*?" For some reason, the audience joined Bob in saying the show's name as if it were the chorus of a song. "Is there some reason you wanted to tell the whole world what Claire did to you?"

"Yes, because she should be held accountable for her actions."

"Makes sense. But you dated her. You had feelings for her. Why not have a private conversation with her off the show? Is it because you *wanted* to humiliate her?"

The crowd gasped; meanwhile, I'd held my breath for so long I was surprised I hadn't passed out. It was like I couldn't breathe until I knew what T had to say.

Finally, T stated, "We were only friends."

"Is that correct, Claire? You two never dated?"

Intense emotion washed over me, and it took every ounce of strength I possessed to keep my tears from flooding my face. "That's correct." My voice came out weak and pathetic, but I quickly found a sliver of courage and spoke louder, with more conviction. "But that doesn't mean I didn't want to date him. Because I did. I was in love with him."

The entire set went eerily quiet.

I turned to the man with Caribbean eyes and a panty-dropping smile and added, "I *am* in love with him."

At this point, no one existed beyond the two of us. The spotlight shone only on us, and there wasn't a hint of sound in the entire studio. Romantic music soared as he stared at me, and I stared at him. Then he opened his mouth to speak.

His lips moved, and his Adam's apple bobbed. But rather than words, the only sounds I could detect were deep, almost hollow pops. Like gunshots. Or a car backfiring. However, it seemed I was the only one who heard them. Once T stopped talking, he stared at me, as if wondering why I wasn't responding to whatever he said.

"What?" I asked, hoping he'd repeat himself.

And he did.

But like last time, instead of words, my ears were filled with pops.

I squeezed my eyes closed, covered my ears with my hands, and screamed. Then I fell off the chair, landing on the floor with a harsh thump. When I opened my eyes, the room was dark. Also, I was in my bedroom, not on a game show.

Without getting up, I sat on the floor with my back against the bed frame and dropped my head into my open palms. Tears filled my eyes and immediately plummeted to my thighs. Strong, deep emotion consumed me until I couldn't breathe without hiccupping.

That's when I heard it. The popping sounds.

Fireworks.

Someone in the neighborhood was celebrating while I cradled my head and bawled my eyes out. All I could think about was how I'd taken everything from the man who was likely sound asleep in his bed next door. I needed to make it right, but as he said in my dream—well, nightmare—there was nothing I could do.

The damage was done.

I WAS dead on my feet, desperate for a hot bath and my bed.

Thanks to the nightmares I had all night, I'd been running on fumes since the moment I woke up this morning. It didn't matter how many cups of coffee I drank while baking, either—I'd lost count after six. My focus had been off all day, and the only task I was capable of completing was fulfilling the Thanksgiving orders for Carla. There were still a few more hours I could've used to bake, but I decided to call it a day shortly before four. There was simply too much on my mind to keep going.

"Is this all you brought?" Carla sounded worried as I carried in only one box of pastries. Although, what shocked me the most was how normal she was acting. Either Travis didn't tell her or… Yeah, there was no other reason she'd be fine around me. "Are you coming back with more?"

I set down the box of holiday orders and centered myself for what could possibly be a worse encounter than the one I'd had here last night with her son. However, I'd had enough time to think about everything, and I knew I wouldn't be able to avoid it.

"Uh…no, ma'am. This was all I was able to do today. Not to mention, I didn't think you'd want me to bring more."

She tilted her head and regarded me with a blank expression. She truly didn't know what I was talking about—which only made this whole thing that much worse. "Why wouldn't I want you to bring your normal order? We've been busier than usual, so without them, we won't have any to sell tomorrow."

"I understand, Mrs. Cabrera, but—"

"What is going on, Claire? You've never called me ma'am, and it's been months since I heard *Mrs. Cabrera* come out of your mouth. This is unlike you."

It was clear that Travis definitely hadn't spoken to her, which made no sense considering his reaction last night. So I twisted my fingers in front of me and took a deep, steadying breath before answering. "I assumed Travis would've said something to you today."

"About what?"

Well, here went nothing. "I'm sorry, but I have betrayed you and your whole family. I can't possibly make it up to you, but I swear, I'll do anything to at least attempt to make it right."

"Start over." She grabbed my wringing hands and led me to the stool behind the front counter. This was the last place I wanted to be. It was like déjà vu, except this time, I was confessing instead of trying to disappear. "How have you betrayed us?"

My eyes stung, alerting me to the impending waterfall about to take over my face. What was worse, though, was the way my voice cracked when I said, "I stole your family's pie recipe…the one you texted to Travis several months ago. It was a misunderstanding, but there's no excuse. I was selfish and impatient and incapable of recognizing how my actions affected others."

I braved a glance her way, surprised to find her expression calm and… normal. She wasn't smiling, but she didn't appear to be shocked by my confession either. Nor did she seem bothered by it. Granted, I wasn't finished with my explanation, and she hadn't spoken yet, so there was still time for her to react the way I'd expected.

"I need you to understand that I have changed the recipe so drastically I don't think it could be considered the same anymore. I'm not excusing my actions or justifying anything. What I did was wrong on so many levels, and I truly am sorry. From the bottom of my heart. I understand the implications of my actions, which is why I didn't come with any pies for tomorrow. I assumed you wouldn't want to share the corner with me any longer."

"Don't be silly, Claire." Her nonchalance blew me away. "Of course I want to. After all, they are *your* pies. It doesn't matter where they originated from; all I care about is how popular they are. Our business has increased dramatically ever since we opened your corner."

Her reaction suddenly made sense.

She didn't want to lose the sales my pastries brought in. I understood her reasoning, but I also knew our relationship would be irrevocably altered, and I wasn't sure if I could handle that. I really valued my time with Carla. Part of me felt like she understood me in ways I hadn't felt since my mom was alive. And being around her, working with her, and *not* having what I'd become so accustomed to, what I'd grown to love the most about our partnership, would only intensify my pain tenfold.

"It absolutely matters where they came from. You and Travis trusted me, and I betrayed your trust." I swiped away a lone tear racing down my cheek. "I truly appreciate your forgiving nature, but I can't let you look past my lies. I'm a fraud. It's time I owned it."

Carla released a heavy sigh, crossed her arms, and stared at her feet for a moment. "Okay, if we're being honest, let me give you my truth." She glanced up again, and in her eyes, I found a comfort I never imagined I'd see again. "I already knew about the recipe."

"You did?" I practically jumped off the stool.

"Yes. I'd be able to sniff out my mama's crust from a mile away. I could tell the filling was new, but I've never had that crust on any pie other than ours."

"And you weren't mad?"

She shrugged. "It doesn't matter now."

"If you knew, why would you offer to sell them in your winery?"

She grabbed my hands and held them between her warm palms. The security that one simple touch gave was more than I could've asked for. "Like I said, Claire, while I recognized the crust, the rest was brand new. Anyone can make a fruit filling, but something about yours made me an instant fan. I was addicted before I finished the first one. And the shapes... It's all so unique I knew they'd do well here."

"How come you never confronted me about it?"

"What would be the point?"

I glanced around the room until my sight settled on the sign we'd made together. Everything about this experience had been a blessing, and it almost killed me to have to give it all up. Regardless of what Carla said, the relationship we'd built these last few months was undoubtedly over. There was no going back now.

"I stole something from you," I reminded her, wondering why I was the only one who understood the severity of what I'd done. "At the time, I wasn't aware the recipe was as old as it is or a family secret. I honestly thought things like that didn't actually exist."

"What do you mean?" she asked with her head tilted and brow furrowed. "You don't have anything that's been passed down from generation to generation?"

I shook my head, ignoring the pity in her stare. "Not as far as I'm aware. If so, it never made it my way. Maybe my mom did, but she didn't have enough time to pass it on to me. We all thought we had more time together."

"I'll be honest, Claire. The fact that you lost your mother so young played a small part in how easily I was able to accept what you did. I don't have a daughter to hand it down to, and you don't have a mother to give you old family treasures. Be it a casserole recipe or a silver platter your great-great-grandfather gave to your great-great-grandmother on their wedding day." She was quite specific, which made me wonder if there was an old platter hidden away in her attic somewhere.

"So you *were* angry with me at the beginning."

Sympathy settled into her already relaxed expression. "I wasn't angry. Maybe a little duped at first, but at the end of the day, I knew in my gut that you weren't scheming us. In my opinion, you took the best part of mine and combined it with an outstanding fruit filling, and then you found a way to make them marketable single servings. I've had that recipe my entire life and never did anything with it other than bake a pie five or six times a year. You had it for a considerably short amount of time and managed to turn it into a very successful small business. How could I possibly be angry about that?"

I was at a loss for words. I'd confessed, and she forgave me. Even though I didn't feel worthy of her mercy, the only thing I could do was accept it and be grateful. I'd be an idiot to turn my back on that kind of compassion, whether I could comprehend it or not.

"Now that we have this out in the open..." Carla started with a singsong voice. "Would it be too much to ask what your secret is?"

"For the filling?" I was surprised to see her nod; this was the last thing I expected her to ask me. "Well, the biggest change is probably in the preparation. I soak the fruit overnight in wine. There are other things, but swapping the apple juice for Moscato made the biggest difference."

"Do you always use the same variety of grape?"

At this point, I didn't care if her motive was to steal my ideas so she could cut me out and sell her own. Truthfully, I'd deserve it. So there was no point in keeping my technique a secret. "No, it all depends on which fruit I use.

Usually darker fruit, darker wine. Lighter fruit, lighter wine. And I pair sweet fruits with dry wine and vice versa. Oh, and I always use Uncorked. I thought it was fitting since the fruit came from your orchard, too."

"It's obvious that you've put a lot of time, effort, and thought into your pies. I can't be upset about that. I can only admire you for it." This woman was seriously amazing. The size of her heart was astounding, but what really blew me away was her willingness to accept me no matter what. Aside from my parents, Piper was the only other person who had ever done that.

Once upon a time, I thought I could add Travis's name to that list. But I couldn't blame him or hold it against him. Carla knew of one lie, whereas Travis had already caught me in two. I couldn't deny that if I'd never lied in the first place, his name would still be on that list.

"Are you serious about all this? Keeping my corner, allowing me to continue to sell my pies here, and not being angry at what I did...you honestly mean it all?"

"Of course I do. It's not easy to come clean about something you did wrong. You owned it, so I can't ask for anything more."

I should've kept my mouth closed, but I couldn't leave it there without always wondering *what if...* "Except I only did so because Travis found out and confronted me last night. If that never happened, I'm not sure if I would've confessed."

"I understand you believe that, but I happen to disagree. We'll never know for sure, although I suspect you would've admitted it eventually. You're a good kid, Claire. You aren't the same person who took the recipe to begin with, even I see that. So I trust that at some point, your guilt would've led you to do the right thing."

While I wanted to reject Carla's forgiveness and acceptance, I knew her decision to keep me around meant Travis couldn't ignore me forever. And if there was any hope of getting him to talk to me—or at least hear me out—I needed to make sure I was constantly present.

Not to mention, I'd given Carla many reasons to turn her back on me, practically telling her to. I'd done everything I could to convince her I wasn't worthy of her compassion, yet she gave it to me anyway. So if she'd felt betrayed by me in the slightest, she would've kicked me out of the shop by now.

In fact, she'd pretty much forced it on me.

"If you're sure about it, I can have more product for you in the morning. It won't be as much as I usually have, but at least the corner won't be empty."

Her eyes softened as she squeezed my hand. "If I didn't know how much work went into baking, I'd happily accept your offer. Unfortunately, I'm well aware of the time and effort required to bake all night long, and I can't allow you to do that. You've been wearing yourself so thin as it is this week trying to fulfill the holiday orders on top of the usual daily sales. Take the night off. We'll survive one day without them."

I would've done it if she wanted me to, but I couldn't lie...the idea of having an early night sounded heavenly.

CHAPTER 22

TRAVIS

"Hey, Trav. You're still here?" Mom lightly knocked on my open office door.

I quickly glanced at the time on my cell and sighed, shocked by how late it was. Ever since the upsetting news Sunday night, hours and minutes became indistinguishable. Actually, days were, too. Since being home was no longer enjoyable, I'd spent most of my time at the winery. But at least I'd managed to catch up on a ton of work.

"Yeah, I'm trying to finish as much as I can before we close for the holiday tomorrow." I didn't need to invite her in because she did so herself.

"Is everything okay with you?" She took the seat across from my desk and regarded me with heavily sympathetic eyes. Before I could ask the reason for the sadness in her expression, she said, "You haven't been the same since your fallout with Claire a few days ago."

Disbelief and annoyance left me speechless. The only noise I managed to produce was a frustrated groan, which became stuck in my throat. I stared at the ceiling, blinking rapidly as if that would offer the insight I sought. Finally, I dropped my chin and returned my gaze to my mother. My sweet, caring mother, who'd obviously been fooled by my thief of a neighbor, too.

"What are you talking about?" Considering I still hadn't said anything to her about Claire or the recipe, I was confused about what and how much she knew.

"Are you trying to tell me you two are fine and nothing happened?"

I wasn't stupid enough to think I could convince her of that, especially since I'd gone missing every day this week at the exact time Claire came to drop off boxes of stolen pies. My mom was at least aware something was up between us.

But I doubted she knew the truth.

"No, Ma. That's not what I'm saying. We ran into a bit of an issue Sunday night, but it's all sorted now." My idea of *sorted* simply meant I'd washed my hands of her.

"That's odd, because she told me something different."

"Yeah, well, she's a liar," I mumbled under my breath.

Mom leaned forward and cupped the back of her ear. "What was that?"

"Nothing. Listen, why don't you tell me what she told you?"

"She said you're not speaking to her."

I bit my tongue, preventing myself from correcting her. Technically, I wasn't refusing to talk to Claire, I was simply ignoring her. She had sent me at least one text every day since Monday. They all basically said the same thing—begging for a conversation. But I didn't trust myself to be that close to her. Even though I was still upset and hurt, I could recognize my weakness creeping in. I was falling in love with her five days ago. So I needed a bit more time to amass the kind of inner strength needed to hinder my feelings from taking over and giving in.

Instead of explaining all that to mom, I asked, "Did she tell you why?"

She waved me off. "I already knew why. She didn't have to tell me."

"Oh, yeah?" I couldn't bite back the sardonic laugh that boomed past my fictitious smile. This wasn't how I imagined I'd inform her of Claire's thieving ways, but if the news ruined her holiday tomorrow, she only had herself to blame. "Please, Ma, tell me what the problem is. I'd love to hear why you think I'm upset with her."

A small grin teased her lips for a split second, long enough for me to see. Not only that, but when she sat back to take a deep breath, readying herself for this conversation, she rolled her shoulders into a rather dominant posture.

People often wondered how my mother survived raising four boys.

This right here is how—we knew who the boss was.

"The problem, Travis, is you're as stubborn as your father."

I leaned into the desk with my forearms on the edges. The pinch kept me grounded for the time being. "This isn't new information. You've known this since I was two. What does it have to do with Claire?"

"Everything." She clearly enjoyed dragging this out. "You found out that she somehow got ahold of my pie recipe and kicked her to the curb. What I don't know, though, is why you're so bothered by it. If anyone should be upset, it'd be me. After all, it was *my* recipe."

The fact that she knew what Claire had done surprised me. Moreover, the fact that she didn't appear pissed off about it completely blew me away. I was so taken aback I needed a few seconds to process it and form a response. "First of all, my issues with Claire extend beyond the recipe. There's a lot more to it, none of which I care to delve into right now. So yeah, I have valid reasons to be upset with her. And second of all, how did you find out?"

"Oh, Travis, I knew way back when you suggested giving the corner to your baker neighbor *friend*." She not only added heavy emphasis to "friend," but she also tilted her head and raised her brows as she said it. Unfortunately, she didn't give me enough time to address it before saying, "I figured it out by the last bite of the first pie you gave me to sample."

My forehead and jaw ached, which I quickly learned was because I'd clenched my teeth together a little too tightly, and utter astonishment left my brows deeply furrowed. I thought the fact that she even knew about the recipe was startling, but this—*how* she figured it out—totally had the initial shock factor beat.

But then she continued. "Also, Claire told me about it on Monday."

Okay, that topped the previous surprises. I was now completely flabbergasted.

"And you're not upset? I don't understand...you told me not too long ago about how the world would end if anyone got ahold of it. So why are you suddenly okay with Claire taking it?"

"I'm not *okay* with her taking it. Obviously, I would never condone stealing and lying. But I'm not upset with her having it because, at the end of the day, her pies are completely different than mine."

I gawked at her, unsure who this woman was, because there was no way she was my mother. It made me wonder what kind of voodoo Claire had done on my mom to make her take her side. "Do you hear yourself? You literally said the problem with other people having it is they'll change it and sell it and make money off it. Which is *exactly* what she's done, yet here you are justifying it."

"Trust me, Travis...I'm just as surprised as you are. The only thing I can come up with is because she made it so much better. She kept all the best parts of mine and perfected the rest. As I sat there and thought about it, I realized those pies would've never existed without her. And now that she's told me what she's done to them, I'm even more proud because she uses our fruits and our wines."

"Amazing, Mom. So basically, what you're trying to tell me is...she's come in and taken over everything, including a recipe that's been passed down in our family for eons, and you're okay with it because it *tastes better*?"

She closed her eyes for a second and pulled in a full breath. "Listen, I understand it doesn't make any sense to you, because it doesn't make any to me, either. Everything I told you about not wanting anyone to have the recipe and all the reasons it can't leave the family were all things told to me by *my* mom, who was told by *her* mom. All I can say is we're put in situations sometimes that make us rethink the things we've been told our entire lives."

"Okay, great. I'm glad you're fine with it. But I'm still not. You've known for however long, and I just found out. You can't expect me to be all hunky-dory about it. She stole from us. She lied to me. Please don't take her side on this."

"I'm not, trust me." Her posture softened, bringing back the supportive and trusting mother who only had my best interests at heart, the one capable of getting answers from her unsuspecting children. "But how come you didn't say anything to me? Why confront her before discussing it with me first?"

"It wasn't like I had time, Ma. Her friend came by to drop off pies and made an offhanded comment, completely unaware of what she was actually telling me. And less than half an hour later, Claire showed up. What would you have wanted me to come to you with? I only had suspicion to go on—no evidence. So I didn't *confront* her. She showed up, and I took the opportunity to *ask* her about it."

Mom nodded slowly while I spoke, letting me know she was paying attention. "But it's Wednesday now. Practically the end of the day, to boot. I've seen you every day this week, Travis. Were you ever going to tell me?"

"Well, at first, I didn't say anything because I wanted to wait until the holidays were over. We've had so much going on, and I figured adding Claire's deception to the pile wasn't the best idea. Plus, she still had orders to fill, and I didn't want to create an issue before everyone who paid for a pie was able to get one."

"I'm sure part of that is true…maybe half of it. But I have a hard time believing you were that concerned about Claire's and my working relationship. If you truly didn't want to rock the boat before Thanksgiving, you would've at least *acted* like everything was fine."

"What are you talking about? I *have* been fine."

"Travis Matthew Cabrera." There came *Mean Carla*—the alter ego of her caring and loving grandmother persona. Mean Carla was the closer; she was sent in to finish things. And the worse part was you never saw her coming. One minute, sunshine; a split second later…the apocalypse. "That's crap, and you know it. You've been the complete opposite of fine. Moping *isn't* fine."

I knew I hadn't been Mr. Go-Getter like usual, but I doubted I'd projected the kind of misery she tried to portray. I was upset, yes. Bothered, absolutely. And sure, even a little sad at the loss of someone I genuinely cared about. But if anyone listened to her, they would've thought I'd spent the last few days crying on my couch in the fetal position.

"All right, all right. I'll give you that; I haven't been acting normal. But I think if you take a step back and look at it through the lens of someone who isn't aware of what's happened, you'd assume I was busy. Which I have been. Maybe even a bit stressed. Which I've also been. But mopey? Not so much."

Mom flicked her wrist dismissively. "Whatever you say, Travis. What do I know? I'm only your mother. As a little boy, whenever you'd cry, I was the only person who unequivocally knew why. I could distinguish between your wails to tell if you were hurt, tired, angry, scared..."

Oh, brother.

"When you got a little older and started working the farm, who was the one who brought you ice packs and heating pads? Me. Why? Because even though you never complained, I could always tell when you were hurting. Just because you're all grown up and out of the house doesn't mean I can't still read you like a book."

Oh yeah, and I forgot to mention that Mean Carla was extremely good at guilt trips. It was her superpower.

"You're absolutely right, Ma. I'm upset about it. What do you want from me?"

She relaxed a little, making me believe she was on the verge of calming down. "I only want to know why you haven't said anything to me. If you'd told me, I could've explained it all, and then maybe you wouldn't be so angry with her."

"That's just it, though...I'm not angry with her." Even I could detect the break in my voice.

"So why aren't you talking to her?"

I stalled for a moment, needing a few deep breaths before expressing out loud, for the first time, how I felt about everything. It was always a lot easier to keep it buried inside. But unfortunately, my mother wouldn't let me.

"For reasons I'll never understand, I simply don't have it in me to be pissed at her. As much as I want to scream and yell...at her, to her, *about* her...I can't. I cared about her, Mom; those types of feelings don't go away overnight. So saying something to you wouldn't have done anything to change how I feel right now."

When I went to bed Sunday night, I was determined to cut her out of my life completely, but as the days waned, so did my resolve. Random thoughts and memories would attack me out of nowhere, leaving me less angry and more distraught over the entire situation.

Claire truly wasn't the same person who took the recipe from my phone. She wasn't even the same person who'd lied about being engaged to me. But as quickly as those realizations came to me, so did the doubts. Such as, *what happens when she lies again?*

As they say... Fool me once, shame on you; fool me twice, shame on me.

207

And regardless of how much I cared about her or missed having her around and in my life, I couldn't see myself giving her a chance to fool me for a third time. Which was why I'd spent the last four days absolutely avoiding her, even if it left me feeling dead inside.

"Well..." Mom shifted to the edge of the chair and leaned forward, taking my hands in hers. "I'm not trying to minimize your feelings of betrayal or the severity of her actions, but considering it's all out there, maybe you both can begin to rebuild your relationship into something stronger with a better foundation."

"There is no relationship and never has been. We were close friends at best. Now we're merely...neighbors." Those words not only tasted nasty coming out, but they also burned my tongue like battery acid.

"Maybe you should look up the definition of *relationship*. Because what I saw between the two of you was a lot more than just close friends or neighbors. I've seen a huge difference in you over the last several months, and the only thing I can pinpoint as the reason is her."

I took a moment to think back over the last four months. The land deal had come into the picture almost immediately following Claire moving in. And with that came stress, stress, and a whole lot more stress.

"I'm not entirely sure what kind of change you're talking about or apparently witnessed, but any difference in me from then to now couldn't possibly have been perceived as for the better. So I can't figure out why you'd think she's done me any favors."

"Why do you say that?" She regarded me with genuine confusion in her gaze.

"Have you not picked up on how anxious I've been?" Surely she had, because I couldn't possibly have been the only person annoyed with my irritable behavior. "I wouldn't be surprised I've developed an ulcer."

"Yes, I picked up on that a couple of days during the expansion talks. But we were all a bit frazzled, Travis. You weren't the only one. If I recall correctly, your father and I were a bundle of nerves at the beginning. It was *your* confident and enthusiastic approach to the land deal that made us feel better and more secure about it all."

I covered my face with both hands and mumbled through my fingers, "Because I was completely clueless about what was going on." I dropped my hands to the desk with a hollow thud and met my mother's puzzled stare. "For whatever reason, I was under the impression this *expansion* was taking place on our own land...that you guys were cutting into some of the unused farmland and reallocating it to the vineyard."

She opened and closed her mouth a few times before deciding to shut it, regarding me with a furrowed brow. But after several seconds, her expression relaxed. "When did you realize we were talking about purchasing the neighbor's land?"

This wasn't at all how I saw this conversation going. Well, technically, I hadn't put too much thought into it because I never planned to tell them unless I absolutely had to. Unfortunately, being mildly depressed, severely sleep-deprived, and—as my mom would say—*mopey* made me say things without thinking. And since I'd already gotten myself into this truth-telling mess, there was no turning back.

I glanced at the calendar on my desk as if checking dates and said, "It was maybe a week or two after the offer was put on the table. Enrique came to give me one of his regular updates on the progress and expressed his concerns. I didn't have a clue what he was talking about, so he explained it. I was never copied on the initial email Dad sent out, so I wasn't aware of any offer, which is why when it was mentioned to me, I assumed you were talking about the farm."

"Why didn't you say anything about it? You never told me about the confusion, and I'm sure your dad would've mentioned it to me if he knew."

"Because, Ma..." I ran my fingers through my hair and groaned. "The ball was already rolling at that point. Not to mention, expanding the vineyard has always been a dream of mine. Saying something would've almost certainly put an end to that option, and who knows how long we'd have to wait for another chance to grow our crops."

She was quiet for a moment; then she sighed. "Let me see if I understand this correctly. You wanted something that would benefit you, so you lied and schemed to make it happen? Wouldn't you call that a selfish decision, one you made without thinking about the repercussions or how it could negatively affect the family?"

"Yes, it was a selfish decision, but I was fully aware of what we stood to face if it backfired. The consequences played in my head over and over again, which was the cause of the majority of my stress. And I never would've let it get to the point of no return. I busted my butt getting a loan for the land, knowing if I couldn't secure something before the deadline, I would have to come clean and deal with the fallout myself."

The room became so silent my ears started to ring. Either that or my blood pressure spiked, and I was on the verge of a stroke. I wasn't sure what the warning signs were, so if that truly was about to happen, I was shit out of luck. Granted, I wasn't so sure I'd leave this conversation in one piece anyway, so technically, I was damned one way or the other.

"It all worked out, so I don't want to beat this into the ground, but I have a lot of questions only you can answer. So please bear with me while I try to piece this all together." She narrowed her gaze and focused on something on my desk while working through her thoughts. Mom wasn't usually one to speak without having fully thought through what she wanted to say, which explained the long pauses between statements. "How did you manage to acquire a loan that size at the last minute?"

I'd already gotten waist-deep in the frigid water; I might as well go in all the way now.

I picked at a piece of imaginary lint on my pants, unable to look at her while I confessed everything that had kept me up at night for the last several months. "Well, the bank gave me an extension on my original loan. But they wouldn't give me enough to cover the deed *and* the expansion costs."

"I'm sorry, but I need you to rewind a moment. I manage all the accounts for Uncorked. I see what's in them, and you deposited your share before we placed the order at the nursery. If you didn't have the money for the crops and irrigation, how did you pay for it? Where did it come from?"

Now my face felt red hot. Burning hot. I wasn't sure if this was an indication that I needed medical assistance or water, but either way, I felt confident I would need an ambulance once I finished telling my mother everything anyway. "Claire."

She was silent for a moment before leaning forward and clasping her hands together on my desk. "Repeat that, please. Did you say Claire?"

Still unable to look at her, I simply nodded.

"How much?"

"All of it."

The most surprising part of it all was the laugh filling every inch of my office. It wasn't her normal laughter, though. It was more maniacal than that. It commanded my attention until I stared at her, filled with concern for her mental health. I was pretty sure I broke her, and unfortunately, I didn't have the faintest idea how to fix it.

Maybe we would need to share the ambulance.

When the laughter finally ceased, she said, "I must've misunderstood something because there's a massive hole in your story. Correct me if I'm wrong, but you haven't spoken to Claire—someone you claim to care about —in *days* because she used a recipe she didn't have any claim to. One that doesn't belong to you, either. And although it all worked out in the end, you can't move beyond the fact that she took it without permission and then lied about it. You don't even care that she's completely changed it and apologized."

She could've stopped talking right there and still managed to get her point across. I knew exactly where this was headed, and despite not wanting to sit through it, I was man enough to accept my penance. Even if my penance was dealing with an insane woman.

I found myself wishing for Mean Carla to come back.

She was much nicer than Crazy Carla.

"Yet this whole time," she carried on, "you've been keeping your own secrets from your father and me...secrets which could've negatively affected not only our family but our financial stability as well. And you kept these secrets and told these lies to get what *you* wanted."

"At first, yeah. But after that, I didn't tell you because I didn't want to let you guys down."

"Do you think it's fair to say Claire didn't tell you what she did because she didn't want to upset you or risk ruining your relationship in any way?" She stared at me, daring me to respond.

Being too chicken shit to answer her question aloud, I nodded. The only thing I could actually say was, "I get it, Ma."

"No, I don't think you do." This was some kind of Crazy Carla, Mean Carla hybrid that I wasn't too fond of. "Not only are you a hypocrite, but you're also an exploiter."

"A what?"

She huffed and shook her head, disappointment in every line on her face. "It was one thing when you were simply punishing her for something you also did. But it became something completely different when you accepted a considerable sum of money from her right before this all happened. Stop thinking about your own feelings right now, Travis. Imagine what she's going through."

"So I'm supposed to ignore her betrayal all because she lent me money?"

"Not at all. You don't have to ignore it, but you also don't have to crucify her for it, either." She shifted to the edge of the seat and held my stare with the compassionate and loving eyes that only belonged to my caring, trusting, and sympathetic mother. "You say you were stressed, but I haven't seen it. And neither has your father. We've seen a much happier and brighter version of our son."

"How so?"

"Well, for one, you weren't spending every second at work. You were also smiling for no reason, and you didn't seem so lonely all the time. I don't care what Claire did—she could've robbed a bank as far as I'm concerned. All that matters to me is what her role in your life has done for you. You're all I care about, Travis. And if she's the reason for all these good transformations, I'm perfectly willing to forgive her for taking *my* recipe."

I honestly didn't have anything to say. It would take a while to process everything she'd said, but I trusted that, sooner or later, I'd be able to face Claire and get this all out in the open. After all, we both deserved to have some sort of resolution to this, even if only for closure.

My mom stood, smoothed her pants to remove any wrinkles she got from sitting, and walked a few steps to the door. "I have lots to do at the house before everyone comes over in the morning, so I'll leave you to lock up. But before I go…"

She tapped her nails on the doorframe, one at a time in rapid succession.

"Remember, I'm your mother. I know what's best for my boys. I would never encourage any of you to do something I didn't strongly believe in. However, with that being said, I only want you to be happy, and I'll accept any decision you make. Even if it goes against my own advice."

And, without so much as a wave goodbye, she was gone.

She came in like a warm summer breeze but quickly became a destructive tornado. Without warning, she ripped the roof off my shelter, knocked down my protective walls, and tore the floor out from beneath me. And as quickly and quietly as she arrived, she left, as if she hadn't just shaken up my entire world.

It seemed my mom and Claire had more in common than I ever realized.

CHAPTER 23
CLAIRE

Even the amazing smell of food as I walked into Gramps's house didn't help my disposition.

If Maureen hadn't put so much time and effort into making Thanksgiving dinner, I would've bailed. The last place I wanted to be was around other people. It was bad enough I'd been here every day for the last week, but I stayed busy in the kitchen, so I was pretty much left alone.

There was no way I'd get any peace today.

"Happy Thanksgiving!" Gramps glanced up from the newspaper at the kitchen table and beamed. "I didn't hear you come in."

I dropped my bag next to an empty chair at the table and gave him a hug. "I let myself in."

"Where's Travis?" Maureen glanced toward the kitchen door, expecting someone else to follow me in. "Did he not come with you?"

"No, I'm pretty sure he's with his family today."

"Pretty sure? Are you two on the outs?" Gramps narrowed his gaze at me, quickly dropping his attention to my left hand, the one still adorned with my mother's ring.

I fiddled with the band before slowly slipping it off my finger and setting it on the glass between us. "I'm sorry, but I have to tell you something."

Maureen shuffled away from the turkey in the oven to stand next to my grandfather. Both sets of aging eyes were on me, filled with unnecessary worry. "You didn't call off the wedding, did you? That would be awful."

As easy as it would've been to go down that route—especially since it had been the plan to begin with—I was well aware I was only in this mess

213

because of that exact line of thinking. Lying wouldn't get me anywhere. My current misery was proof. "Uh, no. It's a little more complicated."

"Well, what is it?"

I was so nervous and scared that my heart tried to burst through my ribcage to escape this potential disaster. "Well, you see, it's, uh… We had a… I um…"

"Spit it out already," Gramps practically scolded. "You're seriously worrying me."

That was the last thing I wanted to do; any sort of stress was horrible for people their ages. So I closed my eyes, pulled in a fast, deep breath, and let *all* the words tumble out before I lost the nerve. "We-were-never-engaged." I cracked open one eye the tiniest bit, enough to assess the damage I created.

"What do you mean?" Maureen's voice sounded soft, slightly concerned.

I waited for Gramps's voice to determine where his mind was, but he never spoke. The silence following Maureen's question caused me to open both eyes. I was a little concerned that I might've given him a heart attack or something equally as bad. But when I found him staring back at me with such disappointment in his eyes, I slapped my hands over my face and fought the urge to cry again. I'd done nothing but cry for days; my tear ducts should've been as dry as the Sahara Desert.

Knowing I needed to face the music—walk the plank, bite the bullet, carry the can—I dropped my arms and focused on slow, even breaths to ensure my words didn't shake when I said, "I lied. To you, to Travis, to his parents, to Piper. To everyone. I lied, and I can't begin to tell you how sorry I am."

"You lied about being engaged?" Gramps finally found his voice, though it sounded normal, not at all matching the confusion in his question. "But Travis was here. I gave him the ring." He pointed to my mother's diamond that still sat on the tabletop between us.

"I know, Gramps. He went along with it to help me."

"Help with what?"

I blew a long stream of air through a small slit between my lips, hoping it would buy me enough time to at least fake courage I didn't have. "Before I go into everything, I need you to understand this all happened *before* I knew why you made me move out. Okay?"

Maureen finally took the seat next to Gramps so they could both stare at me from across the table. Like that didn't make my confession ten times worse—then again, it wasn't like I deserved leniency.

"Okay," they both said almost in unison.

It felt like it'd taken two hours to spit it all out. Unfortunately, I couldn't simply explain the engagement scam, so I had to start from the beginning and disclose everything: the pies, the recipe, the schemes I'd devised so I could get more money. I had to give up the entire lot of lies I'd told over the last several months to fully explain why I'd told my grandfather I was engaged to Travis.

Gramps spent more time staring over my head at the wall behind me and clenching his jaw than he did looking at me. It was devastating. But I had to keep telling myself that I got what I deserved. I'd alienated everyone in my life for a few extra bucks I would've gotten in a couple of years anyway.

"What about the winery? What's going to happen to your business?" Maureen asked, likely verbalizing the questions in Gramps's head he couldn't say out loud.

"Carla said she'd keep me there if it was up to her. We've talked about it, and she's forgiven me, but it all comes down to Travis. She wanted to wait until after the holiday before talking to him, mostly to give him time to calm down a bit. But in the end, if he's adamant about not wanting me there, it looks like I'll have to find somewhere else to sell my pies."

"But she's okay with you continuing to sell them?"

"Well, yeah. I mean, she understands the filling is completely my own, so she doesn't see it as *her* recipe any longer. And while she wasn't thrilled to begin with that I used her crust, she said she quickly became okay with it because the two complement each other so well. The combination gives Cutie Pies something no other bakery has."

My heart warmed anytime I thought about Carla. Not only had she become such an amazing role model for me both personally *and* professionally, but she also managed to fill an uninhabited space in my life I never knew was empty.

But then, I'd be reminded that my relationship with Carla could abruptly end if Travis couldn't find a way to forgive me—or at least look past my transgressions—and my entire body would grow cold.

"Well, that's very good, I guess." Maureen comforted me with her soft words while Gramps continued to stare at everything *but* me. "I'm sure Travis will come around, too. He seemed like such a good boy. And I believe with my whole being that he cares about you...a man doesn't look at a woman the way he looked at you if they're only friends. I trust he'll come around."

"Thanks, Maureen. That means a lot."

Gramps finally shifted his attention from his hands to my face and said, "So you did all this to gain access to your money—or what you perceived to have belonged to you. You told us your pies didn't do well to start off, so how can I trust your business is doing as well as you say it is now? All we have to go on is your word."

Four days ago, I'd witnessed utter betrayal in Travis's stare. The next day, Carla looked at me with pity in her sympathetic gaze. Piper finally came over yesterday to keep me from falling apart. No matter how hard she tried to hide it, disappointment shone back at me as we talked about all the ways I'd ruined everything. However, nothing compared to the mistrust and disillusionment I saw in my grandfather's eyes.

Only one thing had ever caused me more pain.

And that was the death of my parents.

"I understand, Gramps. And if I were you, I'd probably doubt everything I've said, too. But I swear to you, every report I've shown you has been completely accurate. I realize you don't spend time in the kitchen when I'm here baking, but you've helped me take the boxes out to the car many times. I can promise you I wouldn't be spending all my time in front of an oven and all my money on ingredients if I were throwing them out or giving them away. I haven't lied about my sales, but I understand why you'd be leery."

He picked up the ring off the table and held it between his thumb and index as if studying a diamond at a jewelry store before buying it. I couldn't help but imagine he was checking the stone to ensure I hadn't swapped it out for a piece of glass. And if so, I'd hit a new low. One I couldn't imagine climbing out of.

"What have you done with the investment I gave you?"

It felt like I had a pill lodged in my throat, but no matter how hard I swallowed, it didn't go away. Then my ears started to ring, and my sight dimmed. I quickly realized I might've been on the verge of an anxiety attack, so I closed my eyes and took long, slow breaths.

The room became very warm, but before I could switch my focus to the rise in temperature around me, I decided to try something Carla had mentioned weeks ago. I imagined my parents were here, and suddenly, I was consumed by peace I'd never experienced before. Behind my closed eyelids, I pictured the last Thanksgiving I'd spent with my parents. My mom was at the sink while Dad and I sat at the kitchen table to keep her company.

I wasn't sure whether it was some sort of Jedi mind trick or if my angels were physically in this room with me. Either way, it worked. I was calm enough to open my eyes and confident enough to answer my grandfather's question.

I straightened my posture and met his wary stare. "I've put some back into Cutie Pies, moved some to a business savings account..." It would've been so easy to leave it there, trusting he wouldn't ask to see transactions. But I couldn't. I physically felt the presence of my parents on either side of me, which gave me the courage to tell the whole truth. "And the rest I gave to Travis to cover the extra cost of expanding his vineyard."

His eyes practically bulged, though it didn't appear to be out of anger. It was more like absolute disbelief. "How much did you give him?"

"Well, it was a loan, not a gift," I said, dismissing the actual question.

Maureen placed her hand on his arm, and he visibly calmed.

I cleared my throat and sat forward. "I'll admit I didn't have the best intentions when I first asked for the money. I didn't think the baking would amount to anything, and without any skill or trade, I wasn't eligible for decent-paying jobs."

Gramps huffed to himself, likely assuming I was making excuses or justifying my selfish behavior. Which I wasn't. When I made the conscious decision to be honest, I knew I couldn't leave any skeletons in my closet.

"So, basically, I made a business plan with the intention of getting money for doing nothing. But you turned me down, which ended up being a blessing in disguise. Because right after that, I started selling my pies at the winery, and they flew off the shelf. Not only did I experience real success for the first time in my life, but I was also given the opportunity to realize my passion and how much I truly love baking."

"Then why take the check if you didn't need it?"

That answer was both easy *and* hard in equal measures. "Because I did need some of it. Just because I was doing well didn't mean I couldn't do better, and I couldn't make those moves without funding. Not to mention, having a little more cushion in the bank gave me a sense of security, which helped boost my confidence."

"Okay, but you didn't have to take it all."

"You're absolutely right, Gramps. I didn't have to. But I wanted to... because Travis was on the brink of losing his dream for the vineyard. And considering he'd helped me out countless times, I wanted to do the same for him."

"By helping you out, you mean pretending to be your fiancé?"

"As well as being my biggest cheerleader and finding me a place to sell my pies."

"Did he do it *for* the money? Was that part of the deal...fool my grandfather and let me use your winery and I'll pay you?"

"Not at all." Heat consumed my cheeks. While I understood why he'd reach that conclusion, I didn't care for the suspicion he heaved on Travis. It wasn't deserved...I was the one responsible for this mess, not Travis. "He only agreed to help because he's a good guy. That's it. He asked for absolutely nothing in return. In fact, when I offered him the loan, he refused it."

"He clearly didn't if he took it."

This wasn't the argument I wanted to have, especially with Gramps. But I didn't have much of a choice. I'd taken his money, and he had every right in the world to question my motivation for giving it to Travis as well as Travis's motivation for accepting it.

"It's a long story, one I'm not entirely sure I can explain without confusing you even more. But in a nutshell, his parents made certain decisions regarding the expansion, which required him to come up with his share of the funding within days. I honestly believe that if he hadn't been backed into a corner, he never would've taken it."

Just then, the doorbell rang. With a grunt and heavy breathing, Gramps excused himself from the conversation and headed to the front of the house. Meanwhile, Maureen and I remained in the kitchen, awkwardness filling the air.

"He's upset. You know your grandfather…give him a little space to calm down. I think he just needs to process everything. That was a lot to be dumped in someone's lap." She reached across the table and covered my hand with hers. "He likes Travis a lot. He even accredited a lot of your maturity to him, so I think he's more disappointed about there not being a relationship than anything else."

"I get it. And trust me…so am I."

"You cared about him, didn't you?" Her soft eyes nearly made me start crying all over again.

"Yes, I did. A lot."

She squeezed my hand and asked, "I saw the way he looked at you when you were here for the engagement party. Something like that can't be faked, and trust me, I would know. So how come you two never dated?"

I clenched my jaw and took several deep breaths to ward off the shakiness in my voice. "There are probably several factors, but I think the biggest has to be my irrational fear of letting anyone in. I have a hard time trusting people, so I tend to keep everyone at a safe distance. That way, they can't betray or hurt me."

"Let me guess…Travis made his way into your inner circle while you weren't looking?"

I nodded. "Yup. And once he was there, I couldn't do anything about it. I couldn't push him out; the thought of not having him in my life hurt too much. So the only option I was left with was not allowing myself to acknowledge my feelings for him. I figured if I kept telling myself we were only friends, then I wouldn't have to worry about him hurting me."

"What makes you think he would?"

"Would what…hurt me?" I shrugged. "I never actually thought he would, but I also didn't want to give him the opportunity to prove me wrong. There have been lots of people in my life who didn't show their true colors until it was too late."

"So you never allowed yourself to fall for him in case he wasn't as good a guy as you thought?" Skepticism lined her brow and darkened her gaze.

"Well, yeah. Not to mention, if I don't love them, then it won't hurt as bad when they die."

Sadness and sympathy blended together in her softening expression.

"You can't avoid loving someone in case they die. You'll miss out on so much. And who cares who hurt you in the past? None of those people were Travis. He shouldn't pay the price for others' mistakes, nor should he be refused love because you're scared to lose him."

I pulled my hand out from beneath hers to wipe the errant tear that slipped out from the corner of my eye. "I know, Maureen. But unfortunately, I didn't realize that until it was too late. Plus, it kind of worked in my favor this time. I can't even imagine how much pain I'd be in right now if we were dating when he found out I'd taken the recipe off his phone. To be honest, considering how I am with it all right now, I don't think I would've been able to handle anything more."

Maureen checked her wrist and knitted her brows together. "I wonder who was at the door. Your grandfather's been gone a while."

I glanced at the time on the microwave. Without knowing when the door-bell rang, it was hard to discern how long he'd been gone, but I agreed with Maureen…it did seem to be longer than needed to answer the door. It wasn't like we were expecting anyone.

"I'll check. If you leave the kitchen and something starts to beep, I'm the last one you'd want guessing which timer it was and what dish it was for." I laughed as I pushed away from the table. "I'm sure it's just a salesman trying to take advantage of an elderly man in a big house on a holiday."

When I made it to the foyer, the front door was closed. So I cracked it open enough to peek out, wondering if he might've stepped outside. But no one was on the porch or in the driveway. Rather than call for him, I remained completely still and closed my eyes, hoping it would improve my hearing enough to detect the sound of his voice.

Unfortunately, it didn't.

But it did help with one thing. When I opened my eyes, I noticed the office door was closed.

While that wasn't unusual, it caught my attention because it was open when I arrived. And considering I'd headed straight for the kitchen, and we all stayed there until the doorbell rang, the door being closed now *was* unusual.

I quietly made my way down the hallway and stopped in front of the office. But as I leaned forward to put my ear against the cold wood to see if I could hear anything, the door swung open. Luckily, I was able to regain control of my balance before I fell right into my grandfather who now stood in front of me, clearly surprised by my unexpected presence. However, I didn't pay him any attention.

My gaze landed on the tall, handsome man with cyan eyes and a swoon-inducing smile. Except the smile I always looked forward to seeing was nowhere to be found.

"What are you doing here?" I asked quietly, trying to assume the worst so I wouldn't be let down while simultaneously filled with wishful thinking.

Gramps stepped aside and pointed at Travis. "We were discussing the loan and coming up with a repayment plan."

It felt like my body deflated as I sighed. "Oh."

"I'll go see if Maureen needs any help in the kitchen. I'll leave you two alone to talk...I'm sure you have a lot to discuss." Not waiting for me to move, Gramps slipped past me and retreated down the hall.

That left me in the doorway and Travis three feet in front of me.

He was so close, yet completely untouchable.

I expected him to leave as well, but he didn't. Instead, he turned around and stalked to the oversized oak desk that was the centerpiece of both the room and many of my childhood memories. He took a seat and stared at me, a silent invitation to join him. So I did.

But not before I closed the door behind me.

"Apparently, we have a couple people in our lives who want to see us move past this." His voice was low and, surprisingly, not monotone.

I expected to be met with indifference, but that wasn't the case. He wasn't angry or annoyed—at least he didn't appear to be. Granted, he didn't act excited or even happy to be here, so it wasn't all sunshine and rainbows. But at least the air around him wasn't filled with the doom and gloom I thought awaited me.

"What do you mean? Who wants us to move past this?"

Travis rubbed the tops of his thighs as if drying his palms with his khaki slacks. And if so, it was a sign he was nervous. Which was a good thing because it meant we were pretty close to being on an even playing field.

"If we don't at least sit down and have an honest and mature conversation, I'm pretty sure my mom will lock us in a room until we figure it out. And from what your grandfather told me, it sounds like they're in the same boat." He finally met my eyes, and a wave of relief settled him in his seat, ridding his body of its stiffness. "I think my mom might disown me if we don't hash it out."

Piper was right...I'd spent the last eight years pushing away anyone who even resembled a mother. But somehow, Carla had managed to sneak right past my walls without my knowledge. And by the time I'd realized it, it was too late.

And now, it seemed she was rooting for me...like a real mom would.

"Yeah, I think Gramps feels the same about you. I told him everything, and he was furious. I don't think I've ever seen him so angry." I glanced over my shoulder at the closed door and then down to my wringing fingers in my lap. "Maureen says he's probably more upset that we're not together than anything I've lied about."

"Doubtful." His eyes flashed with humor as one corner of his mouth curled. "He's actually on your side, right there with my mom."

"*My* side? That doesn't make any sense. I'm the one who betrayed you, not the other way around, so really, *no one* should be on my side."

He leaned forward, pressing his elbows into his thighs, and briefly dropped his head into his open hands. "They both seem to agree that your actions were wrong, and I have a right to be upset about it all."

I was about to interject, but he grabbed my hand, effectively silencing my comment.

"However…" His gentle eyes hypnotized me the same way his large, warm hand left me motionless. "They're also of the mindset that you're not the same selfish, spoiled, trust-fund baby you were when you made those horrible choices…and I should take that into consideration when deciding where we stand with each other."

"I seriously doubt that's how Gramps feels. I'm not kidding when I say I've never seen him so angry before in my life. And trust me, I've given him plenty of reasons to be."

Travis leaned back, taking his hand with him, and sighed. "I don't know what he said to you, but when he pulled me in here, he didn't act pissed. Granted, he said he was upset I borrowed that kind of money without him knowing, but he didn't sound angry about it. A bit bothered, but that's all."

"Yeah, he seemed to have the biggest reaction to the money part. What did he say to you?"

He began to pick invisible lint off his pants. "That was basically it…he wished we'd come to him about it instead of doing it behind his back. I explained it was never my intention to borrow or take it; otherwise, I probably would've gone to him first."

"Nothing about the engagement?"

"Not really. At the beginning, he mentioned a couple of times how he's sad that we aren't together, but nothing specifically about the engagement. I brought up the ring and told him you wanted to wear it because of what it means to you." He paused, appearing to run through the conversation in his head as if to ensure he'd mentioned everything. "That was about it. We pretty much discussed you and the loan."

I swallowed harshly and asked, "What all did he say about me?"

"Nothing much, just that he's sad we aren't together because he believed being with me played a large role in you becoming a better person." He lifted his gaze, settling his eyes on my face. "I told him he was wrong. You've matured a lot since moving out, but you've *always* been a good person. I also explained that I had nothing to do with your growth and maturity. That was all you."

"You don't think you had anything to do with it?"

221

He shook his head, a smile slowly forming on his kissable lips. "Nah. I was only along for the ride. You're the one who did all the work, not me."

A strong bolt of heated, uncontrollable energy ran through me. It forced me out of my seat and straight into Travis's arms. It was like I had no control over my body. My lips met his, and surprisingly, he kissed me back.

It was slow and tender, full of emotion.

Thankfully, when it ended, he didn't push me away. Instead, he held me in place on his lap but with enough space between our faces to have a conversation. "He's so proud of you, but he's not the only one." He rubbed the tip of his nose against mine, and I doubted I'd ever missed anything more.

"Oh, yeah? Who else is proud of me?"

His lips spread into the panty-dropping smile I thought I'd never see again. "Lots of people," he teased. "But I doubt anyone's more proud of you than I am."

I held his face between my hands. "Does this mean you're not mad at me anymore?"

"No, but I do have one question." His eyes pleaded with mine when he asked, "If I never found out, do you think you would've eventually told me."

I didn't have to ask what he was talking about because his expression said it all. My betrayal still affected him in ways I doubted he'd ever get over. It filled me with pessimism and left me hopeless, but I answered anyway. "To tell you the truth, Travis...probably not. Way down the road, maybe, but I honestly had no intention of ever telling you the truth."

I pulled myself off his lap and leaned against the edge of my grandfather's desk while he continued to watch me from his seat.

"But that doesn't mean I didn't regret it. Because I did. Every single day. I was ashamed of myself for what I did...to you and your family, of all people. And not because you found out, either. I've been plagued with guilt since you told me how sentimental it is to you guys. So please, don't ever think I've spent a single second gloating to myself or feeling like I'd gotten away with anything."

Finally, Travis stood and moved to stand in front of me. He took my hands in his and lowered his chin so he could see my eyes. "Would you have confessed to your grandfather about us?"

My cheeks burned with the heat of humility. "I think I got so comfortable with you that I guess somewhere, in the back of my head, I convinced myself we wouldn't need to tell him because we'd be together anyway."

"Does that mean you liked me?"

I rolled my eyes and leaned back. Ignoring his question, I asked, "What about you? Do you think you'll ever tell your parents about the loan?"

"Already did."

I was so surprised I couldn't do anything for several seconds other than stare with my mouth hanging open. "You did? What'd they say?"

"Well, I told my mom when she came to my office to lecture me about not talking to you. And after she found out about my little secret, she sided with you even more. She thought it was a dick move—my words, not hers—to be so angry with someone who'd given me a personal loan for a couple hundred grand. She also pointed out I was punishing you for deceitful choices made during a selfish moment when I was literally guilty of the exact same thing."

"I like your mom. She's a smart woman," I teased.

He laughed beneath his breath and ran his fingers through the side of his hair. "Where do we stand, Claire?"

"I thought you were the one responsible for figuring that out."

"Well, I'm not foolish enough to assume you'd want to forgive me and move on...*with* me. You're the prize, Claire. Not me."

With my hand flat on his chest, I pushed him back about three steps. "You're kidding, right? What in the world would I have to forgive you for? You didn't do anything."

"I cut you out instead of listening to you and giving you any benefit of the doubt." He wrapped his thick fingers around my wrist, keeping my hand against his chest, and closed the gap between our bodies. "You didn't deserve that, Claire."

My breathing became shaky as I whispered, "Does this mean *you* forgive *me*?"

"Much like with the engagement lie, I understand, and I forgive you...but I don't condone what you did. And to be honest, it might take a while to fully trust you again. Or it might not. But I'm willing to give it a go and see how long it takes."

"So, are we friends again?" Regardless of how confident I felt in the answer, I held my breath anyway.

He lowered his head, bringing his face closer to mine. "If that's what you want, but I was kinda thinking something a bit more than friends."

With our lips barely touching, I asked, "Are you saying you want to date me?"

"Yes, Claire Hansen. That's exactly what I'm saying." His words lined my mouth with a burning heat that ran all throughout my body. It was so hot I had to clench my thighs together, worried we wouldn't make it out of this office.

"Then kiss me already."

He didn't waste a second before lifting me off my feet and setting me on top of the desk. With my legs around his hips, I pulled him into me, feeling his growing hardness against the apex of my thighs.

The last time we were in this same spot, doing the same thing, I hadn't yet discovered what he hid behind his pants, so I didn't have a clue what I was missing when Gramps interrupted. But since then, I'd become quite familiar with his above-average assets.

Which meant I knew *exactly* what I'd be missing when I heard Gramps calling my name as he headed down the hallway. Once again, my grandfather interrupted the hottest make-out session of my life.

We both groaned as we pushed away from each other. Luckily, I managed to slide off the desk a split second before the door opened. I started to suspect he had a camera in here, which was how he knew the exact moment to barge in.

Except, the look on his face and twinkle in his eye told me otherwise.

His timing was horrible, although completely honest.

The goofy grin coloring Gramps's cheeks and brightening his eyes as he glanced between Travis and me confirmed my suspicions. He had called out my name as he approached the office as a courtesy alert, warning me of his proximity.

"Is Travis staying for Thanksgiving dinner?" Hope filled his aging tone.

Travis chuckled to himself and shook his head. At first, my heart sank—and the optimism drained from my grandfather's expression. But then he said, "I sure hope so. My mom told me I needed to make things right with Claire, and if I came back, she'd assume I failed and not give me anything to eat."

"Well, good. I'm glad everything's worked out." He took a step toward the door while keeping his eyes on us. "Now come on, I'm about to carve the turkey."

As we walked down the hallway, Travis grabbed my hand and whispered, "After dinner, what do you think about going home and baking?"

That one question made my clit throb. "How fast can you eat?"

EPILOGUE
TRAVIS

I COULDN'T STOP STARING at her, wondering how in the hell I got so lucky.

She sat across the dinner table talking to my mom, her eyes shimmering like gold in the sunlight. I'd seen a wide range of Claire's emotions in the year since we met, but my favorite had to be happiness. It suited her well. And somehow, I'd managed to keep a smile on her face and a twinkle in her eyes ever since last Thanksgiving.

I loved to watch her interact with my family, especially my mom. Anyone who didn't know us would've assumed they were mother and daughter, and I was the outsider. I couldn't complain about that, though. It wasn't like I was used to being her favorite anyway. But Craig, on the other hand, probably felt a bit left out.

"Did you get everything moved in?" Dad asked, speaking louder than normal to ensure he was heard over the other chatter at the table. Why he thought he had to raise his voice was beyond me. His usual tone could've been heard in the next room over while a stampede of elephants trampled through the kitchen.

I nodded while swallowing my bite so he wouldn't repeat himself, even louder, thinking I hadn't heard him. "Yeah, Pops. It didn't take long, considering Claire only has enough possessions to fill five boxes. She had rented that place fully furnished, so we didn't have to do anything but move over her clothes and toiletries."

Technically, it was a bit more than that, but not by much. I was just happy that I didn't have to move anything around to make room for her in my place. Then again, she'd basically been living there for the last eight months anyway.

225

"I don't understand why you guys didn't just move into her house. Only an idiot would choose a one-bedroom duplex over a mansion." Jake had a bad habit of throwing his two cents into any conversation within earshot.

Although, it was entertaining to watch him get a sharp elbow to his side every time he offered his unwanted opinions. That almost made his commentary worth it.

"What was that for?" he asked, rubbing his ribs as if it'd actually hurt.

"You know what it was for, Jacob Cabrera." Mom glared at my older brother before tossing a wink to the woman who'd elbowed him; she appeared quite satisfied to have backup.

Jake dropped his fork and rolled his eyes. "All I did was ask why they moved into his place instead of her *house*."

I contemplated pointing out the *idiot* remark but decided against it in favor of simply answering my brother. "Well, for starters, I still have seven months left on my lease."

"Well, that was stupid of you to renew your agreement so close to hers ending."

"What can I say, Jake? We all can't be as smart as you." I finished the last spoonful of mashed potatoes on my plate and leaned back in my chair, leveling my eyes on my brother. "And in case you forgot, her grandfather and Maureen live there."

He picked up his last green bean with his fingers and ate it, earning a couple daggers of disapproval from our mother. Ignoring her scowl, he shrugged and added, "All I'm sayin' is that house is big enough for them *and* you. And more than likely several other people, too."

"You're probably right." Claire eyed me with a soft, simple smile and then turned to regard my annoying older brother in the seat next to her. "I'm sure we could all live there with room to spare. But we have a different plan."

My heart pumped harder as my body filled with intense pride for Claire. We had discussed the housing situation many times over the last two months, finally coming to a conclusion this past week. We'd known for a while that her grandfather would stay at the house until at least the end of my lease, but the future of the house had been up in the air from the beginning.

Claire had gone back and forth whether she wanted to keep her family home or sell it. She had pros and cons for both options. I never pushed her one way or the other, knowing we would still have seven months to figure it out. But to my surprise, Claire had come to me last week with a decision, and after questioning it to death to ensure it was what she truly wanted to do, I gave her my full support.

Mom's and Dad's eyes never moved away from Claire's face as she explained. "Travis and I talked about it, and we agreed that it made more sense to get a place of our own once his lease is up."

"Buy or rent?" Mom asked, excitement brightening her eyes.

"Well..." Claire glanced at me for a split second before turning to my mother, who sat on the other side of her. "Cutie Pies has done so well—more than I ever expected. And as you know, Travis has increased sales at the winery at an impressive rate. So we're going to take advantage of the next seven months and save...and then buy a house together."

"And then do what with the big one?"

I groaned at my brother's obsession with her house, but instead of arguing about how annoying he was, I kept my mouth shut so Claire could finish sharing her big news.

"I'll sell it." She winked at me and added, "And then use the money to buy a kitchen. Well, more like buy something I can turn into a big kitchen for all my baking."

Claire's business had grown beyond Tesorita in the last eight months. In addition to the corner at the winery, her pies were now sold in two local bakeries, as well as two others in the next town over. I still had no idea how she managed to bake enough for all five spaces, but she did.

And I couldn't be prouder of her.

Thankfully, Jake didn't question anything else. Instead, everyone on our end of the table congratulated her, showing their excitement with their offerings of well wishes and good luck. Meanwhile, I sat back and enjoyed seeing the love of my life soak up the praise she so well deserved.

"If everyone's done eating, I'll bring out the dessert," Mom said, breaking through the chatter of everyone's side conversations.

I stood and grabbed my empty plate, my heart racing as if I'd chugged nineteen energy drinks. "Let me clear the table, and I'll be in there to give you a hand, Ma."

Just then, Claire stood as well, and I knew she would want to help. She'd baked the pies specially for tonight's family dinner, so it only made sense that she would want to be the one serving them.

But I couldn't let her in the kitchen. I had to stop her. "No, Claire. You made them, so your part's finished. Sit and drink your wine." I quickly grabbed the bottle from in front of Craig and filled her nearly empty glass. I had a feeling the offer of wine would convince her, and as it turned out, it did.

She playfully rolled her eyes and dropped back into her cushioned seat with a teasing huff. "Fine, but that means you're baking tonight," she said softly with fire in her eyes.

"Oh, don't worry, my love. I already planned on it."

Thankfully, Brenden helped clear the table. I'd discussed my plan with him a few days ago, and I was so glad I had because there was no way I would've made it in time without his help. We were able to get the plates and bowls to the kitchen before Mom had a chance to cut all the pies.

I only needed one.

"Hey, now. I haven't cut that one yet," Mom practically scolded when I reached for a tin.

Initially, I'd planned for the berry pie because that was the filling that really got things started for Claire and me. Then I remembered the mess and purple stains, so I'd changed my mind. Apricot was her mom's favorite fruit, so I thought that would be a meaningful choice, almost like having her mom with her. Except she'd decided not to bring any apricot pies—something I'd learned on the drive over. Now, I didn't give a shit what was on the inside. At the end of the day, every filling had some sort of meaning to either her or us. So really, any would do.

"That's okay, Ma. I don't need it cut."

Mom stopped what she was doing and turned to face me, hand on her hip and irritation along her brow. "You're not eating that entire pie, young man."

But I didn't respond. I didn't look at her, didn't shake my head, didn't say a damn word. My pulse was too high to deal with her *and* try to breathe. Luckily, Brenden had stayed back, so he helped handle our mother and keep her off my back.

Finally, when I pulled the diamond ring from my pocket, she shut up.

Technically, she gasped. Then became teary. After that came the swoons and excited blubbering. Honestly, it was all too much to take, but I couldn't deny her this. I would've been just as animated if my heart wasn't currently lodged in my throat.

"I'll go back to the table. That way, if she tries to get up, I can stop her." Brenden patted me on the back and then left me alone with our mother in the kitchen.

"He knew?" Jealousy was not a good color on her.

Honestly, I didn't have enough oxygen in my brain to deal with mom *and* set this up before Claire came in, wondering what happened with her pies. Unfortunately, ignoring her would only make things worse, so I shrugged and said, "Kind of. And before you ask…I didn't tell you because I knew you wouldn't be able to sit through dinner without giving something away."

"Fair enough. So what are you going to do with that?" she asked, pointing to the ring.

Instead of answering her with words, I showed her.

After making a tiny slit in the center of the top crust, I carefully worked the silver band into the opening until the ring was far enough in to stand up but not too far that it would fall in. The entire time, Mom fought hard not to get in the way. There were several times she'd start to reach out, as if to take over and do it herself, but she managed to refrain.

When I finished, I took a step back to admire the brilliant diamond with a pear-shaped emerald on either side that sat perfectly in the center of one of Claire's pies. "What do you think she'll say?"

"I think she'll wonder why you're giving her a ring she already owns. You couldn't have afforded a new one?"

I nearly choked, forgetting that our faux-gagement was the one lie we hadn't confessed to my parents. One day it'd be a funny story to tell our children, but for now...it was better left unsaid. "It's a long story...all you need to know is it was her mom's engagement ring, and her grandfather gave it to me when I asked him for permission to marry her. Now tell me, honestly, do you think she'll say yes?"

Thankfully, the proposal was enough to keep her from questioning anything...*for now.*

"I know for fact she will, son. She's too smart to say anything else." Mom wrapped her arms around my neck and held me tight. That was enough to calm my nerves and give me the courage I'd been searching for since we got in the car tonight to come here.

Releasing my arm from around her waist, I pointed to the other pies and said, "Let's go ahead and take those out, and then we'll come back for the plates and this one."

"You're still going to get down on one knee, right?"

I kissed her on the forehead and smiled. "Don't worry, Ma...you didn't raise a fool."

BEFORE YOU GO...

I've heard that only one out of every two hundred readers leave reviews, good or bad. Authors rely so heavily on readers to help get the word out and let other readers know which books they recommend and why. And reviews are one of the easiest ways to do this. With that being said...I would love you forever if you could please be that one-in-two-hundred reader for me and leave a review on Amazon and Goodreads.

Thank you once again! xx

ACKNOWLEDGMENTS

Being in love has a way of changing your entire life. And nothing was more true for me. After meeting the love of my life, I found myself laughing more, smiling more, and when it came to my writing, I found it difficult to write dark, intense, highly emotional storylines. I tried…and failed. So I decided to stop thinking and just write.

It really shouldn't have come as much of a surprise when I started writing humor. And that was when I decided that romantic comedy was the genre I felt I belonged in all the time.

I honestly couldn't be happier—with my writing *and* my life. I'm finally writing for the love of it again, and for the first time in my life, I feel settled in where I'm at and where I'm headed.

So without further ado, there are a few people who either helped me get here, rooted for me along the way, or had my back from the beginning…

Firstly, Kev—I honestly wouldn't be here without you. I don't know how or when it happened, but it was like a light switch. You took a sad, lost, depressed, unconfident girl and made her a happy, stable, optimistic, confident woman. I can't thank you enough for that. Also…thank you for loving me unlike I've ever been loved before, for loving my kids like they were your own, and for giving me a real home. xx

Marlo—I might've relied a little too heavily on you when it came to this book, but I'm not sorry. You held my hand through the entire thing, and without you, I doubt I would've finished it. Thanks to you, I was able to find my love of writing again. I appreciate you more than you'll ever know. I love you, Lobs.

Crystal—Do you realize you've been by my side since the very beginning? Like, years and years before I ever published my first book. I'm beyond lucky to have you in my life.

Amanda—Thank you so much for letting me use your name as a pen name all those years ago when I didn't have the confidence in myself to be me. You are an inspiration, hence why I used your name lol. It gave me the courage and strength to put myself out there, which makes this book that much more special…because I'm finally putting myself out there. I couldn't have gotten here without you and your support.

Sarah—You've rooted for me from the very beginning. I don't think you know how much that means to me. I've gone through ups and downs in not only my writing but my personal life as well, and you've cheered me on from the sidelines the entire time. You truly are an amazing friend, and I'm beyond sorry that I almost let an insignificant person come between us. She might've come between me and some of my other friends, but the fact that you're still here says a lot about the type of amazing person you are.

Greenleigh—You literally plopped right into my life, but for some reason, it feels like you've always been there. I know you say I'm your mentor (which I think is silly lol) but really, you're my inspiration. You probably don't know it, but being with you through your start in publishing helped give me the courage to step out of the shadow of my pen name and publish something I love as myself. Thank you for that and so much more.

Mimo—You once again saved me from looking like a moron who can't write by proofreading my book. Thank you so much for saving my reputation haha!

My Betas: Lianne, Shannon, Dianna, Jennifer, Kylie, Deana, Kim, Heather, & Stephanie—I know I wasn't consistent with sending chapters, and for that, I'm really really sorry. But the fact that you stuck with me and didn't give up means the absolute world to me!! Your feedback and opinions truly helped shape Travis into the book it is now. When I finally finished every revision, I sat back and looked at the journey from the first word to the last…and I can honestly say the final version is so much stronger, smoother, and more enjoyable, and I wouldn't have this version without each and every one of you. Thank you so freakin' much!!!

Bloggers and Readers—I honestly can't thank you enough for taking a chance on me. Writing has always been a love and passion for me, and I would never be able to do this without you. From the bottom of my heart…thank you!

About the Author

Kaleigh Clark has dreamed of seeing her name on the front of a published romance novel since she was a little girl scribbling loves stories in notebooks instead of doing her homework. In 2014, she made half of her dream come true—she published her first book under a pseudonym. Over the next seven years, Kaleigh had become a bestselling author of more than twenty novels.

Even though Kaleigh had achieved amazing success, she still dreamed of seeing her name on the front of the books she wrote.

After going through a rough period in her personal life, Kaleigh had found the kind of love she'd spent years writing about. So in late 2021, she made the decision to start over and publish romance novels written about the love she has instead of the kind of relationship she only dreamed about. But this time…she'd do so under her name, Kaleigh Clark.

ALSO BY KALEIGH CLARK

The Booze Brothers:
Travis (this book)
Craig (coming summer / fall 2022)
Jake (coming 2023)
Brenden (coming 2023)